THE PRIDE OF THE GREEN BERETS CAPTURES ALL THE FURY AND INTRIGUE OF THE VIET NAM WAR!

Captain Cunningham and his Special Forces team of Green Berets fought more than the Viet Cong in the dangerous jungles of Vietnam.

Back home, the Pentagon vetoed an all-out attack against North Vietnam. On the battlefield, the South Vietnamese often wavered in their own attacks against the enemy. And in Saigon, profiteering and sinister politicking snarled plans for a full-scale onslaught against the VC.

Day after day, Cunningham battled against mortar fire from his enemy and red tape from his allies. Finally he faced a do-or-die battle for survival that would either get him dropped from the Special Forces or make him THE PRIDE OF THE GREEN BERETS!

THE PRIDE OF THE
GREEN BERETS

Peter Derrig

PAPERBACK LIBRARY, Inc.

New York

Chapter 1

His green combat fatigues stained black with sweat, Captain David Cunningham, U.S. Army, stumbled over the uneven terrain, fending the shoulder high elephant grass aside with his carbine. He no longer bothered to try to move quietly. This had become solely a personal struggle to last out the march.

Now he stopped and wiped his forehead and eyes with an already sodden handkerchief. He looked at his raw, dark-red arms and grimaced. The sharp grass was punishing. On either side, Cunningham heard the progress of the battalion but he could not see anyone, even though he was well over six feet tall. The diminutive Vietnamese Civil Guard soldiers remained screened.

Cunningham glanced at the forest rising darkly a mile ahead and then up at the late afternoon sun which kept the temperature over 100°. He knew the humidity was over 95%. Cursing half-heartedly he began to stride through the dry grass.

The pack straps cut into his unaccustomed shoulders and chafed him terribly. The sloppily-packed combat pack bumped his rump at every step. He remembered how nice the weather had been in Illinois three weeks ago. It was September, and the air had been crisp, cool. Autumn had always been his favorite season. But autumn in Viet Nam was something else.

Cunningham, the new commanding officer of the twelve Green Berets in the Special Forces Advisory team with the Vietnamese battalion, first heard and then saw First Lieutenant Robert "Bud" Thompson move back toward him.

"How are you bearing up, Skipper?" Thompson asked, a sympathetic smile on his square face. He fell in beside Cunningham. Even though he was only five feet eight inches

5

tall and had short legs, he was able to match the captain's tired stride.

"I'm pooped, but I'll make it, I guess," Cunningham answered his Executive Officer with a wry smile. The rest of the team members were enlisted men. "I found out one thing these past two days. You sure can get out of shape on an aide's job."

Thompson laughed. "I wouldn't know, but I sure could use some of that duty about now."

Cunningham nodded agreement, saving his breath. Many times over the past eighteen months he had cursed being assigned as aide-de-camp to the Commanding General of the Fifth Army, headquartered at Fort Sheridan in northern Illinois. Annoyance at the flunky's duties and petty detail as well as the boredom had prompted him to volunteer for duty in Viet Nam. After all he was Special Forces trained. And the U.S.A. had only one war going. Martha had objected, but that hadn't stopped him.

Fighting to stay on his feet, Cunningham concentrated on the next patch of grass ahead. He suddenly lifted his head at Thompson's comment.

"Only about ten minutes more, sir. That shade is going to feel good."

Cunningham took a deep breath of the musty hot air and brushed at the cloud of tiny insects buzzing around his head. He started to look around him with relief. He now felt he could spend a little less time worrying about falling down with fatigue and more on the tactical situation.

"How does it look to you?" he asked Thompson. His Executive Officer had been with the team for the past nine or ten months. Cunningham was the replacement for another captain who had been wounded and hospitalized.

The heavy-set first lieutenant frowned thoughtfully. "Not bad. Not bad. They're keeping proper intervals. Communications seem okay. A little too noisy moving, perhaps."

"What's next on the schedule?" Cunningham asked. This was the first time he had been in the field with the Civil Guard Battalion, which was being specially trained as a striking force to take the offensive against the Viet Cong.

"Major Nuan will set up his command post and get his company commanders together. They'll decide on the dispositions of the mortars, heavy and light machine guns, and recoilless rifles, outposts, and roving patrols, and all that."

Cunningham nodded. "I suppose I'd better sit in on that."

Thompson agreed. "Better take Red Kennedy with you. He's got a better understanding of Vietnamese military terms than I have, and he knows all the damn nuances of the language. I'd better round him up now."

Cunningham watched Thompson move swiftly and silently ahead and shook his head in admiration. The Lieutenant wasn't even breathing heavily. His thick legs took his broad body over the ground amazingly fast. Thompson was exactly what he looked like, a bruising, running halfback. He had been All-American at West Point only three years before.

As he neared the wall of tall trees and thick brush Cunningham felt nothing but disappointment with his own physical condition. For the past two weeks he had exercised daily at their base camp at Dan Lac on the coastal lowlands in the northern section of South Viet Nam. But his legs, arms and shoulders were now leaden with fatigue. He had forgotten how much field maneuvers, over tough terrain under a blazing sun, can take out of a man.

Eighteen months before he had been in top shape, fresh from Special Forces school, the Anti-Guerilla Course, Jump school and French and Vietnamese language courses. At school down south everything had been done on the double. Easy living in Illinois and traveling through the midwest with the General on the banquet circuit had destroyed all that.

Cunningham followed Thompson into the forest and halted in the shade of a huge mango tree where the Lieutenant had dropped his pack. He sat down and removed

7

his jungle boots and socks and rubbed his blistered feet. After wiping and powdering them carefully, he donned clean socks and groaned as he put on the boots again. He looked up to see Sergeant Red Kennedy, his Intelligence Specialist, grinning at him.

"They'll toughen up quick, Captain." Kennedy rubbed his fiery red, freckled arms, coated with blond hair and the remainder of a white ointment. "Major Nuan's meeting with his people in a few minutes, Captain. Lieutenant Thompson says I'm to go over there with you."

Cunningham noted the resignation in his voice. Thompson and all the noncoms looked pained whenever Nuan was mentioned, but so far Cunningham had had only a few personal complaints about the South Vietnamese Regular Army (ARVN) officer, who was detailed to train and command the Civil Guards. At Dan Lac he appeared to have a well-organized set-up, business-like, although too much spit-and-polish, Cunningham had decided.

The Civil Guard were provincial troops, like a U.S. State National Guard, except these men were on continuous active service. Their job was to protect the populace. Nuan's battalion members were the elite from the northern provinces, hand-picked to form a search-and-destroy unit.

Wearily Cunningham rose and followed the tall, thin sergeant. Kennedy smiled and spoke to the grinning Vietnamese in their own language. His height and appearance were so different from theirs that it made Cunningham smile. And they knew it and were amused too. But obviously they had the deepest respect for the American. He was an ace jungle fighter and knew the ways of the Communist guerilla Viet Cong backwards and forwards.

Cunningham was suddenly conscious of his own disheveled appearance when he approached Major Nuan, who had changed into a crisp khaki uniform, complete with gold braided cap.

Nuan sat impassively in a canvas deck chair and listened to his company commanders report and give their plans for bivouacking for the night. The Major had a commanding presence, taller than most of the other Vietnamese, and

8

almost roly-poly, Cunningham observed. But he had noticed that Nuan had not worked up much of a sweat marching across country. His deep-set unblinking eyes went from officer to officer as each spoke his piece.

Kennedy kept up a running translation of the Vietnamese for Cunningham's benefit. The Captain was picking up the language quickly, but still many of the colloquialisms escaped him.

After the other officers had left, Major Nuan looked up at Cunningham with a small smile on his face. He turned to one of his coterie of orderlies and waved a hand. An ammunition box was fetched for the American to sit on.

"I am glad you made it all right, Captain Cunningham," Nuan said in excellent English, with only a faint French accent. He looked Cunningham up and down, amused.

"No problems, Major. Another week and I'll be in shape." Cunningham felt annoyed.

Nuan shrugged. "Perhaps, Captain. Perhaps. This is a difficult country for you Caucasians. I think very, very few of you ever become adjusted to our jungles."

Cunningham forced down his irritation and took out his cigarettes. He offered the pack to Major Nuan.

"No, thank you, Cunningham. I prefer this French brand." His orderly was quick with a lighter, going to Nuan first, and then Cunningham.

The American shifted uneasily on the box. Nuan's eyes remained focused on him, as if questioning him.

"Your battalion looked good today, Major," Cunningham finally said, feeling some comment was expected.

Nuan shrugged again. "They should, Captain." The amused look came back to his face and he puffed exaggeratedly at his cigarette. "After all I have trained them for many months. Even these peasants eventually learn."

Cunningham felt his face redden. There he goes again, reminding me he's an old-timer, he thought, and remembered their initial meeting. Nuan had carefully informed him that he had attended the Combat Infantry and Special Forces schools in the United States long before Cunningham, and that he was a graduate of France's St. Cyr military academy.

Nuan casually tossed his half-smoked cigarette over his shoulder where it was immediately scooped up by his orderly, snuffed out and stowed in a pocket. The Major rose abruptly. "If there's nothing else, Cunningham . . ." he said, shifting to French. His attitude was one of dismissal.

Cunningham got up awkwardly, but before he could say a word, Nuan had turned toward his tent. Swearing under his breath he stalked toward Thompson, legs aching with each step, but his shoulders were back and his head up. He sat down on his ground cloth and drank from his canteen.

Thompson looked at him with a half-smile on his face. He exchanged glances with Kennedy, squatting nearby. "How'd it go, Captain?"

His curse was audible this time. "You know damn well what a supercilious bastard Nuan is. He seems to be trying to needle me. And he calls these little guys peasants. Hell, he's more of a Colonialist than the French were. And there's no question but that he thinks he's superior to us Americans." He shook his head, and pounded his fist on his knee. "I wonder what it takes to get through to him?"

They chuckled at him. "I don't think you can, Skipper," Thompson said. "Seriously, our last C.O. tried everything. He was a real gregarious guy. Nuan drove him nuts. He even took the Major some whiskey, but Nuan topped him by producing some fine old French brandy. He's that way in everything."

"Like we're a bunch of amateurs and he's the pro," Kennedy added.

"I guess all I can do is to keep trying, but I see nothing but trouble ahead with that guy," Cunningham said with resignation. "I sure wonder what he'll be like in combat."

"You may never know, Captain," Kennedy said dryly. "I've never seen him in action. We've had a few skirmishes with the Viet Cong, but he's always been somewhere else."

Cunningham assessed the observation objectively, but he decided there were no solid grounds for doubting Nuan's courage. He had read the battle reports. Most of the fire-fights had involved squads or platoons, not even company-sized. The Major's job was to command the battalion. Time will tell, he concluded, glad that the three-day exercise in friendly territory would conclude in the morning.

After Kennedy left, Cunningham moved closer to Thompson. "How do you think our team is shaping up, Bud?" Half of the Green Berets in the advisory team were new replacements.

"Hard to say, yet," Thompson began cautiously. "Thank God we're in depth at the top. Harry Adams and Red Kennedy are the best. Since they've got the key jobs, we're in luck there." A doubtful look appeared on his face. "Chet Smith should work out okay. He's had the experience to handle most of the other jobs. He's got a fine reputation as a demolition man and engineer. . . ."

"And as a booze hound," Cunningham interrupted. "He's in worse shape than I am."

Thompson nodded. "That's about it. Some wife troubles are bothering him, I understand. Well, liquor's scarce most of the time. And if he'll stop griping about being sent out here despite the fact he's only got a few months before he's eligible to retire from the Army, then he should be able to hack it."

"Thayer worries me, too," Cunningham said, nodding toward a man sprawled on his back a few trees distant. The medical sergeant's combat fatigues were completely sweat-soaked and his big stomach heaved up and down as he breathed rapidly.

"Yes, but Doc Elliott can make up for any two medics," Thompson said defensively, nodding toward the diminutive, intense corpsman who was treating one of the Vietnamese soldiers at his makeshift aid station.

"Christopolous and Lord seem to be hitting it off," Cunningham commented, removing his wet shirt.

"They're a good radio team," Thompson said slowly. "But apart . . . well, I wonder."

"I see what you mean. Tiny is sure as hell big enough

11

to haul all of our radio gear, but I understand he's a little slow on the repair end."

"Lord may be small, but he's a whiz at electronics. Anyway he's spending a lot of time teaching Tiny."

Cunningham went to the stream in the middle of the woods and washed his shirt, undershirt and socks. He returned to his pack and put on the last of his clean clothing.

First Sergeant Harry Adams, senior non-commissioned officer in the team, joined him and Thompson. He explained the watch system he had set up for the Americans. One man would check the outposts hourly. Two others would remain awake in the bivouac area occupied by the team. He looked at Thompson and waited.

Thompson carried on. "Captain, Adams and I and our old skipper used to split the watch in three sections, each of us being fully dressed for a third of the night. We can do it that way, or else Harry and I can take it tonight."

"Sounds good to me," Cunningham said smiling, and then grunted to his feet. "I've goofed off long enough. Adams, how about taking me around to the outposts? I'd better know how the hell we're situated, or I'm apt to get lost stumbling around in the dark tonight. Just in case. . ."

Adams and Thompson smiled approvingly. "Good idea, sir," the First Sergeant said. "This is about as safe a spot as we'll find outside base camp but we've learned never to take anything for granted out here." He led the way, weaving through the trees.

Cunningham admired the sergeant's confident movements as much as his leadership ability. He noticed that Adams seemed to know exactly where he was putting each foot down, avoiding brush that would crackle, but still able to make fast progress. The 30-year career man continuously glanced around, at the ground, through the brush, up at the tree foliage. An old hand at jungle fighting, Cunningham decided. Probably he wasn't the brainiest guy in the army at a desk job, but he sure could handle troops in the field.

Adams showed him where the machine guns were dug in at the perimeter of the forest, with log parapets and brush to camouflage them. As they went Adams noted the positions and sentry posts in his ever-present black notebook.

"I've got McDonald and Greer out checking the field of fire for the mortars, Captain," he explained.

Cunningham observed with satisfaction that the Civil Guard officers and noncoms, tiny in their neat but ragged green camouflage uniforms, showed great respect for the big burly first sergeant. Adams' face completely changed when he spoke to them. Normally he looked as sad as a bloodhound, his face deeply creased beside his nose and mouth, and jowly at the jaw line. He had a serious, nononsense attitude that told them he was back of them 100%. Yet there was a gentleness coating his iron-bound authority when he smilingly suggested to the Vietnamese improvements they should make to their defenses. He was raspier to the American enlisted men.

"What'd you think of this training operation, Captain?" Adams asked curiously.

"I think the battalion did a good job. How they'll do in combat is another matter, though," Cunningham concluded. He noted Adams' expression and decided with satisfaction that he had said the right thing.

Thompson had a small fire going when Cunningham returned. He sank to the ground and removed his shoes. While heating a C-ration can of chicken and noodles Cunningham put his head back against the tree and observed the peaceful scene. There were dozens of campfires, screened by shelter halves or ground clothes. The odor of food permeated the area, and the glimmer from the flames threw eerie shadows on the foliage above.

This was the part of the army Cunningham liked best. The field. No, he thought, Martha was wrong. It wasn't stupid to volunteer to come out here now, he decided. Why wait until he was ordered?

Her arguments had a modicum of logic. The aide job was good for his career. If he waited, maybe he'd be promoted to major and then if the war in Viet Nam did continue he'd get a better, safer job. And he'd still have the tour of duty on his army record. It'd be smarter to hold off, she had reasoned, because there might be a cease-fire. They both wanted to start a family, but Martha had declared firmly that it was no dice until he returned from the wars.

For some reason Cunningham could not even get excited thinking about making love to Martha, and he found himself wondering why. He sometimes had the impression she liked to talk about sex more than she enjoyed it——that she just went through the motions to satisfy him. And she generally did, too. Except that it annoyed him to listen to her clinical re-hashing of it afterwards. He was the type who wanted to savor the pleasurable aftermath and turn over and go to sleep.

After they had eaten, Harry Adams rejoined the two officers. "Sir, if you're going to see the Major tonight, I've got a few suggestions about shifting some of the mortar positions. And I just found out that Major Nuan has said there's no need to send any recco patrols outside the perimeter. Now, here's what Stew McDonald and Greer recommend." He flattened his black notebook on his knees so they could see his sketch. They discussed the fields of fire. "So you see, McDonald figures that the range would be quite restricted by these trees here."

Cunningham took the notebook and studied it carefully.

"Say, Harry," Thompson said, "Did you say anything to McDonald about policing up his uniform?"

Adams sighed. "Yes, sir, I did. For about the twentieth time. He almost turns my stomach. He claims that uniform's only two weeks old."

"I don't doubt that, but he hasn't taken the damn thing off, I'll bet. Not even to wash," Thompson said angrily.

"I know it, sir. I'll get him scrubbed down tomorrow after we get back to Dan Lac." Adams shook his head. "He's a damned good heavy weapons man. And he's tough and got a lot of guts. But I don't see how he ever made sergeant. So damn filthy and always running off at the mouth."

Cunningham wearily crossed to Command Post where

Nuan's radio was set up. His nightly conference was usually mercifully brief. Its only purpose was to exchange any late information they might have received from headquarters.

"Good evening, Captain," Nuan said, smiling. "Have a cognac?" Without waiting for an answer he motioned to his orderly to pour from a flask into a small silver cup.

Frowning, Cunningham sat down and looked at Nuan's flushed face. The folding map table was covered with a tablecloth, china dishes and silverware. A fancy leather liquor case looked equally out of place in the forest. My God, Cunningham thought, this is too much. He wondered how many men it took to carry all Nuan's extra equipment. In the background there was soft music coming from a small but expensive transistor radio.

Nuan smiled superiorly. "I know what you are thinking, Captain," he started. "But after all this is a training exercise. Why not observe the amenities, at least on our last evening." He laughed throatily. "I have learned a lot from you Americans, and the British and French. Always go first carriage. I have seen how your generals go to war, with their big trailers, their honor guards, their gourmet chefs, and so on. Ah, your MacArthur and Eisenhower knew how to live." He laughed again and sipped his cognac.

Cunningham drained his cup and set it down. The brandy was excellent, but at the moment he had no taste for it. A beer and a shot would be more appropriate to the setting, he thought.

"Major Nuan," he said seriously, "I'd like to recommend some changes in your mortar positions."

Nuan listened to him in silence, a disinterested expression on his face. "Thank you, Captain Cunningham," he said finally. "I shall consider this. But now, won't you have more cognac?"

Cunningham shook his head. "No sir, thank you. Perhaps you would like me to arrange changing the positions, Major?" he said politely, restraining his anger. He knew Nuan would do nothing unless he forced the issue.

"No, thank you, Captain. I am perfectly capable of doing it myself. If, I say *if*, I decide it should be done."

"But Major Nuan . . ." Cunningham began.

"Captain, please. This discussion is becoming tedious. I don't like to have to remind you that I am in command of this battalion." Suddenly his gaze was challenging.

Cunningham realized the color had drained from his face and he flipped a mental coin. Should he force a show-down or play it cool? He made his lips turn up in a taut smile. He shrugged. "Then don't remind me, Major," he replied off-handedly. He leaned forward and touched the empty cup. "I think I will accept your offer of more cognac, sir."

Nuan motioned almost angrily toward the orderly who nervously poured from the flask. The Major slumped back in his chair, hands clasped over his stomach, lips in a pout, eyes almost screened by thick lashes and heavy lids.

Cunningham tried to keep an amused expression on his face as he drank the brandy, but he felt he was probably not carrying it off well. He rose when the silence became too heavy for him to endure.

"Thank you, Major. The cognac was delicious. I hope you will remember about the mortars."

"Captain Cunningham, you are new out here. Please do not start jumping at shadows. I know this area."

"I realize that, sir. I only hope that it is only shadows that bother me. I would be much more at ease if the mortars were re-positioned and if you sent out patrols tonight."

Nuan sighed, exasperated. "You Americans have an expression, Captain. 'Don't try to teach your grandmother how to suck eggs', I believe it is."

Cunningham's face was emotionless, but his eyes betrayed his anger. "Yes, Major, and there's another. 'A stitch in time saves nine'. Also, 'He who hesitates is lost'. Good night, Major." He turned on his heel and left.

It sure was going by the book, Cunningham thought, still furious, as he rigged his hammock. It was as the instructors at Fort Benning had warned them. Some of them

16

—like Nuan—seemed to resent being helped, even though they knew damn well the fate of their country depended on it. Nuan was a prime example; a Regular Army type, from a high-class old family, who'd been sitting on his ass in Saigon in fancy staff jobs most of the time. Now he was obviously sore at being out here working with the Civil Guard.

Cunningham wondered why, as he climbed into the hammock and pulled the mosquito netting over him. Why did Nuan draw this kind of an assignment? Obviously he disliked these people he was training, and felt far superior to them. It must be politics, Cunningham concluded, closing his eyes. But Nuan had one thing going for him that he, Cunningham, didn't. He was not only an advisor, but he was also in command. But the Americans were neither fish nor fowl. Cunningham could only advise, recommend. He fell asleep, irritated with his position and still wondering about Nuan, the man. Overriding both were fears for the future.

Chapter 2

The heavy hand of Harry Adams shook Cunningham from slumber. In threshing about to get from underneath the mosquito netting he almost fell from the hammock. For a second or two he stood swaying, devoid of any sense of direction.

Apologetically, he finally acknowledged Adams' announcement of the time and the report that there had been no activity during the first third of the night. He quickly searched for his pants and shoes and put them on.

Cunningham had to smile when Red Kennedy stopped by to escort him on the rounds. They had assigned the second most experienced noncom to take the watch with him. Good thinking, he concluded, after the first flush of embarrassment had passed.

Following Kennedy's almost ghostlike movements through the woods, he felt clumsy, shoes snapping twigs, and having to duck suddenly and frequently to avoid low-hanging limbs. They talked in whispers and he listened carefully as Kennedy questioned the sentries and gun crews. He was gratified that he was understanding more of the Vietnamese language as time went on.

Although still dead-tired, Cunningham decided to remain fully awake during his section of the watch and spend the time talking with Kennedy. It was a valuable few hours, for the Intelligence sergeant had more information about Viet Cong habits and tactics and weapons than there was in any book.

Lieutenant Thompson was already dressed when Cunningham went to awaken him for the final shift of the night. He and Adams had the tough periods, while Cunningham had been assigned the soft one, a period when the Viet Cong seldom attacked. He was glad of that, too. As yet he just had not oriented himself quickly enough to the sounds, smells and lay of the land in Viet Nam.

Cunningham started to remove his shoes but at the last minute decided against it. He swung himself fully clad into his hammock after making certain his new model, rapid firing carbine and ammunition belt were within easy reach. That's the secret, he decided. Know what the hell you're going to do first, and where you're heading before you go to sleep. Then you can move instinctively, if there is an attack.

Not long before dawn the sound of gunfire sent him tumbling from the hammock into a crouch on the ground. As he grabbed his weapon he tried to decipher the Civil Guard whistle signals over the staccato barking of the automatic guns. First the deeper throated drumming of the heavy .50 caliber machine guns against the background of light machine guns and rifle fire, then the sound of exploding mortar rounds filled the darkness. Cunningham peered around in bewilderment, unable to get his bearings, wondering if Major Nuan had re-positioned his mortars. Finally he pin-pointed the noise of combat.

The shooting was coming from the far side of the forest, farthest from where he and the other Green Berets had bedded down. Cunningham could see only occasional muzzle flashes through the dense woods, but the light of a mortar starshell helped his sense of direction. He took only a few steps toward the firefight before he halted, uncertainly.

He told himself that Bud Thompson was on duty and automatically would have headed for the scene of action. That was routine. He tried to locate Nuan's command post but all was darkness in that area. It might be smarter, Cunningham reluctantly decided, to check the outposts on this side of the perimeter first.

Fortunately the din of mortar fire cloaked his steps as he approached a heavy machine gun position. Suddenly there were muffled shouts and moans of pain ahead. The faint starlight filtering through the trees showed violent movement which he knew to be hand-to-hand fighting. Finally there was a shot. Then another.

Cunningham wanted to rush forward, but wisely held back, screened by a tree. In the darkness he could not distinguish enemy from friend. He cursed under his breath, unable to decide what to do. Ahead he heard a few grunts, whispers, and the clanking of metal. Raising his carbine and snapping it on automatic fire, he peered ahead and spotted several moving shadows among the trees. Before he could decide whether or not to shoot they had disappeared. He slowly crawled forward until his gun barrel touched something soft. He probed gently but it did not move.

Cunningham cautiously groped with his hand—a uniformed body. He wiped blood from his fingers. It was one of the Civil Guard, with a knife in his chest. He slid around and down into the depression marking the machine gun emplacement. There were three more bodies, one a Viet Cong. Puzzled for a moment, he suddenly turned toward the far side of the bunker. Anger rose in him and he swore. The .50 caliber machine gun and ammunition boxes had disappeared. The clever bastards, he thought.

The attack at the other side of the forest was a diversion. They were after this gun all the time. He jumped to his feet and clambered over the low parapet. Trying to run as silently as possible, he sped toward the edge of the woods. He heard the VC ahead and to his left, moving slower and more noisily than usual. The gun and ammo must be holding them back, he decided, continuing directly to the perimeter. He saw the tall grass in the starlight and cut sharply to the left.

Steadying his carbine against a tree, Cunningham waited. Suddenly the Viet Cong were plainly silhouetted. He opened up. The gun spit its deadly stream of small caliber but high velocity bullets. He sprayed the area until his clip was empty and then dropped to his knees, moved to the left, and reloaded. When he rose and advanced two shots were fired in his direction, but his own carbine fire brought screams of pain. The black-clad figures were all on the ground.

Cunningham yelled in both English and Vietnamese to give his location just in case his men or the Civil Guards had been attracted by the gunfire. He started to move forward but drew back as he saw a shadow in motion. He cursed himself for stupidly revealing his position. From the cover of a tree-trunk, he spotted a dark figure slipping away. This time he fired without hesitating. The man went down, but a stray round hit one of the ammunition boxes. The .50 caliber shells exploded and he was blinded by the flash. He stumbled forward and grabbed a tree for support.

His gun barrel dipped and slapped against something solid in the short grass. Cunningham carefully felt around with his jungle boot. He groaned. Ponji sticks had been planted firmly in the ground in front of him. Two-foot long sharpened bamboo sticks imbedded at an angle so that the unwary moving through the darkness would catch one in the ankle or shin. The tip's probably covered with shit, too, he thought, feeling sick to his stomach. A wound from one would become infected in a matter of hours. And there were probably foot traps in the area too. The VC had had time to dig some of their brush-concealed two-foot-wide holes with sides lined with more bamboo splinters.

Sweat poured down his face as he slowly advanced, feeling with feet and gun barrel for the booby traps. He gave a sigh of relief when he finally came into a cleared area. It was almost his last. He had been concentrating on the ground. Only the snap of a branch saved him. Swinging his carbine upward in the direction of the sound, he saw a dark shape jumping at him. The gun barrel deflected a knife thrust which would have disemboweled him. He barely felt the slash in his shoulder as he pushed hard with the rifle, forcing the Viet Cong back. He pulled the trigger and a dozen bullets ripped the man apart. Cunningham started to where the VC had dropped the machine gun.

On the other side of the forest, Lieutenant Bud Thompson was pinned down. The Viet Cong were firing ahead and he knew other guerillas were near by, waiting.

His patrol of the outposts had begun routinely after an almost sleepless night. Thompson yawned widely and told Stew McDonald to brew some coffee while he made the rounds alone. The 220-pound sergeant was still half-asleep and would have been more of a hindrance than a help, crashing through the underbrush.

Thompson stopped in a small clearing, leaned against a tree and looked up at the dark blue sky filled with shimmering stars. It was still warm and humid. For some reason the night reminded him of Ann. He sniffed. There was a scent of perfume in the air coming from the blossoms in the tree above him. Then it came back to him, the last time he had seen her. It was last December, the night before he had left for Viet Nam. The camelia tree in her back yard had been in bloom.

It had been a rotten weekend, he remembered. Ann's father and mother had put it up to him plainly. She was an only child. They would not give their consent to his marriage to her until he was out of the army.

The memory made him want to escape from the fragrance of the tree. Maybe he should not have been so

21

stubborn, but he had been unable to give his promise to them. It was not that he particularly intended to make a career of the army. He eventually wanted to be a construction engineer, and he also wanted to travel, to see something of the world. If Ann were tied to her mother's apron strings he might as well forget his ambitions. She had to make the choice. It was her parents or him, he had decided, then and there.

Thompson inhaled the scent and sighed. That last night she had given herself to him fully in the pergola with the air fragrant from the camelia blossoms.

But being apart made people do strange things, he now realized. Her letters were uncertain, belying her promise to go with him after his Viet Nam tour, wherever he was assigned, in the army or as a civilian.

Thompson's thoughts might have been with Ann in Georgia, but his senses were automatically attuned to the night in Viet Nam. As he approached the perimeter he felt himself drawn to the shelter of a great tree trunk. He stopped, searched ahead for the sight of the heavy machine gun position, and listened carefully. It was too dark to see anything and there was no difference in the smell of the forest. Yet, there was something wrong and he didn't know what it was. For one thing it was silent; completely still. There were no sounds of small animals rustling through the underbrush, or birds in the branches among the leaves. Usually near a position one could hear the murmur of low voices, some coughing, or the sound of metal against metal. It was as if all forms of life had stopped in their tracks and were listening, waiting for something to happen; as if a danger signal had been sounded.

A moving patch of black, darker even than the forest, was the first tip-off. Thompson slid to his knees and elbows, carbine ready. He listened even harder, holding his breath, motionless. Suddenly he heard the familiar click of a rifle's safety catch being released. Only it came from the wrong direction. Thompson flattened on the ground. There was the sound of a bugle and he saw the flash of gunfire aimed at the gun emplacement. Noise from another nearby concentration of weapons came from a different direction. An attack on two positions, he decided. The Civil Guards were sending back sporadic fire.

Thompson cautiously crawled forward, edging toward where he had heard someone with a rifle. Under these conditions it would be suicidal to charge the gun position, leaving his back unprotected. Suddenly there was a lull in the automatic gunfire. He fumbled in his shirt pocket for his metal whistle. He quickly signalled with a blast on it and hastily moved to another spot and crouched in the shelter of a large thick bush.

A figure moved, not ten feet away. Thompson instinctively fired, beating the enemy's shot by just enough to survive. He sprayed the trees to the right and left and heard shouts of pain. The VC tactics now fell into shape. They were attacking two adjoining gun positions. A third group of Viet Cong had sneaked in between, ready to assist the initial assault, or go either way in case resistance was too stiff in one location or the other.

From the firepower, Thompson estimated the enemy had a platoon size force. A bold maneuver, against a battalion, with little chance of success—unless, he corrected himself, they knew exactly where the Civil Guard perimeter outposts were located and that there were no patrols beyond the forest. He swore softly. It probably meant one of the South Vietnamese had slipped away from the bivouac and passed the information to the VC.

He heard the sound of a shrill whistle and returned the signal. Then he recognized the voices of Adams and Smith to his left, followed by the distinctive noise of their automatic gunfire. He raised his own weapon and fired in the same direction. Carbine empty he ran toward them, dodging through the trees and brush as swiftly as he had moved on the football field.

Harry Adams loomed out of the darkness, and Thompson slid to a halt beside him, going to one knee and reloading his carbine before he spoke. Chet Smith lumbered toward them, panting noisily.

"Harry, go back and circle around," Thompson whispered. "Get some of our boys or the Guard and hit the VC between the machine gun and the sentry position at the fringe of the perimeter. Smitty and I'll start toward you from this side. They may pull back right into us."

Stew McDonald and Dick Greer quietly approached after signalling. Thompson briefed them on the situation and the four Americans spread out on a line and advanced at a crawl.

Thompson heard the *karrump* of grenades exploding ahead and knew Adams was in business. American automatic fire split the night ahead. There were moans and muffled voices and the sounds of men hurriedly pushing through the brush. He raised his carbine expectantly and waited. As the noises drew closer he could also hear shots in the distance. There was at least one U.S. Army weapon similar to his own, judging from the sound. He frowned as he waited. It could be Red Kennedy, or Jake Potter, the other demolition man, or the pair of radio operators. But it was Captain Cunningham who was the center of his disquiet. How was he doing? His hands tightened on his carbine. Well, he thought grimly, we all have to go into action for the first time sooner or later. And there was no use his worrying about Cunningham. They had their own problems right here.

As the sounds drew closer and his muscles tensed Thompson felt a sense of satisfaction. So far everything he had done that night had been automatic, practiced, borne of experience. He had lost the feeling of helplessness he had had when he first came to Viet Nam; the way he knew Cunningham probably felt right now.

On the other side of the forest, Cunningham had almost begun to relax. He was positive the Viet Cong guerillas beside the now-wrecked .50 caliber gun were dead. Still he advanced cautiously. After four paces he paused, listening. A rustling in the brush caught his attention and he jumped back. A long bamboo spear whistled past his head and he fired at the shadow. The VC dropped to the ground, legs jerking spasmodically. Then to the right there was other movement. He shifted his gun barrel and downed a Viet Cong coming at him with upraised knife.

Cunningham leaned against a tree, sweating profusely, trembling all over, almost sick to his stomach. He did not know which way to go. He imagined VC's behind every bush, making every shadow. Another guerilla popped out from among the trees and Cunningham cut him down with a burst, but the man's momentum carried him right into the American officer, forcing him to his knees. Glancing over the inert figure half on top of him, Cunningham spotted a second VC advancing, rifle ready. He heaved the dead Viet Cong aside and opened up. Both bodies crashed to the ground.

He had to stay on all fours for a minute, breathing hard, sweat streaming into his eyes. Slowly and carefully he reached the place where the enemy had dropped the .50 caliber machine gun. The ammo explosion had shattered it. There were four dead Viet Cong and a uniformed Civil Guard on the ground. He bent over the Civil Guard, wondering how he came to be with the others. His hands were not bound and his weapon was in his hand. Cunningham reached to turn him over.

"Don't touch him!" Tiny Christopolous lunged into Cunningham, almost knocking him down. "Move back and watch." Christopolous stepped behind a tree, poked his gun barrel out and fired point-blank at the dead man. There was a muffled explosion and the body was blown upward, blood and innards splashing the trees where he and Cunningham had taken cover.

"Those bastards do that once in awhile," Christopolous explained. "Just as they bug out. Booby trap one of our dead with a live hand grenade. When we move them, zap! We've had it."

"You sure saved my ass that time," Cunningham said.

The radioman looked at Cunningham's blood-stained uniform and then down at the dead. "Looks like you've been having your own private war over here." He warily checked the Viet Cong bodies and the battered machine gun, which he easily picked up with one hand. He extended his other to Cunningham who was sitting gasping against a tree. "Come on, Skipper, that shoulder needs looking after. Doc Elliott and Al Thayer have probably set up shop about now."

Cunningham needed Tiny's assistance to get back to the bivouac area. The loss of blood had left him a little weak although the wound was not deep. What bothered him most was the shakiness in his legs, caused, he decided, by the close call with the grenade.

Doc Elliott had just finished bandaging a flesh wound in Bud Thompson's back. He then went to work on Cunningham.

Thompson passed him a lighted cigarette and reported the action on the far perimeter.

In turn Cunningham briefed him about the attempted capture of the heavy machine gun. "I figure they wanted it for its 7,000-yard range, to use for anti-aircraft fire on our helicopters."

"They must be real hard-up for AA to hit us with that small a force," Thompson said. "They've really got guts. This was a damn well-planned operation, too. Headquarters will want to hear all about it."

Cunningham slowly got to his feet, helped by Doc Elliott. After thanking the medic, he motioned to Thompson to follow him. They sat down by their hammocks in the dim early-morning light.

"Before I go check in with Major Nuan, I want to get started on a few things. Kennedy is probably the one to gather what I want," he said quietly.

Thompson looked at him puzzled. "What do you have in mind?"

"For one thing I want to know just how many of the Civil Guard actually got into the action, and how many rounds they fired. Same for our team. And I want a count of the VC dead. They had to pull out fast, so they must have left some behind. See if you can tell whose rounds got them. The Civil Guard's or ours. Ours leave a pretty distinctive hole."

26

"I see what you're getting at," Thompson began, nodding doubtfully. "How many of the Civil Guard did fight and how much damage did they do, if any. Well, we've tried to find out before about that, to see if some of the Civil Guard just sat back and hoped the VC didn't spot them. We didn't have much luck before, but we'll try again."

"Right. I want to know just how much these Civil Guard Companies have on the ball before we go out on a full-scale strike force operation in VC territory." He got up slowly and painfully, a wry grin on his face.

"And Bud, before the day is over I want to have another session with you. I figure I should have been doing something in the command line rather than running around lost all by myself."

Thompson started to protest, but Cunningham waved him into silence.

"Hell, Bud, it was just pure luck that I ran into the group making off with the machine gun, and you know it. If it hadn't been for Tiny I'd be a dead pigeon now."

"Well, it's pretty hard to figure just what to do in a night attack like this," Thompson said. "One time you need a commander to control things centrally. The next time you need every goddam bit of firepower you can produce." He leaned forward and lowered his voice. "Well, good luck. There's Nuan. From the look on his face I'd say his casualty list is pretty high."

"Too bad it takes a bunch of dead men to open him up," Cunningham said, and he squared his shoulders and walked toward the South Vietnamese major.

For once Nuan's thick, black hair was mussed and his face was sweaty. He was holding a Thompson submachine gun loosely in his hand, and all but screaming at the ARVN Captain who was his Operations Officer. Captain Cau trotted off to gather information for Nuan, who turned now and appeared abashed by Cunningham's presence. Then, as if a mask were pulled over his face, the major gathered himself together. In two swift gestures, he wiped perspiration from his face and smoothed his wrinkled shirt. He grabbed his cap before speaking, as if it were his badge of authority.

"So, Captain, the situation now appears to be in hand. We fought them off at the southwest outposts," Nuan said calmly in English.

"How bad are your casualties, Major?"

"I don't know yet. Not serious, though. The Viet Cong did not come in strength."

"We estimate at least a VC platoon, Major. That's a pretty good-sized force. And we figure you got hit pretty hard over there."

Nuan's eyebrows raised. "You personally were not there then? I wondered, since I expected you to join me here. I hope you found a safe place during the firefight." There was a nasty smile on his face.

Cunningham ignored the thrust. "No, Major, I was busy elsewhere. I located the man of yours who defected and gave our positions to the VC, the one who tipped them off you were sending out no patrols." His tone was coolly straightforward.

It was Nuan's turn to feel his face redden with irritation. "Defector? One of my Civil Guards? Nonsense, Cunningham."

"You may call it nonsense, but I caught him with the VC when they were trying to carry away one of the .50 caliber machine guns."

Nuan was furious. Obviously this action was news to him.

Cunningham explained the situation. "The reason it was not reported to you by your people was that your entire gun crew was killed, and none of the other Civil Guards in the sector bothered to get into the fight," he concluded sarcastically.

Nuan sputtered and asked for additional information.

Moving into the cone of light from the lantern, Cunningham filled him in with the details. He observed, with no little satisfaction, Nuan's gaze fix on his bandaged shoulder. Carefully avoiding mention that he had stumbled on the situation and had almost got himself killed through

28

carelessness, he concluded his story. He had to hand it to Nuan. The Vietnamese didn't bat an eye.

Nuan assumed a sympathetic expression. "I am so sorry that you were injured. A close call. And this was your first run-in with the VC, wasn't it? You did well."

But Cunningham was not to be drawn out this time. He had the upper hand and he felt good about it. "I'll get back to my boys now," he said impassively. "I want to report the attack to Da Nang."

"Is that necessary, Captain? We will be back at Dan Lac by midday."

"Perhaps, Major, perhaps." Cunningham couldn't resist a parting comment. "If we don't get hit again by the Viet Cong. I hope you keep track of all your people and send patrols out ahead of us to the rendezvous area where we meet the trucks." He turned and faded into the darkness, Nuan's retort almost inaudible. By God, he thought, feeling his shoulder, it was almost worth getting knifed to see that bastard lose a little of his cockiness. He went toward Tiny who had turned on the radio transmitter.

As he scribbled his message on a pad of paper, Cunningham thought appreciatively of his radio operator. "You know, Tiny," he began. "I used to get so damn mad at the Chicago Bears fans. They make you think George Halas is the only good football coach in the National Pro League. I had a pretty good bet with one of them on a game you played in. Man, was I happy when you broke through and blocked a field goal which would have won it for the Bears in the last ten seconds. But I'll tell you one thing. Your showing up out there tonight at the perimeter made me a hell of a lot happier."

Tiny Christopolous looked at him, surprised, and then laughed hoarsely. "You're all right, skipper." The smile faded slowly and he gazed into the distance. A look of awe appeared on his face.

"By God, Captain. You know what? That game was only two years ago this Fall. Shit! It seems like a hundred years. Viet Nam. Shit." He spit.

Handing him the message, Cunningham silently agreed. Illinois was farther than three weeks and half-a-globe away for him at the moment.

Chapter 3

Two sets of detailed reports of the firefight went back to Corps and Regimental headquarters from Dan Lac; one Vietnamese and one U.S. Army. Cunningham had to send his in over the protests of Bud Thompson and Red Kennedy. Harry Adams had tended to side with his commanding officer. Cunningham compromised with the dissenters by stating at the beginning of his letter that it was for American consumption only, even though he knew it would probably end up being leaked to the ARVN command.

"I know that this won't make them happy back in Da Nang," he explained to Thompson. "Both Fowler and Boulger will be upset as hell. And the Vietnamese will downgrade it by saying it's just a fresh-caught U.S. Army Adviser complaining." Cunningham paced back and forth in the low, concrete building housing his Control Center and communications equipment while the three Americans listened to him.

"Well," he continued, "I don't give a damn what they think or say. As long as I'm out here I'm going to lay it right on the line. Neither Nuan or his company commanders showed much initiative in taking the offensive after the VC did start to withdraw. That's for sure. And it was our shooting that produced most of the enemy casualties. If one of Nuan's handpicked men hadn't defected and given away our positions we wouldn't have been hit anywhere near so hard."

"Excuse me, Captain," Kennedy began. "The trouble is that we can't absolutely prove any of these claims. And that's where the Major has you right by the gonads. Suspicion is one thing. Concrete evidence is another. He's reporting a lot more VC casualties than we estimate, too, saying they hauled most of their dead and wounded away. Sure, everything points to our being right, but the ARVN High Command has to back Nuan or else they lose face."

"Face, schmace," Cunningham replied, throwing up his arms. "Christ, we're trying to fight a war, not run a cultural psychology class." He turned to them and smiled. "Okay, the report goes in as is, but I promise to be a good boy in the future. I know that my hassling with the Major only makes your training job harder."

Adams' face was creased with worry. "It's more than that, sir. When he gets sore at you he takes it out on the company commanders. Gives them hell. Then he refuses to see them at all. You know what that means. Everybody from there on down gets their asses chewed in succession. First thing you know the morale is all shot." He looked at his watch. "Well, I'd better move. I'm getting the senior noncoms together to give them a pep talk. Maybe that'll help a little."

Cunningham turned his attention back to his Intelligence expert. "Kennedy, I haven't had a chance to ask you since you came back from Da Nang—were you able to pick up anything new? Any rumors?"

The red-head had taken the captured VC weapons to headquarters for examination by American Intelligence officers. "It's just scuttlebutt, Captain, but despite all our air reconnaissance and all the U.S. Marine and Army patrols, they're still getting reports that company-size units of PARVN—Peoples Army of North Viet Nam—are moving across to the coast from Laos. Exactly where these regular Army troops are grouping isn't known. But apparently they'll come in to support the VC in areas they already hold. We may find it tough."

"What do you make of it?" Cunningham urged.

"I'll bet that these regular army people will be more than advisers, operating with small groups of guerillas. My guess is that they'll be kept together in platoons and companies, to operate as units in larger-scale operations with

31

the VC. And they'll concentrate on hitting our American troops just as soon as they start taking the offensive."

"Sounds logical to me," Thompson agreed. "After our bombing runs in North Viet, Ho Chi Minh will need a few victories to build up the morale again. Even if they are costly to his troops."

"Apparently there's quite an argument going on back at headquarters about that and the rest of the VC tactics," Kennedy continued. "Personally, I think that they'll use the hard-core, fanatical and well-trained VC for hit-and-run, small-scale raids at our big bases." He smiled at their doubting faces. "I know, a lot of them will get clobbered. We've got American security troops around the perimeters at Da Nang and elsewhere. But remember, the VC knows the terrain and their intelligence is good. They'll send in their scouts first and know exactly where our outposts are. The Viet Cong'll sneak in close enough to use mortars and grenade launchers on our aircraft, troop billets, and then bug out fast. And the more shooting there is, the better chance they have to escape." He laughed grimly. "And won't that make our people nervous. Besides, think how it will look in the papers back home."

Thompson spoke up again. "I think Red's right. The VC can do a lot of damage by infiltrating with even a squad-size unit. They're sure to know where they're going and probably will get help from a few of their people inside the bases."

"This throws a new light on things, doesn't it?" Cunningham mused, thoughtfully. "Giving the Civil Guard the benefit of the doubt, they probably could do all right against the average bunch of VC guerillas, but against regular Army units, that's another thing."

After Kennedy left, Cunningham brought up the subject again. "You know, Bud, our own safety is involved in this. We'd better work up a damn good team plan for splitting up and going to the strategic places if we run into real rough opposition when we do go out on search-and-clear operations. Stand by the company and platoon commanders to help stiffen their backbone. Take command if nothing else works." He smiled at Thompson's dismay. "Hell, I know it's illegal, but we've got to save our ass. We'll bypass Nuan with this. Hold informal sessions with the c.o.s and noncoms. Get them to trust us as much as possible. So they know we'll stand by them."

"Okay. Why don't you let Adams and Kennedy and I work something out." Thompson looked at his watch and swept the sweat from his forehead with a forefinger. "God, it's hot in here. How about a beer?"

The entire American team ate together at two tables on a porch attached to a thatched-roof mess hall. At night mosquito netting was hung to close in the shelter. They went inside only when it was raining hard, because it also housed the old-fashioned stove, and the thumping of the diesel generator was so loud you almost had to shout to carry on a normal conversation.

Thompson went directly to the battered old refrigerator and got two cans of beer. Cunningham sat down on the porch at a bench at one of the two long tables, removed his sweat-soaked green beret, and sourly looked around the area. At least the swaying of the tree branches made him feel as if there were a little breeze. Nearby, the white-washed concrete-block buildings with either tin or thatched roofs glared in the sunlight. There was activity only at Major Nuan's headquarters.

Well, Cunningham thought, it's primitive as hell but it's about as clean a spot as you'd find in South Viet Nam. He scratched at his prickly heat under his arms and gratefully accepted the can of beer from Thompson. Thank God the generator hasn't crapped out for a couple of days, he thought. Their feeble lights and refrigerator owed it a debt, for a change. Seldom did it run more than thirty-six hours straight without a breakdown.

"I sure hope there's mail on that chopper this afternoon," Thompson said wistfully, sitting down across from him.

"You should get some, the amount you send out," Cunningham teased. He knew his Executive Officer faithfully wrote to his fiancee each evening. But Cunningham didn't

33

want to continue that particular conversation. His conscience was bothering him. It had been two weeks since he'd sent anything off to Martha. She wrote him several times a week. Thompson broke into his thought stream.

"Dave, how did your wife take to army life when you were first married?"

Cunningham was startled at the unexpected question. He considered it for a full half-minute. "Surprisingly well. But then, Martha's folks had traveled all over and taken her and her brothers and sisters along. She's a pretty adaptable person. When she gets to a new place, she makes an effort to get acquainted, finds out the best places to shop and all that. She's pretty eager and a good organizer, so she joins clubs and all that, and works at it. The doors open to her fast."

Suddenly he had a guilty feeling again. Because after he spoke he sensed less than satisfaction with Martha. It bothered him because she was really a good army wife. But what did he want from her? Why was he dissatisfied? Was it because she was just too sociable?

Maybe that was it, he mused. The house had been generally in a state of confusion, with her rushing off to meetings and luncheons, or having them at home. Somehow Martha seemed to be driven to being on a perpetual round of social activities. When he did get back to Fort Sheridan after a trip with the General he got no rest. She generally had a full schedule planned. And what he wanted was to take it easy.

Martha knew how he felt, but it was always the same. It seemed to him as if she did not want to be alone with him. Every evening there was a reception or a cocktail party, and afterwards she would rather eat at the club with other couples, or go out to a local restaurant than be at home with him.

But there was no questioning the value of her role. She was a distinct asset to a career army officer wanting to get ahead. She contributed, he thought, sighing. Boy, how she contributed. Nobody around her got any rest. And she was friends with all the senior officers' wives, from Mrs. General on down.

"How do you think Ann will make out?" Cunningham asked carefully, anxious to keep his mind off Martha, and aware too that Thompson obviously had some misgivings about his girl and their future together.

"I wish I knew. She's awfully close to her family. No brothers or sisters, you know." Thompson explained her parents' attitude.

"If you do get married, Bud, don't live near them. Even if they are real nice," Cunningham advised, suddenly weary and feeling old. Not that he could really blame Martha's folks for anything other than living near Fort Sheridan in Lake Forest. His father-in-law actually was a pretty good scout, though dull as hell, almost totally immersed in his stocks and bonds. Martha's mother was in and out of the Cunningham house all the time. He reddened and glanced at Thompson to see if he had noticed, but his Executive Officer was as deep in his own thoughts.

Cunningham could never forget one occasion. He had come out of the shower, tired and bare-assed naked, thinking he was home alone after a particularly annoying trip to Fort Carson, Colorado. His mother-in-law had been putting Martha's laundry away in her dresser drawers. She had offered no apology for being there. Then, after clinically examining him up and down through her steel-rimmed glasses, she had finally spoken. "Well, I can see what Martha meant. You *are* well-equipped."

Her folks were also embarrassingly free with their money. He and Martha were the only couple of their army rank with a color TV set. Their supplemented income and his aide job were a source of some envy and a lot of back-biting, but he had to admit that Martha had gone about her business with a smile, ignoring all the snide remarks.

Cunningham glanced keenly at the frown Thompson perpetually wore when he was thinking hard. "Look, Bud," he said, "Play it cool. You can drive yourself nuts way out here if you try to second-guess your girl. I remember how I was in Germany after graduation. The year before we got married I almost worried myself sick. You just can't read between the lines of a letter. And the longer you're separated the more you both change. She finds it harder to write, and you start to misunderstand the simple things she puts down on paper. Best thing you can do is to find a date the next time you get to Da Nang or Saigon."

Thompson started to protest.

"Hell, I didn't mean going out and getting laid," Cunningham said, chuckling. "Take a gal out to dinner. Or for drinks. Go some place you can sit around and talk. I don't give a damn if it's just the USO or a church social. But get acquainted with women again. It'll help you keep your perspective."

Cunningham tossed his beer can in the trash barrel and left the porch. But if you can get yourself a piece of tail, he reflected, for God's sake do it. By God, there was nothing like it to give a man something different to think about. You forgot to be a martyr. Your conscience might bother you, but you reasserted your virility. Cunningham sighed, remembering Monique, the restaurant hostess he had met on his way through Saigon. He firmly decided then and there to keep in touch with her by mail. He just might get back to the capital. For a moment he thought wildly of how she had been in bed.

He crossed the sun-baked open area in front of the Civil Guard headquarters, and was surprised to find Major Nuan not only immediately available but also apparently waiting for him. Usually the Major made him cool his heels outside for a few minutes.

"It appears, Captain, that we have a difference of opinion. I am informed by my superiors that the Civil Guard casualty figures of yours are much larger than those I submitted," Nuan began, accusingly.

"Let's put it this way, Major. It's not 'opinion,' it's a difference of arithmetic. Someplace along the line your people must have divided by about two."

Nuan bristled and tapped some papers on his desk.

"No Major, I know exactly how many men you had with you when you started the training exercise. I also know how many men got into those trucks that hauled us out." Nuan tried to interrupt again but Cunningham was not to be put off. "And I know the size of the group you left behind to bring in the bodies. Plus those wounded evacuated. Figure all of those and you come up with the statistics I sent in."

"You're wrong, Cunningham. You're dead wrong. You must have failed to count those I sent back earlier, who became ill or were hurt during the field problem." Nuan watched him closely, his eyes slanted slits.

"No, that won't hack it either, Major," Cunningham replied wearily. "Your medics told Doc Elliott a completely different story. You must have forgotten that you ordered a muster taken right after we got into that forest. Elliott saw the figures." Cunningham shrugged. "Look, what difference does it make now?"

"None to you, Captain. But this is my command. I think you are just trying to make me look bad. And reporting that business about one of my men defecting . . ." Nuan stopped suddenly, face flushed. He had not intended to reveal that he had been forwarded a copy of exactly what Cunningham had sent. A broad smile flowed smoothly on his face.

"But, as you say, Captain Cunningham, let's forget the entire incident." The Major's manner was amiable as they discussed plans for future training. He even extended himself by asking about Cunningham's wounded shoulder.

On his way back to the mess hall for dinner, Cunningham shook his head in disgust. Nuan was too transparent at times, he thought. He knew damn well I wouldn't give in, so he thought he'd try a little honey. Screw him.

Bud Thompson met him with another can of beer and three letters from Martha. Most of the team members straggled onto the porch wearily but were brightened by the mail and the ice-cold beer. There was a lot of chatter as letters were opened and read.

Cunningham glanced at his cursorily and was reminded that Martha was singularly unimaginative when putting anything down on paper. For all she said she could have

37

written a letter in triplicate and mailed it on separate days. He ate when the austere, tasteless meal was announced ready, noticing that most of the others kept on drinking beer or had produced a bottle of something stronger. But tonight intoxicants had no attraction from him. He followed Bud Thompson, who was happily clutching a thick packet of letters, back to the Control Center. Before he left he observed that Chet Smith was sitting in silence, staring into the distance, a full tumbler of brandy in front of him.

There were two tiny bedrooms for the officers in the concrete structure. Thompson's door was already closed although there was a dim light under the door so Cunningham went to his own room which was furnished with a bare minimum. He snapped on the light bulb hanging by its cord from the ceiling and removed his clothing. Weighing the letters from Martha in his hand, he finally tossed them into the open foot locker at the end of his cot. Cunningham lay down, turned on his radio and vaguely listened to the news on Armed Forces Radio. Even the report about more draft card burnings back in the states failed to stir him from the purposeless, irritated attitude which had descended on him. He turned off the light and listened to the music. Already he was covered with sweat and mosquitoes and other insects pestered him although there was netting over the door and the slit that served as a window.

Turning the light on again Cunningham spent a half hour trying to read a detective story but gave it up because his mind wandered. Finally he picked up pen and stationery. He thought guiltily about Martha but started a letter, "Dear Monique . . ." He knew he'd get to see her a lot sooner than his wife, and he recalled his conversation with Thompson. Maybe he shouldn't be so hard up, he reflected, but that was the way it was with a man. You wanted it much worse when there was none around.

The next morning he was in a more optimistic mood and decided to take advantage of Major Nuan's more amenable attitude. Once again he was ushered into his office just as soon as he arrived.

Cunningham broached the probability of increased Viet Cong activity and the possibility of more North Vietnamese regular troops in the country. To his surprise, Nuan agreed. Cunningham plunged on, urging that they intensify the training of the Civil Guard, particularly in counter-attack procedures after they had been pinned down by unexpectedly heavy firepower. Nuan made no comment, so he continued his recommendations, couched in per-suasive phrases. Still Nuan only nodded and remained silent. Cunningham finally faltered in confusion.

"Well, what do you think, sir?"

Nuan shrugged, raising his hands in a Gallic gesture. "It all sounds good, Captain, except I can't see how we will fit it in now that the picture has changed." A superior smile crossed his face and he gave Cunningham an inno-cent look. "Or haven't you had the word, Cunningham? I must say this surprises me. Don't you know we have re-ceived orders to undertake our first search-and-clear operation?"

Cunningham's face reddened and it was all he could do to keep his temper. By God, he thought, jaw muscles bulging as he gritted his teeth, he let me ramble on and on, knowing this all the time. "No sir, I didn't know that," he finally admitted.

Chuckling with gratification at the American's discom-fiture, Nuan nodded toward a chair. "Sit down, Captain. You should have a message on this in a short while. Mean-while, why don't you read my instructions? Then we can discuss what we have to do to prepare for it."

After looking over the brief operation order and exam-ining the tactical map with the Major, Cunningham sent for Thompson, First Sergeant Adams and Red Kennedy. The first step would be to prepare a detailed set of in-structions for the battalion, which would have to be ap-proved by their superiors. Nuan gathered his staff and they assigned certain sections of the order to their respective personnel. The meeting did not break up until lunch time.

Cunningham described to Thompson his initial session with Nuan. "I felt like hitting the little bastard," he concluded.

"Someone at Da Nang must have fouled up, not getting the word to you," Thompson said disgustedly. He called Tiny Christopolous to the Control Center.

The radio operator was not long in raising Lieutenant Colonel Fowler, Cunningham's immediate superior, whose command post was not far from Da Nang.

"I'm sorry, Cunningham," Fowler said. "I just got the damned thing myself. My radio's been fouled up. Colonel Boulger had it flown over. Wanted me to take a look at it first. I'm just about to have it transmitted to you. But the old man said in his note it's almost identical to the one going through ARVN channels."

"It's just that it's embarrassing, Colonel," Cunningham protested once more. "Nuan's tough enough to deal with as it is." He could have bitten his tongue once the words had come out. He was almost certain Major Nuan's people were monitoring all of his radio transmissions.

"Think the Civil Guard can hack this one, Cunningham?" Fowler asked. "Particularly in view of your last report."

"It's a little too early to tell now. I think so. That is, if we find anything there to fight."

Fowler chuckled wryly. "That's your problem, Captain. Yours and Nuan's. It all depends on how good your security is. Good luck."

Cunningham put down the microphone and turned to the rest of the Green Berets who had been assembled by Thompson. He shrugged. "Well, it's laid on. Tiny, get the message down and decode it." He went to the big map hanging on the concrete block wall. "Well, find a seat, men. Here's the story."

The objective area was down the coast from Da Nang, which was south of them. The U.S. Marines had their hands full protecting the big air base and the seaport where supplies were coming in. The Civil Guard was being assigned to go into a Viet Cong-infested staging area, from which hard-core VCs were dispatched on sneak attacks at villages in the southern part of the I Corps area. The CG battalion would go in by helicopters, landing on three sides of a square, to try to drive the enemy back across rice paddies on the fourth side. Back of them were hills rising to small mountains which fronted the shore-line of the sea. The terrain was favorable to the operation because the VC would have no place to go other than over the mountains to the seacoast. The Vietnamese Navy and Marines would be waiting for them there.

"It looks good on paper. Depends a lot on our maintaining the integrity of our three sectors and boxing them in," Cunningham said thoughtfully, tapping the map. "But the element of surprise is absolutely necessary. This grassy plain, which is the Landing Zone—the LZ—isn't wide enough to stop the VC from getting away into the jungle inland if they even have a few hours advance notice of our intentions. And if they get in there, we don't have a goddam chance of hitting them effectively. Nuan says he's been down that way and the jungle is almost impenetrable."

Cunningham looked around the room. His men were patiently listening, faces wet with sweat. "Keep hammering away at the company and platoon commanders and the top noncoms. We must keep this one absolutely quiet." He moved to the center of the room and looked down at his seated members. "Any comments?" As he passed Chet Smith he noticed the man was almost asleep and smelled of liquor.

Kennedy, Jake Potter, the other demolition expert, and Harry Adams were whispering and pointing to the map. Kennedy was elected spokesman. "Sir, it looks to us like there's one mighty important thing we'll have to do. The VC sure must know they're in a vulnerable spot there. Those cliffs go right up where we'll have our left and right flanks, so they won't be able to skirt around us. But they need that rice, so they must accept the risk. They obviously will be well dug in. So it's very likely they have the area mined a lot more heavily than we would normally find."

Cunningham nodded thoughtfully. "I see what you're driving at. The Civil Guard just doesn't have enough trained demolition people now to handle something of that size."

"Right, sir," Potter replied. "That's the problem in a nutshell. I'd suggest we start training some more, down at the platoon level. A whole mess of them. If there's mines there's bound to be casualties when we try to find them. And that's a lot of territory to cross without any natural protection. We'll have to clear a lot of safe paths across simultaneously. That means more trained people, plus some in reserve."

"All right, I'll talk to Major Nuan about that. We'll crank it in as priority in the training. You and Smith had better start this afternoon working out how many you think should take it, and just how detailed the instruction should be."

"What's the intelligence estimate, Captain?" Kennedy asked quietly. "I've heard that's some of the most productive rice farmland in the northern part of the country. And I've also heard rumors that there's some North Vietnamese regulars in there."

"Nuan's message says not, specifically. Just VC guerillas. But I'll check it."

"I'd suggest that, sir. It's one thing going in against even well-fortified VC positions, and it's another if they are manned by a well-armed outfit," Kennedy said, glancing at Adams who was nodding agreement.

"All right, we'll talk more about that later, Red. You stick around, and you too, Harry," Cunningham said to Adams. "The rest of you may as well take it easy this afternoon. It looks like we're going to have to work like hell for the next two or three weeks."

Cunningham watched Smith amble from the room and turned to Adams. "What's with Smitty? He stinks like a brewery. And where did Stew McDonald get that black eye?"

Adams and Kennedy exchanged embarrassed glances. The First Sergeant answered up.

"Smith got a little loaded last night, Captain. Got a 'Dear John' letter from his wife. She's definitely divorcing him. Stew started to needle him about it and Smitty let him have it. We broke it up right away."

Cunningham groaned. "That's all we need. And this isn't the first time Smith's been half-loaded during the day, either. You'd better give him the word, Harry. Either he straightens up, or else." He looked at the two enlisted men keenly. "What's the story about this divorce?"

"Apparently she's got grounds," Kennedy said. "Smitty played around some with the girls while he was tending bar when he was stationed out in San Francisco at the Presidio. Moonlighting, I guess. Well, she got fed up, I'm told, and started to play around too. She's a lot younger than Smitty. Well, he caught her out one night and slapped hell out of her. He ended up in jail. They'd have thrown the book at him if he hadn't had orders out here."

"Right now we've got other problems," Cunningham said disgustedly. "First, I'm going to get us a flight over the objective area, Kennedy. And request that some aerial photos be made. Maybe you'd better go back to Da Nang and nose around some more. See if you can find any basis for the rumor about regular troops down there. And try to scrounge some VC mines to use to teach the Civil Guard how to disarm them." He picked up pencil and paper. "Now, let's set up a training schedule."

At the end of the next week Cunningham reviewed the progress they had made with mixed feelings. Daily hassling with Major Nuan over the wording of the operation order had left him in a constant state of irritation. It was worse because Nuan would deliberately bait him and then finally end up a time consuming session accepting Cunningham's version.

The flight over the objective area had been all too brief, but they had not wanted to raise the VC's suspicions by lingering too long. From the lay of the land, Cunningham had decided the operation certainly was feasible, but that to be successful they would have to take full advantage of surprise.

His discussion of increased security measures with Nuan had been equally aggravating. The Major refused to stop the Civil Guardsmen from leaving the base camp except on patrols. He finally compromised on keeping out the South Vietnamese civilians who brought supplies or worked as cooks, house cleaners, or laundresses. Cunningham had circumvented Nuan by talking with the company commanders individually and stressing the security factor. They agreed to divulge the details of the operation only to their most trusted officers and noncoms and to clamp down on movements of their men from camp without their being under observation and supervision.

Kennedy's report of his survey of the Intelligence offices had been disquieting. The rumor persisted but there was no concrete evidence of regular North Vietnamese Army troops in the area. On the other hand no one could prove they weren't there. At the same time it would be too suspicious to send out even a probing reconnaissance patrol to investigate.

As if preparing for the operation wasn't trouble enough, Cunningham was called to the strategic hamlet near Dan Lac early the next week. The village with a population of 800 was only eighteen months old. The inhabitants were refugees whose farms along the northern coast of the country had been continually harassed by the Viet Cong. The VC had taken their young men, levied taxes, killed their communal chiefs, and forced them to hide them out for days at a time. Under sponsorship of the U.S. Operations Mission (USOM), the farmers were urged to leave their land and gather at the fortified hamlet. There had been a cooperative effort to build houses and to clear nearby fields for the farmers to till. An American-South Vietnamese team of medics, argiculturists and Green Berets had supervised the move and organization of the hamlet. A Self-Defense Force had been trained to handle a variety of weapons and to man the bunkers around the wood and mud-packed wall circling the village. After the people had elected a Chief, Administrator, and Information officer, they settled down to an agrarian life, farming by day, retreating to the safety of the hamlet by night. After the Civil Guard camp at Dan Lac had been built, the Special Forces team had been withdrawn from the village and moved there. The inhabitants were then put under the protection and supervision of Major Nuan and his battalion.

Doc Elliott was waiting for Cunningham and Red Kennedy. The medic was obviously upset and angry.

"What's the trouble now, Doc?" Cunningham asked querulously. He had plenty of work to occupy him back at the base camp.

"The village chief braced me this morning when I came over to hold sick call, Captain," Doc explained. "He's been short-changed. Yesterday the Civil Guard delivered the month's supply of stores—you know, medical supplies, food, shovels, farm equipment, nails, and other hardware. He inventoried the list with his Administrator against what actually came in. When he found there was a shortage, he talked about it to the Civil Guard lieutenant who's been detailed to live over here and train the Self Defense Force. The guy was pretty evasive and bugged out during the night."

"Oh, God," Cunningham groaned. "I suppose you checked the inventory yourself?"

"Yes, sir," Doc Elliott replied. He handed him several sheets of paper. "At the bottom I've listed what's missing."

"Son of a bitch! This is wholesale stealing!" said Cunningham, scanning the lists. "Hell, there must be a shortage of about a third."

Elliott nodded. "That's what I figured." He turned to Kennedy. "Red, tell him about what happened the last time."

Cunningham looked at him curiously.

"This isn't the first occasion, Captain," Kennedy began. "It's happened several times, in much smaller quantities. Then about three months ago, somebody grabbed off a batch about this size. Facts about the theft were taken to Major Nuan. The Civil Guard went through the motions of investigating. Well, the former skipper wasn't satisfied, so he reported it to USOM and to Special Forces at Da Nang. They investigated, but only came up with some suspicions. It was too late, they told me. Nobody'd talk and the thieves had covered their moves all too well. The whole thing was whitewashed and hushed up."

Cunningham swore. "Who the hell did they suspect? The Civil Guard, I suppose."

"Right, sir," Kennedy continued. "The stores were in American hands until they got to Dan Lac. The handlers at Da Nang and the chopper pilots had been making deliveries all over the I Corps area and nothing had disappeared before. So they were clean. Later we noticed that several of Nuan's officers and noncoms disappeared without a word. Nuan said they'd been transferred, and that ended that."

"What do you suggest doing this time, Red?" Cunningham asked.

"Let's not even mention this to Nuan, except that somehow the people at Da Nang didn't deliver enough, and that you're arranging for the rest to be flown in. That should disarm him." Red laughed. "From what you say, he already thinks you're a lightweight. Then send somebody to Da Nang and report the theft to USOM and the Army Security people. Tell them to move in fast and quietly."

Cunningham accepted the suggestion immediately. "Better go, yourself, Red. You can pick up those VC mines at the same time."

Tired after the trek back to Dan Lac through the brush in the ever present heat, Cunningham went to the mess hall and got a cold beer. Stripping off his sodden shirt, he sat in the shade and drank.

Nuan's a lot of screwy things, he thought, but I don't think he'd stoop to stealing. But he knew what the American goods would bring on the black market and how he'd failed to figure out the Major's personality, and he felt more disquieted than ever.

Red Kennedy made the trip to Da Nang the same afternoon and returned the next morning. He brought with him a variety of Viet Cong land mines of various types. At the firing range on the far side of the Dan Lac camp, he completed his first lecture on VC tactics to the demolition men of the Civil Guard A Company.

"Now Sergeant Smith will instruct you in the different types of mines and grenades the Viet Cong use, and tell you how to disarm them." Kennedy looked around in time to see Smith emerge from one of the bunkers and move toward him, lurching a little as he took over in the center of the seated Vietnamese. An interpreter rose to translate for him.

Red Kennedy shook his head as he smelled brandy. He crossed to the place Jake Potter would assemble the men from B Company. Too bad Smith's not more like Jake, he was thinking. Potter was not too quick, and he was certainly taciturn, but he had a way with the Vietnamese. No doubt his appearance was strange to them, and almost fearsome, Kennedy decided. He was tall, had a very long neck, big nose and protruding ears. He gave them instructions in a pidgin mixture of English, French, Vietnamese, and Japanese. Somehow they understood and did twice as much for Jake Potter as they would for any of the other Green Berets.

Perhaps they sensed that he really liked them, Kennedy concluded. Potter obviously thought of them as human beings, not just a faceless bunch of gooks, the way Stew and Smitty did.

Jake Potter greeted him with a somber face, and his expression did not change when Kennedy told him Smith had been drinking heavily.

"I've seen a lot of demo men turn into lushes because they got scared, handling explosives too long, seeing others get zapped," Potter said. "They figure their number would be coming up eventually. Usually did, too. They get too tense."

"But it's more than that with Smitty," Kennedy commented.

Potter nodded. "Part wife trouble. Part getting sent out here just before he retires. And part worrying about how he's going to get along when he gets out of the army."

Kennedy looked at him in surprise. Jake Potter seldom offered an opinion. The last time was when Kennedy had heard him tell Smith to shut up and stop making derogatory remarks about Captain Cunningham. "We're damn lucky to have such a good officer in command of this screwball outfit," Jake had said with finality.

"I wonder why Smith doesn't like the Captain?" Kennedy asked thoughtfully.

"It's not Cunningham himself. Smitty's just got a hard-on for all officers. Goes way back to Korea. A platoon commander pulled out and left him behind after Smitty had been wounded by a mine. The poor second looey didn't have any choice. He had his orders. Smitty managed to crawl back in. Barely escaped being captured. He sure gave that young officer a bad time, though. It was his first time in combat, and he wasn't much good after that, worrying about had he done right or not."

It figured, Kennedy decided. He watched Jake Potter arrange the mines in a row, handling them very carefully, even though they had been de-activated.

"Jake, how much more time do you have in the Army? Going to stay for thirty?" he asked.

"No, siree," Jake Potter positively. "I'll have my twenty in in three years. Then I'm going out."

"What do you intend to do?" Kennedy queried, surprised at his tone.

"First, I'm going to travel. See the parts of the world I've missed. Never been to India or Burma or the Middle-East. I had one tour in Germany, saw most of Europe, but never got to Jugoslavia, Greece or Turkey."

"Then what? After you finish traveling?"

"Well, I've saved my dough. I own a small farm on the

edge of a little town in Wisconsin. Near where my only kin lives. Cousins. Two houses on the place. My one cousin and his wife and kids live in one, rent free. He farms some, but works in town. I'll move into the other house. Go hunting and fishing. Live on my retired pay. Visit the tavern on Saturday night. And forget about the regimentation in the goddam army," he concluded with a tight smile.

His unusually long speech made Kennedy think how little the team members really knew about each other.

"You're not figuring on making the army a career either, are you Red?" Potter said matter-of-factly.

"No, I don't. Why do you ask?" Kennedy said, again faintly surprised at the way the question was put.

"I just figured you were too smart. I don't mean that the army isn't okay, but you just aren't the type. Not that it was so bright your quitting college after two years." Jake Potter smiled apologetically at him. "Even if you did need money you might have got into something that paid more than newspapering. And you probably could have gotten something better. Hell, you made staff sergeant in two hitches, so you must be pretty good at the books." Potter looked down at the mine he was holding and pursued his mouth thoughtfully.

"You know, Red, a fellow like you has no business in the army. Not unless you're running away from something."

"Running away?" Kennedy said curiously. "What do you mean?"

"Well, me, now I'm a drifter. I sort of like to look around. See how people live in other parts of the country, the world. I like to try my hand at different jobs. I know I've no aptitude for college, but I learn a lot as I move around. It took me a long time to make staff. Wouldn't have either, if it hadn't been that some of the officers get impressed with three rows of ribbons on my uniform." Potter chuckled. "Even if most of them don't mean a damn thing. Hell, everybody got one in Korea."

Potter continued. "Well, you're different from the rest of us career guys. Well-educated, well-spoken. I've seen guys like you before, putting in thirty. Most of them stayed in because they were afraid to get out. Didn't want to go back to civilian suit. Some were scared they'd fail in their jobs. Others had already fouled up one or two marriages. Some just didn't want to face responsibilities. Like raising a family or starting a business. Or even becoming an officer. As enlisted men, the army takes care of them, thinks for them. Gets the blame if anything goes wrong."

Kennedy nodded silently. Like being in a womb, he mused. He and Jake Potter actually were a lot alike, he decided. Neither felt he fit into the usual army pattern. They were onlookers, not participators. Maybe that's what he had liked so much about being a newspaper reporter. And why he'd broken up with his girl before he went into the army, barely beating the draft.

"Yes, I guess you're right, Jake. When I come up for rotation I think I'll get assigned to the *Stars and Stripes*. Might as well prepare myself for civilian life, and it's a good newspaper. And I guess I was never happier than when working on a paper, even if you don't make a lot. I liked the life, the people, the excitement. And I like to write."

Jake Potter smiled knowingly. "I figured that. And by God you should do what you want to do. I've been plenty of places I wanted to see, and done things I'd never have known existed if I hadn't left the farm. But sooner or later, it's time to move on. The army, or any service, can only give you so much. And you can give it only so much. When you hit that period, a guy's smarter to make the change. Smitty's way past due, and that's why he's started fouling up and why he's scared."

Their conversation faded as B Company straggled up and surrounded them. Kennedy waited for them all to gather and be seated, and suddenly he sensed a warm feeling of pleasure. At least there was one guy on the team with whom he could talk freely. Harry Adams wasn't the communicative type, and he had his mind solely on the army and his wife and kids. Kennedy felt at ease with Captain Cunningham, but there was the officer-enlisted man gulf between them. Doc Elliott was a little too much of an idealist and do-gooder. He suffered right along with the Vietnamese in their disease and poverty. Strange, he thought, to find so much substance to Jake Potter. He was ashamed he had not recognized it until six months after they had started serving together.

Kennedy smiled at Jake and looked down at the intent brown Vietnamese faces before him and began his lecture.

Chapter 4

The transport helicopters coming into the landing strip at Dan Lac made an impressive sight to anyone who happened to be watching. Vietnamese Air Force T-28s and AD-6s still prowled the air overhead, but the fighters and bombers found no enemy to release their fury on. Dan Lac was a safe area, but the Air Force people took no chances with losing one of their slow-moving choppers to VC gunfire.

The troop loading went off like clockwork. From different directions the Civil Guards raced in groups toward the helicopters while their rotors were still in motion. The banana-shaped H-21s were the first in, having a slower speed. The faster H-34s were next. They carried only seven combat troops and their weapons but they were much more maneuverable.

A huge American-piloted Mojave cargo helicopter hovered and set down. The combined command team with their radio equipment for battalion and American team command posts were loaded. Captain Cunningham was the last aboard.

He moved to a seat forward, opposite Major Nuan, removed his steel helmet, and donned a crash helmet with built-in earphones. Draping a flak-jacket around his shoulders, Cunningham made sure a double-thickness of the armor-plate was beneath him, protecting his genitals.

Then he sat back and breathed a sigh of relief. The operation had finally begun, and he was fairly well satisfied that he and his team had accomplished a lot in preparing for it.

They had rehearsed the landing dispositions once and it had been a success. He smiled, noticing that even Major Nuan wore a pleased, expectant look.

Cunningham was neither bloodthirsty nor foolish enough to want to get shot at, but he hoped they would be able to hit the Viet Cong hard this time. South Viet Nam had not had a victory in the I Corps area for some time. News of one would be a bracer through the northern provinces and hurt Viet Cong morale greatly. They had had their own way too long. Moreover, the Civil Guard strike force had to prove themselves, once and for all. Personally, he felt they were ready to take the offensive. It was on the basis of this opinion voiced to his superiors that Nuan's and his detailed operation order had been approved.

Frowning slightly, Cunningham sensed a few minor misgivings. Intelligence officers at all levels still insisted they would be going up against only Viet Cong guerillas and no North Vietnamese troops. Kennedy was still not convinced, and his doubts had rubbed off on Cunningham. They had tried to prepare for the possibility, anyway, by stressing in the training the need for speed and accuracy in calling for air support.

Cunningham still had his fingers crossed, hoping that the Viet Cong had not been tipped off about the operation. They might be running into an ambush. He looked out the helicopter window and then smiled. The VC would sure take a clobbering. There were fighter-bombers as well as two dozen HU-1B "Huey" well-armed choppers ahead of them. Their combined firepower was awesome. The other alternative pleased him not at all. Maybe the VC had the word and would have simply evaporated into the jungle waiting to fight another day when the odds were better.

Another reason he was relieved the operation was under way was because his team members had started snapping at each other. They were irritable, and plain tired. It had

taken all of Harry Adams' experience and strength to keep
them from punching each other. Even stolid Jake Potter
had threatened to take a swing at Tiny, much to everyone's
amusement. Nor had Al Thayer or Chet Smith been working to get into better physical condition. Jerry Lord had
sweated day and night over the communications equipment
to get it into peak condition. The humidity shortened the
lives of the radios.

The terrain below looked extraordinarily familiar to
Cunningham, as he peered out the window a few minutes
later, although he had only flown over it once before. But
he had spent long hours pouring over aerial photos of the
objective area, taken by high-flying reconnaissance jets.

On three sides of a great group of rice paddies there
was rolling grassland. To the east of the paddies there were
rocky ascending foothills, and beyond them tall spiny
mountain ridges. Back of them there was the sea, lapping
at the bases of the mountains on three sides as they jutted
out like thumbs from the coastline.

The photos had revealed VC entrenchments on the
paddy dikes fronting on the grasslands, but there were
probably dozens more more thickly camouflaged. How
well they were defended and the amount of VC armament
were the unknown quantities.

Cunningham felt it was vital to hit the dikes hard with
air strikes and then for the battalion to attack as swiftly
as possible and take the positions before dark. The agreed-
upon time table called for remaining on the dikes overnight and crossing the paddies the next day when they
again would have the benefit of air support. Cunningham
had little faith in its effectiveness at night.

Once the dikes were secured, an ARVN engineer unit
would move in and clear a landing strip for transport
planes. Reinforcements, supplies and ammunition could be
flown in as needed.

The air armada separated into four sections, with
Cunningham's huge Mojave helicopter, escorted by a pair
of Hueys, bringing up the rear. He soon heard the sound
of bombs exploding as the AD-6s and T-28s began to

plaster the edge of the flatland and the dikes. There was some automatic fire in return, and it made Cunningham grin across at Major Nuan. If the VC still had machine guns emplaced they probably had been caught flat-footed. He peered out again and saw the Hueys go in next with rockets and machine gun firing at a fantastic rate.

Then the transports settled down and began to disgorge the Civil Guard. He could see them scurry into a long line paralleling the VC defenses on the long dike. Then he felt the Mojave's rotors increase their turns and the chopper hovered and descended swiftly, halting a few feet from the ground, and then settled on its skids.

Cunningham leaped from his helicopter door and helped the radiomen lumber to the ground. He waited until all the command group was disembarked, signaled to the chopper pilot, and raced away through the cloud of swirling dust as the Mojave swooped skyward and away. Spotting the sweat soaked figure of Tiny Christopolous visible behind the dubious protection of a small rise, he bent low and ran toward him. He was pleased as he dropped beside Tiny, because he was not even breathing hard after covering fifty yards.

Glancing around he saw that Dick Greer and a Vietnamese crew had set up a light machine gun a few yards away and were peering over the top of the rise. He could hear the sound of the air strike continuing but there was no shooting from the Viet Cong. Greer turned around to Cunningham, smiled and held his palms up. He could see no enemy activity.

"Any reports from the other sectors?" Cunningham asked Tiny Christopolous.

"Lieutenant Thompson reported the company in his sector flushed a few VC coming out of a camouflaged slit trench. Got them all, and no Civil Guard casualties. Harry Adams' outfit hasn't been fired on."

Cunningham grunted with satisfaction. Keeping low, he crossed to where Major Nuan had his radio set up. He frowned as he approached. The position was pretty exposed. Red Kennedy was prone, weapon ready, staring ahead at the dike, and listening to the chatter from Nuan's radio receiver.

Crouching beside Kennedy, Cunningham had him summarize what he had heard. It tallied with his own reports. He was glad he had his team take three radios.

Tiny was with him and Kennedy and Greer in the center sector. Jerry Lord had a second radio on the right with Bud Thompson, Jake Potter and Doc Elliott. The third was in the left sector manned by Harry Adams, with Chet Smith, Stew McDonald, and Al Thayer.

"Major Nuan's telling his boys to move up now," Kennedy said. "They're going to mark their progress with smoke shells from the mortars."

Cunningham nodded approvingly. "Good. Stick with him, Red. Let me know if there's any trouble, or if the advance bogs down." He returned to his former position. "Okay, Tiny, let's go." He signaled to Greer and led the way cautiously toward the distant dike. Ahead were the leading elements of the Civil Guard company responsible for taking the central sector.

They stopped before reaching the top of another rise. Cunningham looked over the crest with his binoculars. He swore. Few of the Civil Guard were moving forward. He could see many of their helmeted heads as they lay in the grass. The sound of heavy machine gun fire reached his ears, and then he saw mortar shells exploding among the Civil Guards. Looking up he saw that there were only a few planes in the air. The bombing and strafing had diminished and the Viet Cong were beginning to fight back.

He slid back and took the microphone from Tiny and called the air controller who was flying lazily about in his L-19 spotter plane. "For God's sake keep the planes coming in until the Civil Guard have advanced further. They can hack us to pieces with their mortars out here in the open."

The air controller's bored voice acknowledged and gave an affirmative.

Cunningham crawled back to the crest and examined

55

the VC firepower coming from the dike. He swore heartily. He could see muzzle flashes all along the dike——.50 calibres, light machine guns, 37 millimeter weapons, and from the sound, several different types of mortars. God damn it, he thought, that meant they were really dug in deep and were as well armed as the Civil Guard.

Kennedy tugged at his foot. "Reports coming in from the front echelon. They're pinned down. I'm worried, Captain."

"Me, too. The VC played it cool. They had a few machine guns in position when the initial air strike hit, but they must have got them under cover when they saw how many planes were coming in. As soon as the raid slowed down they popped up with their weapons."

Kennedy nodded. "This isn't going to be any piece of cake, Captain. Man, they got those positions manned fast. Must be a big complex of deep tunnels in that dike."

"Yeah, I was watching them fire. Good discipline. I guess we're both thinking the same thing."

"Right, Captain. I'll bet dough that there's at least a platoon of regulars with the VC."

Cunningham used his binoculars again. "Damn it, those mortars are getting zeroed in on that first line of Civil Guards. Our boys are sitting ducks." He glanced up angrily and then was slightly mollified as several of the fighter-bombers wheeled in to attack. "Red," he called back. "Call the air controller and see if he can have some of the planes drop napalm in the grass about 50 yards from the dike. Maybe the smoke will blind the VC and then we can move up."

He wiggled back down the slope. Kennedy was putting down the microphone. "Red, better get back to Nuan. Tell him about the napalm. He can lay in some phosphorus rounds with his mortars. He'd better tell his troops to get ready to resume the advance."

Kennedy scurried away and Cunningham returned to his former position. The air strike continued and then he saw the AD-6s swoop down and the napalm bombs tumble from them and explode in giant balls of flame on the ground. Thick black smoke billowed skyward and mercifully screened the Civil Guard in several spots. Cunningham waited and waited for Nuan's mortar fire. As the smoke thinned, the Viet Cong resumed their barrage. There had been no movement of the Civil Guard forward, he noted disgustedly. He glanced impatiently at his watch. It was long after noon. He groaned. They were way behind schedule. He sent Dick Greer to confer with Kennedy.

"Bad news, Captain," Greer said when he returned a half hour later. "Red says Nuan won't move until another smoke screen is laid down."

"Well, what happened before? Good God, they had plenty of time to advance."

"Red said the Major passed the word to move up but the leading elements were too scared to move. He's sent the platoon commanders the word they'll obey the next time or he'll start shooting at them himself."

Cunningham grimly asked the air controller for assistance again. "Try to bring in as many planes with napalm as you can. We must take that dike before it gets dark." He listened to the pilot's complaint, and then said, "I know, I know. They should have moved up the last time. But they didn't."

This air strike was heavier. Nuan had his mortars in action and then there was a sudden wall of thick smoke between the Civil Guard and the enemy. Cunningham observed the troops rise, at first here and there, and then all along the line, and hustle forward. Mortar crews also rushed toward the dike and set up their weapons and fired through the smoke screen onto the dike.

Suddenly there was a chill in the air, a few drops of rain began to fall and a stiff breeze sprung up. The wind strength increased rapidly. Cunningham cursed as it swept across the grass and began to disperse the smoke. Of all the stinking luck, he thought, as he watched the VC guns begin to send a deadly wall of gunfire at the Civil Guard. The momentum of the attack faltered and the South Vietnamese took cover in the grass.

He waited and waited as more napalm was dropped, but

the Civil Guard did not advance. Red Kennedy appeared suddenly and flopped down beside him.

"Captain, Major Nuan says he's going to hold it right here. Says the wind is too strong. He won't pass the order to move until it dies down."

Kennedy returned to the command post and Cunningham lay helplessly watching the Viet Cong sporadically sweep the grass with heavy gunfire. But the high wind continued. And the sun was getting lower.

An hour passed and Red Kennedy reappeared. "You might as well start digging yourself a deep hole, Captain. Nuan's passed the command to maintain these positions."

"Oh, no! The damn fool. Look, the wind's dying down now. If we have more napalm laid down they should make it up to the edge of the dike."

"I know it, Captain, and you know it. I told the Major that. But he's stubborn, you know. Maybe if you'd talk to him . . ."

Cunningham sat up decisively, stowed his binoculars in the case and picked up his carbine. "All right, damn it. I'll give it a try."

Major Nuan sat dejectedly, leaning against the radio transmitter, his face covered with sweat, hair tousled. His clenched fist was beating softly on his steel helmet which was in his lap. He was swearing in French, Cunningham knew, although he could not understand the words. Nuan straightened when he saw him, pushed back his hair and donned his helmet.

Before speaking, the Major lighted one of his French cigarettes with trembling fingers. He looked up at Cunningham with dulled eyes, and listened to him with no change of expression.

"No, Captain," Nuan said, shaking his head. "No, we will not try it again. Not now. This wind is unpredictable. It can come sweeping in again at any time. I will not risk any more of my men." He remained adamant despite Cunningham's arguments.

"Well, what do you intend to do? How long will you

stay put? It's only a few hours until darkness. We have to take the positions before then."

"And why is that, Captain? That is exactly what the Viet Cong will expect us to try. Why should we go in and meet their full firepower?" Nuan's voice suddenly became determined and decisive. "We will attack after dark."

"Oh, no!" Cunningham protested. "That's exactly what they want us to do. Good God, they know we're here in battalion strength, with air support. If we wait until to-night the VC will be able to withdraw and take their weapons with them."

Major Nuan began to resume his usual superior attitude. "Absolutely right, Captain. We will drive them back with few casualties." He smiled. "After all, the object is to drive them out of here. To the sea, where they can properly be confined."

"God damn it, Major. I thought the whole idea was to destroy this outfit and keep the territory for ourselves. It's too chancey the other way. Strike now! Drive them across the paddies. Force them to go while it's still light, and our planes can really give them a going over."

"You don't have to swear, Captain. I know what I am doing. Remember, please, that this operation and this command is my responsibility, and mine alone. I have to weigh the odds and make the final decision. We attack tonight."

Cunningham chewed his lip and after a few seconds his anger began to flow from him. Without another word he started slowly toward Tiny, motioning Kennedy to remain behind. Halfway across the little clearing he thought about going back and arguing some more with Nuan. Slowing, he almost straightened to his full height before he remembered where he was. He started to bend at the waist again, but he was not quick enough. Machine gun bullets kicked up the dirt on the rise at his left and he felt a sharp thrust across his back. He winced but began to run swiftly, keeping as low as possible.

Cursing volubly he sank down beside the radio operator.

"Christ, for a second out there I thought you got hit," Tiny said. "What made you stop, sir?"

"Stupidity, Tiny. Plain stupidity. I was so goddam mad at Nuan." He half-turned to Christopolous and began to unbutton his shirt. "How bad is it?"

"Not too bad, Captain. Creased, that's all. But by God, a half-inch deeper and you'd have had a scrambled spinal column." Tiny swabbed at the long shallow furrow, grinning as Cunningham groaned. "Hurts, doesn't it?" he chuckled.

Bandaged and with shirt back on, Cunningham had Tiny change the frequency of their radio circuit. He contacted headquarters at Da Nang and reported the situation to the U.S. Army Special Forces Advisory group and asked that they intercede with the ARVN to try to force Major Nuan to resume the attack before the sun went down. The answer was not encouraging, but Colonel Fowler would give it a try.

His back hurt, but Cunningham did his part digging a fox-hole big enough to accommodate himself and Tiny.

Finally he sat back and rested as Tiny relayed reports from the other two sectors to him. Both the companies with Bud Thompson and Harry Adams were in similar situations but the Civil Guards had managed to get much closer to the VC lines than they had in the center sector. Small patrols had circled nearer the Viet Cong emplacements, keeping to the tallest grass. They had barely managed to escape, advising that the VC had grenade launchers and recoilless rifles.

Great, just great, Cunningham thought, a sick feeling in the pit of his stomach. As Kennedy had said, this was one of the best armed outfits the Viet Cong had put together. And it would be the Civil Guard that ran into them. Well, he thought, disgustedly, maybe Kennedy could talk Nuan into mounting the attack as early as possible after the sun set. The sooner they hit the more chance there was of catching the VC in the process of withdrawing. He thanked the Lord that they had come in with a whole battalion. The enemy would be able to chew up anything smaller.

Dick Greer crossed to them a half hour later and slid into the foxhole. "No dice, Captain. Red says Major Nuan is going to send out patrols first. Starting about midnight. Red figures the attack won't start until about 3 a.m."

By this time nothing surprised Cunningham. He shook his head, looked at Tiny eating a can of cold C-rations, and settled for a chocolate bar. After it began to get dark and the headquarters at Da Nang had advised that the ARVN refused to countermand Nuan's decision to delay the attack, the three Americans settled back and tried to get some sleep.

The Viet Cong kept them awake firing occasional illuminating rounds from their mortars. They might as well have not bothered in the hours before midnight. The Civil Guard sat tight. The tempo of gunfire increased after the first patrols moved out.

Cunningham looked anxiously skyward. The air support was late. He scanned the black line that marked the dike. There was considerably less firepower, that was evident from the muzzle flashes. But still the Civil Guard recco units were being hit by mortars and machine guns. Only once or twice did he detect the distinctive vermilion splash of color when a grenade launcher was fired.

He heard the planes first rather than saw them. Then the sky was bright from their million-candlepower flares which silhouetted the dike. As they exploded the first series of bombing and rocketing attacks soared down on the VC positions. In the next two hours the enemy guns were silent whenever the bombers and fighters attacked. But they determinedly chattered again after the sorties were completed.

A little after 3 a.m. the Civil Guard began to move forward as mortar shells soared overhead and landed on the VC bunkers. Cunningham halted halfway to the dike and requested flares dropped over the rice paddies and another air strike. He was certain the Viet Cong were withdrawing gradually.

Opposition to the advancing Civil Guard faded. Only occasionally were there the sounds and flashes of a fire-fight. The leading CG elements mounted the dike and found only a few wounded guerillas defending their positions with rifles and pistols.

Before Cunningham could reach the dike word was sent back that the Civil Guard had occupied all the enemy positions. Nuan had directed the attack to halt at the edge of the paddies. Cunningham tiredly had to agree there was little use trying to chase the Viet Cong at night. Even with the brilliant flares, the black-clad VCs were hard to spot against the mud and dark water of the rice fields. He and Tiny and Dick Greer decided to wait where they were until morning, and slept until dawn.

As they moved forward in the early morning, Cunningham was sickened by the sight of many bodies of the Civil Guards lying unattended in front of the dike. The Vietnamese medics were just getting around to treating the wounded.

The broad earthen dike was a network of trenches, bunkers and tunnels. But the only way they could identify the now-vacant gun emplacements was by hundreds of shell cases. The VC had taken their weapons with them. Cunningham had to shake his head with admiration. The circular bunkers had been cleverly camouflaged by bamboo covers topped with grass and brush. The VC gunners had come up into them from tunnels below. They marveled at the backbreaking work that must have gone into constructing the underground maze. Walls and overheads were crudely but effectively shored. First aid stations, ammunition storages, cooking facilities, bunk rooms and command posts had been carved into the earth.

Here and there Cunningham picked up pieces of gear abandoned by the enemy in their orderly withdrawal. After conferring briefly with Kennedy who had been examining another area, they went above ground to the radio. Lieutenant Thompson and First Sergeant Harry Adams reported similar assessments. They had been fighting against more than run-of-the-mill Communist guerillas. Glancing at the pile of equipment, Cunningham grimly set out to find Major Nuan. He wove his way through the tunnels and found him in one of the deepest caverns, the former VC Command Position, judging from appearances.

"Good morning, Captain Cunningham. I am sorry you are just too late. I have finished my breakfast." He motioned to his empty plate on the table. "What do you think of this VC set-up? They lived quite well I should imagine."

"Sure, all the comforts of home." Just like you brought along, he thought silently. He decided to get right to the point before he got angry again. "I think it's time we reassessed the situation, Major. We're way off the time table. And the opposition was a hell of a lot stiffer than we estimated."

His words got no reaction from Nuan.

"I suggest you warn your headquarters that reinforcements may have to be called in," Cunningham continued bluntly.

His remarks raised the Major's eyebrows. He looked amused. "Captain, please. We no more than succeed in the first phase of our operation, than you start to get worried. Remember, this is a battalion-sized operation. True, we are a little behind schedule, but we are at our first objective. We are here in the Viet Cong headquarters, are we not? What more than that can you ask?"

Cunningham's lips tightened. That patronizing attitude had returned. "Major, any time a striking force hits opposition as tough as this and is slowed down as long as we were, then it's time to take a good hard look at the situation. Someplace we figured things wrong." He spoke in measured and patient tones. "The enemy strength is a lot greater than we estimated."

Nuan laughed lightly. "That may be true, but it is not the first time it has happened and it will not be the last. Be flexible, I believe they told us in Combat Infantry School."

"I also remember, Major, that they told us that when we run into as much more firepower than we expected, as we did yesterday, we should re-check the Intelligence estimate."

"Captain, you're jumping at shadows. I suppose that the items of North Vietnamese Peoples Army uniforms and equipment are bothering you."

"You saw them then?"

"Certainly, Cunningham. And what, may I ask, do you read into them?"

"My men and I feel that there is at least one company of regular Army troops with the VC. At the very least a platoon in each sector."

The smile faded from Nuan's face. "Nonsense! The material you saw belonged to the Army Advisory group assigned to this area. A team working in the same capacity as you Americans. They help organize and train."

"I think that's a bunch of crap, Major. I can't buy that at all. If that was the case this is the biggest bunch of advisers in history. And every single one of them must have left pieces of his gear behind. Nuts!"

"Cunningham, I won't tolerate that kind of talk. You're being very disrespectful."

"I'm sorry, Major. I apologize," Cunningham replied with no contrition in his voice. "But I still maintain what I said. This was a well-trained, disciplined unit we were up against." He ticked off the types of weapons they must have had, as evidenced by shell casings.

Nuan sputtered and continued to protest, but it was evident he was now getting worried.

Gradually Cunningham began to have a glimmer of understanding. The Major had already radioed his report to his headquarters and it did not reflect the evidence Cunningham had mentioned. It was the old business of losing face all over again. Nuan was determined not to change his report.

Deciding that further argument was futile, Cunningham decided on a new approach. "Very well, Major. Now, another question. When do you intend to move on?"

Nuan hesitated and appeared to be making the decision right then. "I am sending out patrols today. Across the dikes, primarily. Tonight, unless something turns up, we will attack again. They will not expect us to strike in the darkness." He smiled and rubbed his chubby hands.

Cunningham looked at him doubtfully and weighed the situation in his mind. "But sir, won't we lose the benefit of our air support if we advance at night? That's our big advantage, particularly if we are up against some Regular Army platoons . . ."

Nuan rose abruptly. "Captain, I am at the end of my patience. We already have discussed this. And I am tired of your criticizing everything I intend to do! So please go! I have other matters to attend to."

Cunningham looked at him with astonishment. Nuan's voice had almost risen to a shout. Just as abruptly the Major must have realized he had lost his composure. He walked toward Cunningham, a forced smile on his face.

"Please, Captain. Come back and see me later. I wish to attend to a few details and then lie down. I am very tired. You must be too."

Nodding curtly, Cunningham slowly turned and left the room. He had mixed feelings; some sad, because Nuan was finally realizing he was human and that the burden of command was weighing heavily on him, and some glad, because he had finally gotten under Nuan's skin. So he reflected, the son of a bitch was too proud to admit he had screwed up like Hogan's goat, that he knew damn well he'd run into big trouble. His American and French military education told him that, but his Southeast Asian background forced him to do otherwise. God, he thought, no wonder the ARVN needed the American advisers so badly.

Cunningham yawned after talking again on the radio with Thompson and Adams, and then briefing the team members with him. He sent Kennedy to look over the North Vietnamese Army equipment in Thompson's sector and instructed him to remain there during the next phase of the operation. Dick Greer sleepily came up to the bunker to relieve Tiny, who was asleep in a matter of a minute.

A good idea, Cunningham thought. He spread out his ground cloth and lay down. "I'll need all the strength I can muster tonight," he said to himself. "There's going to be hell to pay."

Chapter 5

Chet Smith and First Sergeant Harry Adams listened to the interpreter while a Civil Guard platoon commander heard a report from a noncom who had led a patrol out along one of the dikes.

"He says it will be very difficult. The VC have been most clever. They have not left a large covering force behind to harass us, but it is well-deployed. Their machine guns have been set up to give them crossfire at the dikes if we use them to advance. Also there are man-traps, punji sticks, and mines all along the paths on top of the dikes running at right angles to this one. When he sent men into the paddies on either side, two were killed there by mines as well. They were placed in the stubble between the puddles of water."

Smith shook his head sadly. The VC had been thorough. They probably had had the dikes already prepared and had retreated right across the paddies in the dark, laying mines behind them as they went.

As they walked away, Adams was deep in thought. "Our only alternative is to form up on a broad line and cross the paddies, too. If we bunch up on the dikes we'll get cut to ribbons one way or the other. Smitty, those mines in the paddies are your problem," he concluded, looking solemn.

"Yeah, I know it. But you bastards aren't exactly getting a cherry." Smith wiped his puffy red face with a wet handkerchief. Then he smiled. "Sorry, Harry. I'm just sounding off. I'm so damned pooped I'm not thinking straight."

"Well, you'd better start right now. Better see first hand

just how tough it will be to spot the mines, particularly at night. Work out some plan with the Civil Guard demo teams. And for God's sake be sure they remember to mark out plainly the lanes they clear or else the follow-up attacking troops will get their asses blown off."

"All right, all right. Leave it to me, Harry," Smith said as Adams left him. He climbed up on a bunker and examined the rice paddy surface carefully with a pair of binoculars. He thought he could see some evidence of digging in several distant places, near the far dike, but sweat ran down into his eyes, obscuring his vision. He cursed and sat down on his ground cloth in the shade. Deciding to take a break, Smith took a few sips from his canteen. He kneaded his leaden legs and stretched, wondering how he'd make it through the heat of the day.

He swore again. That damn Major Nuan and Cunningham, he was thinking, keep us up all last night, work all day today, and tonight we got to fight our way across those stinking fields. "That's the way with them," he told himself angrily. "All they care about is taking some objective so they can go to the General and kiss his ass and get him to pin a medal on them. They put us through the grinder like so many sides of beef. A few of us eventually get through and win the goddam battles for them."

By God, he decided, what he needed right now was a good bracer. He reached down into his combat pack and pulled out a half-pint of brandy. A couple of hookers of this and then he'd get the demo people together and work something out.

The first sip of brandy burned all the way down, and the second swallow warmed his whole system. He immediately felt better. Ten minutes later the bottle was empty. Smith craftily scooped some dirt from the ground and buried it. His head was swimming and he had to lie back in the shade. Almost at once he was asleep.

Smith tossed and turned. The same old nightmare returned, transporting him to Korea. He shivered and moaned. The pain knifed through his ribs and the only warmth he felt was where his life blood was oozing from his side and soaking his winter underwear. He looked wildly around, seeing a grotesque half-figure on the ground ahead, dimly illuminated by a mortar flare. His buddy had been trying to disarm a mine with almost frozen fingers. Smitty had seen it fall from his hands and had burrowed deeper into the snow by the time it had exploded. A chunk of steel had drilled its way through his heavy parka and slammed into his body. He had removed his thick mittens and fumbled with his first aid kit, but it was frozen solid. Screaming for a medic he peered over his shoulder toward the crest of the hill he had just crawled down. Another flare lighted the area and he saw dark shapes silhouetted against the snow, going back up the hill and disappearing from view.

"You bastards," he shouted. "Don't leave me! Don't leave me!" He violently cursed his platoon commander. The sound of a bugle choked off his cries. He swiveled his gaze in the other direction. The damn North Koreans and Chinese were attacking. He could see a wave of them coming down the hill ahead, stumbling in the deep valley snow and starting up toward him. He fumbled for his carbine but his fingers were too stiff to grasp it. The gook figures grew larger and larger. The dragon was coming to get him.

A hand grenade exploded a few yards ahead and the snow stifled his nostrils as he tried to bury his head. He couldn't breath. Then he heard voices speaking a strange language. The picture faded for a minute and he felt a rough hand on his shoulder. He tried to scream but his face was frozen stiff. You bastards, you dirty bastards, leave me be, he thought; let me get back to my platoon, and I'll kill that stinking officer who hauled ass and left me behind. A blinding explosion brought him upright.

Smith was still shivering although ringing wet with sweat. He glanced wildly around and slowly regained his senses, recognizing the bunker. Then he heard another explosion in the distance and finally realized this was not a part of his dream.

He shakily got to his feet and climbed to the top of the

bunker and looked out. Far across the expanse of the paddy he could see tiny green-clad figures crawling from hillock to hillock through the water, ever so slowly. There was another explosion and he jerked involuntarily as a body was tossed aside and fell under a shower of dirt, filth and water.

Those goddam fools, he thought helplessly. Then he glanced skyward. Good God, it was almost sundown, he realized guiltily. And the demolition teams of the Civil Guard were already way out there. He packed swiftly, cursing himself for having overslept, for neglecting to work out a plan with them. Those damn little Civil Guards. Lots of guts, but short on brains. They'd probably lose a lot of men if he didn't get out there fast. I've let those little bastards down, he accused himself.

Smith swung himself to the top of the dike, slid down the slope and began to take long strides from one clump of rice stubble to another, hopping across the shallow brown water in between. Wiping the sweat from his forehead with his sleeve, he watched the Civil Guard and finally figured out what they were up to. The company commander had probably sent out a small number of his best men to locate and disarm mines in three separate lines running toward the far dike. He was chancing on their clearing and marking paths so he could rush squads across the paddy as fast as possible after dark in order to flank the machine guns set up in commanding positions on the dike.

Not too good an idea, he thought, stumbling through the mud, but it was too late to change things now. He was tiring rapidly and already had a cramp in his left calf, and the demo team was still a good piece away. Twilight was setting in. The demo men would probably be pretty cautious now that one mine had blown up. But God help them when the sun set and air support couldn't be called in. The VC would rake the paddy with their machine guns. Trying to move faster, he slipped and fell full length into the water. It took him a few seconds of sliding around to regain his feet. He spat the filthy water disgustedly from his mouth and wiped his face, knowing well what the Vietnamese used for fertilizer.

Smith cursed himself as he ran, seeing that the lane had been inadequately marked with too-thin twine and stakes not buried deep enough. There was no question about it. He should have known his South Vietnamese counterparts would be rattled and badly need his steadying hand. Smith finally reached the Civil Guards clearing the mines. Gasping, he called to the noncom in charge and sat down in the rice stubble.

The Vietnamese sergeant squatted close by, smiling broadly now that Smith was present. Two gold teeth glinted in the dying sunlight. He nodded understanding as he was instructed to drive the stakes farther into the mud and use heavier rope to mark the cleared path. He shook his head when Smitty asked him if he had actually dug up one of the mines and determined the type.

Sighing deeply Smith felt both relieved and dismayed. The Civil Guards were just coming into the minefield, but now it was up to him to take over. "Look, pal. Radio the other two teams. Tell them to be very, very careful. You understand?" he said slowly in English. "Tell them to lash together two of these long stakes. Very tightly. They must wait for me to find one of the mines first. I will say what kind they are. All right?"

The sergeant pointed at the two stakes and frowned. "What for?" he asked Smith.

Between gasps Smith showed him how to poke at the clump of rice stubbles, inserting the pointed end underwater at the base of the hummock. The Vietnamese noncom smiled his understanding and trotted off to his radio operator.

Smith removed his pack and tied it to another stake. His shoulders felt freer and he could drag his gear along behind him. He kept his carbine slung across his back, as high off the ground as possible. His fingers trembled as he lighted a cigarette. He felt like a damn, lonesome, foolish target, sitting out in the middle of the rice paddy. Strange, he thought suddenly, it was kind of peaceful out here. The cigarette butt sizzled as he dipped it in a nearby pool of water. He smiled reassurance at the sergeant watching him encouragingly from a position thirty yards back. "Well, Smith," he told himself, "let's get the show on the road. Enough of these morale-building heroics. It's about time to face the firing squad."

Shoving the long pole ahead of him, he put his knees on one clump of stubble and probed into the hummock ahead. The mud sucked at the stake and when he tried to pull back one knee slipped and he fell face down in the water, barely managing to avoid driving it in deeper. Shit, he thought, regaining his hands-and-knees position and wiping his face, this was going to be tough. He probed again more boldly, using short careful thrusts. No mine there, he estimated. Crawling forward, he felt the dirty water seep warmly around his crotch.

I'm just kidding myself, he decided grimly, poking at the wet brush. With a probe as short as the one he had, he'd get his head blown off if the mines were big ones. Again he swore at himself. He should have had the men bring out longer poles. Sweat streamed down his face and the smell of the human excrement used as fertilizer almost gagged him. He slithered forward, almost automatically. He was so tired he almost missed feeling the stake hit something solid in the next hummock. Cautiously he hauled back and inserted it again. This time he was certain. A mine. He wiped his face, waited a few seconds more, and screwed up his courage.

Smith advanced through the water and examined the stubble with almost caressing fingers. The clump had been torn loose from the roots. He dug his hands underneath it from both sides and carefully felt for the bottom of the mine. A sigh of relief escaped him. It was a small one. The metal cannister was terribly slippery but he managed to get leverage from his elbows and raised it from the muck, with the stubbles still on top. He edged backward, the mine cradled in his hands. He sat down with it on his lap. With two fingers he felt in the mud for the detonator. Its

71

shape was familiar, he thought thankfully. One of the simple ones.

With practiced fingers he held the detonator firmly in place and removed the dirt from around it. He slid a special wrench from his pocket and carefully unscrewed the plunger and removed the fuse. Behind him and to either side the Civil Guard watched him closely. Their gasps of admiration were almost audible when he held the fuse high above his head, smiling. He motioned the sergeant to move up, and explained how the mine worked.

"I know they're all practiced with this type, but tell them again. Now, let's get hustling. It's almost dark. Have more men come up and work along the line. We want to have broader paths. And tell them to keep low. We're going to be within shooting range pretty soon."

The words were no more out of his mouth than he heard the rat-tat-tat of a light machine gun from the dike ahead. He could not spot the exact location of the gun, but he saw the splashes in the paddy water. The range was still short. He called back to the sergeant. "See if you can spot that bastard. Radio the coordinates back to your platoon commander. Maybe they can hit him with one of the 105 mortars."

Conscious of the eyes of the Civil Guard on him, Smith tried to be casual as he picked up the pole again. Somehow he resisted the impulse to hug the filthy stubble and stay there.

The darkness made him more jittery but he knew he had less to worry about from the machine guns. He was a small target and so mud-covered he probably looked like part of the terrain. Even when a gun did go off he kept at his job. Mine after mine was disarmed by his careful fingers and his progress was marked by the Civil Guard following him.

Several explosions among the other two teams made the task more nerve wracking, but he forced himself to move on. Still, the black line marking the dike seemed miles ahead. Guilt again swept over him like a cloud each time a mine blew up. God, if he had only got out into the paddy sooner.

The Civil Guard sergeant cautiously slid up behind him. Harry Adams was requesting information about their progress.

"Tell him if he can delay the attack a couple more hours I can be almost to the edge of the paddy. Depends on if they use illuminating shells or send out patrols to try to stop us."

Deep down Smith knew they would not get the extra time. If Nuan had ordered the Civil Guard to begin the advance at a certain time, he wasn't about to change his mind. So what if a few men in the minefield were sacrificed, he thought, cursing. What the hell did Nuan and Cunningham care about that.

Smith went back to work, deliberately. He was too old a hand to be panicked into trying to rush the job. That could only result in there being one less demo expert clearing the lane.

Fifteen minutes, a half hour, forty-five minutes passed. Suddenly there was the *karrumph* of a mortar from ahead and then the paddy all around Smith was lighted up. He frantically crawled backward as fast as he could. Sure as hell they'd spot him and fire another shell as soon as they changed the elevation of the mortar. The follow-up round exploded very near to where he had been. As the earth shook, he was struck by several pieces of shrapnel. He scarcely felt the stings when the metal slivers followed the shock wave.

Dazed for a minute, Smith raised his face from the water, rolled over, cursing, conscious suddenly of being wounded in several places. He flexed his muscles and moved arms, legs, shoulders and back. Nothing busted, thank God, he realized. He crawled back to his original position. This was going to be a bitch, he thought. The VC had then pretty well zeroed in.

He located another mine. His hands were shaking this time as he unscrewed the detonator, lying prone in the water. He caught his breath and suddenly was concerned

73

about the others. No one was visible to the left. To his right a Civil Guard was also using the flat position to work. This was going to slow things up. He called to the sergeant again and ordered him to bring up more men.

Another starshell burst to one side. The Vietnamese looked at Smith closely. "You're wounded, sir. You'd better go back."

Smith smiled. "Go on back yourself, kid. That's a nasty cut you've got there on your forehead."

Turning over on his belly, Smith again probed for mines. The Civil Guard mortars had been moved up and were firing back at the Viet Cong. That was a help, but he realized he was getting into machine gun range. Occasionally he spotted tracers when they opened up as the star shells slowly parachuted to the ground. Well, it was easier working in the light, he thought wearily. Slowly but surely he was approaching the dike which loomed blacker ahead of him.

Crawl and dig and probe and disarm, and slither up through the water and muck again. Another mine. Still another. They were more frequent now.

A flare directly overhead made Smith want to sink below the shallow water, but he knew it was useless. He was too weak to move fast. A follow-up round exploded just to his left. A piece of shrapnel richocheted off his steel helmet and the force of it almost knocked him out. Simultaneously another fragment slammed into his upper left arm, and several smaller pieces peppered his back.

Smith tried to retain consciousness, but for a full thirty seconds he thought he was lying in the snow on a Korean hillside. He slowly raised his head, realizing that the VC were firing all along the dike. It took a lot of effort but he managed to turn and look back. The Civil Guard platoons were moving forward in force. Another flare exploded behind him and the South Vietnamese dropped. The firing was more intense. Not all of the Civil Guardsmen were able to rise and continue the advance. He sighed helplessly, but he slowly managed to get up on his knees and one elbow, ignoring the increased machine gun fire.

Maybe he could disarm at least one more mine. It might save a few lives. Dizzy, he slipped off the stubble into the water again, almost burying his helmet. He fought his way forward and found another mine, but this time he could use only his right hand to take out the detonator. It seemed to take him forever, and he realized this was his last.

Suddenly the Civil Guard troops were rushing past him, black silhouettes in the light of the flares. He rose to his knees and waved them on, hollering. His head was spinning but he managed to unsling his automatic rifle with his right hand. There were mine, mortar and grenade explosions not far ahead as the South Vietnamese advanced. He struggled to his feet and lumbered forward. Might as well take some of those VC bastards with me, he thought woodenly. His left arm flapped at his side. When another mortar flare illuminated the paddy one of the noncoms recognized him and provided a supporting hand.

They were approaching the dike when a burst of machine gun fire dropped the Civil Guard soldier. They fell into the mud together. Smith tried to rise, but a sudden shot of pain in his upper leg told him he had been hit again. He felt a surge of anger at the Viet Cong and he struggled upright. Spotting the muzzle blast of a VC machine gun close on his right, he opened up with his carbine. The gun bucked crazily in the grip of only one hand, but the stream of high velocity bullets knocked out the enemy gunner. Groping for his ammunition belt, Smith slid sideways and into a shallow shell hole. Crazy minutes passed before he could sort out his head-down position and with one good arm and leg managed to lean his back against one sloping side. The effort was too much. His head fell back and he went out. The nightmare started all over again.

The din of the furious firefight going on only a few yards away took him out of the snowy dream into the slime of the rice paddy. The pain in his arm and leg was excruciating. But the sound of the battle was much more intense. He solemnly debated between trying to re-load his carbine and finding his first aid kit. He had to consciously think in order to move his hand to his belt. The decision was made for him. The kit was torn apart. When he found he had lost the rest of his ammunition he suddenly panicked. He'd die if he did not get medical attention, he thought hysterically.

"Thayer, Thayer, Thayer!" he began to yell. "Al Thayer. Medic! Help me! Help!" screamed Smith. He fainted again but awakened, moaning, when another mortar round exploded near by. Through the crimson haze he vaguely recognized the sticky warmth he felt was his own blood and he began calling for the medic again. Smith stopped in mid-scream, suddenly conscious of being answered.

"Smitty! Smitty! Where the hell are you?" Thayer was calling.

Mustering the last of his strength, Smith yelled back. "Here, Al, here! In this goddam shell hole. Hurry up, Al, you fat bastard!" He tried to lift his rifle but the weapon was too heavy. Suddenly he looked up and saw Thayer standing at the rim of the shallow crater. A star shell exploded directly overhead. The medic remained motionless, transfixed by fear.

"Get down, Al! Get down, quick!" Smith screamed.

It was too late. A mortar round hit just behind Thayer and he seemed to fly all to pieces. A half an arm slammed into Smith's chest and knocked him back. He picked it up and looked at it curiously, hurling it away savagely and wanting to vomit. The exertion made him pass out again.

Harry Adams found him a few minutes later. Smith regained consciousness as the Civil Guard corpsman and Adams were bandaging him. He began to sob and tell Adams about Thayer, but as the sedative took effect, he ended up with blubbering curses at the officer who had abandoned him in Korea. As four Vietnamese struggled to carry him on the litter to the rear, tears streamed from Smith's eyes but otherwise he was motionless.

Stew McDonald lurched up, bearing the heavy radio on his back. He crouched next to Adams. "How does it look with Smitty, Harry?"

"He'll live. They'll have to pour a lot of blood plasma

in him fast, though. Hit in the left arm, and a slug through the meaty part of his thigh. About twenty shrapnel wounds in him. Lost a lot of blood." He rose angrily.

"This was stinking stupid thing to do, attack at night across a mine field. God, look at all those casualties. God, oh God." He wiped his face with a thick calloused hand and rose. "Come on, Stew. Some of our boys are on the dike already. They'll need help mopping up those VC. And we've got another paddy to cross tonight."

On the opposite front the attack was proceeding more smoothly and less costly. Lieutenant Thompson, the CG company commander and Jake Potter had started to plan early in the morning.

Thompson had been set to begin the mine-clearing operation immediately, but Jake Potter had discreetly called him to one side.

"Look, Lieutenant. This is one time you'd better let me take over. This is something I know about. Like it's my profession. It isn't any cavalry charge. When you mess with mines you do it slow and easy."

Thompson's face reddened with embarrassment, but he remained silent while Jake Potter sent men to the rear to cut and bring up long bamboo poles. Thompson chafed at the delay. He wanted to be doing something. Anything. He wanted to keep his mind off the action of the night before.

Previously Bud Thompson had been only in small scale skirmishes in the jungles. Lying in the open grassland with mortar shells exploding around him had been something else again. It was a frightening experience. Never before had he questioned his own courage, but it had been fear of being called a coward that had kept him moving forward. As he looked across the paddy he still felt a little sick to his stomach. Thompson gratefully accepted Jake Potter's advice to stay back while he went out alone to probe for the first mines.

Thompson watched with admiration and fascination as Potter nonchalantly took his long pole into the paddy.

True, he did not stay in one place too long. The VC tried to get him with mortar shells, but he was always one jump ahead of them.

After Potter returned, covered with smelly muck, he briefed the officers and demolition men. "I've marked out a dozen paths to the first row of mines. Let's use twelve two-man teams. I think we can go pretty far across before we're in range of the .50 calibers. But keep low so they'll have a tough job of getting an accurate range for their mortars." He waited while the interpreter translated into Vietnamese. "One man will handle the probe. When he finds a mine, his teammate will come up and mark the spot. Then they'll move along. As soon as a team finds it's within machine gun range, they turn around and start back. Dig up the mines. Take turns. Dig, disarm, and fetch back into the safe area."

Thompson's knees were weak as he crawled across the paddy, observing the teams' progress. Occasionally the VC would lob a mortar shell into the mine field but miraculously no one was hit. Constantly on the move, or prone, the Civil Guard made small targets. Thompson, himself, felt as exposed as a house. He had to force himself to raise his body and cross to another team. He felt only a little better when he saw that Jake Potter was equally cautious.

They had a large sector cleared by late afternoon when Jake Potter called the teams back and made them rest easy.

As soon as the light dimmed, the demolition men went out again. Potter had another pair of Civil Guards follow each team. At regular intervals they dug foxholes, which were filled with seeping water in a matter of minutes. Disarmed mines were tossed to the bottom. The foxholes might be uncomfortably wet but they would provide the Civil Guard with some protection if they got pinned down during the attack.

Thompson could hear heavy gunfire in the distance and knew that in Captain Cunningham's sector the offensive had begun. He calmed the anxious Vietnamese company commander and made him wait until Jake Potter passed back the word.

Across the paddy Thompson saw the Viet Cong open up with flares and then heard the thumping of mortar fragmentation shells and the drumming of the heavy machine guns. Occasionally he could observe the demolition teams advancing, yard by yard. Once he thought he saw Jake Potter's big body. A few minutes later a red flare soared into the sky, indicating all but the last few yards had been cleared of mines.

The company and platoon commanders signaled their troops forward. The Civil Guards ran upright across the paddy as fast as they could and then funneled into the twelve marked lanes.

Thompson had never hustled harder on the football field. He slid a good ten feet and bowled over a slender Vietnamese ahead of him. He helped the youngster to his feet. Then it was run and fall, run and dive. When a mortar flare burst overhead Thompson left his feet and tumbled into a foxhole. He crawled out moments later and raced blindly forward, muddy water blurring his eyesight. He caught a glance of men falling on either side of him as two machine guns converged their fire, but he continued on, afraid to stop. He ran headlong into the side of the dike, one of the first to reach the objective, he suddenly realized.

His pulse was beating wildly and each breath was a painful gasp. He had such a stitch in his side that it almost doubled him over. A bandy-legged Civil Guard noncom joined him, followed by a whole cluster of South Vietnamese. The sergeant screamed at them and started up the slope to the top of the dike. Thompson scrambled up with him and they made a beeline toward a .50 caliber gun firing out onto the paddy.

The VC gun crew spotted them and grabbed their rifles. Thompson reacted immediately. He yanked the CG noncom down and with the same motion flung a grenade at the bunker. The mud was still falling when they plunged into the sand-bagged pit. Thompson felt a blast of gunfire point blank and a slice of pain as his right leg was grazed, but his own carbine was more accurate. The noncom gathered a dozen of his men and they rushed the next position and repeated the destruction.

There were firefights all along the dike, but after an hour the action was only sporadic. The VC, hit in a dozen places, saw how effective the mopping up operation was going, and they began to withdraw, hauling as many of their guns and as much of their ammo as they could carry.

Thompson and the Civil Guard company commander had mortars and heavy machine guns set up and plastered the retreating Viet Cong. Their mortar flares showed the guerillas not stopping at the next dike but continuing their scramble toward the eastern foothills.

Thompson, Red Kennedy and Jake Potter listened to the reports filter in to the company commander who had set up his CP in a large bunker. They exchanged satisfied smiles. Casualties to the Civil Guard had been much lighter than they had expected.

Red Kennedy went off to explore the emplacements and his mud-stained face wore a smug look when he returned a halfhour later. He tossed a stack of papers and some uniform insignia on top of the radio by Thompson.

"There's your evidence, Lieutenant. There was a platoon of North Vietnamese Army regulars here. They were the last ones to bug out. They had pretty heavy casualties, too. There's the platoon roster."

Thompson swore. "Maybe that goddam Nuan will listen to us after this. Red, better pass the word to Captain Cunningham on the radio." He took a long drink from his canteen and then, as he lighted a cigarette, he noticed his hand trembling. He quickly made a fist and glanced up to see if anyone had noticed.

Jake Potter smiled sympathetically at him, and he held out his own hands. "Don't feel bad, Lieutenant. Look at mine." He chuckled wryly. "It isn't so bad when you're actually shooting back at them. It's the before and after that bothers me."

Thompson nodded, not trusting his voice. He remembered crossing the paddy, men to his left and right being hit, and he wondered how he had escaped the crossfire. Next he wondered with surprise how come he had automatically done all the right things in the hand-to-hand fighting.

The sight of Kennedy bandaging Potter's forearm where he had been nicked brought his attention to his own leg. He took out his knife and slit his trousers. The crease was not deep but it was beginning to hurt. Peeling the mud-soaked cloth off had started it bleeding again. Methodically he unfastened his first aid kit and then dropped his trousers and bandaged himself. He would have the medic do a proper job in the morning.

Suddenly he felt relieved. Like everybody else he had worried about getting wounded. Now that it had happened in a full-scale firefight it was like a load off his shoulders. A sense of weariness, mental and physical, began to settle over him. He leaned back and shut his eyes, but the stench of mud and sweat and blood and the dead remained vivid. It wouldn't be so bad, he thought, if this were the end of it. But no, there would be more war tomorrow. And the day after. And as the weeks passed he'd be shot at again and again. He'd wonder each morning if this was the day he was going to run into the final bullet. What a stinking way to live. If this is the way war is and the army is, he decided, they can take it and shove it. Then and there he decided to resign when his tour was completed.

In the central sector Tiny Christopolous slid through the mud and kneeled in a shell hole beside Captain Cunningham. He had to yell to make himself heard over the sound of gunfire.

"Captain, here's the dope from Lieutenant Thompson. They mopped up their area, Red says. No more opposition. Light casualties." He repeated the information about the Regular Army platoon with the guerillas.

Cunningham swore angrily and peered over the edge of the depression looking for Major Nuan. He gave up in disgust. It doesn't make any difference anyhow what we have ahead of us now, he thought. We're committed and he couldn't call the company back if he wanted to.

Ahead the Civil Guard were being cut down in large numbers. The VC mortar flares were very well-timed and aimed. They floated down, constantly lighting the paddy fronting the dike. Fragmentation shells, heavy and light machine gunfire and rifle grenades were concentrated in the last fifty yards. The area was littered with the bodies of the Civil Guards.

"You stick here, Tiny, with the radio. I'd better get up there. A few are getting through. They'll need every goddam gun they can get when they start to hit the strong points."

Tiny shook his head negatively and unstrapped the radio. "I'm coming along. I can always come back after this monster. It's useless right now."

They waited until there was a lull in the VC firing, caused by the Civil Guard mortars finally getting zeroed in on the enemy positions. They scrambled forward, separating, zig-zagging. Cunningham tripped and fell full-length, swore, and then congratulated himself as a stream of machine gun bullets passed over his head. But as he rose he felt a stinging at his cheek and ear and his helmet was thrown from his head. Cunningham scooped it up in one motion and kept running forward. He had it on his head by the time he lay panting at the edge of the dike. With dismay he saw that Tiny had crumpled as a mortar round exploded near by. He sighed with relief when he saw the radio man's huge bulk move, rise and come limping to his side.

"Hit bad?" Cunningham asked anxiously.

Tiny swore. "I don't think so. Got it in the ass. God, I'll never live that down."

They waited a minute to catch their breath and crawled to the top of the dike. By this time, even in the face of greatly diminished strength, the VC resistance was getting lighter.

The bastards must have the word that their buddies in

Thompson's sector have retreated, Cunningham thought. A Viet Cong popped into sight from a bunker and he cut him to ribbons with carbine fire. He and Tiny moved down the dike cautiously, heaving grenades into the gun emplacements as they went. Most were already empty.

The Civil Guards, following them hurriedly, set up their machine guns and mortars and began to fire at the VCs crossing the rice field in hasty retreat. Yet they were carrying most of their weapons. Only wounded riflemen were left behind to keep up the fight as rear guard.

Cunningham and Tiny took a breather after the action ceased. They lighted cigarettes in an abandoned bunker and looked over the radio they had retrieved from the shell hole. As Tiny fiddled with the dials, Cunningham rose and leaned on the sand bags. It was getting light in the east, and through the grayness he could see the bodies lying in the paddy. Occasionally there were screams of pain from the wounded. The medics and litter bearers were splashing through the mud attending to the injured. Cunningham thought of the miasma of death overriding the stink of the paddy, and he was sickened. He quickly lighted a second cigarette off the butt of the first, hoping the smoke would drown out the stench.

He wanted to turn away but the sight of the bodies had a horrible fascination for him. He thanked God one of them wasn't his own. Martha sure as hell was right, he thought, and he vowed to write her and tell her so at the first opportunity. It had been nothing but a damn kid stunt, volunteering for Viet Nam duty. Just because he was bored with the life of an aide. How stupid could a guy be, he wondered. Like he was volunteering for the football team or being the guy to climb the flag pole to pull some Halloween stunt.

Cunningham shook his head, disgusted with himself. On the other hand, maybe this is the best thing that ever happened to me, he mused. If he survived it. A guy had to grow up, to mature, sometime.

Wearily dousing his cigarette he reluctantly decided it was time to find Major Nuan. First he checked with the company commander who sorrowfully gave him his casualty figures. Cunningham was appalled. Tiny caught up with him and reported only a few less dead and wounded Civil Guards in Harry Adams' sector. What bothered him most was the news about Thayer and Smith. The latter had already been evacuated by helicopter.

But Nuan proved to be as cheerful as Cunningham was glum. The Major acknowledged the losses were high, but he insisted they were acceptable. The second phase of the operation was a success and that was the main thing, he claimed.

Cunningham was too tired and disgusted to argue. He followed Nuan along a dike leading to the foothills where the Civil Guard were setting up their defenses. He was only slightly cheered by word that the Viet Cong were still on the run. Getting his feet on the ground—good, solid ground—at the far edge of the rice paddy complex was the only thing that made him feel good. Suddenly some of Nuan's comments started to register in his numbed mind.

"We will send out patrols all day today to reconnoiter ahead, to find out exactly how far the VC have retreated. Tonight we rest here, and then tomorrow morning we will start the advance," Nuan said, almost triumphantly.

"But you'll just give them a chance to get organized and dig in again," Cunningham protested. "Why not move up now, while it's light and we can call in air strikes while they're still retreating?"

"When they are dug in, as you say, Captain, they are immobile, and our superior fire power can overwhelm them. Little by little we will chop them to pieces."

"All right, maybe I used the wrong expression. What I mean is that their commanders will separate them into small but connected units. Set up ambushes for us. Have time to establish strong points. It'll cost you a lot more casualties. And they are already very high now. They still have their heavy weapons, you know."

"That may be true, Cunningham. But they don't have their mine fields. Besides, I intend to bring up my reserves today. That's why we do not resume striking until tomorrow."

Cunningham looked at him aghast. "Good God, Major, you don't have any reserves. Those people back at the air strip are your rear guard. Don't forget that that landing field is our sole source of supply for ammo, food and water. If we lose that we'll really have had it."

"Oh, I intend to leave a token force back there," Nuan replied with a superior smile. "I will accept the risk, which is small. The VC can't move enough forces through that jungle soon enough to do any good. We'll have this group ahead wiped out and be back there before they can. Also, we will request constant aerial surveillance of the area and if they show evidence of gathering, we can always send the reserves back."

"Oh for God's sake, Major, that won't do any good. That cover's too thick for them to see anything from the air. And even if it wasn't they could move by night."

"As you say, Captain, the jungle is very dense. And I'm counting on that very thing to prevent the VC from moving very fast. I estimate it will take them more than a week to muster any large, well-armed force there."

Cunningham stifled any further argument, which he knew would be useless. He could tell from Nuan's expression that he was losing his patience. Excusing himself he trudged off to find Tiny. In the back of his mind he could still remember listening to a diminutive Máo neutralist officer from Laos telling them back at Special Forces school how fast and far the guerillas could move through the jungles, using relays of impressed civilians as porters, wheeling heavily-laden bicycles at a trot over jungle paths. They literally ate up the distances, always on the move, taking their rice and meat on the run. Damn it, he thought, Nuan of all people, a native Vietnamese, should know their capabilities.

Spotting Tiny in the distance, he reluctantly made up his mind to toss the problem back to his superiors at Da Nang, even though he knew they probably couldn't do anything about it. He didn't want to be the perennial cry-baby, but at least he would go on record with a protest. It might be the only thing that would save his skin, his career, if the Viet Cong did turn this into a resounding defeat.

Chapter 6

Lieutenant Colonel George Fowler chewed savagely on his cigar as he listened to Captain Cunningham's report. Static garbled some of the words coming from the radio speaker, but Fowler heard enough to make him groan. He grabbed the microphone and waited for a break in the transmission.

"Hold it, Freeman," he barked to the Special Forces captain starting from the command post. "I want a lift to Da Nang with you."

Roger Freeman, West Point classmate of David Cunningham, nodded and sat down. The radio was suddenly silent.

"All right, Cunningham. Have you finished your sad tale of woe?" Fowler asked grimly.

"That's about it, sir. Our supply lines will be getting longer and longer. We'll have to use more of the battalion to haul stuff up to us. And if we lose the airstrip we'll really have our tails in a sling."

"And your ARVN bright boy is going to use the rear guard as replacements for the casualties?"

"All but a few Colonel. A group about the size of a couple of pro football squads."

Fowler laughed, knowing Tiny Christopolous must have prompted Cunningham.

"I'll be in Da Nang in half an hour," Fowler said. "I'll see what I can do. Don't get your hopes up though. And keep a tight ass, son." He put the microphone down and ran a big hand across his white brush-cut hair. "Shit. Here we go again." He was Cunningham's immediate superior officer and all requests and reports went through his head-quarters, only a few miles from Da Nang.

Captain Freeman looked at the weather-beaten officer sympathetically. "Somebody sure goofed about there not being any regular troops with the VC down there," he said.

"You goddam right. And it was one of those piss-ants in G-2 on your boss's staff. When they first started to talk about this operation I told him he'd better get a crack scout team down there, but oh, no! I don't know why Colonel Boulger won't make them get him better information. If those bastards would get their asses out of Da Nang once in a while and nose around maybe we'd learn a little something." He took the cigar from his mouth and massaged his battered nose. "I'll get my gear and we'll get rolling. I want to talk to Colonel Boulger about this."

Looking incongruous in his jaunty green beret, Fowler drove the jeep to the airstrip in the same rapid, frantic manner he did everything. He was strictly a field man, a pioneer in anti-guerilla warfare dating back to post-World War II in China, and he prided himself on never having set foot in the Pentagon.

"I knew damn well we'd have trouble with that stupid Nuan before we were through with this operation. I never did trust that little bastard. We may get his ass in a bind yet. We're almost certain his Operations Officer was in on that supply theft. I wish to hell the ARVN had kept Nuan in Saigon, 'cause he's better handling the teacup crowd than he is troops."

Freeman laughed and held tight as Fowler roared up to the small helicopter and skidded to a halt. "That Cunningham's a good boy," the Lieutenant Colonel boomed as the rotor blades began to turn.

Freeman nodded. "He graduated near the top of our class."

"I don't give a shit if he never went to grade school," Fowler said belligerently. "When I heard he was coming from an aide's job, I wondered if I was getting some kind of a panty-waist. I liked the way he stood his ground and got the facts after that raid during the training maneuver."

"So did Colonel Boulger," Freeman added.

"By God, he should. I don't know what's getting into some of the jokers coming out of Special Forces school these days. They're scared of their own shadows. Won't speak up. Afraid to get their hands dirty. I can't get a straight answer out of some of them."

Freeman smiled to himself this time. Most of the Special Forces advisory team skippers were scared to death of Fowler. But his bark was worse than his bite, he decided, and the Lieutenant Colonel was finally being recognized as one of the best counter-insurgency and anti-guerilla warfare experts in the army.

After landing at Da Nang, Captain Freeman tried to lead him to Colonel Boulger's outer office but Fowler burst right in ahead of him and swept past a startled warrant officer.

Colonel Boulger looked up in annoyance, reluctantly smiling when he recognized Fowler. He rose to his full six and a half feet and extended a soft large hand. "How are you, George?"

"Fine, boss. Just fine." Fowler sat down without being invited. They had been contemporaries until Fowler had been left behind when they had come up for promotion.

Boulger deserved the silver eagles, Fowler had said. He was pretty fair at soldiering and could sit at the Pentagon conference tables with the best of them, as well.

"What's on your mind this morning, George? Bet it's that search-and-clear operation of the Civil Guards," Boulger said in a soft, southern-accented voice.

"You damn right it is. They got through phase two all right, but they got chewed all to hell doing it. That fool Major Nuan had them attack at night, and now he's up to worse than that." Fowler jumped to his feet and traced the action on a large-scale wall map, explaining about the air strip being left almost undefended. "We've got to make plans to lay on some help for them."

Boulger shook his head. "George, you know damn well my hands are tied until the ARVN asks us to pitch in.

This is their baby and they're going to play it their way."

"Shit! Look, Harry. I didn't say do anything now, but plan. Get our ducks in a row. Dammit, there are good American soldiers out there with the Civil Guards. Some of them have been shot up already. Medic killed and a good demo man seriously wounded. We can't let these boys down."

"All right, all right, George. What do you recommend?" Colonel Boulger leaned back and laced his fingers over his prominent stomach. There was resignation in his voice which indicated he might as well go along with Fowler or he'd never get him out of his hair.

"I know that terrain down there. Jungle on one side of the LZ and paddy on the other. The engineers will finish the strip today and then fly out. If the VC congregate a lot of fire power in the jungle along there they'll be able to shoot up anything coming in to land. And if we lose the strip it will take a full airborne assault landing to take it back."

Boulger shook his head sadly and stroked the silver eagle insignia on his shirt collar.

Fowler continued. "I know, you want to know where the hell we are going to get muscle of that kind." He stabbed his fresh cigar toward the map. "There's an ARVN Ranger outfit here that's just sitting on its ass. I'll bet I can dig up a HU-IB chopper outfit right here from the Marines at Da Nang. The Hueys will be a necessity, and those goddam seagoing bellhops are just crazy enough to risk their asses on something like this. Also there's a new transport helicopter outfit at Chu Lai. Might as well get them blooded right away." His face creased in a broad smile. "There, how does that grab you?"

"I figured you must have something worked out, George. It sounds good, but we'll have to check it out." Boulger turned to Freeman. "Rog, get G-3 to sound out those units. If he needs any more horsepower tell him to use my name. We'll put through the request officially if we find out we need to send them in." The Colonel rose. "I know it's only ten o'clock, George, but I suppose if I twist your arm you'll accept a drink at the club."

Fowler hooted. "By God, I thought you'd never ask me."

Captain Cunningham re-grouped his team the same morning at the edge of the foothills adjoining the great rice paddies. He sent Jake Potter and Jerry Lord back to the airstrip with one of the radios.

"If there's any action at all get the word to me quick," Cunningham directed. "And if you get attacked in force by the VC, get your tails out of there and re-join us. Don't make like heroes."

He patted Jake Potter on the shoulder. "You sure did a hell of a fine job on that mine field, Jake. That company commander's really grateful. A lot of his men owe you their skins.

A shadow crossed Cunningham's face as he turned away thinking about Chet Smith. If he had got off his ass and organized things as well as Jake, the casualties would have been a lot less, he thought. True, Smith had tried to make up for it, but it was too damned late.

Cunningham and Thompson discussed the situation in terms of logistics. "From what you say it's no wonder we're getting short of ammunition," Thompson said. "I guess the only good fire discipline was in my sector."

"Yeah, the Civil Guard sure wasted a lot last night in the central area. Harry Adams said the same thing." Cunningham licked his cracked lips and looked at the sun, already getting high in the cloudless sky. "Water worries me almost as much. We're using up a lot of it just sitting around here today. What's it going to be like tomorrow when we start up those hills with full packs and all our weapons? And that damn brush looks pretty thick in spots."

"Well, the troops moving up from the airstrip are carrying as much water and ammo as they can," Thompson said, optimistically.

Laughing sarcastically, Cunningham waved to the terrain over which they would be marching. "Look at that. Dammit anyway, we could use weapons carriers, tanks, all kinds of vehicles to go up those hills. We could unload them at the airstrip and run them across the dikes. But, no, this is a two-bit operation involving the Civil Guards and the ARVN won't give them a goddam thing more to work with than what they can carry on their backs. Man, I'd give anything to see the 1st Air Cavalry or the Marines come in here now. They'd be on the backs of those VCs so damn fast they wouldn't even have time to reach the mountains."

"What really gripes me," Thompson added, "is that I've seen a hell of a lot of armored vehicles sitting around Saigon, gathering dust and getting rusty."

Cunningham snorted. "Oh no, they couldn't bring that in. That's to protect the wheels running the government. Hell, another junta, with their bellies full of the lousy way things are being run, would probably try another coup if all that firepower wasn't stashed near Saigon." He mopped the sweat from his face. "Come on, Bud, let's try to find some shade. No use boiling out here."

The next morning it seemed even hotter as they trekked up the foothills, brush crackling under their feet. At first it was not too hard going, but as they went upward, the thickets grew more numerous. They had to cut their way through bramble patches and the thick vines hanging from clusters of stunted trees. Each had to be cautiously explored to ensure no Viet Cong were concealed, waiting to attack them after they had passed by. Progress was very slow although few ambushes occurred. The only explosions came from grenades tossed into abandoned caves and foxholes or used to blast paths through the thickest brush.

By nightfall Cunningham found that his prediction had been correct. Water was being used faster than it could be hauled to the battalion. There would be only one canteen apiece for the next day.

The march was started before sunrise the next morning when it was a little cooler. But the terrain was more tortuous and by mid-day the units were progressing only

91

at a snail's pace. Several Civil Guard squads reported contact with the Viet Cong who were using hit-and-run tactics.

Cunningham trudged through a clearing with Tiny Christopolous a few yards to the left. They wearily ignored the clouds of insects stirred up from the dry grass at each footstep. Both were coated with dust, streaked with sweat rivulets on their faces, arms and hands.

Ahead, some of the Civil Guards were carelessly chopping their way into a thicket surrounding several tall trees. The small South Vietnamese were tiring badly under their heavy loads and they had to stop frequently to rest.

There was a series of sudden sharp explosions and Cunningham began to run forward. A Civil Guard came reeling through the brush, streaming blood from a head wound. "Mines, mines!" he cried, warning the others. Doc Elliott raced toward him.

Without hesitation, Cunningham dashed forward, ignoring Tiny's warning. He got to the foot of a large tree and saw several soldiers sprawled dead on the ground. He warily looked around but there was nothing to see. He was peering at the ground ahead of the mine crater when some movement above attracted his attention and he jumped back. There was the crack of a carbine and a chunk of the tree trunk was torn off. Cunningham raised his weapon and sprayed the branches of a nearby tree, using a full clip. There was a cracking of tree limbs and a sniper fell to the ground, limp and lifeless. Before he could re-load, he heard the sound of another shot. Simultaneously he felt a sharp pain on the top of his shoulder. He instinctively swung around and put the tree between him and the direction of fire.

There was a quick burst of automatic fire aimed high by Tiny. Another Viet Cong tumbled from his high perch.

"Goddamit, you gotta watch that, Captain," Tiny admonished. "Those little yellow bastards just sit and wait for some officer to run up to see what happened. Then they let him have it." He yelled for Doc Elliott and led a group of Civil Guard on a search of the area.

Cunningham had a sheepish look on his face as Elliott bandaged his flesh wound.

"You're going to be mighty stiff by morning, Captain," Doc said. "A few inches to the left though and you'd have had another outlet for your windpipe." He smiled sympathetically. "It happens to all of us, Captain. Pretty soon your instincts will tell you when there's trouble nearby."

Tiny approached and grinned as he heard the words. "Yeah, you'll smell the bastards. If you're not in the middle of a rice paddy, that is." Then he was deadly serious. "But take it cool, Captain. Don't rush in that way. Stay back. We don't want to have to break in another new commanding officer." Tiny slipped the radio from his shoulders and sat down under the tree, groaning.

"Your tail still bothering you?" Cunningham asked.

"It sure does. Chafes where the bandage is."

"You two had better take a breather now," Doc Elliott said. "I'll move on up and let Lieutenant Thompson know. You can catch up easy, the way these poor little guys are going. They're really bushed."

Tiny removed his wet shirt and hung it on a bush to dry.

Cunningham looked at his great chest and wide shoulders. "Well, Tiny, there's one consolation for you. This life out here should keep you in shape to go back playing football."

The huge radio operator thought seriously a half minute. "No, Captain, it really doesn't. Oh, my arms, back and shoulders are in condition. I'm keeping my weight down. And my wind is as good as ever. But plodding along like this, same pace, hour by hour, well, it helps the endurance but it sure hurts my speed and agility. Hell, I'll be as easy to get around as a statue."

Cunningham lighted a cigarette and questioned Tiny more about the life of a professional football player. "How come you didn't play much college ball?"

"Quit school after my sophomore season. There was this Greek girl who lived just up the coast from college. We were going together, but her old man had a lot of dough, and my old man was nothing but a steel worker. Me, I had nothing but the jock-strap scholarship. I'd made all-conference that year and was as big as I am now, almost."

"How'd you get next to the pros?" Cunningham plied, curiously. "I would think that would be pretty tough for a sophomore."

"It usually is, but sometimes the direct approach is best. Nowicki, the big fullback with L.A., is from my home town. His pop works with mine. I knew him as a kid. So I went home that winter, joined him and some other guys in a basketball game at the YMCA. It got pretty rough, but I gave as much as I got and I guess it impressed him. So he told me who to see. The scout looked at a couple of game pictures and I got invited to try out."

"How'd they treat you at first?"

Tiny laughed heartily. "Rough. But Nowicki had briefed me pretty good. I had to play well enough to make the squad but I was careful not to rough up any of the first string old-timers." Tiny shifted his seat uneasily. "Funny thing, though. I got the contract, but not soon enough for the reason I was trying so hard. In the meantime my gal married the son of some big movie mogul in Hollywood. Haven't seen her since." He looked at Cunningham. "You play any football, Captain?"

"No, not varsity. 150-pounds at West Point. End. Second team basketball, though. We had a bunch of big ones in my class and I wasn't fast enough to make up for it." Cunningham hesitated and absently looked across the clearing. "I guess it wouldn't have made any difference if I had been taller. I wasn't enough of a competitor in basketball. Football, too. Couldn't get enthused enough about winning."

"That's not unusual, Captain. I guess I felt pretty much the same in college. I wasn't playing for the glory of the school or the team. I just wanted to look good." A big reminiscent grin split his black-whiskered face. "Man, it's sure different in the pro leagues. You know you're going to get a buck if you make it big. You really work your tail off." He sighed and looked at his watch.

94

Cunningham nodded and they rose. Their first steps were awkwardly stiff, but they loosened up as they moved out of the shade and began to sweat profusely once again.

The heat and lack of water forced a halt by mid-afternoon. Tactically they were in exposed positions in most cases. Strung thin in spots, bunched up in others, too tired and thirsty to care. The Americans did their best to organize patrols and station lookouts, but the Civil Guard were almost listless. Even Major Nuan had to agree it was no use to proceed further until more water was hauled up.

Cunningham and his men got little rest that night. All along the line the Viet Cong crept in close and used hand grenades with deadly effect. Then they silently slipped away. The Civil Guard wasted more of their ammunition firing at shadows and each other.

The third day was worse. By noon the soldiers were looking back wishfully hoping for orders to halt or turn back. The encounters with the Viet Cong were fewer than the day before, but the heat took a heavier toll. They were all down to a half canteen of water. The Vietnamese suffered almost as much as the larger Americans. Even Tiny Christopolous was silent and walked very slowly, bowed under the weight of the radio. Occasionally he and Cunningham saw pieces of the Civil Guard's equipment lying on the ground, abandoned.

Cunningham halted in the shade of a huge rock after looking at his watch. He motioned to Tiny. It was time for a radio check with Jerry Lord back at the airstrip.

Tiny raised him after several minutes of swearing at the transmitter, twisting the knobs and jiggling the tubes. "Hold it, big guy," Lord cut in. "Jake and I were trying to raise you. Trouble back here. A lot of three-man patrols were sent out last night. None were back by morning. Jake scouted around and found one wounded, trying to crawl back. He says the jungle is crawling with Viet Cong. They've been infiltrating in small groups. Some have heavy weapons."

Cunningham took the microphone. "But no attack yet, Jerry?"

"No sir, but it's too damn quiet here for my liking. I talked to the air controller and he's got spotter planes keeping an eye on things. I don't know how much good it'll do. That jungle's mighty thick."

"When are your next choppers due in with supplies?"

"In about a half hour, Captain. And we expect one or two Caribous too, shortly," Jerry Lord replied.

Cunningham felt a little more optimistic. The transport plane could carry a big load and still it could land and take off in a very short distance. "What time did the last batch of people leave with water and ammo for us, Jerry?"

"Early this morning, Captain. They were pretty pooped, though. They didn't arrive here until late last night. Almost dead with thirst."

Tiny groaned and shook the little water left in his canteen. "Damn, they won't catch up with us until late tonight."

Cunningham tried to lick his lips but his tongue felt like sandpaper. He called Lord again. "Okay, Jerry. Remember what I said. Bug out if the VC hit. And try to expedite offloading the supplies when they get there. If any of those planes get shot up, those Air Force guys never will come back."

Only the promise of more water that night kept the Civil Guard on the move during the late afternoon. But it was fortunate the Viet Cong chose not to attack them that night. The South Vietnamese could hardly move, rising from the ground only when the cans of water were brought in about midnight.

At daybreak the Americans had to stand by as the Civil Guard officers and noncoms railed and cursed and kicked their men in order to get them on their feet and marching again. The pace was very slow but at least they were moving. News from the airstrip was disquieting. The VC had made several light probing attacks but had pulled back when aircraft had moved in and dropped flares.

The sun was almost directly overhead when Tiny called Cunningham to the radio. "Jerry's reporting that the VCs are firing on the helicopters with mortars and heavy

96

machine guns. Apparently they're well dug in in the jungle because the Hueys are giving them all they've got and still the Viet Cong are plastering the choppers."

"Damn. Did he say if any supplies got landed?"

"Not a thing. Not a goddam can of water, even. The first chopper was just setting down when the VC opened up. Jerry says they saved the crew. Two others were hovering and the bastards got them, too. No survivors. A Huey got hit and had to crash land."

A few minutes later Jerry Lord relayed additional information to Cunningham. "The air controller says AD-6s and T-28s are on the way with napalm. Maybe if we start fires in the grass and along the edge of the jungle we can hold them back. We're laying a smoke barrage around the Huey. One of those big utility helicopters is being flown in to try to pick it up. They did get an evac helicopter in a minute ago and the bodies and the survivors have been taken out."

Twenty yards away Major Nuan was speaking excitedly into his own radio microphone, Cunningham noticed. He was probably getting the same word.

"Okay, Jerry. As soon as that Huey is hauled out of there, make sure the other choppers are destroyed and then get packed up. Move out onto the paddies. And get the hell out of there if the VC come out of the jungle."

Cunningham grimly crossed to Nuan's position. The Major looked no better than he. Nuan's combat fatigues were dirty and sweat-stained and a lock of long hair hung over his forehead. He stopped talking on the radio and tossed the microphone down angrily.

"Well, what do you want, Captain?" he asked curtly.

Cunningham deliberately gave him an I-told-you-so smile. "I just wondered what you were going to do now, Major Nuan?" he began mildly. "Sit here, or go back?"

Nuan's face was mottled with fury. "We do neither, Cunningham," he replied, his voice rising. "Our objective is to wipe out the Viet Cong or to drive them over the mountains." He pounded the top of the radio transmitter with a small grimy hand. "And by the Almighty we will do just that." He rose suddenly and stiffened. "Captain, we march again. Now!" He imperiously turned his back and strode toward his Operations Officer, shouting instructions.

Back beside Tiny, Cunningham lost his feeling of self-satisfaction of having predicted exactly what the Viet Cong would do. "Let's try to get Colonel Fowler on the radio, Tiny."

Cigar bobbing up and down angrily in his mouth, Lieutenant Colonel Fowler yelled into the telephone. "Goddam it, Harry," he said to Colonel Boulger, "You've got to get that airborne assault rolling fast." He rubbed the sweat from his red face and listened. "All right, all right."

His Communications Sergeant came into the office and waved frantically.

"Look, Harry. I'll get back to you," Fowler said hastily. "Cunningham's reporting in now. We'll have it official and then you can get the show on the road." He hung up peremptorily and followed the sergeant.

Fowler listened to Cunningham and grimaced. "That bears out what we got from the Air Force people, Captain. But I'm glad to get the word from you directly. You're smart to have your boys ready to haul ass out of there. The VC are sure to take possession of that real estate."

"I hope we can maintain air reconnaissance around that area, Colonel. We'll need every bit of advance warning we can get if the VCs start to come up to hit us from the rear to take the pressure off the Viet Cong up ahead of us."

"We will, but don't count on too much. If they want to start at night, anything can happen. Now, how's your water and ammo holding out?" Fowler asked.

"Tough. Water, particularly. I figure they may increase their ambushing now, though. Then the ammo will be critical, too."

"I thought that was about it. And now with those choppers down you know how goddam hard it will be to try to get those air people to re-supply you. Well, if you get any bright ideas, let me know. Right now, I'll concentrate on trying to find the muscle to re-take that airstrip."

Fowler went to the map table and scrawled a message describing the situation and dispatched it by radio, making sure the commands who would be requested to provide assault forces would know the serious condition the Civil Guard was in.

"Call me if Cunningham reports again," Fowler said to the sergeant and wearily went back to his office and sat down. He stared at the telephone but decided against bothering Boulger again. He'd have the message in a matter of minutes.

Feeling sorry for Cunningham, he lighted another cigar and leaned back and put his feet on the battered desk. Inwardly he raged against all the Major Nuans in the world, realizing full well that it was his own country's political policies that kept the Americans from taking command. The British didn't make that mistake against the guerillas in Malaya, he thought bitterly. They ran the goddam show. And that's the way things were handled when the 1st Air Cavalry went into action. Like the U.S. Marines. They commanded their own operations, that was for damn sure. And so did the Aussies and the South Koreans. But for poor bastards like Cunningham, they still had to take the crap the ARVN commanders foisted on them, just because the Vietnamese high command was choked with politics and corruption.

Fowler went to the map and thought about the terrain where Cunningham was operating. He shook his head. Tough damn spot to re-supply. The mountains on one side. Viet Cong with heavy weapons strung along the foothills. And the prospects of more VC being able to move into the territory behind the Civil Guard unless that airstrip was recaptured quick. Fowler shuddered, thinking of the casualties the heat and lack of water would cause to the Civil Guard. Well, he thought, I'll just have to sit and wait, and hope that Cunningham will come up with something.

The American advisers wearily trudged up and down

hill with the Civil Guard. At noon there was a brisk fire-fight on the left flank. Nuan had to deploy men from the center units to give them a hand.

Red Kennedy fell in step beside Cunningham. "I'll bet we see more of those, Captain. I was just over on the right. No action there at all. I'll give you odds that the VC will try to break through on the left. They'll concentrate their firepower in one spot to hold us off, and then they'll try to break through on the left flank."

"That figures," Cunningham agreed "They've probably got the word about their buddies at the airstrip, too. They sure as hell don't want to go up in those mountains. They must be as hard up for water as we are."

After thinking about the situation for a few more minutes, Cunningham stopped and took Kennedy and Bud Thompson to one side. He took out his map.

"Now, if we're right, the VC are drifting to mass their weapons to the left of us. That leaves them pretty weak to our right. Agree?"

Kennedy and Thompson nodded their heads and looked at him questioningly.

"Well, if we do a little probing and find that the right flank is fairly free of Viet Cong, there's where the choppers could come in. They could fly along the coast over the water. Then cut in sharp around the mountains. Come in high over our right flank and then set down a few thousand yards back of us." He looked from one to the other. "What do you think?"

"Looks good to me, sir," Thompson agreed.

"It's feasible, all right, sir," Kennedy said. "But first, will the air people risk sending in any more choppers? God, it'll take one helluva bunch to bring in the water we need. Second, will Major Nuan send out the patrols to check the VC on the right?"

"I don't know the answers to either of those, Red, but I sure as hell am going to brace Nuan right now. And if he won't then I'm going to tell him I'm taking the team out of here right now. I'll be damned if I'll risk our asses just so that bastard can save face."

"But you'll get into all kinds of trouble if you do that, Dave," Thompson said anxiously.

"I don't give a shit. All they can do is relieve me and send me to some staff job. It's my responsibility. And if they don't want to take my word for it they can jam this job and the entire Special Forces you-know-where."

Major Nuan turned him down flat. He would not agree to request an air-lift of supplies nor would he send out patrols. "It's not necessary yet, Captain. When I decide our position is untenable then I will do so. But it will only be in case of an emergency."

"Goddamit, Major, this is an emergency. Look around you. Your men are dropping like flies in this heat. And the enemy is sure to put more pressure on us now that they know the other VC are stopping us from getting supplies at the airstrip. Another day of this without water and the Civil Guard won't be able to move, let alone fight."

"Speak for your own men, Cunningham. You Caucasians do not realize the toughness of the Vietnamese. We will fight our way over the mountains without water, if necessary."

"That's a bunch of crap and you know it. Your men are tough, but not as tough as the guerillas who have been living off the land, accustomed to going without water. Your people are used to having full bellies. Think of them, Major. They're human beings. Don't let them die just because you're pig-headed and won't call for help."

"Do not call me names, Cunningham," Nuan yelled angrily. "I am getting damn tired and sick of your whimpering and your insubordination. I will not tolerate it. I am in command here! I say we continue!"

"All right, Major Nuan. If that's your final word, then here's mine. I am going to report this to my headquarters and request an airlift. If it is turned down then I intend to withdraw this Advisory Team from support of the Civil Guard, much as I hate to do it to them. But I have an obligation to my own men. I will not see them sacrificed because of your stupidity and vanity." He turned on his heel and stalked away, his face white with anger.

Cunningham grimly outlined to Colonel Fowler on the radio his conversation with Nuan. He made his request for re-supply by air and outlined his proposed route for the helicopters. He and his team would scout the right flank themselves.

"Okay, Cunningham, I get the picture. I'll do what I can to try to get them to send some of those big Mojave choppers in. And if I don't you have my express permission to get the hell out of there."

Red Kennedy re-appeared an hour later, smiling. He crouched next to Cunningham. "Captain, Harry Adams and I got one of the platoon commanders over on the right to agree to send out a patrol tonight. Harry and Stew and I will go with them."

"How the hell did you arrange that?" Cunningham asked quietly.

"Promised them that they'd get the first water flown in," Kennedy replied, chuckling softly.

By ten o'clock that night the three Americans returned. "It's okay, Captain," Adams whispered hoarsely. "Nothing but a few VCs over there. Riflemen. Snipers. We caught a prisoner. He was all but dying of thirst. It took the last of our water, but we got him to talk. That'll be a safe course for the choppers to take."

Cunningham's satisfaction turned sour an hour later. Jake Potter and Jerry Lord radioed that the Viet Cong were attacking the airstrip guard in full force. The guard was withdrawing across the paddies.

Settling back on his ground cloth, Cunningham felt for his carbine and then tried to get some sleep. He prayed that the VC would not cross the paddies for at least another day or so. Squirming he attempted to get into a more comfortable position. He licked his blistered lips and scratched his growth of beard.

God, wouldn't a nice bath feel good, he thought. Then an ice cold glass of water. Hell, make it a pitcher, he decided. And a nice soft bed in an air-conditioned room, where you didn't have to sleep with mosquito netting. That's what makes this tough. Americans take those things for granted. But we're not alone, he thought disgustedly. Not 400 miles away in Saigon, some of the South Vietnamese were enjoying that kind of comfort, too. Small wonder that they schemed and plotted and became a piece of the whole damn corrupt political system to hold their positions of ease. They knew what it was like out here.

Cunningham smiled. The sage thought wasn't original with him. Monique van Ostrander had warned him about that his first week in the country. She's got these people pegged right, he mused. Then he sighed longingly and looked up at the bright stars. What a woman. Beautiful. The best of East and West. Her mother had come from Thailand, her father had been Dutch-French, a longtime plantation operator in Southeast Asia, she had said. They had been killed in Malaya by guerillas while she was at school in Saigon. An orphan at fourteen. Now she was the popular hostess at the Caravelle roof-top restaurant.

Funny thing how they'd hit it off right away, he mused. Cunningham had been alone at a table in the hotel restaurant. On the spur of the moment he confessed his loneliness and asked her to sit with him when the crowd thinned. Her looks had fascinated him; tawny skin, startlingly blue eyes, framed by slanting eyelids, fringed with long blond lashes. Her hair was blond, piled high. She was tall, with long legs, but tiny hands and feet.

Cunningham could still visualize her nude figure; her magnificent breasts and hips. He groaned with desire, perspiring all the more, and quickly turned on his side and forced himself to stop thinking about her. Damn it, he thought, it's bad enough to be hungry, thirsty, dirty, tired, and disgusted without punishing myself more. By God, though, he firmly decided, I'm going to get down to Saigon just as soon as I can.

Early the next morning the American team members moved out and headed for the rear, leaving only Harry Adams behind to reassure the company commanders they were not deserting the Civil Guard——yet.

Cunningham radioed Colonel Fowler the coordinates of

the landing area he had selected. Fowler tersely acknowledged the message but would give him no definite indication that the flight had actually been scheduled. He simply directed him to stand by the landing position and have it ready.

Shrugging, Cunningham called to Red Kennedy and they decided where they would place the smoke markers and where each of the Americans would take positions to fight off any Viet Cong who might try to down the choppers. Thompson and Doc Elliott returned from making a full circle around the area and reported no enemy contact. Cunningham surveyed his band of five men and wondered if they could hack it. Shit, he thought, why worry. He smiled as wide as his sore lips would permit.

"Let's use up the last of the water and food, you guys," he said cheerfully.

Stew McDonald snorted. "The condemned man ate a hearty meal," he added sarcastically.

At 1100 hours the word finally came from Colonel Fowler. Just in time, thought Cunningham, for their nerves were raw. He delightedly sent a message to Harry Adams.

"Right, Harry. Airlift's laid on. Mojave helicopters. The real big ones. With Hueys for an escort. Mid-afternoon arrival. Jet fighter-bombers from a Navy aircraft carrier will fly cover. And Harry, if Major Nuan says he doesn't want the water, you pass the word quietly to his company and platoon commanders. See what they do."

Two hours later a platoon of Civil Guards arrived at the landing area, eager to help unload.

The first indication Cunningham had that the flight was enroute was the lazy arrival of an L-19 control plane. Tiny set up radio contact with the pilot. Next a section of sleek Navy jets soared over, aluminum skins glistening in the sunlight.

Armed helicopters, the Hueys, buzzed in next, darting over the area rapidly. Cunningham could see gunners at the doors and knew the co-pilots were itching to pull the triggers of their deadly 20 millimeter machine guns.

The Civil Guardsmen gaped at the huge lumbering H-34 Mojave choppers, which were big enough to carry heavy artillery. Six of them were strung out on a long line. As soon as the first touched down, Red Kennedy led a group of the Vietnamese to its side. Cunningham also left his position when he saw Lieutenant Colonel Fowler and Roger Freeman jump to the ground. He met them away from the rotor blast.

Cunningham wasted no time on amenities. He briefed Fowler quickly and sketched out the positions on the map. "That's the story, sir," he concluded.

"Thanks, Cunningham. God, with the heat casualties you've had, plus the others, you're damn lucky the VC haven't got any water supply handy." He started back toward the helicopter. "You're sure you don't want to bring out your team with us now?"

"No, sir. With these supplies we can finish the job, I think. If we pull out, I'm afraid the Civil Guard morale would hit rock bottom. They seem to have lost faith in Major Nuan."

Fowler nodded grimly. "That's an understatement if I ever heard one." He chuckled. "By God, those troops of yours must be thirsty and hungry. I've never seen a chopper unloaded so fast. Now, is there anything else?"

"One question, Colonel. Is anything being done about re-taking the airstrip?"

"I wish to hell I knew. Colonel Boulger and the ARVN staff were still hassling about that when I left. He's almost got them convinced they should send in one of their Special Forces Ranger battalions and get rid of that VC force in the jungle, once and for all. Your battalion sure can't do it now." He shook Cunningham's hand. "Good luck, son. You're doing a damn fine job."

Rog Freeman patted his back. "See you in Da Nang, Dave. Drinks are on me."

The Mojave soared upward with a blast of power and hastily departed, followed by another empty. Another pair immediately landed to be unloaded. And then the third section. More Civil Guard soldiers arrived and there was a steady stream of supplies being hauled back to the main force.

Major Nuan was only reluctantly pleased when he later talked to Cunningham, but he had quickly had the food, water and ammunition distributed. The Civil Guard moved forward in the waning hours of daylight in search of the best defensive positions. The VC surely had seen the big Mojaves and knew it was now or never.

At midnight the Viet Cong struck heavily on the left flank. Cunningham and his entire team were stationed there to back up the waiting Civil Guard. This time the enemy was either too weak or had no spirit left to continue the fight. They simply retreated, leaving their weapons, dead and wounded behind. Or else surrendered.

When it was light, the Americans found dozens of bodies in the typical black-pajama uniforms, looking terribly emaciated, weapons at their sides.

Cunningham mustered his team and was relieved to find that although most of them had been wounded again, none had been hit seriously. Red Kennedy called his attention to the mountains. He adjusted his binoculars and watched carefully. There were dark moving figures, scrambling upwards hastily, making for the passes to the other side.

"Major Nuan's sending patrols up behind them to make sure none slip around us." Kennedy chortled. "Boy, those jokers are in for a big surprise on the other side. Those Marines will chop them to bits."

"Captain," Tiny interrupted, holding up the microphone. "Colonel Fowler wants a report."

Cunningham described the situation. "So they're on the run now, sir."

"Congratulations, Captain. We'll send the choppers back in tomorrow with more supplies to tide you over until you can move back to a better location. In view of all your casualties, we're sending in all the transport helicopters we can lay our hands on."

"What's the story with the airstrip, Colonel?" Cunningham queried anxiously.

"They tried to cross by daylight, but our air strikes drove them back. They got hit hard. Had flare planes over there all night, too. And I and Colonel Boulger won this one, finally. The ARVN Rangers are going in. We should have the field again by tomorrow night."

Three days later Captain Cunningham thankfully watched the first transport helicopter lightly touch down. The Civil Guards quickly moved forward by sections and crawled aboard it and the others that followed. Within two hours the entire battalion was airborne and headed for Dan Lac. This time the American team filled the last helicopter to pull out.

Cunningham breathed a sigh of relief as he caught his last glimpse of the area. What a goddam mess, he thought. The cost had been several hundred dead and wounded, achieved by the Viet Cong and by the terrific heat and lack of water. Many of the living would recover to fight again, but Major Nuan's battalion had been put through the wringer.

And what good had it all been, he wondered. Would the South Vietnamese bring in a force to occupy the area and work the land for their own good? Or would the VC be allowed to return? And there were the weeks of training the Civil Guard that were all shot to hell. He and his team would have all the replacements to work with before the battalion could ever function again as a strike force. Sure as hell there would be a lot of desertions, too, now that the Civil Guards really knew what they were up against.

Cunningham's spirits lifted a little. He would have to report in person to Colonel Fowler and to Colonel Boulger at Da Nang, and after that he'd probably get a week in Saigon while briefing the staff of the Commander-in-Chief.

Saigon, he thought, savoring the name. So he got called on the carpet for hassling with Major Nuan. It would be worth it if he could get together with Monique. He hoped she'd received his letter. His whole body ached for her. But it's more than just feeling the need for a woman. Cunningham sensed that he would crack up if he did not

107

get a change of scenery, a shot at civilization, even if it were only in the primitive surroundings at Da Nang. He knew his team was in the same state. They needed to live like human beings, civilized westerners, for a few days. To have a hot bath and sit on a real flush toilet. To fulfill the urge to get loaded and laid, he concluded dreamily. He began to plan his recreation schedule.

Chapter 7

The base camp at Dan Lac seemed almost like home-sweet-home to the returning American Green Berets. A surgical team from Da Nang was waiting for the battalion to take over for Doc Elliott and the exhausted South Vietnamese medics.

After a bath, a shave, clean bandages, and fresh clothes in that order, Cunningham forced himself to begin thinking about the inevitable report he would have to make. The format was standard, and he knew what he must and would say. First he would have to talk with Major Nuan to learn of his reactions first-hand.

He found the Major in a somber mood.

"Sit down, Captain Cunningham," invited Nuan, spiritlessly. He was hardly the same man who had sat at that same desk and been so insulting to the American officer just a short time before. His uniform clothed a thinner body, and the skin at his chin line drooped. The operation had taken a lot out of him, particularly the super abundance of self-confidence he had readily displayed.

Nuan looked at Cunningham, resignation and sadness in his moist, brooding eyes. "I suppose you came to be congratulated for . . . for . . . what is your phrase?— 'Pulling the fat out of the fire', I think it is. Very well, Captain, I admit it. You were right to send for water and supplies when you did."

Cunningham waited, but then he realized Nuan had gone fully as far as his nature would allow.

"No, sir, I didn't come to say 'I-told-you-so.' That's behind us. But I must report to my headquarters, too." He tried to smile. "It's the curse of all armies, sir."

"I see. You have some questions." Nuan called his orderly. "Please have my Operations Officer report immediately," he directed in Vietnamese. The Major stared out the window while they waited.

The ARVN captain entered and nervously stood at attention before Nuan. His eyes flickered at Captain Cunningham.

"Captain, please cooperate fully with Captain Cunningham. He desires information for his report," Nuan said, waving his dismissal.

Cunningham watched him almost run from the room and his lips tightened. This is the bird, he remembered, that they think was mixed up in those missing supplies for the village.

Major Nuan drew his attention again. "I suggest you list your requirements at once, Captain Cunningham. We leave in the morning. I have been directed to confer with my Corps Commander." Nuan straightened and for a few seconds the old fire was back in his eyes. "I have you to thank for that, Captain. The operation's objectives were fully accomplished, but my superiors are unhappy about you Americans meddling in the command and calling in your helicopters to bring us water and ammunition. My army was perfectly capable of doing this eventually."

"I'm sorry, Major, that this kind of politics must enter into the picture. It shouldn't. We're military men." Cunningham rose and approached the desk. "Besides, what the hell difference does it make who asked for the flight or who provided the choppers? Good God, human lives were involved. We all want the same thing, to beat the Viet Cong with the least damage to ourselves."

Nuan shook his head, a sneer on his face. "You Americans never will learn. It's all black and white to you. You won't understand the complexities of our way of acting and thinking in Viet Nam."

"By God, it is black and white in this case, Major. Either you South Vietnamese want our American aid, our soldiers, our guns and ammo, or else you don't. It's just your damn deviousness. This is a dirty little war, Major. You haven't been able to stop the Viet Cong, even though you have the common complicated mental traits, nuances and intrigues. They do pretty damn well living off the land, relying on second-hand and even ancient weapons. Yet even though we give you the planes and equipment, you still have to call us 'big noses' in to help, and now that we're getting them on the run, you want to reap the credit. You'd be willing for us to go home now, if we'd leave all the strategic hamlets we built, the improved roads and airfields; and you wouldn't have the grace to thank us. For one, I'm getting sick and tired of the whole thing."

Nuan's great anger seemed to make him grow into his clothes. As Cunningham strode to the door, he fired a parting shot. "Captain, I'm getting sick and tired of your sort, too. You think you know so much about us Orientals. Remember one thing, Captain, we Vietnamese are noted for our very long memories. I will not forget that you have circumvented me, been insubordinate and insulting. You have put me in a bad light with my Commanding General. We have a phrase here, too, which means that revenge is sweet."

Cunningham walked quickly out of the room. He was white hot again at both the Major and himself. He knew he shouldn't have stooped to argue with Nuan; it brought him only frustration.

The ARVN Operations Officer pressed copies of the statistical information fawningly on Cunningham. After a few more questions, and nervous, incomplete answers, the American Special Forces officer decided he was in no mood to continue. Bud Thompson could come over in the afternoon to get anything else they needed.

In his own Control Center, he had Harry Adams muster

the Green Berets. With Red Kennedy keeping the record, they went over the events of the operation hour by hour, day by day, for the chronological summary. Thompson and Adams each had prepared action reports, accounts of the combat in their respective sectors during the initial days of the operation.

Cunningham read the sheaf of papers thoroughly and then called several of the men back to give him amplifying information. By noon, he had a pretty complete picture, except for details of the mineclearing efforts made by Smith and the other demo men in Adams' sector. Most of the Vietnamese noncoms had been casualties. After a quick lunch, he sat down with a pencil and a ruled pad of paper and went to work. Thompson was sent to the ARVN headquarters late in the afternoon for additional facts. As Cunningham completed each section he handed it either to Lord or Kennedy who prepared smooth drafts on portable typewriters.

Thompson returned with the desired information, but his comments about the ARVN headquarters' officers bothered Cunningham. Nuan obviously had them on a crash program and it apparently involved getting their action report in to Corps Headquarters simultaneously with Nuan's appearance. The Operations Officer had given Thompson answers to his questions, but with obvious reluctance.

Cunningham slowly re-read what he had written. It sounded a little rough but it was factual. There was no question about it in his mind. It was a near-disaster, no matter how you sliced it. The objective had been obtained, but at what cost? Who was to blame for the casualties being so high? Were the men poorly trained? Had it been lack of equipment? What had gone wrong?

In Cunningham's opinion, Nuan had needlessly sacrificed a large number of his Civil Guards by his headstrong aggressiveness in one case and his failure to keep on the offensive in the other. The heat casualties could have been avoided if water had been brought in sooner, and it would have been feasible to do so. A big mistake was made in taking the protection up to the battalion from the air strip. The result was that it would be many weeks before the Civil Guard could go back into action.

He felt a sense of urgency when he thought of Nuan rushing his report. Cunningham made pertinent extracts from his own report, stamped them "Secret," and dispatched them by radio to Colonel Fowler, with a copy going simultaneously to Colonel Boulger. He knew what the South Vietnamese government had done before, twisting statistics to suit their purposes. Well, I don't give a goddam, he decided. This is one they won't whitewash. Cunningham handed the report to Thompson.

"Bud, please check this over. Make sure it's got 'secret' stamped on each page, that the pages are numbered, and all that crap the Security Manual requires." He smiled. "Get a chopper to pick you up and take it over to Fowler and deliver a copy to Rog Freeman at Da Nang, too. You probably could stand a few snorts at the club there."

Cunningham spent the next three days working with Harry Adams and Kennedy to get their paper work up to date. A rest and recreation schedule was drawn up for each man to get a few days off away from Dan Lac. Training was at a standstill, and as long as the beer rations were flown in, the team members still at the base had no complaint other than the usual heat and insects and poor food.

On the fourth day Captain Cunningham was summarily summoned to Da Nang. Roger Freeman met him at the busy airfield and drove him across the teeming compound in a jeep.

"Man, you sure rattled the cages with that report," his classmate said.

"I just called it as I saw it, Rog. What the hell did Fowler and Boulger expect me to do?" he asked angrily.

"God, don't take it out on me. I'm just Boulger's flunky. All I know is they're both waiting for you. And there's a brigadier general in from Saigon, plus an Air

Force Colonel, both from the Commander-in-Chief's staff."

"What the hell do they want?"

"The general's from Operations and the other guy's the top Public Information Officer out here." They drew up before the long, whitewashed cement building. Freeman looked keenly at Cunningham. "Look, Dave. Try to play it smart, if you know what's good for you. I got a feeling these people from Saigon are out for your scalp."

"So I bugged Nuan. So what?"

"Look, you'd better hear the whole thing from the wheels. I don't understand it all myself. Just don't blow your stack, that's all."

Cunningham followed Captain Freeman into the building.

Colonel Fowler's face was lined with weariness. He introduced Cunningham to Colonel Boulger. "Sit down, Captain. Have a coke or some goddam thing."

They settled into chairs. Cunningham sipped from the cold bottle, grateful for something to hold in his hands.

Colonel Boulger tapped the report lying on his desk. "This is raising a lot of hell. You didn't pull any punches, did you?" He and Fowler were looking at Cunningham anxiously.

"No, sir, I didn't. I thought you would want to know exactly what went on," Cunningham replied evenly. Suddenly the situation was funny. "I figured there were one or two sensitive items in it; so I classified it "Secret." That way there would be restricted handling of it and the ARVN wouldn't get it unless somebody in the U.S. Army wanted them to."

Fowler chortled unabashedly and even Colonel Boulger had to smile. He motioned to Fowler who continued.

"All right, let's get down to cases. Both Colonel Boulger and I have seen lots of them, just like this. But because we have, and just because we haven't been able to improve things as a result, doesn't make us a damn bit happier. I want you to know we don't just sit on these reports. We send them on up the line where, supposedly, they will do the most good. Sometimes there's a different reaction. Right or wrong. That's what the boss and I want to talk about."

Cunningham nodded. There was a tightening in his stomach but at the same time his backbone stiffened. Suddenly there was nothing humorous about anything.

"Colonel Boulger sent a copy of this to Saigon," Fowler continued, "which is standard operating procedure. He endorsed it, urging that your recommendations be given serious consideration. Then some dumb bastard there mouthed off about it to one of the Vietnamese high brass. The word filtered up higher. The Commander-in-Chief was caught off base when he was asked for a copy of it. He hadn't seen it. When he did read it he blew his stack. Primarily because the ARVN knew about it, not because of its contents. Understand?"

Cunningham nodded again.

"Son, what you don't know, too, is that the South Vietnamese government has been playing this operation up to the hilt in the newspapers. They have been pretty jealous about how well the U.S. Marines and Army have done in their own operations. This one—particularly since it involved the Civil Guard—was supposed to show the world that the South Vietnamese were pretty good fighters in their own right. That's why they wanted to use all their own planes, and so on."

Fowler's eyes questioned Cunningham, who felt his spirits sinking. "I hadn't thought about that aspect, sir."

"There's no goddam reason why you should have to, Cunningham," Boulger interjected angrily. "Not at your level. George, here, and I have our troubles, but you're supposed to be free of all this political crap. But . . ." He glanced at Fowler to continue.

"In a few minutes you'll meet the hatchet men from Saigon," Fowler said. "Here's why they're here. The South Vietnamese will try to counter your criticisms by putting out their side of the story in the newspapers in this country. They're scared this will leak to the rest of the world press, what actually happened, I mean. So General Burke and

Colonel Bishop are here to try to smooth everybody's feathers. The Commander-in-Chief has the word directly from Washington to play ball with the ARVN high command. He feels that if your report is made public knowledge, there'll be trouble all around."

Cunningham looked puzzled. "But the report is classified. I can't say anything about it. I don't see how I fit into this picture at all, now."

"Here's the hooker, son," Fowler said disgustedly. "The strategy is to use preventative medicine. You're going to attend a press conference in a little while. You won't be the star attraction, though. You'll be there just to back up Major Nuan's statements."

Cunningham's gasp was not as loud as the sighs of relief from Boulger and the others now that the news was out. Cunningham swallowed a four-letter word and tried to appear casual.

"All right, sir. What am I supposed to do?" he asked.

Boulger took over. "Burke and Bishop will brief you now. A lot will depend on the questions asked by the correspondents, and the answers Nuan gives. Obviously the American newsmen will look to you for verification. Do I make myself clear?" The Colonel waited a few seconds until he had received a strangled affirmative answer.

"Cunningham, I'm sorry to have you go through this, but the word to arrange this came right from the office of the Secretary of Defense."

An hour later Cunningham was nursing a well controlled anger. He had quickly read over a sanitized version of his report given him by General Burke. He was quickly given to understand that the Commander-in-Chief himself had made the deletions and done the editing. Everything derogatory had either been deleted or watered down. Even the estimated casualties of both the Civil Guard and the Viet Cong which he had obtained from Nuan had been changed. Before he left the inquisition, Cunningham was certain of one more thing. Both senior officers from Saigon had fixed their eyes on his captain's insignia, making it plain they were irritated with him for stirring up a hornet's nest, and that if he wanted to remain a captain, he'd better play ball.

Roger Freeman was apologetically silent as he drove Cunningham from the base to the Da Nang Press Center, a few miles away. They followed a sedan bearing the senior officers. After they passed through the barbed wire gate, Freeman stopped before a complex of long, low yellow-stuccoed buildings. Once a French motel, they had an air of genteel poverty. A Public Information Office and press briefing room had been tacked onto one end to service the news correspondents. The arrival of General Burke and Colonels Bishop, Boulger and Fowler had stirred a few newsmen from chairs on the thatch-roofed porch, where they had been having drinks.

General Phuoc, the ARVN I Corps Commander was waiting for them, and it took a good five minutes of hand-shaking among army men and correspondents before Cunningham could get into the room. He was surprised to see so many attending the briefing and then realized how much out of proportion the South Vietnamese had been playing up the story of the operation.

Cunningham managed a bleak smile and cursory hand-shake with Major Nuan who was beaming at all the high brass. He avoided looking directly at the American officer.

Two newsmen waved at Cunningham and he recognized them as being representatives of Chicago area newspapers. He had met them at Fifth Army.

Colonel Bishop introduced Nuan, who was at the center of a long table, General Phuoc, at his left, and Colonel Boulger, at his right. Cunningham's name was added as an afterthought, almost, and he nodded at the roomful of men from his position near the end of the table.

The I Corps Commander briefed the group on the scope and purpose of the operation. He was as smooth and at home in front of the audience as a college professor. Bishop next called on Nuan, after distributing the diluted report to the gathering.

Major Nuan was well rehearsed, that was certain. He added a little more accent to his English than was normal for him, but it added atmosphere as he stopped occasionally to grope for a word.

While Nuan spoke, Cunningham tried to suppress his anger and to figure a way out. He noticed that despite the coolness in Nuan's voice, the Major was nervously fiddling with his lighter and pack of cigarettes.

Unable to find an acceptable alternative, Cunningham jumped nicely through the hoops when he was questioned. As instructed, he was sincere and almost emotional when he verified that the Civil Guard had shown extreme bravery and aggressiveness during the various phases of the action. But when he described how they had continued to attack even though receiving heavy casualties, Colonel Bishop began to try to change the subject.

Dick Sloan, the bearded Chicago *Tribune* correspondent, smiled at him encouragingly and then perused the mimeographed copy of the report. Finally he asked Nuan directly for statistics on Civil Guard losses.

Cunningham's face tightened when he heard the ARVN Major deliberately cut the true figure by over fifty percent. Sloan then turned and asked him for his estimate. For a second Cunningham hesitated.

"Well, sir, I can't say exactly. My men and I were spread too thin to give you an accurate figure. All I know is that every one of my Green Berets are eligible at least once for the Purple Heart as a result of this operation."

Sloan picked up the implication immediately. "Were you wounded, Captain?"

"Three times, sir. Fortunately, nothing serious." He touched the livid mark on his cheek and ear unconsciously.

Sloan looked up at him curiously, opened his mouth as if to ask another question, and then closed it, much to the disappontment of the other newsmen who were waiting to pounce.

Colonel Bishop knew enough to quit when he was ahead. Angry eyes on Cunningham, he declared the briefing at an end. There were unsatisfied murmurs throughout the room, particularly from the old-timers who were exchanging knowing glances.

Cunningham started for the door without a word to anyone. Colonel Boulger clapped him encouragingly on the shoulder. Fowler stopped him with a whisper. "Good show. Go on over to the club. I'll buy!" He winked and turned to face General Burke's irritated expression.

Dick Sloan stopped Cunningham at the jeep and asked him for his address in Illinois and the names of his wife and her parents. He smiled. "They had you in the middle in there, didn't they, Cunningham?" He lowered his voice. "I'd like to talk to you later. I hear you have to go to Saigon tomorrow. See you there. Right now Big Brother's keeping a hard eye on you."

Cunningham turned and saw Colonel Bishop hastily approaching.

"You'd better shove off now, Cunningham," the Public Information Officer said. "I'll have a few more words for you when you come to Saigon. Report to me there after you see General Burke."

Freeman dropped him off at the club, promising to return later. Cunningham felt shaky, drained of all energy. His uniform was sweat-stained. A long gin and tonic made him perk up a little, but he still wondered if he had gone too far or not far enough. Obviously the officers from Saigon weren't happy with him. Yet he, himself, felt a perverse satisfaction in that he had not gone all their way. He had somehow decided he was not going to say an outright lie about the casualty figures. And Colonel Fowler's attitude had shown that he'd said just enough to salve his own conscience, but not so much that they could formally punish him for it.

Fowler and Freeman joined him when he was on his third drink. Freeman tossed him a thin stack of mail. "Thought you'd want this before you go to Saigon. They were going to send it to Dan Lac."

After the waitress had brought a round of drinks, Fowler lifted his glass and smiled broadly. "Well, Captain, cheers. You struck a blow for freedom."

Cunningham questioned him anxiously, and Fowler confirmed his conclusions. "Oh, General Burke and that guy, Bishop, almost bust a gut when you wouldn't verify the Civil Guard casualty figures, but I'll have to hand it to you. You slipped out of it nicely. And they can't court martial you or reprimand you for the way you answered it, by God. I've been in the army long enough to know that. You followed their instructions—to the letter, if not in spirit," he concluded, less enthusiastically.

The words sunk in finally. "I realize what you mean, Colonel," Cunningham began slowly. It was getting a little hard to think straight. In the heat of the afternoon, the gin was taking effect. "They can't do anything to me officially, but, unofficially. . . ."

Fowler nodded slowly. "Right. You didn't back Nuan all the way, so you made the petulant bastards mad. The I Corps Commander, too. General Burke had assured him you'd play ball."

"What more can they do?" Cunningham asked, almost as an afterthought.

"Boulger already has the word from General Phuoc and General Burke. He's got to shanghai you out of this Corps area. You'll probably end up out in the boondocks someplace."

Cunningham exploded. "Boondocks! Where the hell do you think I've been, Colonel? Shit!"

Fowler's laugh was almost a cackle. "Hell, son, you haven't been all over this country like I have. They could send you up into some mountains where the tribesmen haven't ever seen fire, and where you'd have to teach them what to do with a wheel. Dan Lac is a paradise compared to some areas. No, now that you're *persona non grata* in I Corps, General Burke will see that you and your team really get the shaft." He looked to Freeman who silently concurred.

"That's a crock of shit. I don't mind getting the business, but what's the team got to do with it," Cunningham complained.

"They were with you on the operation, and it'd be foolish

119

to think they didn't have the same conclusions you have," Fowler said emphatically. He ordered another round. "Besides, it'd look just too fishy if they dumped you alone."

Cunningham muttered, "Colonel, I thought the goddam army would back an officer up better than this."

Fowler slammed his glass hard on the table. "Cunningham, it's about time you learned the facts of life. When the State Department cookie pushers and the Secretary of the Defense get their noses into our business, and our goddam generals stand still for it, you got as much hope as a virgin in hell." He shook his white head despairingly.

"Well, what's the drill from here on in, Colonel? I hear I'm to go to Saigon tomorrow."

"The Intelligence people want to talk to you. Burke and Bishop will probably chew your ass a little. Then take a few days off. You've earned them."

"And then?" Cunningham asked resignedly.

"I give you two weeks back at Dan Lac before the orders come through. You'll come back here for briefings and then be reassigned; I'd bet down south in the IVth Corps area. Lots of activity being planned there and it's a shitty enough location, so that ought to make them feel they're screwing you." Fowler rose. "Colonel Boulger said to stop by his office on your way back up to Dan Lac from Saigon. He may have some dope for you. Meanwhile, have a ball, son."

Alone, Cunningham swore and ordered another gin and tonic and a bowl of potato chips. The injustice of the whole business made him as angry as he had ever been in his life. It was the team that mattered, he thought. Their morale would really be shattered if they had to move on account of him; they'd drag their feet, grumble, and only do half a job. Who could blame them? Then he wondered about his own future actions.

In the past he had prided himself in doing the best work of which he was capable. Working long hours, seven days a week, busting his ass to get things done right. But now? Hell, if the army wouldn't back him up, why the hell should he beat his brains out. Suddenly he was almost physically sick of the whole affair. He turned to the mail, hoping he could forget about things for a while at least.

The note from his old boss, the Fifth Army Commander, was refreshingly brief and wished him luck. He had the maudlin wish that the General might be in command out in Viet Nam. He wouldn't be so chickenshit, he decided, and then began to wonder. He forced himself to pick up the next letter.

His father and brother didn't have much to say. They were chatty, but about people and events of which he knew nothing, and certainly didn't care. He had been away too long. Cunningham's mother had died while he was at the Military Academy, and he had decided going back home to visit was pointless. His father had been disappointed that he did not want to follow his older brother into his real estate business. His mother had been his only real friend. His father had been too busy moving them from place to place to be ahead of his slightly shady reputation. So Dave Cunningham was a stranger at home with his mother gone. Letters from two former classmates were more interesting. They asked his advice, since they were due for rotation to Viet Nam; they wanted to know what type of duty to buck for. He snorted aloud. By God, he'd give them the word. He'd tell them to make damn certain they didn't get assigned to any Advisory outfit; apply for transfer to a U.S. Army Division. The last Cav, or the 101st Airborne, even to one of the foot-slogging infantry divisions. Anything would be better than having to work with the South Vietnamese Army. If you're going to get shot at, be under the command of your *own* Army officers, die with your buddies. He looked down at the last letter, from his wife, and for the hundredth time thought that he should have listened to her advice and stayed out of Viet Nam.

Martha's impersonal report did nothing to lift his morale at that stage of the game—chit-chat about Fort Sheridan and the North Shore. She sounded martyred when she wrote about how sympathetic everyone was being to her because he was out in Viet Nam. What a bucket of crap, he thought, stuffing her letter with the others in his back pocket.

Roger Freeman arrived simultaneously with the influx for the cocktail hour. Cunningham was already half-loaded, but he was not ready to stop. Finally he talked Freeman into driving him into Da Nang, a filthy town of 200,000 people, swollen with whores, thugs, and black marketeers along with the hundreds of soldiers, sailors, airmen and marines flowing into the area. They visited a couple of honky tonks, which Freeman recommended, and then he urged Cunningham to return to the base for dinner.

Dick Sloan from the *Tribune* joined them at a crowded bar and bought them drinks. Freeman looked at him nervously and insisted they go back to the club to eat. Sloan laughed.

"Why don't you go on, Captain Freeman. I know you don't want to be seen with a dirty old newspaperman. I'll bring Dave back after we've eaten."

Cunningham bought the suggestion immediately.

"How about a couple more at a better place I know? They're just opening up about now. Then we'll go to a real fine Chinese restaurant, best food in town. And the dinner's on me," Sloan smiled agreeably, and Cunningham rose and walked unsteadily after him.

"Dave, how'd you get into this Green Beret outfit anyway?" Sloan asked curiously when they were in the quiet of a bar frequented by Da Nang's business community.

"Well, a couple of years back I found being a platoon commander getting a little wearing. But I couldn't see being a staff corps type or going into something like the Engineers. And, it looked to me like sooner or later the war out here was going to mushroom. They were looking for volunteers for Special Forces training so I put in my papers for it. But then after I completed the courses, I got snagged off to be the General's Aide at Fifth Army Headquarters at Fort Sheridan. This is my first hitch in a Special Forces outfit," Cunningham explained.

"What kind of training did they give you?"

"I guess some of the most intensive and best any of the services offer. Went to Fort Benning first to qualify in parachute jumping. After that to Fort Bragg, North Carolina. Special Warfare Center. Man, they really pour it on you. Anti-guerilla warfare, two different languages, the works."

"Have your men had the same schooling?" Sloan asked.

"Damn right, and they're a smart, tough bunch of guys. They specialized at school, depending on their aptitude and background. They take either the communications, operations, demolition, intelligence, weapons or medic courses. Not only that, they take a second one, so each is an expert in at least two fields. Naturally they also get the language training. And stuff like hand-to-hand combat. They can handle any weapon that's been manufactured. From any country."

"I've seen some of the great work the Green Beret teams have done with the mountain people," Sloan commented as he paid the check and they prepared to leave.

Cunningham snorted. "Yeah, that's what I thought I'd be doing. I really was looking forward to it. Instead I end up doing training with this outfit of Nuan's. Like I was right back with an infantry company again. Shit!" He lurched to his feet, suddenly realizing he was more loaded than he had thought. "Man, I'd better get some food into me pretty soon."

Sloan chuckled at him as they got into a taxi. "We'll eat now." Sloan continued to question him about his team.

"Got a damn fine top sergeant. Harry Adams. He actually runs things. He's an old pro. That's one great thing about the Green Beret teams, Dick. The men are all non-coms. Battle savvy. They've been around the Army quite awhile. They're mature, which makes them better-equipped to deal with the gooks, and especially in training these provincial troops. They can speak to them in their own language, in terms they understand. My boys have all been instructors or else had some teacher training at school." His grin was wry.

"You know, Dick. I had in mind when I volunteered

for the Green Berets training that I'd end up in some kind of glamorous cloak-and-dagger work. Behind the enemy lines, and all that crap. So look what I end up doing. Boy, what I wouldn't give to be in a straight U.S. Army outfit again. Maybe Airborne. Nuts!"

They went into the restaurant and Cunningham turned unerringly for the bar. "I guess I could stand one more before dinner," Cunningham said. "I'm so goddam disgusted with life out here and disenchanted with this assignment that I'd like to take a bath in booze."

The next morning Cunningham was more than a little vague about when or how he had made it back to the transient officers billet. He remembered the large delicious chow they had had, and when he was showering, he suddenly recalled telling Sloan the exact truth about the operation and his feelings toward Nuan and the whole business. His head ached so much and he was so sick to his stomach, however, that he failed to worry much about that.

There was one final chore to be done before he left for Saigon and he only had two hours. He shaved, packed, had coffee and borrowing Freeman's Jeep, he drove to the hospital. To round out his report he had to talk to Chet Smith. Also he realized the Demo man might want something from Dan Lac or Saigon.

Smith was in a bed in a large ward in the newly completed building. "Smitty, how're you getting along?" Cunningham asked, eyeing the bandages that almost completely covered the man.

"Okay, Captain. Glad to hear you all made it. Lieutenant Thompson stopped by and gave me the word."

They exchanged the usual banalities. "I'm not so bad off as I look, Captain," Smith said nervously. "They'll take some of these bandages off this afternoon."

Cunningham took out his notebook. "Smitty, I have a pretty complete report from Harry Adams about the action in your sector, but I'd like for you to fill me in on the mine-clearing detail."

Smith was wary as he spoke, tersely giving a minimum of information.

Cunningham probed further but the response was still ambiguous. After hesitating he finally came to the point. "How come you didn't have the CG demo teams better organized there? What time did you start?"

Hands tightly clenched, knuckles white, Smith was perspiring heavily. Again his reply was vague.

"Well, what time did you actually go into the minefield?" Cunningham asked, his voice heavy with exasperation.

Smith lost control. "Goddamit, Captain, what the hell difference does it make? Say, are you trying to say I wasn't doing my job? What the hell do you know anyway about demolition. God, a guy can only do so much."

"Take it easy, boy. Nobody's accusing you of anything. I just want to find out what happened." He looked Smith in the eye and his tone stiffened. "Now, give me a straight answer. What time did you get out in the minefield?"

"I told you, I don't know! I don't know!" He lay there, turning his head from side to side, avoiding Cunningham's piercing gaze. He sighed deeply. "Christ, Captain, I had to get some sleep sometime. When I woke up I found the Civil Guards already starting to clear the minefield."

"You didn't talk to them before that, then?" Cunningham asked softly.

"What difference does it make?" Smith yelled. "Lay off me, you bastard! You goddam officers are all so goddam smart. You send me out into that stinking slime and I have to feel around in that shit for those lousy mines. All by myself with a bunch of gooks. And the dirty VC shooting. Christ, it isn't my fault Al Thayer got his! It's all your own damn fault! Yours, you bastard! Yours!" He was sobbing and threshing around on the bed.

A nurse came at a run and took one glance at Smith. She shoved Cunningham away quickly. "Get the doctor, quick. He's still got a high fever and infection in his system. We must keep him quiet as possible."

It was just as he had figured, Cunningham realized sadly, leaving the hospital. Adams had reported that when they'd reached Smith after he'd been wounded he stunk of brandy. Obviously, to get enough courage to go out there, he'd loaded up on booze and passed out. Now he blamed himself that some of the Civil Guard were killed, and Al Thayer as well. But now what to do about him was the problem. The Doctor had said that Smith would not be evacuated from the country, but would be returned to duty with the team in less than a month.

Cunningham looked at his watch. Time for a drink and a sandwich at the club, he thought, before plane time. His hands were shaking when he lighted a cigarette, and he realized suddenly how much the encounter with Smith had bothered him. Whenever he sensed the resentment of his rank in an enlisted man he became filled with uneasiness, and a feeling of ineptitude. And at such times he told himself it was guilt. But, guilt about what, he wondered as he drew on his cigarette.

Chapter 8

It was late in the afternoon before Cunningham would allow himself to think about what he was going to do for relaxation in Saigon. He had checked into a spartan room in an officers' hotel, finding it suffocating and antiseptically institutional and crowded. The sessions at the main headquarters of the U.S. Military Assistance Command, Viet Nam (MAC-V), were as grim and tedious as he had expected. Apparently the Intelligence experts could not read. They asked him, time and again, for the same facts he had included in his detailed reports.

Maybe they're justifying their existence, he thought. Or, more likely, salving their consciences for sitting on their fat asses in Saigon by talking with a real live combat officer.

General Burke blew and sputtered and chewed. Cunningham left him feeling that the officer could not even do a decent job of tail-kicking. Colonel Bishop had pompously invoked the stars of his Commander-in-Chief as the finale to his complaining about Cunningham's evasiveness on the casualty figures, but had ruined the whole thing by looking panic-stricken when informed that the General was calling for him. They're all running more scared than I am, Cunningham concluded. He had had a belly-full of the armed services. He returned to the billet to change clothes and forget about the army for a few precious days.

Wearing civilian slacks, light sports jacket, shirt and tie, he decided without hesitation on the Caravelle Hotel as the first stop. He strolled along Duong Tu Do Street appreciatively eyeing the beautiful Vietnamese women, clad in their colorful *au dai*. The light breeze blew their long slit skirts aside, revealing their loose, pajama-like silk trousers. There may be a war in Viet Nam, he mused, but you sure see a lot of smiling faces. The store windows were loaded with expensive goods. It was like being in another country; it was so different from Da Nang and Dan Lac.

Already rock-and-roll music was coming out of the numerous cafes and night clubs. Their garish neon lights would soon be on, making the scene even more unbelievable. But if you look hard, he pondered, the evidence of war was there in the background. There were dozens of uniformed men on the streets, armed guards in front of many of the buildings, iron grillwork over restaurant and bar windows. The day of the sidewalk cafe had faded with the advent of the casually tossed hand grenade.

The Caravelle occupied a prominent corner, towering above the square, solid and secure, made of light colored stone. It was the best—and most expensive—hostelry in the city, its ten floors a tribute to French finance.

Cunningham took the elevator to the roof-top restaurant. There were no diners yet, but he located Monique immediately. She greeted him with a delighted, flashing smile and a warm kiss. He breathed a sigh of relief, for he had almost been afraid she would not recognize him. He remained warily casual, however, as she apologized for already having an engagement that evening. She readily agreed to go out with him the next night. She walked him to the stairway, hugging his arm promisingly. Cunningham felt the old urge as he kissed her goodbye. He stood a moment to watch her ample hips and breasts move.

Remembering Monique in bed—frantic one moment, teasingly caressing the next—he wondered if he could wait another twenty-four hours. In the bar on the floor below he sank into a soft chair at the only empty table and ordered a very dry martini. God, he thought, eyeing the plush surroundings and the gay crowd, this is worth the trip to Saigon itself. Beautiful women of a dozen nationalities were clothed in their best for the cocktail hour. Costumes ranging from Vietnamese to Indian saris, kimonos, cheongsan, and Paris creations. He almost did not notice Dick Sloan approaching. Cunningham waved him to a vacant chair.

The correspondent attracted a waiter immediately. "I see you're participating in our favorite Saigon sport," Sloan said, with a chuckle, "girl-watching."

Cunningham smiled at him nervously. "It sure beats Viet Cong-watching." He had had a nagging worry in the back of his mind for the past 12 hours about the bearded *Chicago Tribune* representative, or more particularly, just how much Sloan believed of what he had drunkenly told him the night before. "When did you get in from Da Nang?" Cunningham asked.

"Just a couple of hours ago." Sloan waited until the waiter left their drinks. He reached into his pocket and brought forth a sheaf of onion-skin paper. "Maybe you'd like to see these, Dave." He tossed them across the table, an amused look in his eyes. "You probably don't remember, but I told you last night about this time that I had filed a piece about your team's action with the Civil Guard. Called it in here from Da Nang. Had an answer waiting for me when I returned this afternoon. My publisher's happy as hell about it. The reaction in the Midwest was very good. Incidentally, he knows your father-in-law. Talked to him on the phone about this. Asked me to pass the regards of your wife and your folks."

Cunningham absently thanked him and rapidly scanned the news story. He was embarrassed by the time he finished it. "Well, this is something. Thanks for the fine write-up about my guys. They'll appreciate it, I know." He tried to get across to Sloan that perhaps too much had been made of his own role. He stopped when he saw the bored look on the newsman's face. Obviously he had heard the complaint hundreds of times.

"What's this one?" Cunningham asked, picking up the next story.

"Dave, I couldn't stand still for that crap Nuan handed out yesterday afternoon. I had the young Chinese fellow who works for me up there with me yesterday. I sent him over to Dan Lac right after the news conference. He came back about noon today and gave me a full report."

Cunningham leaned forward, curiosity rising. "And. . . ?"

"He verified what you told me last night. He got the proof that Nuan falsified the true figures on his casualties by about 60 percent." Sloan laughed sarcastically. "It cost me a few bucks in bribes and for the booze he brought in, but he got the ungarbled word from the officers and senior non-coms in nothing flat. Apparently they don't have any more love for Nuan than you do. He even managed to get a look at each company commander's report of casualties to Nuan."

Cunningham groaned silently as he read, and he finally put down the story, feeling a little sick. "Well, it's all there, Dick," he admitted. "But I sure hope to hell that Burke and Bishop don't think I gave you this information."

Sloan laughed. "Don't worry about that, kid. I knew they'd get you over a barrel if I credited you. That's why I didn't even refer to you by name. I just got off the phone with Bishop. I called him right after I cabled the piece. I told him exactly where I got my information, and I said that if he gave you a bad time over this I'd get every news guy I know here to send in a protest to Washington, asking for his dismissal. That ought to keep that stuffy bastard off your back. He knows I could crucify him if I wrote a story about how he masterminded this little caper."

Cunningham let out a sigh of relief. "I guess I owe you one." He signaled for another round. "I know I was out of line shooting my mouth off to you last night. But I'm not sorry."

"Don't worry about it. Hell, you should have known I wouldn't print anything about what you said. Not without checking with you." Sloan had a wry look on his face. "Look, just because this story is getting out, don't think the system will be changed. The same kind of officers as Nuan will get the commands. Hell, this is the way of life out here. They're corrupt and they're opportunists. Nuan has powerful connections. He was scheduled to move up fast under this new regime. He would have before, but one of his relatives was a little suspect of retaining allegiance to the Diem family. That's all settled now. He's one reason the ARVN gave so much publicity to this operation, by the way."

Cunningham voiced his surprise.

"Don't think a breath of the true story will ever appear in the newspapers out here. They may keep Nuan on ice for a while, but the politicians backing him will have him on the way up again. And, incidentally, watch out for him while you're out here. He's got a lot of power and influence. He'll try to get even with you."

"I guess I really have my ass in a sling any way you look at it," Cunningham said as they went down in the elevator. "Nuan on one side and the wheels at MAC-V headquarters on the other."

"Dave, you might as well forget it for the time being. Come on, we'll have dinner. There's a good French restaurant near here. You have to climb one of those iron, circular staircases like they have in lighthouses to get to the dining room from the bar, but the food's worth it."

As Cunningham expected, he was called to the Public Information Office the next morning and quizzed by

Colonel Bishop. He found it easy to deny any knowledge of Dick Sloan's article. The newsman picked him up at his billet in the afternoon. They drove down along the Saigon river to the Navy Exchange in Sloan's small Renault.

"Dick, I can't figure out what the hell the navy is doing running all the services and billets in this town," Cunningham said.

Sloan laughed. "That was a Pentagon brainstorm. Back in '61 or '62 when they started to beef up the U.S. Advisory group they tried to keep the facts away from the press. They wouldn't admit just how many people they had out here. So there wouldn't be so many army people to see on the streets, some jerk back in Washington came up with the idea of putting the navy in charge of logistics here in Saigon. The navy guys run the housing, the PX, Commissary, and all the rest. I agree that it's ridiculous."

While Sloan went for his ration of liquor, Cunningham shopped for souvenirs but he followed the newsman's suggestion to look around in the city stores first. On the spur of the moment he purchased a tape recorder and some 35mm. film for his own use. He was browsing at the racks of paperback books when Sloan re-joined him.

"Here's a liquor ration card for you. I know the Commander in charge here. It's pretty damn expensive on the open market." Sloan led the way to his car. "Now, how about a swim and some lunch. Let me introduce you to the Racquet Club. It's the posh spot here. The French run it, as they have for years. I'll get you a guest card."

Cunningham could feel himself unwind in the pleasant surroundings. He began to think of himself as a human being once more, not a khaki-clad cipher. Sloan laughed at his comment and asked his plans for the rest of his leave period. Cunningham told him something about Monique.

"Say, that's a mighty nice gal," the newsman said, eyebrows raised in surprise. "I asked her out once, but she quoted some old Vietnamese expression about ancients with frosted beards." He chuckled, stroking his white whiskers. "Say, I'm taking the evening plane to Bangkok. I've got to cover that Southeast Asia Treaty Organization meeting. I won't be back until next week. Why don't you use my apartment. It's not much but it's better than living in a four-man room in that billet. You can use my car, too."

Cunningham accepted the offer happily. They picked up his gear and drove to the apartment house in a Saigon residential section favored by diplomats from the embassies in the capital. He helped Sloan pack and dropped him outside the city at the airport. On the way back he was stopped at several check points by Vietnamese soldiers and asked to produce his identification.

The evening with Monique was an unqualified success. He economized with before-dinner drinks at the roof-top officers club at the Brinks Officers Billet. There was a nice cool breeze and the view was lovely. The city was aglow with neon as they drove across to Cho Lon, the Chinese section of Saigon, across the river. On Sloan's recommendation, he had made reservations at the justly-famed My Luong houseboat restaurant.

Monique was instantly recognized and the Chinese *maitre d'* immediately escorted them to a prime table. It was a colorful place, beautifully decorated in Chinese style. They chose their fish course from the tank wheeled to their table. The live fish were shimmering as they darted about in the water and Cunningham wished he did not have to select one. Crispy duck and all the trimmings were served and they did not have dessert until almost three hours had passed.

A good listener, Monique made him feel they had been friends for years. She readily agreed to coffee and after-dinner drinks at the apartment.

Cunningham turned on the lamps and Monique explored the two rooms and kitchen. The ceilings were typically high and the shuttered windows large. The furniture was definitely old French colonial, but Sloan had had it reupholstered with colorful oriental cloth. In the old-fashioned kitchen, Monique made strong coffee while Cunningham poured cognac.

132

As he carried a tray into the living room, she investigated the bath and bedroom. He heard her opening and shutting cabinet doors and drawers.

"Your Dick Sloan not only must have quite a good income," she called, "but he must be a ladies' man. I guess he won't mind if I borrow one of these robes." She emerged diaphanously covered in a filmy flowing negligee. "Why don't you change too. It's warm and that fan doesn't do much good." Extended down from the ceiling, its blades turned negligently, barely stirring the air. There was one in each of the rooms.

Monique laughed merrily at him. His robe had apparently been tailored for a Vietnamese. It came only to midthigh. "Well, at least it will be cool," she teased.

As he drank the brandy, Cunningham was reminded of Major Nuan. He found himself telling Monique about him and the last operation.

"Sloan is right, Dave," she commented seriously, her accent a quaint combination of Dutch, French and Thai. "I know of this Nuan. His family was closely allied to the Vietnamese royal family for many, many years. And they are important financially, too. One of his uncles is an important Buddhist bishop. I think the Major could be very dangerous to you."

"Don't worry about me. I can take care of myself," he replied stubbornly.

She laughed at him and rose. When she bent over to pick up his glass from the coffee table her gown gaped revealingly.

Cunningham had to restrain himself. She was perfectly silhouetted in the lamplight and was fully aware of it, he decided as she looked at him with amusement.

Monique brought him another brandy and sat down beside him. She ruffled his brush-cut hair with a small hand. "Dave, you really are a baby. A man like Nuan would eat you alive. Like this." She nibbled his ear but pulled back laughingly from his grasp. "To deal with Nuan you must be a hard-headed, unscrupulous, a realist." She passed his glass to him. "This is the last for you, my dear.

I don't want you drunk. Not tonight." There was a twinkle in her beautiful slanted eyes. "I feel wicked tonight, Dave. Perhaps it is because you are so unlike the Nuans of the world. So young. So soft. So unspoiled."

"I'm hard as nails. And I'm older than you are."

"Perhaps in years. But women age quickly here in Southeast Asia. Particularly when one is orphaned at 14 and left with only a little money." She ran her long, red fingernails caressingly across his cheek.

"But do not feel sorry for me. That is unnecessary. I have worked hard, but I have invested well. Before long, with help from my financial guardian, I shall have my own restaurant." She sighed deeply and her breasts were clearly outlined through the robe. "Times have changed out here, though. You Americans have helped do that. A woman of part Caucasian blood and part Oriental is now accepted. Perhaps not everywhere, unless one is very rich. And that is what I intend to be."

Monique laughed throatily. "But I am getting too serious." She leaned across and kissed his cheek. Her movement revealed a long, well-rounded leg, tanned a shade darker than the rest of her tawny body.

Cunningham could resist no longer. He kissed her passionately, feeling her breast rise tautly under his hand. Her hand moved to his knee and upward, searching under his robe. She moaned softly, gradually removing her lips from his until only her tongue touched them.

"Come. Must I carry you to the bedroom?" She rose, robe undone, and stood before him, hands on bare hips, legs akimbo. "Or perhaps you have found the village women at Dan Lac more desirable these past few weeks."

He chased her, laughing, into the next room. It was almost daylight before she would let him sleep, satiated, dreamless.

Monique was a different person at breakfast. Tilt-nosed, rosy, and glowing. Proper. There was none of the abandon showing that she had demonstrated during their love-making.

Their conversation was light; the omlette she made was

fluffy; and Cunningham felt at peace with the world. Now this, he thought, was the kind of a woman I should have married. There was a mercurial quality about Monique. Cheerfully straightforward one moment, the ultimate in sex-appeal the next, friendly and business-like at another time. He moved across the room and, as if reading his mind, she tossed a bright smile at him over her shoulder. He lifted her long blond hair and kissed her neck, putting his arms around her waist. She sighed and put down the dish she was holding.

He caressed the rise of her belly and slid his hand onto her bare skin. Her curls were crisp under his fingers as he grasped her roundness firmly. He felt her buttocks tighten and move back against his hardness.

"Mmmm, you have," she murmured, turning, "been leading a monastic life."

Cunningham had to break the speed limit to get her to the Caravelle in time for work at noon. He spent the day idly, driving about Saigon, having a dip at the Racquet Club, window-shopping, waiting for Monique.

After a late dinner at the Caravelle they crossed to the Brinks Officers Club bar for drinks. The city was moon-drenched and beautiful from the roof-top vantage point. Palm trees waved gently in the breeze.

"Peaceful, isn't it?" Cunningham said softly as they looked over the railing. Moonlight was reflected on the Saigon river and it shimmered and changed from silver to black and back to silver again.

"On the surface, yes, I think so," Monique idly replied.

"What do you mean by that?" he asked curiously.

"It's hard to explain. To the newcomer, the city looks like that. Gay by day, lovely and serene by night. But we old hands know different. We accept the beauty but we are ever-conscious of the ugly undercurrents always present, of what is going on below the surface. Saigon is like that. Lulling a visitor like a woman in a beautiful mask. But underneath she is ugly, seething, corrupt, trying to pull you down, always grasping at you. Sometimes I hate her."

Cunningham was surprised at the vehemence in her voice, but when he began to question her further she asked him to get her another drink. At the bar, he heard the club manager in conversation with two officers from the Provost Marshal's staff. After they left he motioned to the sergeant.

"What's this about another bombing?"

"Yes, sir. Just down the street. At that enlisted men's billet near the Majestic Hotel. Luckily there was a dance tonight and only a few men were in their rooms. Nobody killed, but three seriously injured."

Cunningham relayed the information to Monique. She merely shrugged. It was old stuff to her. "It's been happening here in Saigon for years. As long as I can remember. First to the French. And now to your people. In Viet Nam life's cheap."

There were an unusual number of armed police in the streets. Cunningham was forced to stop the Renault at almost every intersection and identify himself to either Vietnamese police or soldiers, or else to American Military Police. Truckloads of soldiers were being moved through the city.

In the distance they heard the sound of an explosion. Three speeding jeeps passed them. A few blocks ahead Cunningham had to stop for another road block. He talked to the husky master sergeant as he showed him his ID card.

"Another bombing, Captain," the noncom explained. "At a party at one of the Colonels' houses. He's on the MAC-V staff. Somebody tossed a sack of hand grenades over the wall. Nobody seriously hurt but a few got cut by flying glass when the windows were blown out. That's the sixth incident tonight."

"I wonder why the Viet Cong always seem to pull a whole bunch of these in one night. Then it's quiet for a week," Cunningham asked Monique.

"It's simple. Each by itself is nothing. Many together in a few hours are very newsworthy. It's good propaganda for the VC. It is reported all over the world that the Communists can come right into the capital at will and thumb

136

their noses at both the South Vietnamese and the Americans."

"What I can't figure out is why they can't keep the VC out of Saigon. Hell, they seem to come in even carrying great big bombs," Cunningham said angrily.

Monique laughed lightly. "You are naive, Dave. It is an impossible job. Look at how much food, alone, must come into the city. Each bag of rice cannot be opened and examined. And it is not the nature of the Vietnamese to want to do this, anyway."

"What do you mean?"

"Darling, the black market has been in existence here for many, many years. Before World War II. Everyone dabbles in it. It is the livelihood for thousands. True, a lot of Viet Cong propaganda and explosives and weapons might be found, but also so would a great deal of contraband. That would not prove very popular. Besides, the main targets are you Americans, and no one cares about the few Vietnamese who do get killed."

"You certainly seem to know a lot about this. And you have a very fatalistic attitude," Cunningham said, restraining himself from sounding bitter.

Monique squeezed his arm as he drove into the apartment house courtyard. "Just because I am a woman, do not think I cannot be realistic. I hear much at the Caravelle. About deals and things that would make your stomach turn, my soft one," she said laughing softly.

Cunningham had to admit that she was right. This was a whole new world to him. He knew it existed, but he had never been a participant in its griminess.

As they mounted the stairs to Sloan's apartment he had a sudden thought. "That's right, you do hear a lot of things at the Caravelle. How about keeping your ears open. I'd like to know if Nuan is engaged in the black market." He told her about the theft of supplies from the village near Dan Lac.

"I doubt that I would overhear anything about that," she replied quickly. "It is too commonplace. Besides, there probably would be no point of bringing those things to

Saigon. They would likely be sold right in Da Nang, or up north at Hue. That is the usual procedure, I am told." She smiled softly at him, and slid her arms around his waist. "Let's talk about something else now."

The next day was his last in Saigon. In celebration Monique arranged for someone to take her place at the Caravelle.

"First thing I have to do this morning," began Cunningham, "Is to get some money changed."

"How much will you need?" Monique asked with sudden interest.

"Oh, I guess a couple of hundred dollars worth." Cunningham ticked off the items on his shopping list.

Monique nodded. "That should be more than enough. Where do you intend to get your dollars exchanged for piastres?"

"Oh, the Army Finance Center, I suppose."

"That's silly. They have to follow the official rate of exchange set by the government. Look, when we get downtown you give me your traveler's checks and I'll get you four times the official rate."

"Well, if you think it's okay," Cunningham said hesitantly. He knew the armed services were cracking down on black market currency finagling.

"Certainly it will be all right. How do you think the Americans stationed here in Saigon can afford to eat and drink at the Caravelle and the other expensive places? Even your high pay wouldn't allow you to do that several nights a week." Monique laughed. "Selling American dollars and Post Exchange goods on the black market seems to be everybody's principal hobby out here."

As they went through the shops and Cunningham saw the large amount of American goods on the counters he had to agree with Monique. In the market stalls of Cho Lon, particularly, he saw "U.S. Army" stamped on dozens of items. He shook his head. The South Vietnamese government had stated its intentions to crack down on black marketeering and corruption in order to stabilize the economy, but there was plenty of evidence around in plain sight to show that somebody was looking the other way.

Monique helped him pick out the gifts he wanted to send back to the states and had them wrapped for shipment. Cunningham felt a little embarrassed when he addressed one package to his wife. But she's 10,000 miles away, he thought, and I haven't much time. Any further misgivings were erased by the sight of Monique in a bikini when they swam at the Racquet Club.

After changing they headed for the dining room, where they had to wait for a table. Part of the club was reserved for an official luncheon hosted by the French Ambassador. Several of the guests passed and spoke to Monique. A murmur of excitement swept through the room and heads turned as an old bearded Chinese dressed in a richly embroidered mandarin coat was ushered in with a large retinue. He bowed deeply to Monique and spoke to her in Cantonese. She curtsied and replied most respectfully in the same language.

"You seem to know everybody in Saigon," Cunningham complained, half teasing.

"Don't be bitter, dear. Remember, I'm almost a native."

"Who was that old guy with the wispy chin whiskers? He looked like someone out of one of those old paintings," he commented.

Monique laughed. "Very astute comment, although you don't know it. He is the Number One among the Chinese in Southeast Asia. Extremely wise and most well thought of. He is very wealthy. He runs Cho Lon."

Cunningham's eyebrows rose.

Her face was serious. "He is a very fine man. Deeply honored by all. Your ambassador relies a great deal on his advice. And, in a way, he serves as a go-between."

"What do you mean?"

"He has contacts in Peking, Hong Kong, Indonesia, and North Viet Nam. All over the Orient. He can pass things along—both ways—that they don't want to go through diplomatic channels."

"You seem to know a lot about him," Cunningham said as they were escorted to a table.

"I owe him much," Monique said softly, leaning across the table toward him. "After my parents died, my relatives on both sides wanted to send me away to a convent in Paris, while they scrambled among themselves for what money was left. I went to the Number One for advice and assistance. I had heard much about him from one of my Chinese girl friends. I was not one of his people and he did not know me, yet he treated me as an adult. He praised my determination and bolstered my courage. I needed that badly at that time. He invested my money, helped me finish school, and saw that I found employment." She chuckled and gazed across the room as if remembering. "Believe me, he made me work. To know the value of a franc, a dollar, a piastre." Suddenly her face grew taut.

"What's the matter?"

"Here comes your Major Nuan," she breathed, nodding her head.

Cunningham did not turn around but followed her moving eyes. He felt an arm brush his shoulder and looked up.

"'Scusez moi, m'sieu," Nuan said automatically, and then glanced down. His face reddened with recognition.

"Well, hello, Major," Cunningham said, rising. "How are you?"

Nuan ignored his extended hand. "Very well, Captain."

Cunningham was amused at his obvious embarrassment. "Won't you sit down, Major? Having trouble finding a table?" He was delighted at the reaction he got.

Nuan was flustered and at a loss for words. "Well, no, Cunningham . . . Ah, thanks, though . . . You see I have to . . . ah . . ."

"Oh, I beg your pardon, Major. Let me make the introductions." He turned to Monique. "Miss van Ostrander, this is Major Nuan. An old friend." He suddenly noticed her white face and looked back to Nuan.

The Major's face was wearing a haughty, unsmiling look. He was not even looking at Monique. "Some other time, Captain. Excuse me now. I must go." He marched away before Cunningham could say a word.

Why that impolite bastard, he thought, sitting down.

"Just because he doesn't like me he shouldn't skip the amenities," he said.

Monique looked down at her plate. "Dave, it isn't you. It's me. The old-line Vietnamese are like a lot of the French and the British. They do not care for us half-castes."

"Well, that's the damnedest thing I ever heard of," he replied hotly. Then part of his anger was directed at himself. He should have thought of that, should not have caused her to be embarrassed. Good God, he thought, will I ever stop being so damn *gauche?* Will I ever fully understand the way they think out here?

Monique reached across and patted his hand understandingly. "Forget it, Dave. We must not be unhappy on this last day." There was a brittle cheerfulness to her laugh. "Besides, meeting Nuan may be the best thing that ever happened."

The arrival of the waiters with their lunch prevented him from asking her what she meant.

The evening was almost a solemn occasion. They had dinner at the apartment. Cunningham felt more comfortable with her than he had with any other woman, he concluded. She was so natural, so perceptive of his moods, and she behaved and talked accordingly. Tonight she was almost silent. It's strange, he thought. On such short acquaintance, we're so close; a feeling a couple gets normally only after very long friendship.

Her loving was tender their final night together. And in the early morning she prepared his breakfast without speaking. It was as if they were afraid to break the spell.

There were tears in her eyes when she kissed him goodby at the airfield. "Come back, darling. Come back. As soon as you can." Monique turned and almost ran to the Renault. She drove off without looking back.

Chapter 9

The mass of green and khaki uniforms at Da Nang did nothing to raise Cunningham's spirits as he rode to Special Forces headquarters. Thoughts of Monique and the good life in Saigon were fresh in his mind, but they were gradually being replaced by the stark realization that he had to go back to Dan Lac.

Colonel Boulger was away from the base, but Roger Freeman informed him that no decision had been made about where to send Cunningham and his team. He confirmed that Major Nuan would not return to Dan Lac.

"He doesn't have any permanent assignment yet. With the Joint Staff in Saigon on temporary duty. So things should be a little easier for you," Freeman commented cheerfully. "Say, here's something that might be of interest. We've turned the information over to the Security people. The AID representative checked back on that shipment of supplies for the village near you. They had just started a new color-coding system at the USOM depot. To keep the different batches separated. When word of the theft got back to them, they stopped using blue ink. All the stuff for Dan Lac was marked with this number, and in blue. Sooner or later the investigators should find some of it turning up in the black market."

Cunningham looked over the correspondence and made several notes on a sheet of paper and stuffed it in his pocket. "We'll keep our eyes open up there," he said, thanking Freeman. "Now, can I use your jeep? I want to see how my sergeant is getting along in the hospital."

It took him longer to reach the hospital than he had anticipated. Smith was a walking patient, he was informed, nearly ready for release. Cunningham noted the head nurse's frown when she advised him he probably could find his man at one of the nearby recreation centers.

Smith was at the enlisted men's club, sitting at the bar, drunkenly arguing with another man. Cunningham slid on to the next stool. Smith stared at him owlishly, but he accepted the offer of a drink. Making small talk, Cunningham looked him over closely. He had a small bandage on his neck, his arm was in a sling, and there was the bulge of more dressings under one pants leg. He had gained weight and his complexion was pasty.

A look of hostility preceded Smith's first remarks. "Look, Skipper. Knock off all that crap. I know that as C.O. of the team you figured you had to come over here to see how I was getting along, to find out when you could put me back to work again. Well, you've gone through the motions. So why don't you shove now and let me alone, like a good boy."

Cunningham chuckled half-heartedly, trying to pass off the words as a joke. "What's with you, Smitty? No need to get sore at me. I'm headed for Dan Lac and wondered if you wanted me to have anything sent down."

"Like shit you did. You just want to bug me again like you did the other day. You just can't wait to needle me," Smith said sarcastically.

"Well, why be sore at me? It was my job to ask you about the operation."

"You damned right I'm sore at you. The army says I got to treat you with respect because you're a damn officer. I have to salute you and all that crap. But there isn't a goddam regulation that says I can't be sore at you or that I have to like you!" He moved his face belligerently close to Cunningham's. "And by God, I don't like any officer who says I screwed off and didn't do my job, who blames me for all the CG casualties in that damn minefield. So blow, Captain! Scram!" With his good right arm, Smith pushed him violently.

Cunningham went over backwards as the stool tilted and he ended up on his back on the floor. He was ready to roll since Smith had stepped down and was poised over him. Cunningham forced a hard smile on his face and motioned the bartender and two other sergeants away.

"Okay, Smith. Have it your own way. I guess this hospital duty's made you pretty nervous and touchy." Cunningham rose and brushed off his pants. "Well, live it up in Saigon and get it all out of your system." He turned and casually retreated from the large room, conscious of the inquiring stares from the men at the tables.

His face was still red and his ears burning with embarrassment when he arrived at Dan Lac. He described the situation freely to Bud Thompson.

"I didn't know what the hell to do after he pushed me. I felt like clobbering the bastard, but you can't hit a man with only one arm. Maybe I should have got the MPs and put him on report for assaulting an officer. But . . ." Cunningham stopped and shrugged.

Thompson was sympathetic. "You did right, sir. Nothing to gain the other way. Maybe if he relaxes when he gets to Saigon he'll be all right. But I do think we should see what can be done about transferring him someplace. Even if he is a short-timer we can't afford even one foul-up in the outfit."

"All right," Cunningham agreed reluctantly. "You're right. And it would be better for Smitty too. Maybe we can get him a staff job some place for these last few months before he retires." He smiled. "So what else is new?"

"We've got some more problems over in the village. Nuan's Operations Officer is temporarily in command here. He never has replaced that officer who's supposed to live at the village. And he doesn't bother to send any of the Civil Guard over, even when the Viet Cong are reported in the vicinity. That's made the VC bolder. They've sent threats and harassed the peasants out in the fields. I've been keeping a man in the village each night for the last few days." He glanced keenly at Cunningham. "What's the dope from Da Nang and Saigon?"

"Well, I suppose I have to tell you the bad news sooner or later," Cunningham replied.

"You mean about the team being transferred somewhere else?" Thompson asked casually, a smile on his face.

"You already know about it?"

144

"Fowler dropped by to give us the word. He got the whole team together and told us the whole story. He sure had some nice things to say about you."

"How did the men take it?" Cunningham asked anxiously.

Thompson laughed. "Don't worry, Skipper. They're with you all the way. In fact they've got a welcome-home dinner planned for you tonight, with wine and all the trimmings."

Cunningham breathed a sigh of relief. "God, that's a load off my mind. It sure is stinking for them to get screwed for something I did."

"We don't think so, sir. We're damn proud of what you did. It took a lot of guts."

Changing the subject hurriedly, Cunningham asked about the Civil Guard.

"Not much we can do with them now. There have been no new replacements. A lot of them are away on leave. I doubt if there will be any new men sent here until a new ARVN commanding officer takes over," Thompson said.

"If that's the case let's spend as much time as we can with the villagers. At least when we leave they'll have some faith in the Americans, even if they don't in Nuan and the Civil Guard."

"I was going to propose that myself, Dave. Harry Adams and I have a list of projects we could work on. We were just waiting till you returned."

Cunningham and Thompson worked on a plan of action the rest of the afternoon. After the festive dinner, Cunningham adjourned to his hot, stuffy room, feeling tipsy. He wrote a long rambling letter to Monique. As an afterthought he told her about the blue serial numbers on the missing sacks, boxes and pieces of equipment. "If you see any of them floating around in the shops," he wrote, "let me know. Maybe your Number One Chinese friend might help you keep an eye out for them."

Writing to thank Dick Sloan for the use of his apartment, Cunningham passed him the same information. There, he thought, craftily and drunkenly, that's one way

145

to keep Nuan off my back. If I can get the goods on him or one of his staff, then he'll be in no position to give me the business. He finally went to sleep feeling maudlin and guilty over not having written to his wife for more than ten days.

The team went to the nearby village the next morning. Cunningham was surprised that the people's morale had dropped so much. Even the village chief, who had been supported and elected because of his common sense and militant attitude toward the Viet Cong, appeared listless.

"Captain, I do not know how long I can hold them together. They are very frightened. They have lost confidence in the government. No longer do we see the Civil Guard, and the province administrator who used to visit us at least once a week no longer does so. We wonder if we will be protected if the Viet Cong come."

The slightly built white-haired man shrugged and looked even more uneasy. "As for me, I believe my days are numbered. The Viet Cong have made it known that they intend to kill me and my family."

Cunningham felt very sorry for the chief, for he knew the VC generally made good their threats, one way or another. The chief could not remain within the walls forever, and the guerillas would patiently wait and wait. It took a lot of guts for someone to agree to take the job as chief, for the man who did knew he had laid his life on the line.

For the next two weeks Cunningham's team spent practically all their time in the village. The sand-bagged bunkers were enlarged, bamboo walls repaired, more coils of barbed wire strung, accordion fashion, outside the wall, and thousands of ponji sticks embedded in the ground at the edge of the jungle.

Stew McDonald and Dick Greer tirelessly drilled the 20-man Self Defense Force noncoms and held daily target practice. They scrounged several outdated light machine guns from Da Nang and set them up in sand-bagged slit trenches inside the walls so there would be crossfire at the four entrances through the village fortifications.

Jake Potter rigged a system of trip flares which would be set off by anyone approaching through the jungles at night. A minefield was also emplaced, connected with batteries so that it could be set off from inside the village.

Angered at the way the Civil Guard medics had neglected the populace, Doc Elliott worked overtime treating the people. The children, particularly, needed his healing hands and medicines.

After fourteen days, Cunningham surveyed the situation and was satisfied that the Green Berets had made a significant contribution to the village welfare. The people were not only in better physical condition but also their morale was much higher. Tiny Christopolous interrupted his inspection trip by summoning him to the meeting house where the village radio was located.

"Harry Adams just passed the word from the base. Message from Da Nang. A chopper is bringing in supplies tomorrow and we have orders to return in it. All of us. Plus all our official files, codes, and that stuff."

Cunningham groaned. That meant a new team would not be sent out for a few days, at least. All I can do, he decided, is to try to get some of the Civil Guard company commanders to take an interest in the village, keep an eye on it, and come running if the VC attack.

The team prepared to pack out all their equipment and began to make their formal goodbyes to the village officials. Almost everybody came in from the fields to throng around the departing Americans. The gratitude of the village chief, his daughter, widow of a victim of the Viet Cong, and her small son, was particularly warmly expressed to Cunningham and the others. And that, he realized later, was probably why he allowed Doc Elliott to remain overnight to check his most serious patients one last time.

The team gathered in the recreation area at Dan Lac late in the afternoon, agreeing to drink the rest of their beer. The prospects of a few days in the relative comfort of Da Nang competed as a topic of conversation with speculation about their next assignment. The talk went on well into the night.

Ernest Thomas (Doc) Elliott was sure of only one thing. He was the best enlisted army medical corpsman in Viet Nam. And he wanted only one thing—to be a full-fledged medical doctor. A modest man, he had only a single affectation. Instead of carrying the usual G.I. khaki colored medical kit on his rounds he toted a black leather bag, the kind a general practitioner uses on calls. In it were a lot of non-standard items, including a stethoscope.

Doc set the leather bag and his carbine wearily on the table near the radio transmitter at one end of the long house. The villagers met there to discuss important things. It served as a school, headquarters for the Self Defense Force, and first aid station, also. The SDF radio operator on watch, distinguishable from the rest of the people only by his green fatigue cap and ammo belt, was half asleep, Doc noted absently. He sat down, turned up the kerosene lantern and got out his green ledger-type notebook.

With meticulous handwriting and thoroughness he logged the name, diagnosis and medicine he had just dispensed to the sick child at the other end of the village. Mixed with the resignation he felt because of their leaving was a grim determination to return some day. They just won't change overnight, he told himself. For thousands of years these people have neglected their ailments, gone without medical attention, applied their own remedies based as much on superstition and tradition as anything. Why should they turn to anyone when they became ill? Particularly a long-nosed American? Sickness they accepted as inevitable as the monsoon season. Doc had only been partially successful in getting them to come to him when a malady first struck. Many of them still waited too long, and then expected a miracle.

But Doc felt a sense of pride as he looked at the hundreds of entries in his book. He had learned a tremendous amount about tropical medicine and ailments in the last three years. Few doctors could compare with him, he fully realized with no undue modesty. It was fact. He had performed miracles, or what seemed like them, thanks to proper diagnosis and treatment with new drugs.

148

Doc was very tired. His patients during the day had numbered over a hundred. He heated water on a single-burner kerosene stove and carefully washed his undershirt and fatigue shirt. He was always in full, clean uniform when he treated his patients. They might be filthy themselves, but he knew his neat appearance and confident, gentle manner had a lot to do with his success in getting the natives to come to him.

Listening to the British broadcasting short wave news on his transistor radio, he sipped from a mug of coffee. Why did he bother, he wondered. The news of the outside world meant little to him. Not with things as they were in Viet Nam. The people were so pathetically in need of medical attention. He turned off the radio. It sure is quiet tonight, he suddenly thought, draining his cup. Then he stiffened and listened hard. It was too still, he decided, and a shiver crept up his spine. His hand unconsciously reached for his carbine. He spoke sharply to the radio operator, rousing him.

"If you hear any shooting, radio Dan Lac right away. You hear?" Then Doc shortened the lantern wick, put on a shirt and went to the doorway.

No dogs barked. No animals or birds shuttled about. There were not even the usual cries of small babies. Doc slung his ammo belt over his shoulder and stepped down to the ground. Something moved him toward the south end of the village. He had taken only a dozen steps when the night was rent by explosions and bursting flares. As he ran toward the south gate he waited for the chatter of the Self Defense Force machine guns. But he heard only the sound of mortar fire and hand grenades.

Doc groaned as he neared the gate. The two light machine gun positions had been hit hard already. He raised his carbine as black clad Viet Cong filtered through the dust and smoke inside the bamboo fence. They had made it across the mines at the gate and knocked out the machine gun positions.

He emptied a full clip from his carbine and was satisfied as he dropped to one knee and reloaded. Several VC had gone down. He waited but no more of the enemy appeared. But he did not know how many had already come through the gate. As he turned there were more explosions, this time outside the west wall. Doc outdistanced several SDF troopers who had appeared and climbed to a parapet inside the wall. Two dozen VCs emerged from the jungle and flung straw mats over the barbed wire, shattered by mortar shells. He waited until they were on the mats and then opened fire. The SDFs lobbed hand grenades across at the remaining guerillas. The survivors melted back into the jungle, hauling their dead and wounded.

Gunfire back at the south gate drew Doc's attention but he saw flames rising from the ammunition storage shed area and raced toward it. He snapped several shots at Viet Cong emerging from the bunkered structure and killed another who turned to explode the ammo with a grenade. Working fast he organized a fire-fighting party, while he sent others to the south gate.

Doc was panting, smoke-blackened and singed by the time the fire was under control. If the ammunition had blown up, the village would have been destroyed. There was silence among the knot of people at the south gate as he approached. The two SDF he had left there were dead, and beheaded. The gravest thing that can happen to a Vietnamese, he knew, was having his head cut off. Not just because his life ends, but because forever his spirit, which has escaped from his body, will be seeking happiness without finding it.

One of the SDF who had been on watch outside the walls at a gun position staggered through the gate, seriously wounded. Before he fell in front of Doc Elliott he pointed mutely outside the gate and sobbed.

Doc ran out into the darkness and almost stumbled over a body only thirty yards away. He carefully snapped on his flashlight and shielded its glow. As quickly he turned it off, and he felt vomit rising to his throat. He swallowed and breathed deeply for a minute, shamed. He had never been effected this way before. Finally he lighted two other nearby figures, one large and one tiny. The chief, his

150

daughter and grandson were horribly mutilated. Slowly he turned and went back into the village and stopped by the administrative official, second in charge behind the chief. He nodded and motioned without speaking and walked toward the long house, carbine almost trailing in the dirt.

The radio operator handed him the microphone and he was in contact with Cunningham at Dan Lac.

"They were after the guns and ammo, Captain," he reported dully. "They had the machine gun positions at the south gate zeroed in with their mortars. Hit the outside bunkers simultaneously. Killed the guards and got their weapons. We stopped them from coming through the west wall. I guess they were trying to get to the long house to knock out the radio. They were hauling away some guns and ammo when I got there."

Doc had to force himself to continue and his words were halting. "They got the chief and his family. Cut off his head and hands. Stuffed his genitals in his mouth. Beheaded the kid, too. Ripped out the mother's guts." He lost his self-control. "Oh God, Captain. It was terrible. The dirty, filthy bastards!"

Cunningham tried to placate him but his words fell on deaf ears. Doc Elliott had seldom felt such anger or sorrow.

In a way it was like the feeling he had had when the medical board at college at the end of his next-to-last year had told him he was not being continued. They had said his aptitude for becoming a medical doctor was too low, that he'd never make the grade. True, he found book learning very hard. His marks were less than mediocre. But the desire and the aptitude were there, he had railed, losing his temper. The more he talked the firmer the board members were convinced that he was unstable. All the years of working at sometimes as many as four outside jobs to pay for his schooling had gone down the drain; as well as all his wonderful dreams.

Doc listened to Cunningham say the Civil Guard would move out at once to try to locate the Viet Cong and the team would arrive after daylight. But what did that matter, he asked himself. What did anything matter now? He put his head down in his arms and sobbed quietly for a few minutes.

Finally he raised his head and wiped his eyes, conscious that there were a cluster of villagers outside the doorway. He knew why and was angry with himself for neglecting the wounded for so long. He picked up his carbine and looked at the black medical bag with distaste. For the first time he hated to pick it up. He had to do so, he knew, and he had to force himself to move outside to treat the wounded. Maybe he didn't have the aptitude after all, he thought, going out to the porch.

But his pace grew firm and his shoulders straightened. No, by God, it's not true, he thought. I've gone through too much to let one incident like this throw me. I'll help these people. I'll do what I can. And after my tour in Viet Nam is up I will go home and go back to school, and when I am a doctor I will come back. They will still need me then.

The Civil Guard came and manned the gun positions while Doc worked through the night. Cunningham and the team arrived after sunrise, but he barely acknowledged their presence. There was too much to be done and too little time, he knew.

In the afternoon word came that the helicopter was arriving. The team would have to leave for Dan Lac to catch the flight to Da Nang.

After Doc Elliott had said goodbye to the villagers and gone through the gate he could still feel their accusing eyes on his back; silently accusing him of abandoning them.

The march of the Green Berets back to Dan Lac was made in silence. The men knew how Doc felt and they were affected the same way. Doc moved up close beside Red Kennedy and Harry Adams as if by sharing their feelings the guilt would somehow diminish. God, what a dirty little war, Doc thought, cursing the Viet Cong, the Communists, the whole world, and himself.

152

Cunningham was one of the eight Special Forces team commanding officers attending the briefing in the stifling Operations Room. The Green Beret Captains were outnumbered by the briefers, who had flown to Da Nang from Saigon, much to the dismay of the young officers who had anticipated going up to the capital for a few days of soft living.

Lieutenant Colonel Fowler had made the introductions, his disgust with the staff types evident from the expression on his face. Cunningham had not expected him to be present. At the first coffee break he told Fowler as much.

"Son, sometimes you want something so hard and so long that you forget about the consequences. I was passed over for selection to Colonel twice. But I still kept hoping for the silver eagles. I just got the word they're coming. They needed a new bird Colonel to oversee this operation as liaison with the IV Corps area commander and adviser to the ARVN Division Commander down on the Ca Mau peninsula." He shrugged and made a face.

"Well, ah, congratulations, sir, I guess . . ." Cunningham spoke hesitantly, not knowing exactly what comment to make.

"Shit," replied Fowler with a wry grin.

The sun beat down on the corrugated iron roof and the briefers droned on. Cunningham wished they would shut up and let him and the other Captains read the fat operations orders piled on a table in the corner. Already he was fed up with Da Nang. The simple uncomplicated life at Dan Lac was preferable, after a few days, to the hustle and bustle of the great complex of military commands which had grown out of a medium-sized South Vietnamese Army base. The city itself was impossible, its population tripled, attracted from all over the north part of the country by the plethora of uniformed men from a half dozen nations, representing every type of military service.

Only when the lights were put out and slides projected on the screen did Cunningham return his attention to the briefing. So far the speakers had talked only about the offensive segments of the operation in the southernmost part of South Viet Nam.

The area had remained almost constantly in the hands of the Viet Cong, even during the French occupation. Sporadically, after American arms and assistance had come into Viet Nam in large quantities, the ARVN would sweep in to the peninsula in strength. Somehow they were never able to surprise the Communists. All that would remain were old men farmers, women and children. A few caches of rice and a few ancient weapons were all that were ever destroyed. Then the ARVN would pull out and return to the relative comforts of their well-protected bases around Saigon. And the VC, biding their time, would slip back to their former positions. They controlled the villagers, extracted their own taxes, and filled their ranks with the young boys as they matured. The Communists had the only organized force in the area and they were smart enough to wield their strength with restraint. Only occasionally did they have to resort to terror and strong-arm tactics.

The high command in Saigon was determined to drive the Viet Cong out, once and for all this time. Several regiments of American and crack ARVN troops would participate in the search and clear operations. They would go in by air and hit hard and fast. Their strength would be on a greater scale than attempted before and they would cover every small hamlet on the southern end of the peninsula. Then the Green Berets would come in, supported by ARVN infantrymen, to occupy the villages and tiny hamlets. A massive civil assistance program would go into effect. If the farmers could be made to realize the benefits of their standard of living they would gain by keeping out the Viet Cong and cooperating with the South Vietnamese government, there was at least an even chance the area would remain free of Communist influence.

Cunningham groaned when he saw the colored slides. It would be a miserable countryside in which to operate. The cleared areas were water-covered rice paddies. The farmers lived in small clusters of houses either on stilts or

154

on earthen works raised above water level. The mangrove swamps so prevalent were all but impenetrable, ideal hiding places for the elusive VC.

The Green Beret Captains looked at each other in dismay. Some of them had worked with the primitive mountain tribes, but at least the highlands were cooler and dryer. And living a few feet above water on the banks of a canal with a rice paddy in the back yard did not make for very sanitary or healthy conditions on the Ca Mau peninsula.

The briefing officer had more bad news. "The concept we have agreed on in Saigon is this. This is the third set of teams we are assigning to the area. Each team leader will be assigned a sector of responsibility. There will be several small hamlets to be occupied in each sector so you will have to split up your teams." He waited until the groans stopped. "Each hamlet will be guarded by a squad of ARVN troops who will help you train the basic elements of Self Defense Forces, and who will serve as security guards." There were grumbles of doubt interrupting him this time.

Cunningham left the briefing with Roger Freeman. "Rog, I sure hate to tell my team about this." He hefted the bulky operation order.

Freeman agreed. He had a pair of the envelopes containing the orders in his hands. "I'll be going through this training with you, too. I'm going to be Colonel Fowler's G-3, I'm sorry to say." He adjusted his green beret. "Dave, let's stow this crap in my safe in the office and have a few cold ones at the club."

"Damn good idea. Maybe I'm just putting this off, but I think I'll wait until tomorrow before giving the boys the bad news. Let them have one last blast before we have to go to work."

They managed to get to the club early enough to snag two bar stools.

"You said Colonel Fowler had clued you in on the training sked. How does it look?" Cunningham asked.

"Rugged. They're bringing up some ARVN officers

who've operated down there. And they're going to make each team member an expert in tropical diseases. We'll all get refreshers in drainage and sanitation problems." Freeman chuckled. "One of the biggest headaches for you team leaders will be the paper work. You'll have to figure out a list of supplies and all that for each one of your hamlets. They'll make them up in separate packages and have them flown in to you."

Cunningham shook his head in dismay. "Good God, we'll be working in the dark. How the hell will we know exactly what we'll need?"

"Play the old Army game, Dave. Get up a list of bare essentials first, then double it, and add everything else under the sun you figure you just might possibly have use for. To hell with the cost."

There was a dubious note of agreement in Cunningham's resigned nod. He leaned forward thoughtfully. "Rog, how does the Colonel feel about the VC? I understand the theory all right, but does the Viet Cong? Does he figure enough forces are being left behind to make the VC really stay out of the area? Good God, they need that rice down there really bad."

"He says a lot will depend on the dispositions of the ARVN left behind. They will have at least one Division supporting your sectors. If the Corps and Division Commander keep the ARVN on the move, staying on the offensive, really staying mobile, then there's a good chance of picking the VC off as they try to slip back in. Before they get re-grouped."

"Seems to me there are one helluva lot of 'if's' about this whole damn business. After my last experience with ARVN officers, I hate like hell to have to rely on them."

Freeman laughed. "Brace yourself, Dave. Here's one item of information I forgot to pass along to you. The people from Saigon here told Colonel Fowler that your old buddy, Major Nuan, is now a Colonel. He won't be going back to Dan Lac. He's got a plush staff job in Saigon."

"Son of a bitch!" Cunningham continued to swear. He

beckoned to the bartender. "That calls for a couple of doubles." He raised the glass, a sardonic look on his face. "Well, my team will sure as hell hate to hear about this, too. By God, I'd like to get even with that little bastard if it was the last thing I could do." He gulped the whiskey and grimaced. Waving to the bartender again he ordered more drinks. "I really feel like pinning a good one on tonight. I've had about all of this crap I can stand."

Several hours later he helped Freeman to his room. Cunningham was full of liquor but still cold sober. He went to his own cot, undressed, draped the mosquito netting carefully over the bunk frame and lay back. He laughed silently at himself. At his thoughts. He had made his bed and now he had to lie in it. He had volunteered for Viet Nam duty, over Martha's protests, her advice. And damn good advice it had been, too. She knew him better than he knew himself, he suddenly realized, and the thought angered him. He went to sleep feeling terribly sad and he didn't know why.

Cunningham's Green Berets gathered at 1000 hours the next morning in the small office assigned the team. All were freshly combed and shaven and wearing newly-laundered fatigues. Cunningham focused bloodshot eyes on them and saw universal hangovers equalling his own.

"The first order of the day, Adams," Cunningham began with a croak in his voice, "is for you and your men to scrounge a coffee pot and the fixings. And some ice water." He smiled bleakly and could feel the men relax.

A half hour later he began his briefing, repeating in 60 minutes what he had had to listen to for several hours. He could feel their doubt rising as he spoke.

"All right, gather around and take a look at your new homes. Here are the pictures. You might as well know the worst." He spread the photographs on the long table.

The general feeling was that they were really getting shafted, that the small hamlets would be terribly hard to defend if the VC attacked in any kind of strength; but Cunningham got unexpected help from Kennedy.

"It can be done, you guys. Down on the peninsula, north

157

of where we'll be, a Chinese priest made a go of it. From scratch," Kennedy explained. "This joker came into Viet Nam a few years back with two or three hundred refugees, Chinese. They'd come down across the border of Red China and got refuge first in North Viet Nam, but then the Commies took over; so he moved out to Cambodia. Then he got permission to go into South Viet Nam. I guess they figured if they let him stay down in the Ca Mau peninsula he wouldn't be around long anyway. But this tough old guy was a former Chinese Army chaplain. He'd fought the Japs and the ChiComs. He still has a big fortified village and his own little army. Damn fine soldiers. I heard that a lot of the ARVN were against him because he was so damn successful. His town is built on two sides of a canal, in the midst of rice paddies, just like any one of these. But he doesn't just man outposts around the village. He sends out roving patrols looking for the VC and attacking them. Especially at night. Gives them hell. He had to beg, borrow and steal weapons at first, but when he showed results the Americans practically forced the ARVN to support him."

Cunningham nodded. "That's the general pattern we are to follow. We've got to fortify the hamlets first thing. Work out a system of protecting the villagers inside them as well as out in the rice fields. Also we'll have to train a nucleus of them to handle the guns we bring in with us. We'll have a civic action program in each hamlet, and it'll probably take a sector-wide cooperative effort to get it going. One thing, there aren't any roads down there, and we won't have choppers available much. We'll have to use the waterways—canals and rivers—and our radios to maintain contact between the net of hamlets."

He held up the thick operation order. "I can see we all don't feel too damn good today, so we'll spend it on paper work. I want each of you to read this thoroughly. Tomorrow morning we'll have a skull session and ask and answer questions. In the afternoon we'll begin by drawing up our initial requisition list. I want to get that in as early as possible. Ahead of the other teams. We can always augment it as we go along. But it'll be first come, first served. Then day after tomorrow we'll start classwork." He tossed the order to Harry Adams. "Lieutenant Thompson and I read this over this morning. You and the rest of the gang take it today. See you all at 0800 hours in the morning."

Cunningham smiled broadly. "Maybe it'd be smart if we all took it easy tonight and get a good sleep."

The beer at the Officers Club was fairly cold and they drank from the cans greedily. Cunningham looked across at Lieutenant Thompson with a smile. "How was Saigon, Bud?"

Thompson glanced at him quickly and reddened. He had flown into Da Nang the evening before. "I called Monique for you. She sends her love." He looked embarrassedly down at his beer can. "I took your advice. She fixed me up with a date. One of the waitresses from the Caravelle. We had a ball." Suddenly he was serious.

"I'm afraid Smith may get in a hell of a lot of trouble in Saigon. He's really been whooping it up. He got next to one of the doctors from the hospital and he gave him an extension on his R and R. He's loaded all the time, they say, and is running around with a pretty rough bunch of characters. I tried to find him. Talked to the sergeant at the billet he's assigned to. He only comes back there to get into clean clothes and dump his dirty laundry."

"Any chance of getting him reassigned elsewhere?" Cunningham asked. "You said you were going to check on that."

"I stopped by the Personnel Center. There wouldn't have been any trouble at all before, but now he's getting quite a reputation. I doubt that any of the commands in Saigon will take him. I'll try again here at Da Nang, though."

Cunningham amusedly returned to the initial topic. "Did a little female companionship make you feel any better about things?"

Laughing lightly, Thompson flushed. "Damn right. Especially with this upcoming operation." He stared off

159

into space. When he continued his tone was wry. "Even though I am suffering pangs of remorse."

Cunningham chuckled sympathetically. "I know what you mean. But better a pang in your remorse than somewhere else."

Sergeant Chester Smith had the combined inborn suspicion and cunning of an incurable drunk and a con artist. Since he had had another run-in with the Military Police the night before, was still half-loaded, and headed for an illegal financial transaction, Smith had reason to be cautious. He left the Enlisted Transient Billet to which he had been assigned in Saigon. Despite the urge he passed up the entrance to the bar down the street. As usual he was beseiged at the corner by a throng of shoeshine boys. He stopped suddenly and leaned against a building, nodding to one of the tiny black-haired Vietnamese boys.

A casual quick glance backward revealed a husky crewcut American in civilian clothes quickly step into a doorway. Smith grinned to himself. His young shadower must have had only the short course of the Army Criminal Investigation Division.

After handing the boy a handful of piastres Smith sauntered down the street, feeling the perspiration spring out on his face and body under his sport shirt. It was not just the hot sun and high humidity. His hangover helped, but mostly he felt the pressing of his obligations and his lack of discretion the previous night. He cursed himself and headed for the air-conditioned bar of the Majestic Hotel.

A sigh of relief accompanied his first gulp of cold Danish beer. He wanted to order a shot of whiskey on the side but he refrained because the Army CID man was watching from the lobby. It would not do to appear too affluent. He shifted his arm uncomfortably. The clean white bandage and sling were binding. As he had intended, the bartender inquired. He explained being wounded and then hurting the arm in a hassle the night before. The bartender smiled sympathetically and bought him another beer.

Smith would have liked to tarry but he knew business came before pleasure. It had taken all his will power to get up in the steaming barracks-type room to which he had been returned by the MPs after they had picked him up. But he had had a date with a certain medical corpsman at the dispensary. While shaving in the latrine he had made a big show of voicing to other men that his arm was hurt again. Then he had gone to the medics. He had winced at the proper time as a bored doctor probed, accepted the prescription blank for pain-killer pills, and gone down the hall to be re-bandaged by the corpsman who had treated him on his second day in Saigon. The medical tech sergeant was an old buddy from Korea and Japan. Over a good many drinks they had seen in each other the makings of a method to improve their respective financial status. The corpsman had access to medical supplies which sold well on the black market. But he was smart enough to know that because of his position he was probably under surveillance whenever he started to walk out of the building. In Smith he had the means to get the medicine out of the dispensary when he came in to have his wounds checked.

Unconsciously Smith stroked the bandage again, feeling the highly-prized vials of anti-biotics secured beneath the cloth. He drained his glass. Time to lose the shadow and make contact with the Korean, Sook Kim, another veteran of the black market during the Korean war, both in his homeland and in Japan. Smith had been wary in looking for the right man to take the goods off his hands. He had been tempted by several Vietnamese and Chinese, but either they had been too ready to do business, or else the price wasn't right. Since he had known Sook Kim from the old days, he had immediately made the arrangements. This was the last shipment. And he had to be doubly careful. The MPs had searched him after the fight in the Wild West Bar and knew exactly how much money he had. That he had been in company with two Korean girls supplied by Sook Kim must have registered with the CID right away. There were few rackets in which they were not engaged, from prostitution to dope peddling.

Outside the hotel, Smith crammed his bulk into one of the small blue and white Renault taxis and directed the driver to the Navy Exchange. On arrival he gave careful instructions and a big tip to the driver. The store was jammed with military personnel in all types of uniform. Smith wandered around as if shopping, keeping an eye on the following CID man and at the same time edging toward the stockroom door. When the crush of shoppers was considerable, he slipped through the door and raced around to another access to the retail store, ignoring the curious stares of the Vietnamese stock clerks. He made it in time to see his shadow enter by the other door. Smith quickly went to a side exit and got into the waiting taxi.

He switched cabs twice and then went back to the Majestic. In the men's room he removed the small packages from the bandage. After readjusting the sling he put the vials inside his shirt and went into the lobby and purchased a canvas Pan American Airlines duffel bag. The switch was made in a busy waterfront bar down the street. Smith walked out with a similar flight bag full of greenbacks, leaving the other, containing the medical supplies, behind with his contact.

Selecting a small but exclusive restaurant featuring French cuisine, Smith boldly got a corner table. He delayed by ordering several brandies and soda. Then he slowly ate his lunch, watching the cafe empty of patrons. When the waiter went to get his coffee, he put the flight bag on his lap, covered by the table cloth and transferred half the money into the sling. Next he took a taxi to the Caravelle hotel and checked the airlines bag. He picked up an envelope at the desk, wrote the medic's name on it, and placed the claim check inside.

Smith's hands were trembling and he was soaked with perspiration after he left the envelope at the medical corpsman's billet. He forced himself to bypass the inviting, cool interior of a bar, and went to a jewelry store, where he examined several ornate carved jewel boxes. He ignored the decorations and carefully looked at the locks. He

162

selected the one with the strongest and most intricate locking device.

In the privacy of another men's room toilet stall, he filled the box with money from his sling, re-wrapped the box, and addressed it to himself, care of the Green Beret team at Da Nang. He could hold out no longer. After gulping a cold beer in the hotel bar, he felt himself relax. The bartender provided a length of twine and he wrapped it around the package.

Smith chuckled to himself as he had another beer, accompanied by a shot of brandy. Why not mail it right under the noses of the top brass, he thought. He taxied to the Army Post Office branch at the Military Advisory Command Headquarters. Barely suppressing a smile, he insured it for $25.00 and breathed a sigh of relief as the postal clerk took the package.

Back at the Majestic Hotel, Smith ditched the bandage and sling and grabbed a secluded table in the bar. He soaked up the coolness from the air conditioning and several drinks. Gradually his nervous edge wore off. He chuckled softly. He'd had a great time during the rest and recreation period and he had a hell of a stake built up as well. A half dozen packages had gone to Da Nang. Between the Vietnamese silk embroidered pictures of exotic birds, rolled and mailed in a cardboard cylinder, between the pages of some books, and concealed among other souvenirs, Smith already had a down-payment for a small saloon back in San Francisco. And if he played his cards right during the rest of his tour he'd find other opportunities to increase the amount. Little by little he would buy money orders and send them back to his bank.

There was a smirk on his face as he ordered another drink. Barbara would be damn sorry she had decided to divorce him when he came back and set himself up in business. With his retirement pay and a place of his own he'd have a goddam good life. And maybe, just out of meanness, he'd call her up and offer her a job as a waitress.

Smith thought about her beautiful body and felt the old urge come back. He left a hefty tip and clumsily left

the room. It was about time to find someplace a little live-
lier. A joint with a little action. Maybe call on Sook Kim
and say goodby. He could probably dig up a couple of
gals.

The evening was a blur of pretty girls, noisy juke boxes
and dozens of drinks. Smith, Sook Kim, two Australian
paratroopers and another Green Beret sergeant ended up
in the House of Mirrors, a revitalized version of a once-
famous French brothel in Saigon. The place was jumping.
Several South Vietnamese officers were already living it
up with the staff—girls of a dozen nationalities and shades.

Smith caught the eye of a tall Danish girl. When her
Vietnamese escort left the table, she glanced at the big
American sergeant. He nodded and with unspoken but
mutual assent they moved simultaneously from the room.
Her room upstairs was small but well-appointed and the
bed was clean. Her body was magnificent, but she needed
every bit of her experience to arouse Smith's alcohol-
sodden body. The beautiful Dane was almost sorry she
got him started. His endurance matched his size and she
was gasping for breath by the time he was satisfied.

When they returned to the main room, the South
Vietnamese officer whom she had deserted grabbed her
angrily by the arm. He wore the garb of the elite Ranger
Division, but it made no difference to Smith. He pushed
the small man aside. Then he was faced by two more of
the ARVN's friends as well. From hot words to shoving
to fists, the hassle progressed. The Australians, Sook Kim,
and the American sergeant joyfully came to Smith's aid.

It might have ended with a bunch of broken jaws and
a lot of damaged furniture and glassware, but the screaming of the frightened girls brought a truck load of patrolling
armed soldiers into the building. After the first shot, Smith
and the others knew they were fighting for their lives. They
smashed the lamps first, taking their chances in the dark.
Their powerful blows were now meant to main or kill. But
the odds were too rough, Smith realized.

He grabbed a heavy chair and heaved it through a glass
door leading to the patio. Yelling for his friends to follow,

he plunged through and raced toward the wall around the brothel. Going through the front gate was out of the question. The Army vehicle was there and he could hear its radio blaring a response to a riot call. In the distance he could make out the sound of sirens. Sook Kim grabbed him by the arm.

"Shall we try the wall?" Smith asked.

"God no! Broken glass imbedded in it, probably. And maybe barbed wire. Quick, this way. I remember a small back door to the wall."

Smith led the way through. They ran as fast as they could down an alley. The other American sergeant pulled up short.

"Smitty, they'll block off all the streets. We'll never make it."

Sook Kim agreed. "We'd better split up. I know some people living in the neighborhood. Being an oriental I can move in with them for a few hours."

One of the Australians spoke up. "Hey, mates, there's another spot around here. I don't know exactly where, but I had a few bloody good drinks there and a nice girl."

"Listen. Isn't that the sound of music?" said the other Aussie suddenly.

The sound of a rock and roll recording could be heard faintly, coming from ahead. They automatically started to move again.

"Here, the house inside this wall," Smith. said softly. He looked around quickly, hastened by the sounds of more sirens approaching. "Over the wall, boys." He spotted a tree looming ahead and quickly leaped for a low-hanging branch. Painfully, he hauled himself up. "Watch the glass," he whispered. He kicked at the shards and stepped across and lowered himself into a garden. The others followed and they circled the house. Smith silenced the armed doorman with a $10 bill and they were allowed inside. The Madame acted frightened at their appearance but a fistfull of bills changed her mind.

She ushered them into a private room. Smith smiled. Sook Kim was no longer with them. He could not afford to mess with the South Vietnamese police at all. The four battered soldiers took turns cleaning up their clothing as best they could and wiping the blood from their cuts and bruises.

"Well, you guys, let's have a couple of good big drinks. I think we just have time before the MPs figure out where we've disappeared to. They'll search every house in the area."

They were drinking and laughing with four girls as the American Military Police and a pair of South Vietnamese soldiers burst into the room. Smith suddenly cursed, finally conscious of the fact that he still had two or three hundred dollars in greenbacks in his pocket.

In the Provost Marshal's office the quartet vehemently denied being involved in the brawl, but it was obvious that they had been in a fight some place. Smith suddenly became very sober when they were informed that several of the Vietnamese had been seriously injured. If any died, there would be a full fledged investigation.

Smith kept insisting that the fight had been among the four of them and that he had won the money in a crap game. The latter they could not disprove, and he had a feeling that the girls at the House of Mirrors would not identify them and that the South Vietnamese officers who had been there would not relish any official inquiry.

Forty-eight hours later Smith breathed a sigh of relief. The injured men were recovering. The only charge against him was possessing an illegal amount of American currency. Since he had already been in the guard house for more than two days, he was sent up to Da Nang along with others on a disciplinary status. The order read that he was to have no further R and R tours in Saigon during the rest of his tour of duty in the country.

Word of Smith's troubles preceded him north. The grapevine brought it initially to Harry Adams who passed it to Lieutenant Thompson. An official query to Saigon confirmed it.

Captain Cunningham grimaced when Thompson gave

him the bad news. "I suppose this will mean what I think it does."

Thompson nodded. "Yes, sir. Personnel got a message about him, and the CID checked his gear at the hospital barracks. Didn't find anything though. But everybody on this damn base will know what's up. We don't have a chance in hell of getting him transferred to anybody here."

Cunningham's mouth tightened. "Well, by God, when he does get back we'll work his ass off and keep a close watch on him. No booze, understand? And I'm really going to give him holy hell. One more stunt like this and I'll throw the book at him even if it does cost him his retirement."

Harry Adams brought the Captain further news about Smith two days later. "I don't know what those people in the hospital personnel office are thinking about. Smitty came in by plane late yesterday. He had to go back over there to check out and pick up his duffel bag. Those dumb bastards let him talk them into waiting to discharge him until this morning and let him go to the noncom club. One of the boys saw him. He was drunk as a goat."

"When will he arrive over here?" Cunningham asked disgustedly.

"Sometime around noon."

"When he does come to the office you take the others out and I'll see if I can give him a good enough ass-chewing to make him straighten up. It'll be up to you to keep an eye on him. I can't be around day and night. Let me know the first time he steps out of line."

When Cunningham approached the office later he could hear the sound of coarse laughter. Smith was regaling Stew McDonald and Tiny Christopolous with his Saigon adventures.

Adams approached along the corridor and Cunningham motioned him into the room ahead. After Adams had led Tiny from the office, Cunningham opened up on Smith with both barrels.

"You think all that in Saigon was pretty goddam funny, don't you Smith?" he said caustically.

167

Smith's face whitened, perspiration streaming down his forehead as he stood at rigid attention. He shook his head. "No sir, I don't."

"It sure sounded like it. I don't know what the hell's the matter with you, Sergeant. You're in the Army almost 20 years and you turn out to be a foul up. You jeopardize your career, your discharge from the Army. You give this team a bad name. I don't see how you've lasted in the Green Berets this long. Good God, I was all set to try to get you transferred out of this outfit to a staff job so you could take it easy the last months of the tour out here. Now nobody will touch you with a ten foot pole."

"But Captain, I haven't any charges against me from the deal in Saigon," Smith protested sullenly.

"Horse shit. You know damn well you were involved in that fight, and so does the U.S. Army, even though they can't prove it. And they know that you're smart enough to be goddam familiar with the currency restrictions we're operating under out here. Why didn't you shoot crap with MPC—Military Payment Certificates—or haven't you heard that we use them, sergeant? Crap. They've got you dead to rights on that."

"Well sir, it wasn't very much money," Smith said lamely.

"Don't hand me that, Smith. You got into trouble with the MPs a couple of times before that big brawl in Saigon. The report is that you've been spending money like a drunken sailor all during your R and R. I checked. You haven't drawn any more than a hundred bucks pay from the finance office for the last couple of months. Nuts, you're not that good a gambler, Smith. I don't know exactly what you were up to but I'll bet it was something crooked."

Cunningham looked at him hard and saw that the words were having no effect. He was just wasting his breath.

"All right, Smith. You're back on duty with the team. We've got a rotten operation coming up, and you'd better do your share or I'll hit you with everything in the book. Screw up just once and you've had it. I don't care if it means a court martial for you and the loss of all your retirement benefits. I won't see a good team of Green Berets get fouled up just because of one man who won't carry his weight. You're a mature man. You know the Army, and you know the work we're doing. So you shape up, or else!"

Smith stubbornly looked him right in the eye. "Yes, sir!" he snapped.

"All right, Smith, report to Adams and try to catch up on what this deal is all about."

Cunningham resignedly left the office. He knew that Smith would do just as much as he pleased, and no more. And there wasn't a damn thing Cunningham could do about it until Smith broke some regulation. By that time it might be too late. Maybe, just maybe, he thought, we'll be lucky, and he will cut down on his drinking until his time is up and we can ship him home.

Chapter 10

Tiny Christopolous scratched thoughtfully at the inch-long growth of curly black beard on his face. He looked awesomely huge alongside Jerry Lord, his 250-pound bulk looming over his fellow radioman's slender form.

"You really think it's okay to suggest it to the Captain?" Lord asked, peering up at Tiny owlishly through his steel-rimmed glasses.

"Damn right. If we're going to be split up, then every damn one of the guys in the team should be able to service these radios, including him. You can't come running every damn time something breaks down." Tiny grinned. "And despite all the work you've done with me, Jerry, you know as well as I do that half the time I wouldn't be able to fix them anyway."

Tiny straightened as Cunningham came into the office. "Tell him now, Jerry." The big ex-football player waited patiently as Lord gathered up his courage and went to Captain Cunningham. He shook his head as he listened to Lord make his suggestion in apologetic and faltering terms. Shit, he thought, the kid is still afraid of the skipper. And mostly of himself, he decided, rising. He crossed to them.

"It sounds like a good idea, Captain," Tiny said encouragingly. "Jerry's made up this list for me. We could get it copied. It has on it most of the troubles that could happen to any of our communications equipment. Also some maintenance hints. Things to do daily, weekly, and so on, to keep them running better."

Cunningham's annoyed look faded. He sighed. "Okay, I'll buy it, Jerry. You figure that if we have the pieces of equipment here you can brief us well enough in three or four sessions to keep the gear in operation. I sure don't know where we're going to squeeze it in, but I have to agree with you." Cunningham smiled. "Okay. Work out the details with Lieutenant Thompson and Harry Adams. Maybe right after that special session we have on putting together those prefab bridges over canals. Or else just before it. Jake Potter's running that one."

Eyes glowing with pleasure, Lord bustled out to find Sergeant Adams.

Tiny grinned easily at Cunningham who sat down heavily in a chair. He dumped his green beret on the table and fished the training schedule out of his shirt pocket.

"Getting a little rough, Captain?" Tiny asked sympathetically.

Cunningham nodded. "There's so damn much we need to know before going down to the peninsula. But some of this refresher training on tactics is exactly the same as we got at Special Forces school. A damn waste of time here."

"Jerry has been a big help to me," Tiny commented. "He's a damn fine kid, Captain."

"He sure is a worker, I'll say that." Cunningham grinned at Tiny. "At first I wondered how he ever got into the Green Berets. He's pretty slender and you can't exactly say he's very aggressive."

170

"Don't underestimate him," Tiny replied without hesitation. "He's a tough little guy. It's just that he's shy. Particularly with officers and senior NCOs."

"What does he do for relaxation?" Cunningham asked curiously.

"Oh, he goes over to the rec hall with us for a beer now and then. When he goes off the base he wanders around with the rest of us for awhile, but mostly he pokes around the shops, talks to the natives, asks them all kinds of questions. What this and that are used for. He knows almost as much about their customs as Red and Doc.

Cunningham chuckled. "We sure have a varied bunch in this team." He looked at Christopolous, suddenly serious. "How do you think Doc is coming along?" He had been worried about the medical corpsman since the Viet Cong attack on the village near Dan Lac. Doc Elliott had been morose, disinterested in anything, and withdrawn since the incident. Cunningham knew Tiny would give him a straight and astute estimate.

"He seems to be perking up, Captain. Since you set up a series of lectures on the different tropical diseases and other things we might run into in the hamlets and how to treat them he has snapped out of it. I think that once we get back to work down there, he'll be running with the ball again."

Two days later Jerry Lord stood nervously in front of his fellow team mates. Beside him on a table were four different radio sets of the type they would be using. He was almost sorry he had suggested giving the Green Berets the extra instruction on repairing the electronic gear. He had always hated getting up in front of an audience.

His ears reddened as he remembered waiting to explain his entry at a regional science fair when he was in high school back in Iowa. He had been scheduled to speak next. From the wings of the stage he had looked out at the sea of strange faces. Suddenly he had felt urine seep from him and warmly trickle down his leg. He had turned and run for the toilet. What he recalled most were the shaming remarks and taunts his instructor, who had had to take his place onstage, had made. It was the last such event he had ever entered.

Lord swallowed deeply. He turned to the radio sets themselves and continued. As his hands touched the various parts he began to relax. They were his babies and no one knew them like he did. He reviewed the various components and indicated what was most likely to go haywire and how to repair them.

Young as he was, Lord was an electronics whiz. When the other kids on the block of the small town where he had lived had been out playing football, he was tinkering with the ham radio he had built from the parts of old sets dredged from a second-hand store and a junk shop. Unfortunately his father's feed and grain business had succumbed to branches of chain stores located in the nearby city. Going to college had been out of the question.

Jerry had gone to work for a television repairman in the city, a veteran of the Korean war. Observing the boy's talent, he had suggested that Lord go into the service to get the additional knowledge he wanted so badly. Jerry had waited until he had saved quite a bit of money and then contributed it to the household fund to help make up for the lower pay he would be getting in the Army. After basic radio school he had wanted to go into radar, but his senior instructor had other ideas and two quotas to fill. Lord would remain at the school and teach, or else volunteer for the Green Berets. He chose the latter.

Strangely enough Jerry Lord had taken to the training. The physical conditioning program showed him that he was more athletically inclined than he had thought. He was pleased that his body had toughened and his endurance increased. He was 15 pounds heavier when the course was completed, and it was all muscle. The radio training was a snap, for the equipment was relatively simple. He had had French in high school and his only trouble in the language course had been one of accent. Vietnamese was tougher, but he had almost a photographic memory and he retained the vocabulary better than most.

The weapons training, his secondary specialty, was tougher. Within a week he could assemble and take apart and service every piece of ordnance equipment, but it took him longer to become accustomed to firing the weapons on the range. Little by little he got over being gunshy. The course in hand-to-hand combat had made him a little sick to his stomach but he had mastered it.

Like everyone else Lord had wondered how he would react in actual combat. But in the first firefight in Viet Nam everything had happened so fast and he had returned fire so automatically there was no sensation of having killed another human being. As time went on the fighting became just another part of the job. His spare hours were spent on a correspondence course in electronics and radio engineering. Sooner or later he had to make a decision, he knew. Remain in the army and hope for more education, or get out and try to work his way through college. The G.I. Bill would pay part of the tab, but he had his mother, his partially invalided father, and three younger sisters to think about.

"The rest of the session and the one this afternoon will consist of my bugging these sets, and each of you figuring out what's wrong with them. Sergeant Adams has posted the schedule for the individual instruction." Lord heard the groans of protest and stiffened. "Look, you guys. Being able to repair one of these radios in a hell of a hurry may mean your lives if the VC attack your hamlet. You may need to put through an urgent call for air support, or something. Now I don't want any of your blood on my hands, so pay attention."

Cunningham looked up at Lord in surprise. There was a bite in his tone. The Captain rose. "You heard what he said, you jokers. So get with it." He smiled encouragingly at Lord and walked to him. "That was a fine start, Jerry. I think even Stew McDonald and Chet Smith understood it. That's pretty good with the hangovers they obviously have." He grinned as he spoke but the sarcasm and disapproval in his voice were evident to everyone in the room.

McDonald laughed harder than the others, but Smith

looked angrily and defiantly at Cunningham, his face red.

After the radio series, Doc Elliott took over with his short course in tropical medicine. Initially he was casual in his approach, but as he used slides showing Vietnamese suffering from various illnesses he became more animated. There were smiles on the faces of the Green Berets when he finished his first session. Not because of the subject matter, but because they knew Doc Elliott was now his former self.

Jake Potter, as usual, had thoroughly investigated not only the problems of construction in the damp soil in the south but also ways and means of helping the farmers plant and harvest their rice crop. By combining the Vietnamese ways with modern weapons and materials, they could do much to improve the lot of the natives.

Cunningham and the other team commanders joined Colonel Fowler in the Operations Center the next week when the offensive phase of the plan began. The initial reports were encouraging. Simultaneously over the southern portion of the Ca Mau peninsula, the Americans, ARVN Rangers and crack troops from other countries struck swiftly at the Viet Cong. The air was dotted with transport helicopters, supported by Hueys and fixed-wing fighter bombers flying from fields ashore and aircraft carriers at sea. At first the VC had had to stand and fight, their backs to the wall. But by forty-eight hours later there was only infrequent contact with the Communists. The VC were evaporating into the sanctuary of the mangrove or blending into the native population. The South Vietnamese River patrol craft followed them on the canals and rivers, but the enemy kept on the move.

Gathering the Green Berets in the office, Cunningham briefed them on the situation. "Frankly I don't much like the looks of the whole damn thing. You'd think the VC casualties would be much higher, with all the troops and planes we had in this operation. Of course the terrain is in their favor. And sure as hell they knew sooner or later we'd go in in force. They probably had a well-organized plan of withdrawal. So far Intelligence reports the VC had a system of occupation down there just about like what we'll have. There's one good aspect, though. The VC did have to leave behind a lot of weapons and ammo. They just couldn't carry much with them across those paddies and in their small boats. The ARVN are going through each village and hamlet with a fine tooth comb to try to sanitize the area. That should give us some time in our favor. Even if a lot of the Victor Charlies did escape, they can't try to fight their way back in until they smuggle in more guns and ammo. We should be able to get pretty well along in our civic action projects by that time."

Moving to the map on the wall he continued. "Based on what has been reported about our sector by the ARVN political intelligence people, this is the way we'll be organized. I'll set up my headquarters in this village here, with Red Kennedy as my liaison with three sub-sectors. He'll be free to nose around the whole area and to coordinate mutual cooperation on some of our projects. Lieutenant Thompson, Harry Adams and Jake Potter will be in charge of the three sub-sectors, in addition to having the responsibility for their own hamlet. Tiny and Dick Greer will be here and here, working under the supervision of Lieutenant Thompson. Jake Potter will be here, and Jerry Lord and Doc Elliott in these hamlets. Harry Adams will have his sub-sector headquarters down here, with Stew there, and Smith here."

Cunningham put down the pointer and picked up several folders. "In these there's a report of what action occurred in each hamlet and dope from the intelligence people about each of them. Also they're flying up with some more up-to-date pictures." Cunningham, checking coordinates from a sheet of paper, went back to the map and marked several spots on it. "They'll set up helicopter pads, a small airstrip, and base a few Vietnamese Navy craft at the locations I've indicated." He glanced from face to face. "The formal training is over now, but I want each of you to know these folders by heart. Check your requisition lists once more, too. Set up some sort of filing system in a box to take with you, and start to pack your personal gear.

We can't tell when we might get orders to move." He handed the folders to Harry Adams. "Okay, Harry, pass these around please." Motioning to Thompson to accompany him he put on his green beret. "See you all after chow."

Lieutenant Thompson matched Cunningham's long stride down the hall and out the front door. The mid-day sun hit them full force. The officers club was only slightly cooler, but the beer had been on ice.

"I thought we'd better get the hell out of there, Bud," Cunningham said smiling. "Sure as the devil there will be a lot of gripes about the way I've assigned them. They might as well get the chance to get them off their chests now."

Thompson grunted agreement. "It never fails. They haven't even been in the area yet, but they'll figure that some other hamlet is better." He frowned. "You know of course where the biggest howl will come."

Cunningham nodded grimly. "Sure, Chet Smith will be mad as hell that I made Jake Potter a sub-sector leader instead of him. I know he is senior to Jake, but I just can't trust the son of a bitch. Besides, I gave Harry Adams a tough area. There were a lot of hard core VC in there. He, Stew and Smith all have a lot of experience. By this time they can smell any VC trying to infiltrate. And they're older. They'll have easier going in getting the villagers to cooperate. They've worked with teams in Viet Nam when this strategic hamlet program was first started south of here."

"I know it, and you know it, but I still bet that Stew and Smith are plenty pissed off right now about being stuck the farthest from civilization," Thompson replied with a grin. "Come on, let's have another brew. I don't think we're going to be around to enjoy this soft life much longer."

After a leisurely lunch they returned to the office building. Cunningham's lips tightened. Chet Smith and Stew McDonald were waiting for them at the entrance. Cunningham could smell whiskey fumes when Smith said he wanted to talk to him.

"All right, Smith, let's have it."

"Well, Captain, Stew and I think we've been shafted." McDonald nodded agreement, moving a trifle unsteadily on his feet. "Yes, sir, first of all I outrank Jake Potter," Smith continued. "I should have been a sub-sector commander instead of him. And you stuck Stew and me in the worst damn area in our whole sector. Christ, any kid can see that it'll be the first ones the VC will try to move in on. It seems to me that in view of our long years of service—years of getting our asses shot at—that we are entitled to something a little better. Let some of the kids be on the griddle for a change."

"All right, Smith, I'll give it to you straight," Cunningham began. "The reason I picked Potter over you is because he is dependable. And you're not, by a damn sight. I'll consider myself lucky if you can hack the job in that one hamlet. God knows you should be able to. I put you there, and Stew in the same general area, because they are tough ones. Sure, they're isolated. But the job of this team is to keep the VC out of the whole sector. The most experienced men get the roughest spots, because our overall security depends on maintaining its integrity in all locations." He felt inclined to wipe the surly sneer off Smith's face with a fist, but he patiently continued.

"It isn't just this team, Smith. Check with any of the others. The C.O.s have done the same damn things as I have. You've been around the Army long enough to know the system. Anyway, this is the way it's going to be in my team. If you don't like it, put in for a transfer. I'll sure as hell recommend it. But it won't do you any good, Smith. Like I told you before. Nobody in Viet Nam will take you off my hands. So you might as well grin and bear it."

Cunningham stared him down. "All right, let's go into the office and get to work on those folders."

By 4 p.m. the print was swimming before Cunningham's eyes. Sweat was dripping off his face. He looked around the room. Stew McDonald and Smith were asleep, and several others were on the verge. He motioned to Harry

Adams. "Okay, let's call it a day. Trying to get anything done in this heat is stupid. We'll go at it again about six in the morning and work until noon." He leaned toward Adams. "Sorry to saddle you with those two, Harry," he said, motioning toward McDonald and Smith.

The top sergeant smiled grimly. "I understand, Captain. But they'll shape up or I'll beat hell out of them, you can bet on that." He stretched. "God, I'll be glad to see the last of this office. This waiting around is getting on everybody's nerves."

Two days following, the Green Berets were all packed. Their gear was loaded into a transport plane. They were all soaked with perspiration before the steaming plane took off. It was a long flight before they reached their first stop, Soc Trang, southwest of Saigon. There the team picked up their radios, ammunition, and initial food supplies. A quartet of huge helicopters next hauled them to Loc Than down on the Ca Mau peninsula, where a detachment of smaller choppers were based. The sun was low before they got unloaded and found bunk space in the tent city which had sprung up during the offensive operation.

Cunningham conferred with the helicopter unit skipper and groaned, but he accepted the inevitable. Somewhere along the line, somebody had not passed the word about the exact plan. The choppers would take the team members to the hamlets where Cunningham, Thompson, Adams and Potter would be located, but there were no suitable landing spots yet prepared at the other places. The rest of the Green Berets would have to haul their supplies and equipment down by boat. And re-supply would be the same until they got launching pads constructed. To make matters worse, the bulk of their supplies had been sent mistakenly to Quan Lon, headquarters for the ARVN Division which would provide the security troops for the southern peninsula.

The team members accepted the word impassively; they were old hands at Army routine. They laughed when Cunningham concluded with the usual, "Sorry 'bout that" expression. If something had not been screwed up they would have been worried. Cunningham managed to get off a message to Roger Freeman who was already at Can Tho, farther north on the peninsula, headquarters for the IV Corps area. Maybe he could get the supply situation unscrambled.

After a breakfast of canned frankfurters and beans the next morning, Cunningham and Kennedy loaded their gear aboard a small helicopter and crawled in. The Captain shook his head as he looked down at the terrain they flew over. Flat and wet. Laced by rivers, streams, and canals. Loaded with rice paddies. An occasional mangrove swamp reared its green thick head above the water. A cluster of farmhouses showed here and there along canal banks, and even out in the middle of the rice fields, like an island. Far ahead he could spot the deep blue of the ocean. He looked down at Thuong Ninh with interest. Strictly speaking it was not a hamlet but a village of 800 people where he would make his headquarters. In some areas of Viet Nam a village like this would be a part of a working government-organized political section in which there were several hamlets under the supervision of the village administrator. He, in turn, reported to the governor of the province, similar in form to a state government in the U.S.

A muddy earthen helicopter landing area had been hastily built by the occupying ARVN troops. Cunningham spotted a cluster of Biet Dong Quan uniforms and breathed a sigh of relief. The ARVN Special Forces were damn good soldiers. Their officers would have the village well in hand. He was greeted warmly by the Ranger Major commanding the battalion headquarters in the area. His men quickly unloaded Cunningham's equipment and trotted off with it to the large thatch-roofed house on the bank of the canal.

Major Ngo smiled broadly. "The VC used it as their headquarters. The people are used to it. We cleaned it up and enlarged it a little. Can't have you losing face," he said in fairly good English. "You'll need a tin roof though.

It'll be hotter, but at least you won't get burned to a crisp by a well-placed tracer or gasoline bomb."

Cunningham was pleased with the house, which was perched higher above water level than most of the others. The log walls were double thickness and the big open windows had shutters as well as split bamboo shades. He quickly noted with approval that the small market place and few stores were across the canal. At least he wouldn't be bothered by their smell. As it was the odor of the nearby rice paddies and murky water flowing languidly in front of the house was stinking enough.

The Major briefed Cunningham thoroughly over cups of tea on the search and destroy operation in the area. The American Green Beret saw that the Vietnamese was a tough, thorough officer.

"How long can you stay around?" Cunningham asked.

Major Ngo shook his head. "Only until the two squads of ARVN infantry arrive from Song Hao. That's where the infantry company and a weapons company are located. Near the chopper base at Loc Than. Unfortunately there's no road connecting them. At Song Hao they supposedly have your sector zeroed in with their heavy weapons so that you can get fast call fire on the approaches if the VC try to come back. I'm sorry, Captain, but if I were you I'd check that myself. Frankly, I have my doubts about the quality of the security force you're going to have. They are rather inexperienced."

"When will the squads arrive?"

"They should have day before yesterday. The Navy patrol was supposed to bring them down by boat. But no sign of them yet. I checked by radio. They've left Song Hao, all right, but I suspect they holed up someplace along the river."

After Cunningham returned from a tour of inspection with Major Ngo, Red Kennedy reported he had the two radios in working order. And with the help of the ARVN Rangers he had started construction of a small ammunition bunker in back of the house.

Later in the afternoon, Major Ngo assembled the village

elders in the community meeting hall and introduced Captain Cunningham. They greeted him with formality and toasts with *ruou rep,* a sickening liquor made from fermented glutinous rice. Each house featured a great clay vase-like container of the liquor. The more jars one had, the more prestige and importance he was accorded.

The faces of the old men were expressionless. They kept warily watching Ngo who told them what Cunningham's function would be. The American took over and briefed them on his intentions. He spoke their language slowly and carefully. Major Ngo concluded the session. His voice was sharp and he did not bother to conceal his contempt for them. He laid it on the line. They would not resist the Americans and they would cooperate, or else!

The Major apologized to Cunningham when they were back in the house. "The Viet Cong have them well indoctrinated. They resisted giving my men any help at all when we arrived, so we had to be a little rough on them. All they understand is force." He shrugged. "Frankly, Captain, I do not envy you your job. These people are ignorant and backward. They have been dominated by the VC for years. They will not change overnight. All they want to do is to live, to grow their rice, to maintain their family relationships as they have done for hundreds of years. They care nothing about politics. Their water buffalos are more important." Ngo's face was grimly serious as he leaned toward Cunningham. "But do not think for a minute that the VC will not try to retake this area. They need the rice grown here badly. It feeds the bellies of the VC farther north in other areas."

"Where do you think they went into hiding, Major?" Cunningham asked.

"There are many opinions about that. Naturally, some are back in the mangroves, but since they are helpless without heavy weapons and ammunition, it is probable that most went someplace else seeking a haven. At Corps headquarters some seem to think they filtered northward and have gone over the border to Cambodia, where they will procure more arms and prepare to return. Others think

181

they went into the swamps and then are gradually drifting toward the western seacoast where they will re-group and be re-armed by sea, returning up the canal and river complex."

"Doesn't the Navy patrol the coast and the waterways?" Cunningham queried.

"Yes, but at sea there are hundreds of fishing boats. They can't search every one. And the radar on your destroyers cannot pick up the small wooden sampans sailing close in to land at night. There are literally thousands of small boats plying the inland waterways, too. And the Navy River Patrol does not have many boats to cover all this territory."

Cunningham nodded thoughtfully and sighed. "I have to agree. An attack will come sooner or later. It is inevitable. The question is, when?"

Major Ngo chuckled softly. "As long as you approach the job with that in mind you will do all right, Captain." He rose. "Now, let me be the host tonight. It so happens I have a bottle of scotch with me. We have time for a drink before we eat. My cook is preparing *cha-gio,* egg-roll of a sort, you know, and *cha lua,* a fried pork sausage with cinnamon. Also some sea swallow soup that is delicious. If you have some crackers in your C-rations, we can spread them with *banh beotom,* a very tasty shrimp paste. Makes a fine hors' d'oeuvre with a drink." He smiled. "Of course there's *nuoc man,* but I don't know if you've developed a taste for our fermented fish sauce yet."

Cunningham smiled back. "As a matter of fact I have. I liked it before I found out how it was prepared." He did not admit he had to concentrate on not remembering that it was made out of rotten fish, heads, guts, and all.

Sitting on the porch overlooking the canal, Cunningham watched the sun get lower. Conversation with Major Ngo was pleasant although it had taken an unreal turn. Ngo talked about his recent tour as an instructor at the Green Beret training camp at Fort Bragg, North Carolina. When he returned to Viet Nam he had immediately been assigned to the Rangers and had been in several operations.

Learning that Cunningham had been in Saigon, his home city, recently, he eagerly plied him with questions about it. So he told the American about things stateside, and Cunningham told him about the pleasures of the Vietnamese capital.

It was not until noon the next day that the 24-man contingent of ARVN soldiers arrived in two weather-beaten heavily-rusted landing craft. The senior sergeant, looking worse for wear, pleaded a breakdown of the engines for their delay. His English was halting, but when Red Kennedy began barking orders in rapid Vietnamese he grinned and got his men into action. Major Ngo listened amusedly, but he did not interfere. The two squads were under Cunningham's orders and he was happy not to have anything to do with the motley group.

Early the next day, Major Ngo and his Rangers left by helicopter and landing craft. Cunningham went back inside his headquarters house and looked across at Red Kennedy. They both had helpless expressions, and the sight of the other and the similarity made both of them laugh heartily.

"Well, Red, I guess we might as well get operational, since we're now in the saddle and holding the reins. Let's get our files unpacked, maps up, and all that crap up."

Chapter 11

Cunningham's team had been designated "Green Charlie" as a code name. His radio call sign had the word "Leader" tacked to it. The other members of his team in the various hamlets were called "Green Charlie," followed by a number. Geographically not much distance separated the Green Berets, but physically they were isolated. There were no connecting roads. Only the rivers and canals. Helicopters provided the only quick means of transportation and the choppers at Loc Than were in great demand. They would be lucky to get supplies flown in, let alone transport for

Cunningham to make inspection trips. He went out on the porch and watched with amazement as three youngsters were crossing the filthy canal waters in a round boat made of bamboo woven together and caulked with the milky sap from the gum tree. They were standing and paddling energetically but not moving very fast. He was hard put to understand how the tub-like craft would be kept headed in the direction they wanted to go.

Moored to a tiny wood landing down from the house was a long metal piroque, double-ended and low in the water except at the curved bow and stern. He guessed if he wanted to go any place he'd have to learn to use it, a version of the native boat, similarly fashioned but either sculled or poled. For the metal craft someone had dreamed up a method of attaching a small, low-powered outboard motor so the piroque could crab at a slow speed through the turgid water.

Back inside he sat down at the rough table and got out pencil and paper. Even if they had not received their materials at least he could start to plan. First of all he had to inspect the ARVN soldiers, their gear and billets, and give Master Sergeant Nhon his instructions for keeping men on watch at each end of the village during the day and doubling the number each night, as well as sending out small roving patrols around the perimeter.

Guard posts, gun emplacements, and an earthen wall would have to be built, with help from the villagers. Maybe three observation towers, higher than the houses. Once these basic things were done and a routine had been established they could begin their civic action program. But the village elders had to have some part in this, he decided. And he would have to go slow in cultivating their interest and convincing them of his good intentions. Once the work in their behalf started, he and Kennedy could commence recruiting and training men for the Self Defense Force, which would augment his own slender resources.

It was late in the evening when Cunningham and Kennedy finally sat down to dinner. They were tired and dirty. Kennedy had purchased kitchen utensils and hired a woman to do the cooking. They decided to try to vary their diet of C-rations with local food. They had heard that fish and shrimp were plentiful, and there were several kinds of tasty fruit, including pineapple. Initially Kennedy would supervise the cook until Cunningham mastered more of the language of the kitchen.

Kennedy looked around the large room, lighted by kerosene lamps. There was a breeze coming through the insect-netting covered windows and doors. "This is kind of cozy, Captain," Red said, leaning back contentedly.

"It is, at that," Cunningham replied. "I sure hope the VC don't hit us tonight. I'm pooped. That bunk looks mighty inviting." Their cots were placed at either corner at the front of the room. Split bamboo screens could be lowered from the ceiling to the floor to give them each privacy.

This won't be bad at all, Kennedy decided. The Captain was easy to get along with and certainly open to suggestion. They made a good team, he thought. He sighed aloud.

Cunningham chuckled. "I guess you must be thinking what I am. God, there's so much to be done."

"And so little time to do it," Kennedy added. "If we could count on having a month, a whole month to get things organized and constructed here, I think we'd have a fighting chance of keeping the VC out."

"Well, Red, if we're lucky we will." Cunningham mentally added that a lot depended on the type of support they got from the South Vietnamese army units.

Lights out and each on his own air mattress on a folding cot, Kennedy tried to sleep. It was still hot under the mosquito netting but it was a necessity. The night sounds are different down here, he idly reflected. If you took away the stink this could be a cabin alongside some stream in the western United States, he thought, hearing the water lap against the bank. It was on one such fishing trip after he had finished basic training and had been assigned to the public information office, he recalled, that he had come back from ten days furlough firmly decisive on what he wanted to do in the Army. He had had a wonderful time in the coolness of the California redwood forests, after having baked in the southeast part of the country. Kennedy had done a series of articles on the Green Berets' training. The general had liked them and suggested Kennedy join the elite group. The lanky redhead lay in his Viet Nam bunk and wondered exactly what had made him decide to accept the offer. Probably because he had hated the chickenshit associated with duty at the headquarters office.

At least in Special Forces there was opportunity for a man to express his individuality. No parade ground. No big brass everlasting chipping about proper uniforms. No guard duty at the gate. No writing poop about the officers' wives club for the station paper or covering ribbon-cutting ceremonies. He had to smile when he thought about it. When he had worked on a civilian newspaper in California he had run into the same thing though. Some of the assignments given him had almost bored him to death. How many dozen dinner speeches had he sat through. And club meetings. But later on the jobs got better as his reporting skill improved. Man, he thought, how I'd like to smell the odor of a composing room again. But did he want to go back to the newspaper, he wondered. He had quite a bit of time in the Army and he was advancing up the promotion ladder fast. Probably he could get commissioned, sooner or later, if he wanted to. He'd make as good an officer as lots he had met. But would the Army begin to bore him? No, he decided slowly, probably not. But maybe after this tour I should try to get assigned to the *Stars & Stripes,* the Army paper. Maybe in Japan, or in Europe. That way he could finish his hitch and still find out if he would like working on a paper again. Also he could sharpen up his writing. Plenty of time to think about it, though. And now he liked the present freedom of the Green Berets. Deep down, however, he knew he personally needed some work with more discipline for his own good. Something with more pattern. He needed purpose and form for his life, or else he'd end up a rolling stone. He went to sleep remembering Jake Potter's comments about his being out of place in the career Army.

Cunningham found Sergeant Nhon a savvy, battle-hardened noncom. Moreover he was from peasant stock from the delta land. He knew the area and the rice farmers. And he had built fortifications around villages like Thuong Ninh before. A bandy-legged, short but husky man, the Sergeant was proud of his gold front teeth. It was obvious he had full control over and the respect of his men. Cunningham found their weapons surprisingly clean and well-cared for and their gear neatly arranged in their billets. Half were living at each end of the village. Kennedy and Nhon immediately went into a huddle to set up liaison with the civilian population and develop an intelligence network.

When Cunningham learned by radio that the supplies were being sent down the river network by barge, Nhon and Kennedy came up with a suggestion: Consult the village astrologer and find out what date he considered most propitious under the stars for the arrival of the materials. The superstitious Vietnamese listened solemnly when he made his prediction and Cunningham delayed the delivery for 24 hours to make it coincide.

The village was flag-bedecked when the barge hove into sight. The natives cheered when it was tied up at the bank. All hands joined in to unload the crates. Kennedy and Cunningham got to work on the electrical generator first. Next they unpacked a motion picture projector, screen and films and set them up in the market place. After dark the citizens of Thuong Ninh saw their first movies. They knew about radio. Each night the Viet Cong had tuned in the Communist "Radio Liberation" broadcast from Tayninh province for the people all over the delta area. But motion pictures were something else again. Kennedy used only one propaganda film and showed cartoons the rest of the time. The villagers howled with delight, captivated by Donald Duck and the others.

The two tired American Green Berets returned to their house convinced they had taken a big stride forward with the villagers. The civic action program could now progress at full speed.

There was a never-ending procession of detail to attend to, but as the days went by Cunningham found satisfaction in the sweat and energy expended. Particularly as the mass of slant-eyed faces emerged as individuals to him. First the village elders, person by person, became something more than the Army handbook's phrase, "Indigenous personnel," natives. Mr. Quon was really very jolly, had a large family, and was on his third wife. Another was painfully shy at first in front of the long-nosed Americans, but he had a surprisingly large amount of information about the United States and an insatiable curiosity about some of the things he had heard which were beyond his comprehension. Cunningham was pleased with his evening visits, for he always brought a question, a picture, or a page from an English-language book. The Captain often was hard-pressed to answer some of the queries. He also came to recognize the women, and particularly the children. The latter were unabashedly taken by the huge Americans, but the women, except for the very old, remained silent and inscrutable.

More than once Kennedy and Cunningham had discussed the matter. They would observe a group of young native women laughing and talking animatedly, their dark eyes flashing, their words rapid. But with the approach of the Americans they would lapse into silence and lower their eyes. Only occasionally would they see the girls caste a sideways glance which showed they were aware of the existence of the white-faces. Of course, there were exceptions.

Radio reports to Cunningham from the sub-sector commanders were necessarily guarded. The Viet Cong probably were monitoring them. The Green Berets had arranged a helicopter mail exchange weekly among the hamlets. Lieutenant Thompson reported that Tiny Christopolous and Dick Greer apparently had sensed the same feelings of urgency. They were putting in 18-hour days.

Things were going well in Harry Adams' area, but the occasional Vietnamese Navy patrol boat generally had a variety of products for sale, including whiskey. Adams was keeping a close watch on Stew McDonald and Chet Smith but a few times they had gone on a bat when they had been working on projects needing both their efforts together. Otherwise their progress had equalled the rest of the Green Berets. Their long experience and know-how in dealing with the natives had also worked wonders. Adams sounded one note of caution. There was no question but that they had improved the lot of the villagers but he doubted that in his sub-sector any of them had been won over to the side of the government, as opposed to the Viet Cong. They remembered all too well the efficiency of the VC. They had seen government troops come and go before, but the VC always returned to stay for a long time. They fully expected it to happen again.

As Cunningham had expected, the efforts of the trio in Jake Potter's area had been little short of miraculous. They were located closer together, so Jake was able to use the team approach. Benefitting from Doc Elliott's medical know-how to the fullest. The mothers of the youngsters had been particularly appreciative. And Jerry Lord's small school system had also been a winner. Jake Potter had one disquieting note. The Green Berets and squads of ARVN soldiers had been authorized to hire native women to cook and launder for them. In most cases the village elders had selected old widows, but the woman working for Lord was young and attractive, with a five-year-old son. Reportedly her husband had been killed by the Viet Cong, according to Lord, but when Potter had visited the hamlet he had not liked the situation. Sergeant Dien, the squad leader, had things too well organized and had taken almost too much of the detail from Lord. But he obviously had full control of the village senior administrators.

Cunningham read between the lines. Jerry Lord was a good man, but he was young and inexperienced. It probably would be best if he sent Red Kennedy over there unexpectedly to stay for a few days and take a close look.

At the same time, the leader of Green Charlie team had other things on his mind. The word had come in that Colonel Fowler and Captain Freeman were due in shortly on an inspection tour. And Dick Sloan, the Chicago news correspondent, had written that he would make a visit.

Pondering the message and the letter, Cunningham wondered if maybe he had been a little too glowing in his reports of the team's accomplishments to the Colonel. From two of the chopper pilots he had heard that some of the other teams were having big troubles. And also disquieting was that Sloan's letter had indicated he was engaged in writing about the black market and he was having plenty of difficulties. The late afternoon radio reports took his attention. At the end of the day he breathed a sigh of relief. Another 24 hours had passed. Still the Viet Cong had not attacked.

The VCs were far from Jerry Lord's mind. It had been a long tiring day, but the bridge across the canal had been completed. He removed his glasses and wiped the sweat from his eyes. He felt quite pleased. His bridge was finished even before the one in Jake Potter's hamlet. He smiled at Sergeant Dien and Corporal Hau.

"Fellows, we've earned a drink. Come on over to the house. And I've got a couple of bottles left for the rest of the squad."

Lord did not notice Dien's face tighten as he shook his head negatively at his Corporal. "We will come, sir," Dien said smoothly in almost perfect English. "But I think I'd better wait until after the men eat to give them the liquor. We have another hard day tomorrow." Dien would give them one bottle and sell the other in the village market. He smilingly followed Lord to the spacious house which was his headquarters.

Bich Hong was solicitously waiting for them. As usual she had boiled water in the morning and had a pan of ice cubes waiting, made by the ancient refrigerator he had renovated with spare parts and equipment procured from some mysterious source by Sergeant Dien. She smiled at him shyly and poured cognac and coke for himself and the two ARVN noncoms.

The men settled down in the crude but comfortable chairs to begin what had become a late afternoon ritual. Sergeant Dien had a great amount of reserve, but Corporal Hau was his own age and also had a great interest in electricity and electronics. He had not been originally a squad member, but he had turned up as a replacement after one of Dien's men had become ill the week after Lord arrived at the hamlet. Lord thought it was a shame to waste Hau's talents as an assistant squad leader when he had been to basic radio school in Saigon. Obviously he had the mental capacity to go further. Lord had shrugged it off as just another foul-up typical of any army and was glad for Hau's company. Dien was not much of a conversationalist, while Hau was cheerful and outgoing. Lord thought he was lucky to have him and Bich Hong around. It would have been lonesome as hell otherwise.

Stretching out his legs, Jerry Lord appreciatively watched the young woman make preparations for dinner. As usual her long, glistening black hair was freshly combed and pinned up. She was one of the most beautiful oriental women he had ever seen. Delicate, like the rose she was named for. She prepared for his home-coming by changing from the black silk trousers and white blouse she wore during the day, to the *au dai,* which brought a touch of Saigon sophistication to the rural village. From what Dien had told Lord, she had been left penniless in her village not far from the capital when her husband had been killed. She had returned to her parents but they had been as poor as she. Bich Hong had worked in the fields and part-time in the village store, run by a Chinese merchant. One day after she had come to cook and clean for him Lord had seen her boy playing at one end of the village near a broken down shack. One look inside and he was horrified. Not that it wasn't clean, but its walls and floor were almost rotted away and the thatched roof was open to the sun and rain in spots. Sergeant Dien, who had been with him, had immediately suggested they make an addition to Lord's quarters for Bich Hong and the boy.

Lord felt woozy from the drinks and a big dinner, but he forced himself to turn up the kerosene lamp and sit down and write his weekly report. Half-way through he lighted the stove and heated water. He was typing the letter to Jake Potter when he heard Bich Hong pad into the room and turn off the stove.

"I'd like some coffee," he said, glancing around. Then he did a double take. She was perfectly silhouetted by the lamp by the stove. Her beautifully formed body was visible under the filmy cotton night dress. Lord blushed and turned back to the typewriter. But he could not keep his eyes off her when she brought the coffee. She returned with a cup of tea and sat opposite him. He tried, but he was unable to look away from her brown-nippled breasts. They raised toward him as if in a challenge. When he met her penetrating gaze she smiled faintly and put her hand on his.

Lord found himself shaking, almost uncontrollably. He had had a woman before, but never like this. The back seat of a car, or in the hills under the stars after a picnic, with most of their clothes on.

Bich Hong reached across and turned off the lamp. She gently pulled him to his feet and led him across the room to his bunk. Slowly and deliberately she slipped out of her gown and then got on her knees before him as he sat on the cot. Her touch was almost excruciating as she removed his clothing. She caressed the length of his body, pushing him backward. Then she rose and crossed the room and turned off the other lamp.

The ferocity of her lovemaking astounded him. He could not believe this was the same Bich Hong. But he quickly found himself responding and reaching a height of passion he did not know he possessed. The writhing of her perspiration-wet body finally subsided and Jerry Lord dozed momentarily. Her caressing hands aroused him once more but it was a moment before he realized where they were. Her tiny insistent fingers and searching lips made him groan with pleasure and they joined once more. Her slender body was light as a feather on his and their loving was long and leisurely.

For the first time since he had come to the hamlet, he was not awakened by the sunrise. He stretched luxuriously and then realized Bich Hong was not beside him. A flush crept on his face. Now what the hell had he got himself into, he wondered. Sacking out with his cook. What would their relationship be like now. He'd always heard that it was bad practice to mess around with the help. Particularly indigenous personnel. But then he recalled their lovemaking. He quickly turned over on his stomach. God, what a woman. For a fleeting second he wondered where she'd learned all the magic she'd practiced on him, but he banished the thought from his mind. He heard her shuffling approach and forced himself to look up at her. Her smile was brief and mysterious as she put down fresh underwear, socks, and fatigues on the chair by his bed. By the time he was dressed she had his breakfast on the table.

Jerry ate in silence and accepted a second cup of coffee, finally able to meet her impassive gaze. She acted no different than she had other mornings.

"Sir," she said, coming from the door, "Sergeant Dien is outside."

"Thank you, Bich Hong," he managed, knowing his ears had reddened. "Please ask him to come in."

Lord did not notice the exchange of knowing glances as the ARVN sergeant passed her.

"I'll be right with you Dien, as soon as I finish typing this report. Better have your squad look around the area. The chopper is due in later this morning. We don't want the VC sniping at it, or we'll never get any more supplies."

Dien bowed solemnly. "Yes, Sergeant. You might as well remain here with your papers until it is time. It is going to be very hot today. I already have a group of the villagers at work. Making desks for the new school."

Thanks. I am running a little late this morning," Lord said, not recognizing the suppressed grin on the husky sergeant's face.

193

The day passed slowly for Jerry Lord. The helicopter was late arriving and the news from Jake Potter about Colonel Fowler's impending visit the next week bothered him. He was always nervous when the big brass were about, even a good egg like the senior Green Beret. Sergeant Dien frowned thoughtfully when Lord told him about it. They were sitting on the headquarters' porch. It was stifling in the late afternoon. The clouds hung low, and their rolling blackness was reflected in the canal waters.

"God, if it's going to rain, I sure wish it would hurry up," Lord complained. He put down his brandy and canned juice, half-drunk. Bich Hong came hurriedly when he called. There was irritation in his voice. He was tired and his prickly heat rash was bothering him a lot. The oppressive humidity and low-hanging clouds seemed to amplify the stench coming from the placid greasy-looking canal and rice paddies. Even the sight of Bich Hong did not lift his spirits.

Suddenly he was bored with the business conversation with Dien and wished he had brought Corporal Hau. No, he thought, it's more than that. It was the lack of American companionship that bothered him. But why today, he wondered. Was it because of last night with the girl, or was he just getting sick and tired of dealing with the poverty and filth of Viet Nam.

Suddenly the skies opened and the downpour began, a cloudburst. Dien sensed Lord's dissatisfaction and when he followed him inside he did not sit down. "I must see that the sentries have not left their posts because of the rain, Sergeant Lord," Dien said, moving toward the rear door. Bich Hong was lowering the bamboo shades to keep out the rain. She followed Dien outside. The pounding rain muffled their brief conversation from Lord's ears. She nodded when Dien told her to meet him later that night at the store of the Chinese merchant.

Bich Hong thoughtfully looked back inside where the American was wearily removing his shoes and socks. She moved a bamboo pipe from where it was directing the flow of water off the eaves, and then it began to fill a large tin tub. She went back inside.

"If you wish to eat now, your bath will be ready by the time you finish," Bich Hong told him.

He smiled gratefully at her, stripped off his shirt, and went to the radio. Time for the radio check. He ate and was half asleep when she pulled the tub into the room. She removed his sweat-soaked undershirt and helped him strip to the bone. Her hands were gentle on his skin as he settled back into the cool water. She brought another bucket and poured it over his shoulders after she had soaped and scrubbed his skin. The khaki-colored towel was rough on his body as she dried him thoroughly. He couldn't help himself. When her hands tenderly moved down from his muscle ribbed stomach he felt the desire for her rise, and she abetted it, her fingernails tracing a pattern which gave him goosebumps. They moved to the bed.

By 9 p.m. he was sound asleep. Bich Hong carefully raised the mosquito netting and slipped off the bunk. Without putting on any lights, she hurriedly dressed and padded barefooted out of the house. Her steps were sure as she crossed the new bridge and went directly to the tiny store. There were only three waiting for her to come to the meeting: Sergeant Dien, the Chinese storekeeper and the number one son of a village elder.

"The civic action program of the American must continue," Dien began with obvious authority. "This Colonel Fowler must see great progress. He must believe there is great cooperation here." The Chinese nodded agreement.

"But this Sergeant Lord is becoming friends with many of the people," the young man continued. "We cannot delay too long. My father and the other old men see all the improvements and all the goods the Americans send. They cannot help but become impressed. We must act soon."

The Chinese merchant counseled patience. "Remember, our comrades are not yet ready to return. Once this Colonel makes his visit and departs, Sergeant Dien can slow the work. Sabotage it. While Bich Hong and Corporal Hau take the mind of the American off his projects, Dien can also see that the supplies are diverted to our own use."

The girl reddened and averted her gaze. She hated the role to which she was assigned. At the urging and finally direct order of Dien and her Chinese employer she had accepted it. More than once before the Viet Cong had made her do similar things. Once she'd even had to work in a brothel. It had all started when she had joined the Communists in anger after her husband had been killed by the Americans in a raid on a VC outpost.

At first she had hated the sight of Jerry Lord, but strangely enough when she had followed orders and seduced him there had been something about his gentleness that had touched her. And she had come to realize that his desire to assist the Vietnamese people was both sincere and deep-seated. For the first time she had some slight doubts about the Viet Cong's motives and ability to do even half as much.

Back at Lord's house she shook the moisture from her hair and stole closer to his bunk. His breathing was deep and regular. She felt the urge to touch his face, his big nose. Inside of her was a sense of shame and she turned and went to her own room.

Chapter 12

Cunningham looked across the table at Dick Sloan with pleasure. Red Kennedy was gone on an inspection trip in advance of Colonel Fowler and in a week the company of Sergeant Nhon had worn thin. The bottle of scotch between them was an added dividend, the present of the newsman.

"Well, Dick, what brings you way down here to the boondocks? I don't suppose you'd like to do a story on the glamorous lives of us Green Berets who are lying around in this lap of luxury."

Sloan laughed and looked around the almost spartan room. "The word has filtered back that you boys are doing a terrific job down here. I saw Colonel Fowler on my way down. He's real proud of you, Dave."

"Thanks," Cunningham said dryly. "I'll believe it when that tough old cookie tells me that after his inspection trip."

He described to Sloan the extent of the work of his team. The reporter took notes and looked at the map with interest. Cunningham next showed him some before and after photos his men had sent in.

After dinner Cunningham could not wait any longer. "Now, what's the story about my friend Major Nuan?"

"Well, he's partly a reason I'm down here. I thought it was getting a little unhealthy in Saigon." Sloan dug a news article from his typewriter case. "I checked into that boy's activities. It took a little bribery, but these jokers would sell their mother for a couple of bucks. I tied Nuan's relatives in business in Saigon into the supplies missing from up at Dan Lac. Those numbers you sent me were the deciding factor. Strangely enough I was able to pinpoint their arrival in Saigon with the day that Nuan flew down in a supposedly empty plane. Those materials were dumped on the black market in wholesale lots through his relatives' connections. And I got next to a joker at the airfield who worked on offloading the cargo from Nuan's plane. It went into Army trucks and disappeared." He shrugged. "As you can see from the story I wrote, I couldn't accuse him directly, but I sure as hell pointed out the coincidences involved."

Cunningham read the clipping and whistled.

"So now the South Vietnamese government is threatening to throw me out of the country. Our Ambassador is sore as hell at me, I guess, but what the hell. It's the stated policy of the new government to close down this corruption and black marketing, so they ought to do something about it. The native papers in Saigon are sure lambasting me. Trying to discredit my stories. But my editor has been in contact with the White House and our Illinois Senators.

I'm sorry that our Ambassador is caught in the middle, but if I get the boot from this country, sure as hell there will be a congressional investigation. And our Administration knows they can't stand another one."

"Man, you sure must have done a lot of spade work to get all this dope," Cunningham commented admiringly.

"Hell, I was a police reporter when I first started out in Chicago. You develop a nose for this stuff." Sloan chuckled. "Besides, you sure helped out."

"You mean the numbers?"

"That and your knowing Monique. She's really got connections in Saigon. I hate to say it, Dave, but she has some pretty shady friends. That Chinese pal of hers has his finger in about every big black market deal in the country. But she hates Nuan, for some reason. She put me in touch with some others who have no love for him and they were the ones who spilled the beans. For a big price, of course."

Cunningham shook his head. "I wouldn't count on their not grabbing your passport and sending you out. It's happened before."

Sloan agreed. "If I could have got to talk to someone who was in on the transfer of the materials from those Army trucks I'd have proof positive. I've got a lot of snoopers working on it, but so far no soap."

"Did you ask Monique about that angle?"

"No, she did enough already. I figured if she got any more involved she'd get in too deep. I happen to know that she's a little worried as it is. She's transferred a lot of funds to Swiss banks."

Cunningham's eyebrows raised. "I had no idea she was that well off."

Sloan looked at him cynically. "That's Saigon, Dave. She's got a good deal there in the capital. Her job permits her to have a lot of contacts. She can operate openly, and who can prove anything about the people she meets at the hotel. The Caravelle's a natural. She's mighty shrewd, too, you must have learned that."

The correspondent turned the conversation to the Viet

Cong. "All I've heard are rumors, but there are lots of reports floating around that it won't be long before the VC start to try to move back in down here on the Ca Mau peninsula."

"So far there isn't any direct evidence of it, Dick. But I just take it for granted."

Sloan nodded. "That's smart. The longer you Green Berets hang tough here, the more face the VC lose. The harder it will be for them to regain control of the people. But you guys have your necks out a long way."

"You're telling me. As each week goes by, I get a little more careful about going out at night. We're really spread thin, and . . ."

"And you don't even know if there are any of the old VCs who are still here in this village. Or if some of the ARVN are their boys."

"That's right. Worse yet, there seems to be a division of opinion among the Intelligence people as to the route the Viet Cong will take to come back in. From the north, Cambodia, or in by sampan from the south and west. Watching both approaches spreads our recco people out. The approach of the monsoon season worries me, too. No air surveillance then." They continued the discussion far into the night.

The next morning Cunningham took Sloan around the village. The newsman's enthusiasm was reassuring. An old hand in Southeast Asia, he nodded approvingly at the ARVN medic working in the sparsely furnished but well-stocked dispensary. There was a variety of patients by age, sex, and physical condition. A good sign. The ARVN and the Green Berets were getting across the message about the benefits of early treatment.

Sanitary conditions in the village had improved immeasurably. A system of small canals for sewage had been constructed. Efforts were being made to purify the water supply. Their next stop was the newly re-furbished school.

"See how damn crowded it is, Dick? These little kids are really eager to read and write, but we sure have a problem. The A.I.D. people have come up with a simple syllabus—a teacher's aid—but the problem is elementary school books in the Vietnamese language. They're in damn short supply. If we had some to teach reading to people of various age groups it would be easier. I'm no educator, but I'd bet they'd learn faster if we had something like comic books. With illustrations which would appeal to the kids. They'd learn to read and write in their own language soon enough."

"That's a damn good idea. But you'd need hundreds of thousands."

"Sure, I realize that. But what the hell, look at the comic pages your newspaper prints every Sunday. And all the other supplements. If all the papers in the U.S.A. got together they could do the job in no time."

Sloan laughed. "You know, that isn't a bad idea. I'll mention that to my publisher."

Kennedy and I use old American 1st grade textbooks to teach English, but I still think the first thing to do is to teach them their own language."

"Don't the VC do anything like that down here?" Sloan asked.

Cunningham reached in his back pocket and took out a small, four-page newspaper. "You may have seen a copy of this. The *Gia Phong Viet Nam,* meaning "Long Live Viet Nam." It's the VC newspaper down here on the peninsula. See the poor grade of paper? They print thousands of these underground and send them down the rivers to the hamlets. They're smuggled in, if necessary, and given to their supporters who can read. They use them to give information of a propaganda nature, of course, to the farmers. They also teach kids to read. And the content serves to indoctrinate them early. But it's selective and at best a haphazard project."

"Where'd you get this one?" Sloan asked curiously.

"We're spot checking the boat traffic. Ran across a handful of these accidentally. First ones we've seen since we got down here." He pointed to the biggest print. "That says the VC are preparing to return; that the villagers are to stand ready."

"I can see why you've been working so hard to get the village defenses completed," Sloan said.

They toured the chest-high earthen wall around the village and then watched Sergeant Nhon and another noncom showing a group of young and middle-aged villagers how to use various types of weapons.

"We're really just getting started. It complicates matters, but we can't let them hang onto the weapons at night yet. Just during the training, until we get to know them better, when we have no doubts about trusting them. We don't want them turning on us. The system we'd use now is for each of the ARVN soldiers to haul extra weapons to assigned outposts and pass them out there in the event of an attack."

"You know, Dave, I think I will do a series on your team. I've got my camera and plenty of film."

"Sounds good by me. I'll get you a chopper ride to another hamlet. You just might catch up with Colonel Fowler someplace along the line. He's got his own helicopter and can expedite your moving around."

Cunningham returned to his headquarters to send the necessary messages. Sloan was a good guy and the Green Berets as a whole would benefit from his articles, he decided. So damn many of the Army staff types were always sniping at the Special Forces. Saying they were getting too much money and prestige and the cream of the personnel. To hell with them, he thought. We produce, and that's what counts.

Toward the end of a nervous week of waiting, Cunningham watched Red Kennedy arrive back at Thuong Ninh by piroque with the two ARVN soldiers who had accompanied him on the tour of the hamlets. As the long narrow boat approached the canal landing, Kennedy grinned up at him and waved.

Cunningham had a cold beer waiting for his Intelligence expert. "Well, how did it go?" he asked anxiously.

"They were all primed for the inspection, Captain. Colonel Fowler was just arriving at Lieutenant Thompson's as I was leaving. Captain Freeman said it went well when they were in Harry Adams' sub-sector."

Cunningham breathed a sigh of relief and sat back, relaxed.

Kennedy laughed at his expression. "I thought you'd be glad to hear that. Harry must have thrown the fear of God into Stew and Smitty. Stew even had on a clean uniform." He began to describe his visits to the hamlets in detail.

"In my opinion, Captain," Kennedy concluded, "The guys have done a damn fine job in a mighty short time."

"Any evidence of the VC in the hamlets? Or elsewhere? Any rumors?"

"Very little, Captain. I picked up a few of these in different places." Kennedy showed him several copies of the Viet Cong newspaper. "They're still preaching the same old story. Like MacArthur they will return." There was a frown on his face. "I know the guys have been working mighty hard and that they have a lot of experience. But it just isn't like the VC to stay completely doggo, not to stir up anything at all, give us some troubles, as a symbol if nothing else."

"That bothers me too, Red. I just can't believe that all of them got the hell out of the country."

"That's another thing, Captain. The two ARVN with me got the same impression I did. The villagers are quiet, but sometimes act like they're scared. Looking over their shoulders out at the mangrove swamps, as if they're being watched. We picked up a few of Lieutenant Thompson's squad and took a couple of other boats and ran a sweep in that dense swamp area west of Binh Chan. Naturally there wasn't a soul around. We couldn't penetrate very deep, of course, but there was plenty of evidence men had been recently camping back in there."

"And you figure they're just biding their time? Waiting to be rearmed?"

"Yes sir, and watching what we're doing. Sooner or later one of our patrols will run across one of the piroques or barges loaded with guns. Maybe they'll bring them down from the north by the bicycle load and then bring them into the swamps by foot, an armload at a time. Sure, I know, Captain. It'd take days, and they'd have to pack in howitzers, recoiless rifles and ammo, but it's coming. That's for sure."

Cunningham shrugged helplessly. "I agree, Red. But what the hell more can we do? Except keep a close eye on things, and be a sitting duck when they do take the offensive."

"Right, sir. That's exactly what we will be. But there should be a massive effort by the ARVN to stop the flow of weapons into the peninsula."

"Red, you know it, and I know it, and Colonel Fowler knows it. The trouble is the General Staff in Saigon won't send down any more forces. And the ARVN Division down here isn't aggressive enough. Not enough recco patrols are being sent out. They're already protesting about furnishing the squads with the Green Berets. And they claim even if they were at full strength it'd be impossible to stop the constant trickle of guns coming in. They don't have enough confidence in their own ability down here. And it's a lot more comfortable sitting in the larger villages than it is out patrolling the canals and combing the swamps." Cunningham angrily threw his empty beer can across the room into the trash basket. "Ah to hell with rehashing all this. We end up talking in circles. Red, let's have a couple of more beers. And I'll tell you about Sloan's visit."

Forty-eight hours later they were warned by Lieutenant Thompson that Colonel Fowler was enroute. He reported that apparently Fowler had been satisfied with the work done in his, Dick Greer's and Tiny Christopolous' hamlets.

Sergeant Nhon had his squads deployed around the helicopter landing pad, weapons ready, just in case of a Viet Cong surprise attack. Nhon saluted Cunningham and smiled broadly. "All is in readiness, Captain." He fell into line beside him and Kennedy, but he kept glancing around at his men, alert for any indication that they were not on the job. A large crowd of youngsters gathered nearby, eagerly awaiting the arrival of the chopper, which never failed to start them hollering with delight.

As the helicopter hovered, gunners at each door with their automatic rifles ready, Cunningham could see Colonel Fowler unbuckling his seat belt, wipe his face with his green beret, and then settle it jauntily on his head. From long force of habit he jumped from the chopper when it was still five feet from the ground and ran toward the trio awaiting him, followed by Captain Freeman.

Fowler waved a hand returning Cunningham's salute and his face broke into a wide grin. "Come on, Dave. Let's get out of this goddam heat." He strode alongside the Captain and slapped him heartily on the back. "By God, kid, your team has done a mighty great job. Green Charlie is the best goddam bunch of Green Berets I've seen down here."

Cunningham's step was jaunty as he led the way into his headquarters. Fowler didn't hesitate. He tossed his beret on the table and headed for a waiting bucket of ice filled with beer cans. He opened one and did not take it from his lips before he had finished half of it. He polished off the other half without moving. Grabbing another, he used the opener and moved to the table and sat down.

"Tell your lads to stand easy, Dave. I've seen enough. I don't need to look around this village. I will, as a matter of show, but that's all." His weather-beaten face crinkled in a big smile. "I meant what I said. Your sector is a showplace. And I told that Dick Sloan so, too." He turned to Roger Freeman.

"I want you to send a couple of messages. First, to the General in Saigon. I'd like his civic action and G-3 people to fly down here to see this operation." He looked up at Cunningham. "Maybe to that Lieutenant Thompson's hamlet, Binh Chan. He's a West Pointer, isn't he? Good. Also, I want the chief of the Green Beret team training to come down and get some movies. Go into several of the hamlets in Cunningham's sector. It should have been done before. We did it up in the highlands with the mountain tribesmen, but it's a different operation in the delta. Completely." He snorted.

"What gripes me is how in hell Green Charlie turned out so much better than the other teams down here. God knows you've got a couple of screw-ups down in Adams' sub-sector. And those kids, Lord and Greer, are hardly dry behind the ears. But by God, they're all doing a terrific job." He slapped the table hard.

Roger Freeman concurred. "Colonel, I think it's because things are so much better organized in this sector. The planning, the way they went at the work, the reports, and the checking on progress. Dave here has utilized the combined skills of his men the best of all."

Cunningham was embarrassed but highly pleased. He started to change his mind at Fowler's next words, but then the full impact struck.

"Rog, I think you and I will stick down here for a couple of days. I don't have much liking for that goddam weasling Division Commander up at headquarters, anyway. Dave, I'd like you and Kennedy here to go up to Saigon and sit down with the Chief of Training and the motion picture boys and tell them what they ought to shoot down here. Help them make up a schedule. Meanwhile I can take care of the brass that comes down."

The thought of the paper work involved made Cunningham want to groan, but the prospects of a little free time in Saigon was mighty attractive. Already there was a big smile on Kennedy's freckled, sunburned face. Red had worked hard, particularly the last week, and he deserved a break.

Cunningham nodded. "Maybe before I go you could give me some suggestions of things you think should be photographed, Colonel."

"Damn right." The Colonel looked at his watch. "Kennedy, why don't you get the two of you packed now. Dave, you and I can open some more beer and then work on a list of items to be covered. You can fly over to Soc Trang this afternoon and make your way up to Saigon in the morning."

Three hours later, Fowler clapped Cunningham on the back. "Belt a few down for me, Dave. I figure you should be able to make the job in Saigon last for at least three or four days. So don't hurry back. You need a little R and R." He looked hard at the tall Captain. "You've lost a lot of weight, son. You've got to be careful about that down in this heat and constant dampness. Eat like hell even if you have to force yourself. If your resistance gets low, you sure as the devil will pick up some kind of crud." They shook hands.

Fowler watched the two Green Berets get into the helicopter. He shook his head suddenly and went back into the headquarters with Freeman. "There goes a damn good man. And some of these old-timers say this new breed doesn't have what it takes. Crap! But I wish to hell I didn't have to leave guys like him spread out all over the map, living in conditions like this. The VC will hit back, sure as hell, and some of them are sure to get zapped."

Chapter 13

Cunningham appeared at the Military Advisory headquarters, suddenly very conscious of his appearance in contrast with the staff officers he saw. He needed a haircut, his face was burned almost black, and his calloused hands and split nails still had the earth of the Ca Mau peninsula ground into them. He felt strangely light-footed wearing low black Army shoes instead of his combat boots.

Colonel Fowler had paved the way with an enthusiastic message and Cunningham and Kennedy were warmly greeted in Saigon by the Training Section staff. They drew up a work schedule that looked ridiculously easy. Cunningham did not know whether it was because of the staff's sympathy for the pair who had to return to the Green Charlie area, or because they didn't want to change their usual soft routine.

At noon Cunningham got to a telephone and called Monique. She greeted him with a strange mixture of warmth and reluctance.His proposal to eat a late dinner with her at the Caravelle was turned down quickly, but she agreed to meet him at the Brinks Officers Club after work. In one way he was irritated, but in another relieved. He owed Kennedy a good dinner. Red had volunteered to take their bags and register them at a hotel, both having decided to make the most of the short stay in the capital. The billeting officer had gone out of his way to secure them rooms at the Majestic.

The Chinese food at Cheap Charlie's was excellent, and the restaurant was convenient to the officers' billet. Following after-dinner drinks, Kennedy and Cunningham parted at the door. Red had declared a serious intention of going out on the town and getting thoroughly loaded.

When Monique entered the club, it took all of Cunningham's restraint to keep from grabbing her. She looked marvelous in a white linen dress that contrasted nicely with her tawny skin. He immediately escorted her away from the bar, and the envious eyes of his fellow officers, to a table outside on the terrace overlooking the city.

It took several drinks before she overcame a curious nervousness and was her old self.

"I'm sorry I couldn't give you advance notice that I was coming, Monique," he said, drinking in her candle-lighted beauty. Suddenly he was unsure of himself and their relationship and his feeling of gaucheness returned. Maybe he was expecting too much; perhaps she was tired of him. But she must have sensed his thoughts, and she patted his hand.

"Let's go," she whispered.

"I'm staying at the Majestic . . ." Cunningham began.

"No, let's go to my house," she replied with a soft smile.

Outside the billet she shook her head when he was going to wave down a taxi. They walked around to the Caravelle where she carefully selected a driver from the rank of cars.

Cunningham whistled softly when they rode through a gate guarded by an armed man. The house inside the high thick walls was spacious. She was pleased at his reaction when they were admitted inside by a maid servant.

"Man, this is some better than Dick Sloan's apartment. Do you have the whole house?"

She nodded and in Vietnamese told the maid to bring drinks into the living room. The room was beautifully and expensively furnished in an Oriental motif. He accepted a tall gin and tonic and settled down beside Monique on a large couch, looking around with appreciation.

"There were apartments in this house when I originally bought it, but I gradually converted it to the way it is now. After a busy day at the Caravelle it's nice to come home to," she explained.

A disturbed thought crossed his mind when he remembered his conversation with Dick Sloan. He commented on several pieces of old China porcelain.

Monique, delighted at his interest, took him on a tour of the room, pointing out various bric-a-brac and explaining their vintage. She had a costly collection of jade statuettes and very old Chinese vases. "It's my hobby, I guess. And a good investment," she added shrewdly. "Every year they are worth more. Little by little I have purchased them. Advised by the Chinese gentleman you saw at the tennis club. He is an expert. A lot of these pieces were brought to Viet Nam by refugees from China when the Communists took over from Chiang Kai-shek."

Cunningham was surprised and pleased at this unknown side of Monique. Her face fairly glowed when she talked about a beautiful screen on the wall at one end of the large room. She was obviously very proud of her possessions. Finally she put down her glass and apologized.

"Dear, I'm sorry. You must be terribly tired. And here I've been chattering on and on. Come, I've had Tuyet prepare your bath." She took his hand and looked at it closely, running her fingers over the thick callouses. "You poor guy. You have been working hard."

He walked up the stairs beside her, hand in hand.

"I should think you'd hire the village people to do the manual labor," she commented, still stroking his hand with her fingers.

He shook his head. "It just doesn't work that way. If we get out there beside them and use a pick and shovel, and show them how to handle tools, they get the idea quicker, and they know we are sincere in our intentions."

Monique laughed lightly, almost derisively. "I doubt that, dear. I've lived in this country for a long time, and it's been my experience that if a Caucasian or a high-born Vietnamese stoops to labor alongside a peasant, then the peasant has nothing but disdain for him."

Her tone irritated Cunningham. "That sounds like a typical Saigon attitude. That may be the way things are here in the city, where all you hear is this talk about losing face. But it's one hell of a different story out there in the boondocks. It's about time some of the government officials realized that, and got off their fannies and went down to see how the peasants, as you call them, live and work and think. Until they do, the farmers will never feel any obligation to the government."

Her soft laugh sounded like she was humoring a small boy. He could not help but continue as a result. "I'm serious. Look, Monique. Living here like this, working at the Caravelle, how the hell would you know how the people in the countryside feel? You live in different worlds. They're a different breed of cat, too, from the laborers here in Saigon. They've got a lot more dignity. A feeling of individuality. They figure they're as good as the next guy, even if he is loaded with money."

Her bedroom was ultra-feminine and he felt like he was entering another world, too. The bathroom was huge and the tub and other fittings opulent. Cunningham sank into the warm water gratefully and soaked. Monique continued the discussion through the open doorway, but he suddenly felt himself too tired to listen.

Clad in a diaphanous, soft-pink negligee, she leaned against the wall inside the bathroom and laughed at him.

"Come on, sleepy-head. Hurry up. You can't lie there all night."

It took all his strength to rise and towel himself.

"My God, you're thin," she said accusingly as she watched him. "You can see every rib."

"Well, that C-ration diet can't quite compare with the Caravelle," he replied smiling. "And I can see the difference." Cunningham deliberately let his eyes scan her full body. He felt the weariness slipping away, replaced with desire.

She looked at his lean tanned body and then where it was snow-white where his shorts had covered it while he worked in the sun. Her voice was sensual. "Hurry darling. Let's not waste that beautiful thing." She turned and removed the robe before sliding beneath the sheet on the huge bed.

Cunningham tossed the towel into the hamper although he was still damp-skinned, and hurriedly followed.

Her alarm clock awakened them at 6 a.m. Cunningham was so tired he was barely able to get out of bed. She had indicated it would be best if he left her house very early and returned to his hotel. When he was fully dressed the maid entered with a cup of hot coffee.

"The taxi is waiting for you, darling," Monique said, a trace of a worried frown on her face. It was obvious she was trying to hurry him. He gulped the rest of the coffee, revived by the burning in his throat. He kissed her lightly after receiving her promise to dine with him and went outside into the early morning air.

Cunningham was surprised to see the same driver, his face sleep-lined, in the same taxi they had arrived in the night before. Monique must have aranged for him to return, he decided, but the cabbie refused his money and told him he had stayed at the house and had been paid in advance. Cunningham shook his head, bewildered, and went to his room in the Majestic.

Both he and Kennedy looked the worse for wear when they arrived at headquarters at 9 a.m. They completed almost the entire plan for the motion picture taking by late afternoon. After cold beers at the hotel bar, Cunningham telephoned Monique. Again she refused to have dinner with him at the Caravelle, saying she would wait and they would eat at her home later. He ordered sandwiches for himself and Kennedy and afterward they both decided to take a nap before going out for the evening.

Cunningham felt refreshed when he arrived by taxi at her home that night. Monique swept into the room wearing the *au dai* costume of the Vietnamese women, except that it was made from exceptionally thin material. The floor-length slit skirt and long-sleeved tight blouse were of a blue that matched her lovely eyes. As they embraced he could feel that she wore nothing under the blouse or the long white trousers.

Her eyes mischievous, Monique pushed him away gently and called to her maid. The drinks were icy and delicious. The French cuisine on which they dined was light and outstanding as was the wine. While they were eating she plied him with questions about the Green Charlie members and their work.

When he casually said Dick Sloan was doing a series of articles about them, she suddenly was withdrawn. He could not help mentioning Sloan's articles about Nuan and the black market. She nodded absently, as if she already knew about them.

"By the way, have you heard anything about Nuan?" he asked. "I suppose he's still here in Saigon."

Her face showed her distaste for the man. "Yes, but not for long. That is the rumor, anyhow. He will be transferred." Her tone was positive.

"I sure wish Sloan could get out of this mess. If he could pin down where those Army trucks were unloaded and who hauled them to the black market outlets he would be in the clear."

Monique looked thoughtful. "I suppose he would want to talk to someone who actually saw the transfer made, someone who was there?"

"Right. He said he wouldn't have to print the man's name, but he might have to give it to our Ambassador."

"It would be difficult to arrange, but not impossible." Monique's tone was crisp and she finally rose. "Come, let's have coffee in the living room." A few minutes later she excused herself and left. He sipped at his snifter of fine cognac and savored it along with the luxurious surroundings.

"It will be done," she said decisively when she returned. She handed him a piece of paper. "Have Dick Sloan contact this man at this address when he returns. He will be taken to one of the Vietnamese who helped move the supplies to the other trucks, and then unload them at their destinations." She held out her hand. "Enough of that. It is done. Let us have another brandy in bed."

Cunningham's glass remained half-full on the bedside table all night. This time their embrace had been less frantic but more long-lasting. She alternately teased and restrained him. He was almost exhausted when the anxious muscular quivering of her hips and her grip on him tightened convulsively and their rhythm was matched at full stroke. He did not remember her setting it, but her alarm sounded an hour earlier than the morning before. The touch of her lips on his body and the tickle of her long hair as it swept over him told him why. Again he was almost groggy when he stumbled out to the waiting taxi.

As had been arranged, Cunningham and Kennedy completed their work by noon and returned to the hotel. A couple of pick-me-ups and lunch refreshed them and they went shopping. On a chance that Sloan had returned, Cunningham called his office. To his surprise, Dick answered and they arranged to meet at the Caravelle bar later in the afternoon.

Leaving Kennedy to procure a table, Cunningham climbed the stairs to the hotel restaurant. The place was almost deserted, and he thought it strange that Monique dismissed him so hurriedly, pleading she was too busy to talk. She hastily but reluctantly agreed to meet him at Brinks and then they would go to her house. But she was insistent she would not go night-clubbing.

Dick Sloan was sitting with Kennedy down in the

lounge. His white beard contrasted with his freshly tanned skin. He greeted Cunningham with enthusiasm.

"Dave, I think I got a helluva story. Good interview with Colonel Fowler, too. He sure thinks a lot of you."

After the drinks were brought and they were alone, Cunningham dug into his pocket and leaned across the table. "You did a favor for me, so I'll do one for you. Monique came through for you again. Here's where you can get the dope about the black market transfer. I don't know if the guy has any information about whether Nuan was actually present at the time, but at least you should be able to prove he was lax as hell about what was on his plane and where it went."

Sloan was delighted with the information. "Well, I hope Monique doesn't get in any trouble over this. I'd drop the whole thing, but the pressure's getting stronger on me." He invited the two to a night on the town and to accompany him to interview the man about the stolen supplies. Cunningham reluctantly turned him down, explaining about his date with Monique. He turned to Kennedy.

"Red, why don't you go along. It's our last night in Saigon. God knows when we'll get back."

"All right, sir, if it's okay with you, Dick."

"Great. Look, I'll get on the phone right away and make the initial contact. They'll probably want a meeting some place after dark." He looked thoughtfully at Kennedy. "Red, if I lend you a light-weight sport coat, would you carry my miniature tape recorder? I'll pretend to take notes, but we'll also have the conversation verbatim. Maybe you might have to translate for me, too. My Vietnamese is a little slow."

After Sloan left, Kennedy looked doubtfully across at Cunningham. "You know, sir, somebody could get into a real mess over this. Your lady friend, maybe. And certainly the guy that talks. If Sloan has to reveal his name he's a dead pigeon. I hope your Monique has a lot of powerful friends in Saigon. She may need them."

Cunningham's brows furrowed. "Maybe I shouldn't

have mentioned it to her. But I counted on her being able to take care of herself." He commented about her Chinese friend.

"I've heard of him," Kennedy said thoughtfully. "Supposedly he's got a piece of everything crooked in this city. And his influence stretches all over the country." He shrugged. "For her sake I hope he's on her side."

Sloan and Kennedy left Cunningham in front of the hotel and got into the newsman's Renault. Sloan stopped at his office to get the tape recorder and jacket. Red Kennedy took the wheel and followed Sloan's directions. It was dark and the garish neon signs cast a weird glow on the towering palm trees. They stopped in front of a bar and a Vietnamese hurriedly came out of the shadows and got into the back seat.

In the rear view mirror Kennedy could see that he was tough-looking and broad-shouldered in his white shirt. When dickering over money, he spoke English moderately well, using American serviceman's vernacular.

There was only a feeble glow of light where the Vietnamese told him to stop and park. They were in the dock area which was almost deserted at this time of night. Kennedy warily followed the other two into a small dirty restaurant, smelling of greasy Vietnamese cooking. Their escort faded into the darkness of a rear room and beckoned to them.

Kennedy looked around. The restaurant was completely vacant. The remains of two meals were on the empty counter and cooking utensils were on the cabinet behind it. He reached across with a long arm and quickly grabbed a wicked looking kitchen knife and slid it up his sleeve. It would be better than nothing and in the darkness of the other room he did not know what they were getting into. It might be some sort of a trap.

A small kerosene lamp provided the only illumination in a storeroom in the back of the building. An elderly man was sitting in the corner on a straw mat, looking frightened half to death. Their escort was talking to him urgently but quietly. Money exchanged hands and the old man nodded.

Kennedy snapped on the tape recorder and translated the man's comments for Sloan and put his questions into Vietnamese. The escort remained at the door into the restaurant, obviously on the look-out. He shifted from foot to foot nervously, ignoring the interrogation. After five minutes he turned and urged Sloan to hurry. But the reporter was thorough and deliberate. Finally at the end of 15 minutes Sloan was satisfied. He slipped the old man extra money.

Suddenly Kennedy heard a noise outside in the alley. He could see nothing through the dirty window, but he reached across and clutched the escort by the shoulder. They listened carefully and then there was the definite sound of running footsteps fading into the distance.

They hurriedly went out the front door of the restaurant and got into the car. As soon as they arrived among the bright lights of the business district, the worried escort had Kennedy stop, and he all but ran away from the car.

"Well, now that's a hell of a thing," Sloan commented as they drove on. "He sure acted panicked."

Kennedy nodded. "Can't say I felt too damn good about it myself." He chuckled and shook the knife from his sleeve and handed it to Sloan. "Here's a souvenir. Better toss it out the window." He explained where he had procured it. They stopped at the office and Sloan carefully locked the tapes and his notes in the safe and they returned to Tu Do street. Kennedy's fears evaporated with a huge dinner and a swinging nightclub show, with a hostess at his side. After all, the evening was being paid for by Sloan's expense account.

At the Officers Club Cunningham knew he had been drinking too much while awaiting Monique. But a long bull session with another Green Beret had encouraged the flow of liquor.

Monique joined him at the bar and insisted on remaining there. A close look at her convinced him she had had a few herself, and it irritated him that she had tarried on the way over. But she was gay and the talk was interesting and light. They stayed until closing time. She was amorous in the taxi while they were being driven to her home.

Insisting on more drinks, she delayed eating for another hour the cold supper the maid had left out for them. Cunningham began to wonder if his legs would carry him up the stairs. He glanced at his watch. It was already two o'clock and if she made him leave at six, he would have little enough time with her on his last night in the city.

Finally she led the way upstairs, each carrying another glass of liquor. He gratefully got out of his clothes and lay down on the bed, knowing he was too drunk to be able to do much if he did have a desire for sex. Only the display of Monique's body as she undressed made him keep his eyes open. She stopped at the foot of the bed and tickled his feet and made her way up his long body, a squirming mass of warm desirable woman, preceded by a caressing touch which finally aroused him almost to the bursting point. She was on him at once, first this way, then that.

Pillows and sheets on the bed were askew and rumpled when she finally allowed him to sink into a deep sleep. Never had he felt such a sense of having been thoroughly seduced. His eyes closed to shut out the light, and he changed his mind, a smile on his face. Raped, he decided. That's it. I've been raped. And in positions he had never would have believed possible.

The alarm went off again at six, but when he started to get up she pushed him back, leaning over him, her breasts soft against his face. He was so tired and spent her hands and the sight of her body failed to stir him initially. When she changed her tactics he started to become alive. The touch of her lips and tongue on his sensitive skin set him on fire and he was at rigid attention.

Still nude she went downstairs with him at eight. She arched herself against him as they kissed one last time at the door. Her buttocks firm in his hands, Cunningham felt himself aroused once more, but the hurt it caused made him retreat.

Kennedy laughed at his sallow face when he got back to

the Majestic. Red was already packed and had checked out at the desk. Wearily Cunningham got his gear together and they started for the airport. He slept during the entire flight to Soc Trang.

Thank God, Cunningham thought, when they were advised they could not be flown back to Thuong Ninh until the next day because of bad weather. He went to bed right after dinner and slept straight through until breakfast.

Chapter 14

Cunningham felt almost a human being by the time the helicopter landed at Thuong Ninh. He looked out the door and saw Roger Freeman standing on the field with Sergeant Nhon.

"The Colonel had to go back to Quon Lon," Captain Freeman explained as they crossed to the headquarters house. "All hell's broken loose at the ARVN Division headquarters." He glanced sidewise at Cunningham. "Brace yourself, Dave. They've got a new Chief of Staff to the Division Commander. Your old buddy, Colonel Nuan!"

Cunningham uttered a long string of oaths.

"Well, they knew they had to get him out of Saigon a week ago when our Ambassador absolutely raised hell about the government's plan to kick Dick Sloan out of the country," Freeman explained. "Colonel Fowler guesses Nuan had so much on his superiors that they were forced to give him a good job. In effect this is another promotion. And it'll keep him on ice, out of the capital, for awhile. The Chief of Staff that was up at Quan Lon was dead on his ass anyway and due to be replaced. Now Nuan's got the Division Commander practically all talked into using some different tactics."

"What do you mean?" Cunningham asked curiously.

"Another development since you left is that they picked

up a couple of defectors from the VC. They say that weapons are now being sent into the peninsula on a large scale, but they don't know exactly how or where. Nuan wants to pull out all the ARVN squads from the hamlets and mount a full division-strength search operation up towards the Cambodian border. He claims he knows for sure that that's the route they're using for re-supply of arms. A lot of other people disagree with him. So Colonel Fowler went back up to find out what exactly the story is and how the Division Commander feels about it."

Cunningham groaned aloud. "This sure changes the picture."

Freeman agreed. "I'm sorry, Dave, but I have to shove off now. The Colonel told me to get up there with him just as soon as you came back." He continued to brief Cunningham on what had been happening in the sector. "That's about it, except that we're getting some monsoon rains earlier than we expected. They're ass-deep in water down in Sergeant Adams sub-sector. Oh yes, a message came in this morning. I relayed it to Bud Thompson. The motion picture camera crew will fly in tomorrow. With the weather the way it is predicted for farther south, I don't see any use of them visiting Smith or Potter, do you?"

Cunningham shook his head. "No, and we made provisions for that. They should be able to get everything from Bud, and maybe end up here shooting a couple of sequences."

After Freeman's departure, Cunningham and Kennedy discussed the situation as they looked over the reports of the past few days. Red passed him the Vietnamese Navy weather data.

"Look at this. They've been getting heavy rain all along the southwest coast. Visibility lousy. That means the Viet Cong could land arms anyplace along there and transfer them to river craft." Kennedy went to the map. "The river patrols could be passed too, if they used this route." He traced with his finger. "Captain, if the weather does break down there, I suggest we ask Colonel Fowler to

218

arrange for some helicopter reconnaissance and to try to get the river patrols increased."

"All right, Red. If they used a maximum effort and examined all boat traffic on the waterways for a few days, we might find something out for sure."

News the next day was also disquieting. Harry Adams sent up a box by helicopter. Inside they found a wicked VC weapon, a plank imbedded with numerous six-inch spikes, hammered all the way through with points exposed fully. Several had been found in the paddies buried in the mud, spike points upward, just under the surface. Several villagers had stepped on them and been wounded. It was the first actual evidence of renewed Viet Cong offensive activity. Bud Thompson reported by radio that farmers in his sub-sector had informed the Green Berets that many strangers were passing through the area and several unidentified piroques had been spotted traversing the canals during a rain squall.

A note from Roger Freeman later in the week provided Cunningham with the biggest blow of all. Colonel Fowler had been able only to get a compromise with the ARVN Division Commander. All the ARVN infantry squads stationed with the Green Charlie hamlets would remain in place, except the second one with Cunningham. But the company of foot soldiers stationed near Thuong Ninh at Song Hao would be withdrawn, plus all but one platoon of the artillery company. To cap it off, Colonel Nuan had prevailed with the Division Commander, and the whole outfit would move out soon toward the Cambodian border.

"Son of a bitch," Cunningham said, crumpling the letter. "We'll be worse off now than if the squads had been pulled out instead. I was counting on those troops to be air-lifted from Song Hao by chopper if any of our hamlets got hit. And cutting our long-range heavy weapons support by 75 percent will really hurt."

"Particularly if this damn rain continues," Kennedy said. The big drops were pounding on the new corrugated iron roof of the house. "We'd get no air support in weather like this."

219

Cunningham did all he could to make the best of the new situation. He increased the reports to him from the sub-sector commanders to three a day and sent each of the Green Berets a new plan of action in case they were attacked and outnumbered without benefit of artillery support. He listened worriedly to Harry Adams' radioed complaints about failure of helicopter re-supply missions in the face of heavy rains and winds in his area.

"I'll do the best I can, Harry. But you know the chopper pilots. If it really is an emergency they'll come out, but not before. And I hate to ask this, with the weather the way it is, but you'd better send one of your Green Charlies on recco for a couple of days. Concentrate on the canals and river."

Adams' groan was clearly audible from the radio speaker. "All right, sir," Adams replied reluctantly. "I guess I can best send Stew. But he's going to kick like a bay steer."

They discussed plans for the reconnaissance operation. "How about this, sir," Adams decided. "I'll send one boat, equipped with outboard motor, with Stew and a couple of his men. He can pick up another pair from Chet Smith."

Cunningham signed off and looked at Red Kennedy's doubtful expression. "Sure, I know the noise of the outboard will warn anyone he's coming," the Captain explained, "But this way he can cover a lot more territory faster. In the day time any VC boats wouldn't be able to hear him approaching in time to pull in to the bank and camouflage their own boat. And at night Stew couldn't spot them anyway."

"I guess you're right, sir. If nothing else he will slow them up. Delay their getting to where they're going. Maybe we can stop Colonel Nuan from going north if we produce some actual evidence the VC are infiltrating from the south part of the peninsula," Kennedy said hopefully.

"That's wishful thinking, Red. I'll bet they have this timed to hit us before the real monsoon season sets in for good. They'll want to be back in control of this whole area. And with the weather the way it is now, they can be sure that we won't be supported by air strikes and that we can't airlift in another big bunch of troops to help us."

Cunningham settled uncomfortably in his bunk that night. Everything he touched was damp and clammy. And he knew he would have to wear wet clothes the next day. Nothing would get fully dry. He scratched at his prickly heat and thought longingly of Monique's bathtub. His conscience bothered him. He had not written her since returning to Thuong Ninh. He examined his feelings about her, realizing they had been mixed up since that last night. It had been as if she had wanted to eat him alive. Or leave him with a high point never again to be reached between them. Like a final curtain. As the rain drumming on the roof lulled him into a deep sleep, he was still wondering.

In Saigon later that week Dick Sloan looked curiously at the letter with the unfamiliar handwriting that had come in the mail. There was no return address, but it had been posted in Saigon and had lain in his office for three days while he was up at Da Nang. He had felt free to travel about the country and maintain his contacts now that he was no longer *persona non grata* with the government and his visa was no longer in danger.

He opened the thick envelope. There was another inside, addressed, to his astonishment, to Captain David Cunningham. He looked at the sheet of paper which had been wrapped around it. It was a brief note from Monique, merely asking Sloan to mail the letter to Cunningham through U.S. mail channels, which were unavailable to her. Sloan frowned. Strange, he thought. She could drop it off at one of the billets, or get one of her regular American customers at the Caravelle to mail it. Or she could have called Sloan and asked him to pick it up. His Chinese employee advised him Monique had not telephoned during his absence.

Sloan looked at his watch and went out to his car. Might as well have lunch at the Caravelle, he decided, and he could ask her about this.

Monique was not at the restaurant and the woman replacing her was strangely evasive. He finally had to go to the hotel manager to find out what had happened to her. She had telephoned in her resignation from the job to one of the employees, with no explanation at all. And when the manager had tried to reach her by telephone the next day to urge her to come back, there had been no answer.

The sky was threatening rain as he drove to her house. He parked in front and walked to the gate in the wall. It was unattended and ajar. No one answered his repeated knocks on the door. He tried the knob and found the door unlocked. Cautiously he entered and looked around the first floor. Despite the daylight, the living room curtains were drawn and two lamps were turned on. Everything was in perfect order. The dishes all washed and put away. The upstairs was also vacant. A light was on in one room and a bathroom. A bed was turned down. It was obviously Monique's bedroom. There were clothes in her full closet, and he could see a matched set of luggage gathering dust in one corner. No pieces were missing as far as he could tell.

He closed the outside door behind him and went to the houses on either side. In answer to his questions, the servants there said they had not seen her or her maid or cook for several days. The gateman had also been absent. Sloan returned to his office mystified. He settled back after making several telephone calls. The American Army Criminal Investigation Division officer, a Central Intelligence man, and his informants in the South Vietnamese and Saigon police forces would check into her absence for him. He deliberated about mailing the letter to Cunningham and decided to wait until he had further information.

In the next forty-eight hours his contacts all reported they had drawn nothing but blanks. Sloan remembered something Cunningham had said about her being close friends with the Number One Chinese in Saigon. He got his assistant to make an appointment for him with the man, although the young news reporter advised against it.

The venerable Chinese was the picture of old world courtesy, serving him the customary cup of tea before they began their conversation in earnest. But during the verbal sparring, he proved more than a match for Sloan in evasiveness. He tried various solutions to the mystery of Monique's disappearance on Sloan for size, but when the newsman found arguments against their being possible, he retreated into Oriental inscrutability. Frustrated, Sloan returned to his office and pecked out a letter to Cunningham, telling him what little he knew. Well, he thought, mailing the letter at the U.S. Army Post Office, maybe the Captain has heard something else from her, or else the explanation is in her letter to him.

That afternoon Sloan was summoned to the Saigon Police Headquarters by his friend for an unofficial meeting. It had been reported that the newspaperman had been seen picking up a Vietnamese of disreputable character in front of a bar several nights before. After Sloan admitted as much, they politely asked him to accompany them to the morgue to look at several bodies who had been the victims of foul play.

Sloan's gasp told them what they wanted to know. The man who had escorted him and Red Kennedy was there, throat cut. He had been fished out of a canal. What they did not learn from him was that he recognized another body, too. It was the old man who had informed him that night about the transfer of American supplies to the black market. He denied knowing anything about the death of his escort, and since the man had been seen several times by others since Sloan had met with him, the police made no attempt to detain the newsman.

Back at his office, Sloan made one firm decision: To drop the whole business of Nuan, the black market and Monique. Life was too short, and Saigon was too much like Chicago in the old days. Life was cheap. After all, his job was to report on American activities in Viet Nam and the progress of the war. His life wouldn't be worth a plugged nickel if he continued probing, he realized.

Far down on the Ca Mau peninsula, Sergeant Chester Smith looked out at the rain and cursed. Over the sound of the rain on the metal roof he yelled at the woman who served as his cook, laundress and current mistress. She quickly poured brandy into a cup and added a little ice water. Peering at the brown bottle she shook her head worriedly. It was almost empty and it was the last one. Smith would be ugly if he did not get more. The rain had stopped the helicopter from coming. Smith was expecting, she knew, the arrival of another American by boat, but he probably would be delayed by the cloudburst.

Smith accepted the glass without a glance and continued to watch the canal waters. What a stupid idea of Cunningham's, he thought, to send Stew out in weather like this. But as far as he was personally concerned, it was a godsend. He was almost out of liquor and McDonald was bringing some from his own supply. That meant he was saved a damn wet trip. The only source elsewhere, other than that brought in by chopper, was the Vietnamese River Patrol and they were smart enough to stay high and dry in their base headquarters a few miles south.

Turning, Smith looked at the big calendar he had drawn up and hung on the wall of the room. He smiled. He could do this last goddam month in the damn Army standing on his head. But what a shitty place to spend it, he thought. Water in the rice paddy was almost up to his back steps. When he did go out the mud was almost up to his knees. And probably back in the mangroves there was a company of Viet Cong troops just waiting to strike. Well, he conceded, that stupid Captain Cunningham had at least said they could bug out if they were attacked. That screwed up ARVN squad of his in the hamlet would probably run at the first shot, leaving the Self Defense Force unit helpless. He looked down at the small dock. His piroque was bobbing in the canal waters and under rubber ponchos were the outboard motor, cans of gas, and plenty of ammo and chow. He was ready, and, by God, he'd give the VCs a run for their money. He had traced his escape route more than once and Stew had agreed to the plan. They'd join forces and try to link up with Harry Adams. The three of them might be able to fight their way up to

Khanh My where Jake Potter had a well-fortified chopper landing area.

Smith scratched himself and swore. His money belt was chafing him terribly, but he wouldn't take it off for anything, including a piece of tail. He smiled. Now the cook had a raw belly, too. It was a damn good idea, he thought, holding out that cache of Viet Cong weapons he had discovered hidden in the hamlet. There was a good market for them at the helicopter base. He knew the pilots were doubling their money, selling the Chinese, Czech and Russian-made rifles for souvenirs, but they paid in good hard cash. Greenbacks, too, not MPC, and since they had all the booze they wanted, cheap, they were happy to share it with him. They had even taken out several boxes for shipment back to San Francisco and given him the receipts. He had completely dismantled a Czech machine gun and wrapped each piece separately. It would make a nice display in his bar, along with the two Viet Cong flags he had.

It was a comfortable feeling, he decided, pouring himself another drink, to know that the negotiations for purchase of the tavern were proceeding nicely. His former boss in San Francisco was doing the dickering for him and a retired Army legal officer was handling the paper work. He kneaded his beefy face with satisfaction as he thought how his wife would react when she heard he was in business for himself. Then he remembered he had forgotten to fill out the papers she had mailed him. They were necessary for her to get the divorce. He drank deeply. To hell with them, and her. Can't mail them today anyway. No chopper's flying in this downpour.

Smith was almost asleep in his chair an hour later when he heard the putt-putt-putt of an outboard motor. There's old Stew, he thought, arriving in the nick of time. He tossed the empty brandy bottle out the window and stumbled out on the porch and waited for the piroque to dock.

Stew McDonald followed him into the house, wringing wet and cursing because of it. Without a glance at the woman he stripped to the skin and sat down with a wheeze.

225

He pointed to his soggy duffel bag. Smith opened it and dug for a pair of bottles. He handed them to the cook who made them drinks.

"I guess I'd better tell Harry you're here, Stew," Smith said, going to the radio. He handed the microphone to McDonald when Adams asked if he had found any Viet Cong.

"Not a goddam thing, Harry. We searched a lot of boats but they were clean. Did hear several reports of a lot of strangers around, some wading it through the paddies, in two's or three's, others sculling along the canals. More boat traffic, overall, than usual, I understand."

When Adams asked their plans, Smith eyed the two bottles and looked outside. The rain was slowing and it appeared to be less cloudy. He motioned for the mike. "Stew's soaking wet, Harry. I'll take the last stretch down to the River Patrol base," he volunteered. He knew he'd need more liquor, anyway. What Stew had brought would disappear overnight. "I'll start out early tomorrow."

McDonald was grateful for the offer. He rubbed his big bare paunch thoughtfully. "I sure don't like the signs, old buddy. I'll bet the VC will be in shape to hit us in a minimum of two weeks."

Smith agreed. "How's your SDF force coming along?"

"The little bastards can march all right, and hit a stationary target on the firing range, but I bet they run like hell if the VCs come along. The best men in the hamlet wouldn't join up for anything. Those gooks are too smart for that."

"Mine, too," Smith said laughing. "Old Colonel Fowler thought they looked pretty good. But he didn't know the trouble I had recruiting them or making them stick around during firing practice. Christ, they're gunshy. And my ARVN squad's almost as bad."

"I can't say the same thing. My boys are pretty sharp and tough. They won't bug out. My sergeant's got them so goddam afraid of him they'd rather take on the Victor Charlies."

"Well, that's the final report of the day, how about a little drinkee?" Smith asked, opening one of the bottles.

"You son of a bitch, I thought you'd never ask. And how about a towel?" Stew dried his big body thoroughly and eyed the cook who was preparing the evening meal. "How's the broad? She's better looking than mine. A little older, though." He laughed hoarsely.

Smith grinned. "You'll find out tonight. After I get finished."

Stew looked at the calendar. "Not long to go, eh? How about sending her up to me when your time is up?"

"Sure, but you wouldn't need a new one if you weren't hung like a horse." He called to the cook. "What do you think of that?" he asked in Vietnamese.

She glanced around, stared wide-eyed, covered her mouth with her hand, giggled appreciatively, and ducked her head.

The two men killed half a bottle of brandy before dinner, and half the other later, when they were joined by the woman.

It was almost 3 a.m. when Smith awakened. The sight of the naked bodies of Stew and the cook almost sickened him and he drank thirstily from the water jug. Outside the moon was shining. Smith looked thoughtfully down at his boat and then tilted the liquor bottle and gulped. The alcohol burned all the way down. But after a couple more snorts, he felt better. Hell, he decided, why wait. Why not leave now. Have a couple more shots; take some with me in a canteen; then shove off. He got his clothes on and then wrote Stew a note.

By the time he got two of his ARVN squad members moving and into the boat with him it was almost daylight. The piroque slowly chugged away from the dock. Smith was asleep within a half hour, arm over his eyes.

The two ARVN soldiers sighted several small craft move into the reeds at the side of the canal far ahead as they approached, but Smith did not respond to their calls. They looked at each other and shrugged. The piroque chugged on and one of the ARVN managed to dislodge the canteen from under Smith's arm. They were half drunk by the time he awakened and finished off the liquor.

The South Vietnamese Navy men were happy to see the American sergeant. They quickly accepted his dollars for a case of whiskey they had stolen off American sailors with the River Patrol. And he accepted their offer of several drinks. His ARVN soldiers were included in the invitation. It was a gay three-some who embarked in the boat and slowly made their way back up the canal at dusk.

Smith cursed when it began to rain again, but he decided to continue on. Stew would get sore if he wasn't back with the booze. Suddenly he began to wonder if Stew had been sober enough to report in for them to Harry Adams on schedule. Once or twice he thought he heard gunfire in the distance behind him, but the rain was pelting down so hard it was impossible to be sure. Smith swore and stretched out in the bow of the boat and decided to catch a few winks.

The outboard engine drove the piroque slowly up the canal. The ARVN soldier amidships was asleep sitting up. The second trooper huddled at the tiller, rain dripping from his poncho. He couldn't see a boat-length ahead. His eyes began to close and his head drooped. His body shifted slightly as he went to sleep. Little by little the piroque closed the distance between the middle of the canal and the right hand bank. The boat lurched when the bow plowed through the reeds into shallow water and the stern swung to the right. The engine's propeller churned but it could not cut the tough weeds. The motor sputtered and finally died.

The ARVN at the tiller jerked awake and looked around with dismay. For a second he didn't remember where he was. Suddenly the rain eased and he could see the houses of the hamlet looming ahead less than 100 yards away. He leaned down and shook Smith by the shoulder.

"Sergeant Smith. Smith. Wake up. The motor has stopped. We are almost home." He finally had to yell to bring Smith to his senses.

Smith finally sat up and looked around in bewilderment. He cursed the ARVN for running them aground and kicked the other soldier awake. Grabbing an oar, he probed the water. They were stuck hard and fast.

"All right, goddamit. You bastard, you got us on here, now get your ass out and up on the bank. Walk on in and get some help and we'll haul this stinking boat into deeper water." He heard the man splash into the shallow water and disappear in the darkness. Slowly Smith's head cleared. As it did the hackles along his spine began to rise. Something was wrong here. He peered ahead at the village and suddenly knew what was amiss. No lights at all. Not a one. Not even the flicker of a cooking fire visible through a window. Then he heard a sudden scream ahead on the bank of the canal and then all was silent again. No sound of his man walking through the grass.

Smith touched the other ARVN and motioned. They quietly uncovered their weapons and picked up their ammo belts. "You go first, quietly," Smith whispered.

The ARVN tried to get into the water as silently as possible, but he slipped in the mud and fell backwards with a splash. Almost immediately there were several rifle shots fired from the bank at the piroque. Smith acted automatically, toppling right into the water, weapon clutched in his hand, putting the boat between him and his assailants. He could hear the ARVN noisily trying to regain his footing. There was another burst of firing and the soldier fell back into the water, motionless.

Ahead in the village there were other gunshots and then Smith heard the sound of a machine gun. One of ours, he thought. At least the ARVN squad outpost sentry was alert. Other gunfire took Smith's attention and he frowned. The chatter of shots was unmistakable. A weapon like his own. Must be Stew, he decided grimly. I've got to get up there. There was no more firing in the direction of the piroque. Slowly Smith rose. He grabbed the side of the boat and it floated toward him, lighter with the three men out of it. Little by little he eased it out of the reeds into deeper water. Finally he hauled himself aboard and lay flat for a second. Then he sat up and grabbed the oar. He used it to pole it forward. He concentrated on what he was doing, trying to ignore the sound of the firefight as he approached.

Smith had a sinking feeling in his stomach as he began to recognize where he was exactly in the outskirts of the hamlet. The shooting was concentrated in two spots. At the ARVN squad's billet and at his own house. The ARVN machine gun was now silent.

He was gasping from the exertion but managed to get past the area where the billet was being attacked and finally eased the piroque to a landing before his house. He got on the dock and crouched and listened. The gunfire was heaviest at the rear of his house, with Stew's weapon firing burst after burst. There were only sporadic shots from the canal side.

By God, Smith thought, that's a Browning automatic rifle (BAR) being fired from the house up front. One of the ARVN must be with Stew, he decided gratefully. His hopes rose and he quietly stole across the plank and climbed the bank. He saw a dark shape moving toward the house, screened from whoever was shooting from the door. He decided to let go with his own weapon. It would tell Stew and the ARVN with the BAR that he was coming.

Smith carefully aimed and cut the Viet Cong down. He raced toward the house and gained the steps, but he had to duck and hold his position when the BAR opened up. He glanced behind him just in time to see the muzzle blast from another VC. Smith fired quickly, but it was not soon enough. A slug slammed into his chest and knocked him backward. For a second a red film passed over his eyes and he thought he was back in Korea. When he came to a few seconds later he realized he still had his rifle tightly in his hands. A pair of shadows were creeping through the grass toward him. It took great effort but he managed to fire at them and then scrambled up onto the porch. Lying gasping he realized the situation had changed. The BAR fire was now coming from the other side of the house. And he could no longer hear the sound of Stew's automatic

230

rifle. Between bursts Smith shouted in Vietnamese that he was coming in. He was hurt bad, he knew, feeling the warm blood seeping down his belly. The wound did not pain him and he was scared. His whole chest was numb.

Smith hauled himself across the porch and slithered through the back entrance. Suddenly he knew what he had to do. The firing was more intense at the back of the house. He crawled on hands and knees to the right and pulled himself onto a chair by the radio. He turned on the transmitter and then swung toward the door, gasping for breath. Suddenly he saw a shadow on the porch and fired hastily. A body fell to the floor, almost inside the door.

With satisfaction, Smith picked up the microphone, still holding his rifle pointed at the doorway with the other hand. "Green Charlie Four, Green Charlie Four. This is Green Charlie Six. Emergency, emergency." He knew Harry Adams' receiver was left on permanently. Smith shook his head. There was movement outside and then the firing at the rear intensified. Harry'd better hurry up, he thought, hoping the VC didn't toss in a hand grenade. Then he decided they would not, hoping to capture the radio intact.

Smith heard Adams' voice just as he was firing at another man who had gained the porch. "We're getting hit hard, Harry," Smith said with a gasp. "Must be at least a company size unit from the sound of the gunfire. Stew got zapped just after I came back and got in the house. There's apparently only one ARVN and me left, and I can't last much longer." He said the last without thinking, and the sudden realization that this was the end was almost too much for him. He was barely able to remain upright in the chair. "Sorry 'bout that, Harry. Tell the boys to haul ass. . . ." Smith faltered. Before he could continue a figure appeared at the door. They fired simultaneously.

Falling backwards, Smith crashed to the floor. His weapon had slipped from his hand. He groped weakly for it but the effort was too much. He made one last automatic lurch and his hand touched an open ammo box on the floor beside the radio. Reaching inside, Smith grasped a hand grenade. He rolled over and pulled the pin. At least the bastards won't get the radio, he thought, and let it roll toward several Viet Cong coming through the door, firing at him. It was his last thought.

At Cai Tho, Harry Adams listened grimly and then stared at the silent speaker. Shit, he thought, both those poor bastards bought it. He quickly turned to the other radio connecting him with Cunningham and the other sub-sector commanders.

"Green Charlie Leader, Green Charlie Leader, this is Green Charlie Four. Emergency. Emergency. Attention Green Charlie One and Seven." He waited for Cunning-ham's reply, knowing also that Jake Potter and Lieutenant Thompson would be getting up and manning their radios.

While he waited Harry Adams yelled at his cook who slept at the back of the house. The old woman emerged rubbing her eyes. He directed her to go and wake up the ARVN squad leader and send him over.

After Cunningham acknowledged, Adams described the situation. "From what Smitty said before he got zapped, this must be the beginning of the all-out attack. In view of that I suggest we execute the emergency plan, sir."

The ARVN sergeant came running into the house. Harry Adams quickly told him to get his squad going and to alert the Self Defense Force.

Cunningham's reply was not long coming. "All Green Charlies, I concur with Green Charlie Four. Execute the emergency plan. Use your own discretion. Keep me in-formed and stay by your radios until you decide to bug out."

Harry Adams acknowledged and then listened to the voices of Lieutenant Thompson and Jake Potter. His movements were crisply efficient, born of planning and long experience. He sent his cook to the home of one of her friends. The VC would kill her if they knew she had worked for the American. First he rigged demolition charges in each radio and then in the ammunition bunker behind the house.

The first item he put into his combat pack was a picture of his large family. After spending a lingering, lonely few seconds looking at it, he stuffed his pockets with official papers wrapped in plastic bags. Assigning one of the ARVN to monitor the radio, Adams made the rounds of the village defenses. He was pleased to see that even the SDF recruits were eagerly alert and ready. After ensuring that all the ARVN knew exactly what to do if they were attacked and forced to pull back, Adams went down to the canal and examined once more the four piroques which they would use to evacuate from the village. There was a branch off the main canal only a short distance away which they would use. The VC would probably expect them to go down the broader waterway and would have an ambush set. By traveling on the smaller canal they could get to the river and have a better chance to escape.

Suddenly he heard the sound of gunfire on the far side of the village. Adams ran for the house. He got inside in time to hear Lieutenant Thompson's voice. "Green Charlie Leader, Green Charlie Two has just reported being hit by a company size force."

Adams looked quickly at his map. Dick Greer was being attacked and he was in a hamlet a little to the northeast. A pattern was developing. The Viet Cong were moving up from the southwest, probably right across the peninsula. He picked up the microphone and advised Cunningham that Cai Tho was also under fire.

Captain Cunningham wearily acknowledged. "Stand by your radios, all Green Charlies and prepare to get moving immediately."

Chapter 15

Jerry Lord sleepily padded across the room to his radio and answered Jake Potter, his sub-sector commander.

"Green Charlie Eight and Green Charlie Nine, the men

in Harry Adams' area have been hit bad. Dick Greer's hamlet is also under attack. Go on full alert. We're probably next. Acknowledge."

Lord replied immediately, with Doc Elliott answering up finally.

After putting the mike down, Lord moaned both from the news and because of the way he felt. He had a terrible headache and his tongue was thick. Sergeant Dien, Corporal Cau, Bich Hong and he had been up late. The slender radio technician knew he had had too much to drink but it had been a pleasant evening. Even Dien had been cheerful and had joined in the conversation. Jerry Lord drank two glasses of water while trying to figure out what to do first. He finally returned to the bed and awakened Bich Hong.

"I have to stay by the radio," he explained. "Please go get Sergeant Dien."

There was a frightened look on her face as she sat upright. The sheet slipped from her naked breasts and Lord was almost tempted to tell her to stay where she was.

Bich Hong dressed quickly and started for the door. She startled Lord by returning and putting her arms around him. Bich Hong kissed him and then looked up at him, tears streaming down her lovely face. "Goodby, Jerry Lord. Thank you, my love. Thank you." Then she ran from the room.

Lord did not yet have all his clothes on when Sergeant Dien came into the room, fully clad in combat gear. Lord explained the situation as he put on his boots. "Better alert your men and the Self Defense Force."

"Yes, sir," Dien replied crisply.

Lord didn't see the elated expression on his face as he quickly departed.

Ten minutes later Dien returned. "The men are all on station, Sergeant Lord."

"Thank you, Dien. That was quick work." Lord looked indecisively at his combat pack and weapons and then at the radio. "I suppose I should go out and take a look around."

234

"I would suggest, Sergeant Lord, that you remain here in case any messages come in. I will check with you every few minutes. Corporal Cau is with the men."

Lord began packing, wondering where Bich Hong was as he searched for his gear. Dien returned and sat down, his carbine across his knees.

Jake Potter kept passing to him information he received from Cunningham and Thompson. Lord did not pay much attention but Sergeant Dien listened intently.

An hour passed. Lord paced the room worriedly. Still no action around his hamlet. Sergeant Dien sat as rigid as a statue. Corporal Cau entered and told Dien that all was well outside. Dien visibly relaxed and a smile played on his face.

The voice of Doc Elliott reporting his village under attack brought Dien to his feet. He trained his carbine on Lord, who looked at him in amazement. There was no doubt about the expression on his face.

"Dien, what the hell is this all about?" Lord asked needlessly.

"Yes, sergeant, as you finally have guessed, this place is also under attack. But you will not report it. In fact it is already in the hands of the Peoples' Army. You are my prisoner."

"What the devil do you mean?"

"The ARVN squad, except for my comrade, Corporal Cau, have been captured. And the Self Defense Force is helpless without their weapons. I am in control of this hamlet." He laughed suddenly and the high pitched sound astonished Lord. It was the first time he had ever heard him relax in merriment.

"Why you dirty conniving bastard, I'll . . ." Lord began.

"You'll do what, Sergeant Lord. No, don't move toward your weapons, or I will cut you down. You will be a valuable prisoner, so I don't want to do that. I am certain you will eventually be cooperative and give us a great deal of information about your electronic equipment." Dien laughed again. "You American fool. This was so easy. I am almost sorry for you, Lord. Frankly, I had almost hoped you would realize how we were duping you, so that I would have to kill you. But you became so preoccupied with my other comrade, Bich Hong, that there was nothing we could not do behind your back."

"Bich Hong! Good God!" An anguished look crossed Lord's face as the full realization of what had and was happening sank into his mind. They had him and his radio and all his equipment. He knew he had to do something, but what? If he could only get to the radio or to his rifle across the room.

"Green Charlie Eight, this is Green Charlie Seven, over." Jake Potter's voice broke the silence. Lord took an involuntary step toward the set.

"Wait, Sergeant Lord." There was an indecisive look on Dien's face. "All right, pick up the microphone. But if you say one word about the situation here I will kill you." He held the muzzle of his carbine against Lord's chest and poked him firmly twice.

"Green Charlie Seven, this is Green Charlie Eight. Over," Lord said quietly.

"Jerry, I just got the word to execute emergency plan. Bug out, boy. I'll be waiting for you. Acknowledge." The speaker was silent.

Perspiration streamed down Lord's face. He looked questioningly at Dien who jabbed him again with the carbine.

"You heard him, Lord. Acknowledge. That's all!"

Lord pushed the muzzle away and turned toward the radio and leaned down on the table it rested on. He slid his hand toward a switch, shielded from Dien's view. He made up his mind. He had been betrayed by Bich Hong. Weakened by her. Betrayed by himself. What might the Viet Cong make him do. He was weak, weak, weak. Lord began to speak into the microphone.

"Green Charlie Seven, this is Green Charlie Eight. They've already taken over here, Jake. I'm a prisoner of Dien. He's a VC . . ."

Dien's finger pressed the trigger and he fired point blank at Lord. The American sergeant got it in the guts. A second round spun him, but not before he had flipped the switch. He was smiling as he sank to the floor, unconscious of more bullets slamming into his chest. Wait'll they try to turn that back on, he thought as he went out. The lousy bastards.

Sergeant Dien stepped over Lord's body and looked anxiously at the radio. He was satisfied that none of his rounds had damaged it. But the indicator light was out and there was no noise, not even static, coming from the speaker. Corporal Cau ran in, drawn by the gunfire.

"See if you can get this operating again, Cau. I want to be able to continue to listen to the Americans." He looked around. Bich Hong had entered and was looking down sadly at Lord's body. Dien laughed at her.

Cau snapped the switch. The booby-trapped radio erupted as the demolition charge exploded. The shattered bodies of Dien, Cau, and Bich Hong joined Lord's on the floor and then the four were consumed by the fierce flames that swept through the house.

At Thuong Ninh Captain Cunningham helplessly paced the floor of his headquarters. There wasn't anything else he could do, he knew. The ARVN weapons platoon had zeroed in the approaches to his village with test rounds. All his outposts were manned and Red Kennedy was on continuous patrol. He cursed. The lives of damn good men and all this work had gone down the drain. If Nuan's Division had stayed in the area, they would have had a chance of keeping the VC out. They might not have risked attacking if the company had remained at Song Hao, and the rest of the Division on call not too far away. Now there wasn't a chance of retaking the hamlets already occupied. He ticked off the names. Stew McDonald and Chet Smith first. Dick Greer in Thompson's sector next. And then Jake Potter's report about Jerry Lord. Well, at least the kid's not a prisoner, he thought. Jake had known about the booby trap and had heard the explosion.

Now every damn hamlet but his own was under seige. He wondered how many others would make it out.

Cunningham looked out the window and gratefully noted the first strains of morning twilight showing up in the east. He poured another cup of coffee. It was bitter and hot and matched his mood. He sat down by the radios and looked at the map. His surviving Green Berets had all moved out of their hamlets and were headed toward Thuong Ninh as planned. There was only one ray of optimism in his thoughts. If the Viet Cong did not attack his village in the next hour it was probable that they hadn't yet moved this far north. That would give his men the daylight hours to travel. And the rain they had reported would give them cover. The squall line was moving toward Thuong Ninh, but the prediction for the following night was good. With the help of the artillery Cunningham felt they could hold out at least one night. If any of the other Americans arrived, and if they brought any of their ARVN, the odds would be more equal.

Roger Freeman's voice from the speaker broke his train of thought. "Green Charlie Leader, I finally got your reports to Colonel Fowler with the Division. He has talked to the Division Commander and they're making a 180 degree turn. Depending on the weather, he's going to try to arrange a chopper lift of a company down to Song Hao. He says for you to use your own discretion about moving up there from Thuong Ninh. It looks like we've had it all over the south part of the peninsula." He concluded with a report on the high fatality rate among the other Green Beret teams scattered around, who had been hit simultaneously with Green Charlie.

Cunningham groaned. Good God, he thought, this was a massacre. And his team was in better shape than most, so far as he knew. He spoke into the mike. "Thanks for the dope, Rog. But I'm going nowhere until my boys get here. I have one more casualty to report. Green Charlie Eight."

The sun rose at Thuong Ninh and the early morning rain began to pound on the metal roof. Cunningham wearily stretched out on his bunk, fully clad, his rifle close at hand.

Lieutenant Bud Thompson had left Binh Chan with the only four survivors of his ARVN squad. He looked anxiously down at the small amount of cargo covered by the ponchos. Viet Cong grenades had destroyed the other boats. They had had to leave a lot of the ammo behind to make room for the five men and the gasoline cans in the piroque.

He swore at the heavy rain which made the visibility almost zero. It seemed that they were barely making any headway as the outboard motor labored to haul the heavy load through the water. As it was, they were damn lucky to have escaped, he decided. Maybe he should have pulled out earlier, but he had wanted to see what could be done for Dick Greer, he remembered. The night had been one long nightmare and it wasn't over yet. They had one critical point to pass before they could join up with Tiny Christopolous and the ARVN he managed to bring out.

One thing he had learned during the fight. As far as the Army was concerned, he'd had it. When his obligated service was concluded he wanted out. He did not mind working in under-privileged countries. In fact he got a great deal of satisfaction from improving the lot of these backward people. But the killing was another thing. As soon as he got back to civilization the first thing he was going to do, he vowed, was to write Ann and tell her he intended to leave the Army. Thompson frowned. Her latest letter was in his shirt pocket. Probably soaked by now, he thought.

Her missive had disturbed him terribly. Every day they were apart he could feel her growing more and more influenced by her parents. Being turned against him and his desire to take her away from them. He'd probably get a few days in Saigon soon, he figured, since Cunningham had had the last R and R time. He'd call her on the radio telephone, no matter what it cost. Maybe the sound of his voice would accomplish what his letters had not. Oh, he had no doubts but that she still loved him. But it was turning out that it would be marriage only on her terms. Settle down near her parents. Yeah, he concluded, and vegetate.

Become a clot. Shit. His brow smoothed. Now that he had decided against the Army, he'd tell her and part of the pressure would be off her. Maybe he should go further. Imply he would accept her terms. Get a job near her home. Once they were married he could bring her around to his way of thinking. He smiled happily, and then the realization of his present predicament erased the thoughts of Ann.

The ARVN corporal behind him in the boat tapped his shoulder and pointed ahead. Barely visible were a cluster of a half-dozen small farm houses on either bank of the canal. Bud Thompson stiffened. He knew this was the critical point. Once past the tiny hamlet it should be clear sailing. They would turn a few hundred yards down where another canal would take them to the river. And somewhere on that canal they should meet up with Tiny.

Thompson felt insecure with the ARVNs. It was so damn much more comforting to go into a fight with a buddy by your side. He checked his automatic rifle and turned to the corporal.

"Have your men get their weapons ready. The BAR to the left. I will fire to the right if we are attacked from both sides. We must split our fire in that case."

He peered through the rain at the houses. No sign of movement or activity. They almost look abandoned, he thought, but you can never tell. The course of the boat was right down the middle of the narrow canal and they would have to pass through what could be a perfect place to set up an ambush. A look at a map would tell any VC that they would have to come this way. Suddenly, as the houses were very close, Thompson had the urge to laugh. Just like the old cowboy and Indian movies. They'll be waiting for us at the pass. Yeah, he thought wryly, but I sure as hell don't see any cavalry coming to the rescue.

The piroque plodded along, past the first house, then the second, and the third. All hell broke loose. From the doorways of every house on both sides gunfire poured down on the hapless quintet. Thompson's rapid fire swept from house to house, joined by the BAR and three M-1

240

rifles. But the VC were well-concealed, while the American and the ARVN soldiers were almost sitting ducks.

"Give 'em hell!" Thompson yelled uncontrollably as he loaded another clip. He glanced back and saw two of the riflemen slumped over. The corporal now had the BAR and was firing furiously. Thompson raised his automatic rifle again and watched a VC tumble to the bank after his burst. He glanced ahead. Only one more house to pass and they'd be in the clear. Suddenly he saw the barrel of a recoilless rifle appear around the corner of a building. Thompson quickly fired and smiled grimly at the explosion.

He died with the smile on his face, never knowing what hit him. The round that slammed into his forehead was fired from an old French Lebel rifle. Thompson slid backward onto the corporal, pushing him aside just in time to avoid another whizzing bullet. The BAR kept chattering even after the ARVN noncom was hit in the shoulder. The piroque putted on through the rain, past the last house, to the connecting canal. The corporal wearily made the turn and then stolidly staunched the flow of blood from his shoulder. He gripped the tiller tightly and looked down at his cargo of dead. He was the only survivor.

Two hours later Tiny Christopolous heard the outboard motor as he stumbled along the canal bank. He yelled and yelled, but the corporal's head did not turn. His eyes were still fixed glassily on the other dead in the boat. Tiny splashed out into the canal and as he pulled the piroque toward the bank, the corporal toppled over, out of the boat, and fell into the water like a stone.

Tears came into Tiny's eyes when he recognized Lieutenant Thompson. He wearily sat down on the bank and tried to figure out what to do. His own boat had been sunk in a similar ambush and he had had to swim for it. His hopes had risen when he had seen the approaching piroque. But now he was still alone.

Worse yet, the VC were probably out scouting for any survivors. And undoubtedly this particular boat. Well, he thought, at least I have weapons now. After hesitating he went to Thompson and removed his pack and the con-

241

tents of his pockets. He took the bodies from the boat and hid them in the reeds. If he got back he could guide a helicopter in to pick them up. Then he sank the piroque, after removing the BAR, Thompson's rifle, and the ammunition. Slinging the pack on his back and the BAR over one big shoulder, Tiny continued his trek along the bank. He knew he made a big, plainly visible target, but he was counting on the rain to provide some cover. And he was confident he could make as good time as any pursuing Viet Cong. He'd try to pick up a boat when he got to the river.

Pick 'em up, and lay 'em down, he chanted, over and over. That's the thing. Concentrate on moving first one foot and then the other. He felt a little weak from loss of blood, but the wound in one arm and another in his side had stopped flowing. There was a determined set to his black-bearded chin as he stalked through the mud. No little yellow bastards are going to stop this guy, he vowed. Anything the gooks can do I can do better. This old Greek is a match for them all, he thought. Then he smiled as he caught himself wishing he had something to eat.

Hell's fire, you're in good shape, Tiny, he told himself, if you can worry about your big stomach. Thank God you've got enough beef on you so there's plenty in reserve.

The mud slowed him down, but he covered three miles in the next hour and a half. He could see trees lining the river and he cursed. The rain was letting up a little. He'd have to be very careful as he approached the end of the canal. There was a damn good possibility that the VC realized this was another strategic spot on the escape route and would have it covered with heavy weapons from the banks of the watery crossroads.

When the rain diminished even more, Christopolous grimaced and stepped off the bank into the rice paddy opposite the canal. The reeds were high and provided good cover, but the gluey mud sucked at his boots at every step. He had to stop for a couple of minutes to regain his breath, but he kept his gaze on the trees and finally con-

tinued plowing ahead. As he neared the thicket he deliberately slowed and cautiously advanced a step at a time.

Tiny halted and listened. There was the sound of voices
ahead. A few steps further on he stopped again. No doubt
about it. Sounded like someone shouting orders. He had
to hold himself in check. The loneliness of his situation
made him long to rush forward to find human companionship even if they were VC. No, dammit, he ordered himself, take it easy. You've come this far so don't blow the
whole deal. Do like you did on the football field. When
you see an opposing lineman making a mistake, don't
charge in blindly the first time. Set a trap. Make the most
of it. Set him up. Then spring the runner through for a
score. It's that six points that counts.

Peering through the reeds, Tiny could see several
figures on the river bank among the trees. Looks like
they're setting up a .50 caliber machine gun, he decided.
Not many of them either. Maybe a dozen. He ducked and
moved forward slowly, hoping that the sloshing of his
body through the mud and water would not betray him.
He stayed close to the canal bank. Finally he was at the
edge of the thicket of stunted trees and brush. Tiny climbed
cautiously out of the paddy and crawled to the protective
cover of a bush and stretched out on the ground. While
he regained his strength he mapped out a path to the
river's edge.

He wrinkled his nose. There was something more in the
air than the stench of the paddy. Ahhh, food. That's it, he
decided. Food. The smell of cooking. He glanced at his
watch. Time for their midday meal. They've probably
been sent to set up a permanent outpost here. Digging in.
To command the river traffic. And I'll bet they have a boat
down there, to go out and examine any boats passing by.
Those clever bastards. And right now they're all sitting
around the fire eating chow.

Tiny got to his hands and knees decisively. Now's the
time, he thought. He ran to the shelter of a big tree and
halted momentarily. The voices were louder and the smell
of food stronger. His next light-footed movements were

toward the cover of a large bush. Now he could understand the conversation in Vietnamese. There was no movement he could hear. The men seemed to be clustered down the bank a few feet. He dropped and crawled forward.

Risking being seen, Tiny readied the automatic rifle and then the BAR and slowly lifted his head. There were ten black pajama-clad men squatting around a small fire, shoveling rice into their mouths and talking. Near them was the heavy machine gun, in a good position to shoot out onto the river.

Tiny breathed deeply, slung the BAR over his shoulder, and set the other rifle on automatic fire. He crept forward, got into a crouch and rushed down the slope at full speed.

Ten startled faces turned toward the huge mud-stained figure racing toward them. The sight made them freeze. Before they could move, Tiny was spraying them with lead. He stopped for only a half minute to fire more at each prone figure, and then raced on down the bank. Only a slender piroque was there, bobbing gently in the water. Tiny deliberately went back up the bank. Ignoring the bodies, he picked up the bubbling pot and squatted by the fire and began to eat. The grisly company bothered him not at all. His appetite was good.

Ten minutes later he was full and the pot was empty. He tossed the men's rifles far into the river and gathered up the machine gun and ammunition and took them to the boat. Awkwardly at first, he rowed up the river, finally gaining good speed. Well, he thought grimly, even if they have the river guarded I'll have a chance with all these weapons.

When he rounded a bend he found it tough going against the swifter current. Finally he had to pull in to the river bank and rest. He was almost asleep when a familiar noise made him sit up. A damn outboard motor, he decided almost immediately. He'd never heard of the Viet Cong having any of them, but then they might have captured one last night. He set up the machine gun among the trees lining the river bank. We'll see soon enough if they're enemy or friendly, he thought.

Waiting nervously Tiny was finally able to distinguish a string of four boats, all with motors. He had almost decided they were VCs when he spotted Jake Potter's lanky form in the lead boat. He cupped his hands around his mouth and moved into the open, yelling Potter's name.

The little convoy changed course and Tiny could see about 20 weapons swing toward him. He kept hollering as he watched the small craft through the light rain. His face lighted up. Harry Adams was there and so was Doc Elliott. He was suddenly thankful for the latter, conscious of the stiffness and pain in his side and upper arm. Maybe if Doc went to work on him he could stop any infection.

After the initial joyful greetings they were sobered by the realization that they were the sole survivors of the Viet Cong surprise attacks. As Doc Elliott cleansed and re-bandaged his wounds Tiny told them about finding Lieutenant Thompson.

Harry Adams looked at his map and then at his watch. "We'd better get moving as soon as possible. We should be able to make it to Thuong Ninh by dark. If we can't we'd better hole up someplace. We don't want to walk in there just as the VC are attacking."

"How do we know they didn't hit the Captain and Red last night?" Tiny asked.

"Well, it figures, that's all. The first VC strike was farthest south. Seemed to come up farther north in waves. You can only go so far in a night. And it'll take a good-sized unit to have a chance against the Captain with his big SDF outfit. Also the support of artillery from Song Hao. No, I think the VCs are probably mustering their forces to go in either tonight or tomorrow night."

Jake Potter agreed. "I guess I had the last radio communication with the Captain. When I told him about Jerry Lord. Everything was quiet with Thuong Ninh at that time. And everywhere else the attacks were already in progress."

"How did you make out, Jake?" Tiny asked.

"Not too bad. I think the VCs got screwed up in their

timing at my hamlet. We were all loaded and ready to go in the boats before they fired their first shot."

Harry Adams nodded. "That must be right. You got underway quite a while after I did. I didn't get hit hard though until we were in our boats."

Doc Elliott's lips were tightened into a grim line as he finished caring for Tiny. "The bastards really had my place zeroed in. They knew exactly what they were doing. Where everything was. They came in hard and fast on a direct line. Luckily the day before I'd decided to move the boats to the north end of the village. I barely had time to destroy the ammo and the radio and haul ass. Luckily it was raining and blowing so hard we had cover down the canal." He swore angrily. "Some of the villagers must have tipped them off about our setup. And after all I did for those gook bastards down there."

"Well, let's go," Tiny said, rising. He felt a little shaky in the knees. He was glad he didn't have to row any more. "I'll transfer the .50 caliber and sink my boat."

The convoy moved out slowly, an American in each boat. The heavy machine gun was cradled on Tiny Christopolous' lap, ready for any opposition.

Chapter 16

Cunningham and Red Kennedy stood in their headquarters looking out the window, pleased expressions on their faces. The rain had stopped and there was a bare patch of blue sky showing among the clouds.

"God, if this good weather can only hold I'll bet the Viet Cong won't dare attack," Cunningham said.

"Sure, and the choppers should be able to bring in that ARVN company down to Song Hao." Kennedy sighed deeply. "It sure would be nice to be able to count on having air support in the morning, even if they do try to knock us off tonight."

The radio receiver came to life and they turned from the window. Roger Freeman advised Cunningham a helicopter load of supplies and extra ammunition was being sent down, plus several pack radios.

"Any news about that ARVN outfit Colonel Fowler was trying to get moved?" Cunningham asked.

"Nothing so far. So I doubt if it will get transported today. There's heavy weather moving into that area. But the Colonel says it should be good tomorrow."

Cunningham put down the microphone feeling more optimistic. Kennedy was already going out the door to prepare for the arrival of the helicopter. Not much needed to be done for the ARVN squad and the entire Self Defense Force were deployed around the village. All Kennedy needed was a working party to unload the chopper. Cunningham went to the kitchen and opened a can of C-rations, suddenly hungry. He had eaten almost nothing during the day. When he heard the sound of the aircraft's engine he joined Kennedy at the landing area.

As the supplies were being piled on the ground the helicopter crew chief jumped down and came toward Cunningham.

"Sir, we circled the area before we came in. About three or four miles along the canal we spotted four piroques. I recognized one of your men. That big pro football player, Tiny. Guy with a black beard. There were three other white guys with him. Altogether about 20 men."

Cunningham thanked him profusely. The chopper took off and he and Kennedy started toward their house.

"I've got a mess of mail here, Captain," Red said, handing him a pouch.

"Good news, Red. They saw Tiny in one of four boats headed toward us. About three miles away. Said there were three other Americans."

"Terrific! Say how about my taking a couple of men and going down to meet them. I can scout the area at the same time."

"All right, Red, but be careful. Every man counts now," Cunningham said. He watched Kennedy move off at a trot.

Inside he sadly sorted the mail for his team. A big legal-looking envelope for Smith. A scented letter postmarked Georgia for Bud Thompson from Ann. He wondered if Bud would be one of the men with Tiny. Letters for Stew, Jerry Lord and Dick Greer were piled with the one for Smith. He quietly put them away.

He took his own mail and sat down on the porch. There was still plenty of light to read by and a nice cool breeze was blowing. Martha's letter was cheerful if uninformative. She wondered if he had any idea when his tour might be completed and where he would next be assigned. He sighed. He wished he knew himself. He opened the thick envelope from Dick Sloan and then was surprised to find Monique's letter inside.

Sloan's note was brief and to the point. It reported his investigation of Monique's disappearance. He hastily opened the other envelope. Monique's handwriting looked like she had been in a hurry. She sent her love, first of all. Then he frowned. It was imperative, she wrote, that she leave Saigon at once. She could not state the reason, but there was one. She would write again after she had relocated. Her destination might be out of the country—Bangkok or Hong Kong. She closed by reminding him of their last night together and hoping he would always remember her, no matter what.

Cunningham tapped the letters thoughtfully on his knee. Probably nothing to worry about after all, he thought at first. She just skipped out of the country. Then his brow furrowed. That would be impossible, he decided. She'd have to have a passport and go through customs, and certainly the airlines would have a record of her departure. Son of a bitch, he thought, now I've got something else to worry about. Suddenly he felt guilty, sensing that her disappearance had been probably the result of his asking her to help Dick Sloan. He thought of Nuan angrily. Now he had another reason for wanting to get even with him.

An hour later in the fading light, Cunningham heard the sound of outboard motors and went down to the canal bank. Kennedy led the procession up to him.

"That's the lot, Captain," Red said softly.

Cunningham cursed. Only 17 ARVN surviving out of 108. And four Green Berets out of nine. Oh my God. He solemnly shook hands with Harry Adams, Doc Elliott, Jake Potter and Tiny Christopolous.

"What the hell you been doing, Tiny? Making like a footslogger?" Cunningham asked. Tiny was encrusted with mud from head to toe. "And where the hell did you get that?" The .50 caliber machine gun was tucked under one huge arm. "Come on, you guys. I've got a bottle open."

Cunningham made notes while the men reported as they drank and then ate. Doc Elliott, the only one unscathed, began to patch them up after each had showered. Adams had a deep flesh wound in his thigh but he still moved around freely. Jake's shoulder had a crease and his forearm was cut. Tiny also had been plain lucky. Cunningham breathed a sigh of relief. He might need these men to fight again, and soon.

"All right, fellows. Better turn in now. We'll roll you out if there's any action," he said. He turned to Kennedy. "How are the ARVN they brought in?"

"A couple seriously wounded. One may not live." Kennedy chuckled. "The rest are ready to take on the VC again. The squad here is treating them like heroes." Kennedy looked down at the envelope in Cunningham's hand. Addressed to Thompson. "Sorry about the Lieutenant, sir," Red said sympathetically.

"You goddam right it's too bad. And about Jerry Lord, and Stew McDonald, and Dick Greer, and Chet Smith. Son of a bitch!" Cunningham turned away quickly and began to bundle up Thompson's effects and put them with the other letters. He did not want Kennedy to see the tears in his eyes. "You'd better catch a little shut-eye too, Red. I'll call you about 0200 hours. Then you can take the watch."

Cunningham made a drink of whiskey and water and took the cup outside and sat on the porch. Those poor bastards, he thought, tears streaming down his face. Bud wanting to marry his southern gal and wanting to be a good engineer. God, what a hell of a thing to make civilized Americans go through. The goddam VC and the goddam war. God, oh God, how I want to get out of this country. How could I have been so stupid as to volunteer for this duty. Then he wiped his eyes and sat back and relaxed.

Well, he thought, I picked my career in the Army. And so do all the second lieutenants. All so damn dumb and foolish. Maybe it is patriotism, but when they decide on active duty in the Army they don't know what war is all about. And that's what they're preparing for all the time they serve. Sure, somebody has to go to war, to defend the country. Duty. Yeah, he concluded bitterly thinking of the letters he would have to write to wives and mothers. Duty, shit! A wonderful word until you know exactly what's involved. He drained his glass.

Cunningham made the rounds of the village defenses again at midnight. It was a beautiful starry night. The South Vietnamese troops were edgy and restless. He reassured them as he stopped at each outpost and gun emplacement. When he returned to his headquarters he checked in by radio with the artillery platoon at Song Hao, and then with the chopper base at Loc Than. After the latter conversation he felt a little better. A helicopter reconnaissance flight had just returned after a long sweep around the area. Nothing was moving around Thuong Ninh as far as the crew could see. It took a lot of men, weapons and ammo to mount an attack on a village the size of the village. Cunningham finally began to relax. He chatted with Roger Freeman before going to awaken Kennedy.

"I was just going to call you, Dave. Colonel Fowler just radioed that they will start moving the company down tomorrow as soon as the weather clears. He'll be in the first one out. He's going to come in here first and then swing down to see you. He says he wants you to hold out just as long as possible. That's the direct order from Saigon." Freeman chuckled wryly. "But he says use your own discretion. You know what that means."

"Yeah, it means if I bug out I'll be the one to get my

ass in a sling as long as I'm in command of the Americans here. But Rog, I don't give a shit. If I think things are getting too tough, I'm going to do just that. Haul ass. Three of my men who did make it back are wounded. So are some of the ARVN. So tell Fowler not to expect any goddam miracles."

Cunningham was still tired when he got up the next morning. He first ensured that there would be no movement of civilians in or out of the village. Then he checked the schedule to make certain that small patrols would keep searching the area outside the village perimeter. Satisfied with Sergeant Nhon's arrangements, he next gathered his Green Berets.

"I hate to ask it of you guys," he told the four men who had returned. "But I'll have to have you turn to today. Here's the plan of the village. First, familiarize yourself with it. Then Harry, I'd like you to assign each of the men a post. Just sit tight and watch. No work involved. Make sure the ARVN and SDF people in your area are on the ball. The sight of you will tell them that we're with them all the way. This waiting around has made them nervous as hell." He smiled at them. "And me, too. Red here will alternate with me roving around. We'll bring the chow to you. And the beer. I don't think we have anything to worry about during daylight but you never can tell."

They all nodded agreement in unison, as if to say, how true, how true.

That night things were even more tense. On the outer edge of the village one of the Self Defense Force started to shoot at the shadow of a tree blowing in the breeze and in 30 seconds 20 guns were firing blindly at nothing. Sergeant Nhon, Kennedy and Harry Adams had to spend an hour calming them down. At daylight, Cunningham made a personal inspection of the perimeter and found exactly nothing.

He returned to the headquarters with mixed feelings. The last part of the night had been cloudy and rainy. No choppers had been out on patrol. But one platoon had been flown into Song Hao the previous afternoon. And he

251

felt more secure now that Colonel Fowler was at the Quan Lon Division headquarters. Fowler had already informed him two or three more platoons would be sent down during the day.

Cunningham felt almost relieved when two probing attacks were made by the Viet Cong at midnight. On the east side, the ARVN, led by Tiny Christopolous, fought off two or three squads who pulled out so fast they left several of their dead. On the west side it was a different story. The SDF-manned outpost had almost been over-run and would have been if Sergeant Nhon and Harry Adams had not rushed up with automatic weapons and grenades and driven the VC off. As it was, Cunningham was not positive that some of the enemy had not managed to infiltrate through the gap and were in hiding in the village. He doubled the guard at the ammunition bunkers, just in case, and posted sentries around the barracks where the off-duty soldiers were sleeping.

"That's the story, sir," Cunningham told Fowler by radio. "I'll let you know if anything else occurs."

"Thanks, boy," Fowler replied. "I'll be down there late this afternoon unless this goddam rain doesn't stop. I don't like to bug you, Dave, but hang tough in there. I have another piece of news. When the rest of the artillery company is re-positioned at Song Hao, Colonel Nuan will be with it. The Division Commander's making him personally responsible that you get the right kind of support." Fowler laughed. "You don't have to thank me for nothing, boy."

Cunningham put down the microphone, a doubtful expression on his face. He knew from past performance what he could expect from Nuan. Nothing but shit. But if it meant the ARVN Colonel's army reputation he'd probably have to do the right thing. Besides, Cunningham concluded, Fowler will be here to keep an eye on things. Nuan wouldn't dare cross him. Still, he was on pins and needles all day.

The night was stormy and pitch black. Cunningham wearily slogged toward the southern perimeter about 10 o'clock, head bent against the rain which had continued through the day and evening. Rivulets of water ran down his helmet onto his neck, under his poncho, and down his back. He shivered and struggled to keep his footing in the mud and still hang onto his rifle.

Suddenly he heard a strangled cry ahead and then shots rang out. He raced forward, weapon ready. For an instant a dark shape was visible on top of the shoulder-high breastwork and Cunningham fired. All along the wall there was hand-to-hand fighting as the VCs slithered into the ARVN and SDF positions, almost undetected. Cunningham halted and began to send burst after burst along the top of the wall. Then he heard shooting to the east and west, but much as he wanted to retreat he had to maintain his position. Red Kennedy came racing to his support. Without a word they separated a distance apart and kept up a steady stream of fire trying to keep any more VC from crossing the parapet. The South Vietnamese would have to do what they could to cut down the men already over.

Cunningham winced as a slug ripped through his poncho and nicked his arm, but he fired at the flash and the enemy dropped. Suddenly the surviving VC started back over the wall. He and Kennedy got several before the action quieted.

Leaving Red to help mop up, Cunningham quickly went to the eastern sector. The attack had been of the same type, and here also the fierce close combat by the ARVN combined successfully with the American firepower to drive back the VC. It was the same story on the west side.

Doc Elliott bandaged a pensive Cunningham. He turned to Harry Adams who was manning the radio. "Harry, I'll bet money they aren't through for tonight. Two will get you ten that they'll use grenades and maybe mortars next time."

"I agree." Adams smiled suddenly. "Look, why not try this. We used it once in Korea in a similar situation. Let's have our men go over to the other side of the wall. It's so damn dark out and raining so hard that the VC won't be the wiser. If they lob grenades over the wall, there won't be anyone there. Then when they follow it up with a rush, our boys can cut them down."

"Well, by God, that's good. How about getting the rest of the guys together and giving them the word?"

The Viet Cong hit again at 2 a.m. Cunningham remained in the headquarters. He heard the sound of grenades exploding just inside the walls. Then there was sudden silence. Simultaneously at the sound of a bugle gunfire opened up on three sides of the village.

A half hour later a mud-streaked Red Kennedy came into the house. He had a broad smile on his face. "It worked, Captain. Just like Harry said. This time we shot the shit out of them. And only a few of the SDF got hit. None bad, thank God."

Cunningham sat thoughtfully as Kennedy removed his soaked clothing. "Red, why do you suppose they haven't come around to the north?"

Kennedy stopped, surprised. "Why, I don't know," he began slowly. Then he brightened. "It could be they have the word that the ARVN are back in strength at Song Hao. That they figure they might come down by boat or across country to beef up the force here."

"Mmmm, that could be it. But it seems to me they'd make at least some show of strength there. To show us we're encircled."

A third VC attack was mounted at 4 a.m., but it stopped as suddenly as it started when the clouds parted and the visibility was good. This time the enemy used mortar fire, recoilless rifles and grenade launchers.

"They haven't much cover out there, Captain," Harry Adams commented. "Not protection from our counter-fire. One of the ARVN on the watch tower pin-pointed one of their mortars and one of our shells hit dead center. I saw that myself. But the VCs sure pulled back fast when the visibility got good. Too fast for me to call in the artillery support."

Cunningham sighed. "Well, we'd better pray the weather clears for good. They're getting dug in deeper out there every minute we can't call for any air support. And if they can creep up so goddam close without our spotting them, the artillery can't be used for fear of hitting our own people. Worse yet, little by little they'll wear us down."

Every available man was on watch in the afternoon after Cunningham was alerted that Colonel Fowler was coming in by helicopter, come hell or high water.

Cunningham was alone at the landing pad when the chopper swept in and dropped. Fowler leaped to the ground and ran to his side. The helicopter swooped upward, but it was only 50 feet in the air when they heard the heavy drumming sound of .50 caliber machine guns. They gasped as they saw tracers from three different points drift toward the moving chopper.

"Oh, my God," Cunningham breathed. Then the sound of his mortars firing took his attention. Thank God, he thought, they were really on the ball, picking out the locations of the .50s that fast. Suddenly overhead there was a burst of flame and the helicopter lurched sideways. It was a ball of exploding fire by the time it hit the ground just inside the wall.

Fowler and Cunningham ran toward the burning helicopter, knowing full well there was no use. Wreckage was strewn over a wide area. By the time they got the fire out, they found only the charred remains of the crew.

Berating himself for having exposed the crewmen and angry at the VC in general, Fowler got on the radio to Song Hao and ordered the artillery to plaster the surrounding area. He ordered Cunningham to remain in the headquarters and for the rest to take cover and grimly mounted one of the spotting towers to observe the barrage. Minutes later artillery shells began to rain down on the paddies and dikes on three sides of Thuong Ninh.

When he finally rejoined Cunningham after it began to rain again and he could see no more, Fowler felt a little better. "Now maybe those sonsabitches will behave and keep their heads down. At least they know what firepower we have available." He pounded the table. "But, by God, unless this weather changes, I'm going to make Nuan order that company to start down her overland. I've had enough of this shit."

But the rains continued. Three more attacks, preceded by heavy weapons fire, were beaten off that night. The poor visibility made it next to impossible to pinpoint the enemy gun positions for the artillery.

Colonel Fowler's face was drooping with fatigue the next morning as they made the rounds. Eight men had been killed during the night, and more than a dozen wounded badly enough to be out of the fight, Cunningham reported. He was still mystified by the lack of an attack from the north.

"I guess you're probably right that they're scared we'll bring in reinforcements from Song Hao," Fowler said, glancing skyward. "Anyhow, there's no chance of anything flying today."

"No, sir, and the weather prediction is bad," Cunningham said grimly. "Colonel, I respectfully suggest that we're going to need help. At the rate we're going we won't be able to hold here more than a couple of more days."

"You're right, son," Fowler said resignedly. "And even if we do wait that long, we'll need support even to evacuate from the village." He turned back toward the headquarters building. "I'll get on the honker right now and get the word to the Division Commander, Nuan, and also Saigon. This goddam set-up is hopeless."

It took over half a day of haggling with Fowler remaining adamant in his recommendations. The ARVN company, supported by a heavy weapons platoon, was ordered to advance to the direct support of the Thuong Ninh garrison. Fowler had had to agree to hold the line as long as possible for their arrival, but he bluntly told Saigon that they'd pull out sooner if they had to. He would not promise a thing.

Cunningham got grim satisfaction to learn that Colonel Nuan had been directed to personally lead the company overland. He chuckled. "Now that bastard will have to get off his ass and do a little foot-slogging himself."

Fowler shook his head. "No, no, that jerk will probably

256

come in by yacht down the canal, if I know him. But I promise you, son, if he screws this up I'll have his ass if it's the last thing I do."

Sure you will, thought Cunningham, if you're alive to do it. If they get here 48 hours as they say, I'll put in with you. Not the slow way they move. He did not voice his opinion. He knew Fowler recognized the messed-up situation the same as he did.

Chapter 17

From the time the VCs opened fire at midnight, it was evident they had a lot more strength. But the rain hampered their attack as much as it did the defenders. The hundreds of rounds fired and the barrage of mortar fire added to the casualty list inside the walls.

At 4 a.m. the enemy tried an end run. A suicide squad slipped up the canal in small boats. Fortunately Jake Potter was on roving patrol. There was a lull in the firing and he heard splashing as they poled the piroques. Jake quickly rounded up Red Kennedy and four ARVN soldiers. When the Viet Cong climbed up the bank they were met by the explosions of a dozen hand grenades and concentrated automatic weapons fire. The VC got off only a few rounds but Jake Potter caught one in the arm.

As a parting gesture before daybreak, the Viet Cong lobbed mortar shells indiscriminantly into the village. Doc Elliott and the South Vietnamese medics had a long line of civilians to treat, also.

Cunningham sent for Red Kennedy at mid-morning. "I hate to get you up, Red, but the Colonel wants you to type up a report for him. Don't say anything yet, but we'll probably haul ass tonight unless the situation changes. He talked to Colonel Nuan, who said the company was starting to move out. But Fowler doubts it. He's got a chopper from Loc Tan going over there now to see what's what.

Make plenty of copies of the report so each of us can take one to make damn sure at least one gets back to Saigon. It's going to be a blisterer."

The noon news on the Armed Forces Radio broadcast was full of information about the fight at Thuong Ninh. The seige was getting world-wide attention. The announcer said that reinforcements were on the way, and Cunning-hom groaned. Goddam it, he thought, the VC listen to these broadcasts too.

Fowler swore too when Cunningham told him about the newscast. "That tears it. The Viet Cong will ambush the hell out of Nuan's force and slow it down to a crawl. I wonder what in hell that stupid PIO in Saigon let that dope out for?" He went to the radio and got Rog Freeman at Division headquarters at Quan Lon. "Rog, take a message for the Division Commander, and relay a copy to Saigon." After he concluded his words of protest, he asked, "Anything new up there?"

"I hate to tell you this, Colonel, but Saigon is sending a planeload of newspapermen in here. I'm to get them to Song Hao by helicopters. Some of them want to move south with Colonel Nuan."

"Well, I'll be goddamed," Fowler complained. "That's all we need. A bunch of goddam correspondents. All we need now are circus wagons in the relief force. Look, Rog, you go down to Song Hao with them. Take a radio along. Keep reporting Nuan's progress. If he knows you've got your eye on him he may hurry things up."

Fowler turned to Cunningham. "Make plans for a bug-out tonight, Dave. As soon as it's dark. Any ideas on how to handle it?"

"Well, a few go first with the walking wounded. By boat. We'll let them get a good head start. With luck they can make it to that branch canal. Then we follow in three increments, going out the north end of the village. Fan out then and run for it over the dikes. We'll set up a rendezvous point for daylight. Together we should be able to hold them off until dark. Then we move again. Some

258

place along the line we should meet up with the lead units of Nuan's ARVN."

"Sounds good. Get at it, Dave. I'll lead one group. You another. Adams the third? What about men to accompany the wounded?"

"Well, I thought Doc Elliott and Sergeant Nhon. Nhon knows the area very well." Cunningham hesitated. "Colonel, as much as I hate to, I'm going to tell the new village chief we're pulling out. I'll ask him if he wants to go with the wounded. He's a dead pigeon if he doesn't."

Fowler nodded. "It's going to be tough on all the ones who cooperated with you." He sighed deeply. "Nuan's being so slow and this goddam rain have combined to beat us. God only knows when we'll take Thuong Ninh again. With the VC in the village, we'd need a regiment to take it back. And no time for that now that the monsoons seem to have started for good." He turned to Kennedy. "All right, Red. Let's get on with this report."

Cunningham visited the head of the village, who quickly agreed to leave with them. Then the Captain gathered the Green Berets and Sergeant Nhon. They began to work out the evacuation plan details. Doc Elliott was the first to protest. He wanted to remain until the last, but Cunningham was adamant.

"Doc, better decide as soon as possible those that will be fit enough to travel. And Nhon, you see to the boats just as soon as the sun goes down."

He took the plan to Fowler, who also objected violently. "Goddam it, Dave, I should be the one to go out last."

"No, sir, I will be, with Red Kennedy. As it is, Harry Adams and Tiny will have to follow their group and catch up. At the end we'll need all the fire power we can get, just in case. And then we'll really have to run for it."

Fowler reluctantly agreed. He realized he would only slow them down. He was still in pretty good shape but he knew he did not have their endurance. "What about all our gear, and ammo and weapons?"

"Jake Potter is rigging demolition charges, timed for a half hour after we leave. They also can be set off by anyone going over the wall. We've also got a building on the north side of the village loaded with explosives. As we pull back we'll dump every weapon and all the ammo we can't carry with us in there."

Fowler was satisfied. "There isn't anything more we can do now. Let's have a brew."

Late in the afternoon Roger Freeman contacted headquarters by radio. The signal from his own set was weak. "I didn't want to use the ARVN gear," he reported. "The point units of the company have left. Nuan himself is still here, holding forth with the newspapermen. By the way, Dave, Dick Sloan is here. Says hello to you and Colonel Fowler. We should leave with the main body in about an hour." He gave them a series of map coordinates and times. "That's the route we'll take and when Nuan's company commander estimates we'll reach the points. What are your plans?"

Fowler snatched the microphone from Kennedy's hand. "If anybody asks—particularly those newshounds or Nuan—tell them we're holding tough here. Plenty of ammo, morale good, and all that crap." He winked at Cunningham. "Rog, report in every hour, on the hour."

"I'll bet the VC are sure as hell monitoring our broadcasts. Or they have several of their own men in that ARVN outfit at Song Hao," Fowler said to Cunningham who agreed.

They plotted the route the ARVN would take. "Hell, at that rate they could not possibly get down here in less than two days without any opposition. Anyway, if we can get this far by tomorrow morning, we should be able to get artillery support," Cunningham said grimly.

"That looks like a good spot to rendezvous in the morning, Dave. That stretch of higher land."

"Yes, sir. Let's just hope all this damn rain hasn't inundated it." He rose. "We're eating early tonight, Colonel. The cocktail hour starts right now, and the boys have a real spread arranged for dinner."

Fowler laughed nastily. "I know, the condemned man ate a hearty meal." He watched the Green Berets file into the house and accept glasses of whiskey. Fowler shook his head and chuckled. "Christ, just like in the movies. Everybody shaven and in clean clothes. Just before the battle, mother, and all that shit."

They laughed with him and their nervousness began to disappear. Fowler regaled them with stories about his earlier experiences in Viet Nam. Cunningham drew Jake Potter aside and spoke softly to him.

"Jake, I want you to stick close by the Colonel tonight. He's tough all right, but don't let him set too fast a pace at first. I don't want you to have to be carrying him at the end. He's no young chicken any more."

Potter nodded. "You can count on me, sir. He's a right good guy, Captain. Glad to be going with him. He'll do damn well, I know, if we run into trouble."

After a big dinner the Green Berets dispersed to check the outposts as usual. Only this time each carried extra ammunition and their combat packs under their ponchos.

After dark Cunningham went to the first aid station where Doc Elliott had gathered the wounded ARVN and Self Defense Force soldiers.

"We're ready to go now, sir," Elliott said. "Sergeant Nhon has the weapons and medical supplies at the boats already. He made up fake identify cards for the men we're leaving behind and put them in among the civilians who were wounded last night."

Cunningham nodded and held out his hand. "Good luck, Doc." They shook hands solemnly and Elliott led his group out the door.

When the boats were filled, Doc conferred briefly with Sergeant Nhon who would be in the lead piroque. "Remember, Nhon. Use the oars until we've gone quite a way. If the VC attacks back here, or if we're hit, then get your motor going fast and move out. Okay?"

Elliott got into the last boat. The convoy slowly and silently moved off, the wounded with whole upper bodies and arms rowing. The rain pelted down but the men sat still, grateful for the concealing curtain. They were almost a mile from the village when the VC mortar barrage started. Ahead of Elliott, Nhon started his outboard motor. The others followed suit.

An hour later he heard Nhon slow down. They were coming to a bend in the canal. From this point on they would be headed almost directly north. But if they were going to run into trouble this would be the place, Doc and Nhon decided.

The Viet Cong must have not been on the ball, because half of the piroques had made the turn before the enemy opened up. Elliott's boat was illuminated by a mortar flare and he heard and saw the fire of a .50 caliber machine gun. There were screams of pain from two boats ahead. A recoilless rifle and a grenade launcher began to fire. Elliott braced himself and aimed at the machine gun. As soon as he saw it explode he turned his automatic rifle on the flashes from the other heavy weapons. The men with him in the boat were also firing. The VC firepower was cut almost to nothing. It seemed to take an eternity, but the piroques passed the turn. Suddenly a mortar round exploded directly on the boat ahead. The craft disappeared in a cloud of smoke and water. Doc swore and slowed. He pulled to the far side of the canal and stopped. There was no sound of any survivors so he re-started the engine and continued on up the canal, swearing. So close to making it without a casualty and a lucky shot like that takes the lives of six men.

Elliott settled back. Their chances were now very good. They should be able to link up with patrolling units of the ARVN company first thing in the morning at this rate. He could hear the sounds of the battle raging back at Thuong Ninh and wondered how many of the Green Berets he'd see again.

Colonel Fowler looked around the headquarters one last time and nodded to Jake Potter who was waiting for him. "As soon as Freeman reports in we'll bug out."

On the hour Freeman called and reported his position. Fowler marked it on his map and re-folded it and put it in his pocket. "All right, Rog, now on your next report, use this frequency." He repeated the megacycles that Jake Potter, who had a pack radio on his back, relayed to him.

"I don't understand, sir," Freeman said, startled.

"Goddamit, think a minute," Fowler snapped. "What's on your own back? So don't ask questions. Maybe I'll have more to tell you about midnight." He tersely closed the conversation and then donned his own pack and picked up his weapon. "Okay, Jake, let's gather our boys."

The rain beat a tattoo on their steel helmets as they stalked through the mud to the north end of the village. In five minutes a mixture of ARVN and SDFs joined them at the wall.

"All right, let's go. Don't bunch up too much, but don't lose sight of the man ahead. We'll have to move fast along the dike at first, but then we can spread out a little more after that."

They made the first thousand yards without incident. Suddenly Fowler halted the group. "Quiet," he whispered, listening hard. There was something ahead, he sensed. He turned to Jake. "I'm going to take a look-see. Stand fast."

Potter tried to protest but Fowler faded into the blackness of the night. The Colonel was silent as a cat, listening at each step. Then he heard a voice. Finally his eyes located a lean-to shelter directly in his path. A small VC outpost, he decided. Then there was a flicker of light as a match was struck. He saw a cloud of cigarette smoke and the faces of two men sitting on straw mats, a light machine gun between them. Grimly, Fowler slung his rifle over his shoulder and hauled out his large sheath knife. Moving to the far side of the dike he carefully walked toward the small shelter, approaching it from the side. One of the men said something and the other laughed.

Fowler pounced on them. His knife blade plunged into the back of one, and then he was on the other. A karate chop killed him instantly. Fowler got his knife and made sure of both of them. He silently took the machine gun apart and tossed vital parts out into the rice paddy waters. Then he rejoined the group.

"Okay, Jake, let's move on."

"Find something, Colonel?" Jake asked. He had been worried because the Colonel had been gone a long time.

"Yeah. Outpost. Two VCs. All clear now." Fowler's pace was fast. He figured the enemy had a string of these machine guns placed on the dikes north of the village. Fowler stopped again a few minutes later. "Jake, better get on the radio and call the others about the outposts. They probably will run into them about the same distance from the village as we did." Smart of the VC, he thought as they started out again. That's why there had been no attacking from the north. The VC wanted to keep concealed their machine guns so they could catch either any reinforcements coming up or any of us leaving the village in their crossfire. But they probably didn't expect us to move out tonight in this rain. It took another hour to make another mile, and Fowler began to set a slower pace. They had a long way to go before morning, and they'd need their strength. However, now it looked as though their opposition would be light, if not nil.

Back at Thuong Ninh the Viet Cong had followed their initial barrage with another sneaking charge at the walls on the south end of the village. The defenders were expecting it and were braced. Mortar shells and grenades exploded in the path of the attackers and only a few had to be cut down with machine gun and rifle fire. The VC withdrew. There was another probe on the east side, but once more the enemy had no stomach for the withering firepower that Cunningham rushed to support the outposts there.

Cunningham called to Harry Adams. "Better get your ARVN noncom to start out with your group. Once they're out on the dike, you and Tiny pull out, one along the east side and the other on the west. Good luck, Harry." He slapped the big man's shoulder.

As he anticipated, the VCs came at the west wall next. He gathered the rest of his men there on the double. Finally when the strike had been beaten back and all was silent except for an occasional mortar shell exploding, Cunningham looked at his watch.

"All right, you guys. Let's go," he called softly in Vietnamese. He could guess that the Viet Cong leaders were massing their men and exhorting them to advance no matter how intense the opposition was. They'll try to overpower us by sheer numbers, Cunningham mused. The remaining ARVN and SDF were gathering up their gear plus the mortars, machine guns and other heavy weapons. They carried them hastily to the north end of the village and dumped them into the mined building and then ran quietly for the wall.

"Red, I'll lead, you take the rear. Now, let's haul ass." Cunningham slipped through the opening and with a long but noiseless stride headed for his designated route. Kennedy moved up beside him after they had gone a few hundred yards.

"Better slow down, Captain, and let me reconnoiter ahead." Kennedy said he would take an ARVN soldier with him.

Cunningham agreed and halted the rest of the group. He fidgeted as the minutes went by. Finally he spotted the red glow of a flashlight coming toward them rapidly. The ARVN with the light arrived with a broad smile. He made a slicing motion across his neck and beckoned.

A half-mile more progress was made before Cunningham heard the sound of the VCs firing again back at Thuong Ninh. His jaw muscles worked grimly. They really would have to make time now. The Viet Cong would attack and find them gone and realize immediately what had happened. Patrols would be sent out in pursuit. He decided to take a chance and changed his pace to a loping trot.

The firing behind them intensified and finally died down to nothing. "Look at that," Kennedy called.

Flames shot into the air and huge explosions rent the silence of the night. The demolition charges set in the village had been set off by the leading Viet Cong going over the walls. It gave Cunningham a feeling of satisfaction. A few minutes later they saw three red flares arch above Thuong Ninh and explode. Damn, a signal of some sort, he thought. Meaning they have taken the village and we're gone. Any other gun positions ahead will be alerted now.

They had gone another mile before Cunningham pulled up short. He had almost fallen into a break in the dike. "We're going to have to wade it, men," he whispered. He slid down into the waist deep water, cursing. The deep mud sucked at his feet. He felt sorry for the South Vietnamese who would follow him. The water would be up to their chests. His progress was very slow as he was keeping a careful watch on the dike ahead. Then he stopped. A lean-to was up there on the bank ahead. He decided to remain in the water and try to bypass it. His rifle was ready as were the guns of the men following.

Cunningham almost made it past. But one of the VCs stepped out into the rain and urinated. When he turned to go back in he spotted the figures in the water. As he shouted, Cunningham's rifle spurted fire and the man dropped. All his group hustled for the bank of the dike and slithered upward.

Kennedy made it first. His shots hit the other gunner as he was swiveling his machine gun around.

Cunningham was panting as he congratulated Kennedy. "But now the fat's in the fire. I don't think the VC back in the village would spot our shots, but any outpost ahead knows we're coming."

"Look, Captain, why don't we try this? There's another dike up ahead, running at right angles to this. Let's go west awhile and then cut back to the north. We'll have a little farther to go to the rendezvous, but it might be safer."

"Good idea, Red." A few minutes later Cunningham was even more grateful he had taken the suggestion. This dike had a better walking surface and they made good time. Finally they turned north again and once more were lucky. The knee-high grass gave them good footing. As it turned out, they hit the slope leading to the meeting place before Harry Adams and Tiny.

It was a gloomy morning twilight when Cunningham signaled ahead with his flashlight. He sighed with relief when Fowler gave the answering blinks.

Fowler's face looked drawn and ashen in the gray dawn. He was still breathing heavily as he sat huddled in his poncho on his ground cloth.

Cunningham described his pull-out and heard Fowler's account. So far, so good, the Captain thought. Not a casualty.

An hour later Harry Adams and Tiny Christopolous slowly led their men to the group. They had run right into a machine gun emplacement that had been dug into the surface of the dike. He had lost four men and three others were wounded. The latter had slowed their progress during the rest of the arduous trek.

Cunningham let the men rest for an hour. "All right, Harry, start them digging in. The only cover we have is this high grass. We'll hide out here all day and move out tonight again and try to locate Nuan's force the next morning."

After carefully examining the area, Cunningham selected the highest point of land as a command post. They camouflaged it with grass on four sides. He knew they each had to get as much rest as possible, so he had only one man on watch at a time. Anything moving for miles around could be seen from the position in clear weather, but there was still almost a half-mile visibility in the rain.

Cunningham listened to Fowler talk to Freeman on the radio.

"Now listen carefully, Rog. You give Nuan our present position. Tell him and those reporters with you that we had to bug out." He described the situation back at the village and at their current location. "If I guess right, the VC will try to get between you and us as fast as possible. I think we're okay for today, but I'm worried about tomorrow morning. You sure aren't making very good time."

"This is a pretty slow moving outfit, Colonel," Freeman concurred. "The artillery pieces are holding us up.

I have some more news, sir. We just got the word that Doc Elliott and the wounded have made contact with one of the patrols. They're sending the wounded on back. Your man will join me in about an hour."

The Green Berets were elated to hear that Elliott and the others had reached safety. Now they had only their own skins to worry about.

Cunningham wearily settled down in his foxhole and shut his eyes. He was terribly tired, but sleep would not come. Forty-eight hours, he thought. If we can hold out that long we've got it made. Sure as hell this team has had it. Maybe I can get us some fat-cat training job until my tour is up. Man, will I ever be glad to see Martha again, he thought. And then he was surprised at himself. Well, maybe it's just the idea of being out of Viet Nam and having the comforts of home again. He finally dozed off.

Chapter 18

In the fading light, Cunningham and Fowler studied the map. "Well, tomorrow morning's going to tell the story, Colonel," Cunningham commented glumly.

Fowler growled agreement. "Any way you slice it, son, we're going to be out in the open at daybreak. Alone. I've already asked Nuan to send a couple of faster moving patrols ahead to meet up with us. They should be able to flush out any VC ambush and at least give us some warning."

Red Kennedy joined them. "One of the SDF says there's a tiny hamlet, actually only a few farmhouses, on our route." He pointed their location out on the map.

"Yeah, and it'll be between us and Nuan in the morning. It's right on our track," Cunningham said thoughtfully. "A sweet place to hit us, and we don't have any other route to take."

The rain fell all through the night as they marched

onward. Fowler and Cunningham led the band. Their progress was slow because they had to stop occasionally to permit the wounded men to rest.

Cunningham gathered the Green Berets when he saw the first strains of light in the east. "We'll take the point since we've got the most firepower. In an hour we'll be close to the village so don't bunch up too much.

They gained the last dike leading toward the farm houses. It was fully light and the nervous strain was apparent on each weary face. Cunningham peered ahead. He suddenly saw a flash and yelled a warning even before he heard the karrumph of the mortar. His men dove for the sides of the dike. The round exploded past Cunningham among a knot of South Vietnamese soldiers who disappeared in smoke.

"Stay down! Stay down!" Cunningham yelled. He heard the opening rounds from a .50 caliber machine gun and groaned. It was shooting from a good angle and could almost hit the sides of the dike. He carefully raised his head and looked to either side. He caught sight of movement on the next dike to the left. He raised his weapon cautiously and then saw a light machine gun being set up. Aiming carefully he shot the gunner down with the first burst.

More mortar shells were being walked up and down the dike, but all his men were down along the banks. Something had to be done fast. The men would have some protection, but they sure as hell were pinned down. He called to Colonel Fowler. "Think we might have some artillery units close enough to call in some fire on those houses?"

"I'll see, Dave." Tiny's pack radio was passed up to the Colonel, who explained the situation to Roger Freeman, giving him both the coordinates of the houses and their own position.

Five minutes later Freeman called back. "Can do, Colonel. They horsed four pieces of artillery ahead of the main body. They ran into pretty good terrain. Just within range now, and getting set up. I passed the position to Colonel Nuan and he's relaying it to the unit ahead."

Doc Elliott and Dick Sloan sat half-heartedly digging at congealed frankfurters and beans, while Sergeant Nhon ate his inevitable rice with relish. Elliott looked across and saw Freeman talking to Colonel Nuan excitedly. The Colonel and the Captain were looking at a map. "Hey, Nhon, how about finding out what's up?" Elliott asked curiously.

The sergeant smiled, wiped the food from his face, and trotted off. He talked first to Captain Freeman and then followed the Colonel who went to his Operations Officer at the radio.

Meanwhile Doc got out his own map and showed it to the newspaperman. "I'd guess the Green Berets are about here, sir. And we're here. We should join up by noon."

Nhon came trotting back, a puzzled look on his face. "Captain Freeman says Colonel Fowler reports they are pinned down on a dike." He leaned down to the map and pointed. "VC here."

"Oh my God! How bad is it?" Sloan asked.

"Mortar and heavy machine gun fire. From farmhouses. Here. Or was it here?" He frowned. "I do not understand this. Colonel Nuan ordered artillery. But he gave these coordinates as target. Not coordinates of the houses which are closer to us."

"You must have heard wrong, Nhon," Doc said jokingly.

Sergeant Nhon shook his head solemnly. "No sir, Doc. I hear right. Something is wrong. Fishy, like you say."

Sloan and Elliott chuckled. Doc finally rose, tossing the C-ration can aside. "I'll see what Freeman has to say." He waited until the Captain had completed his radio transmission. "What's the story, sir?"

Freeman repeated what Nhon had said about Fowler and Cunningham's group being under fire. He listened casually while Elliott told him what Nhon had brought back about the coordinates. "Oh, no, that couldn't be possible. Colonel Nuan wrote down the numbers. They were the same as mine." He looked thoughtful. "Doc, how about checking it out with the Operations Officer, though. Christ, this would be a fatal mistake."

270

Elliott was listening with horror to the Operations Officer who showed him the coordinates they were firing at when he heard the first shots from the artillery ahead. He ran across to Freeman. "God, Captain! They got it just back-asswards! They're shooting at our people!"

Freeman grabbed for his radio. "Get Nuan and have him countermand his order! Hurry!" Then he yelled a warning into the microphone. "Green Charlie, Green Charlie, acknowledge," he repeated over and over. There was no answer.

Colonel Fowler had turned to Cunningham in his position further ahead on the bank. They had all clawed at the dirt under them and were a little better protected. "It won't be long now. We'll just hang tight until the artillery flattens those damn houses. I'll send in spots to Freeman." He still had the radio.

They heard the sound of artillery firing and then the screech of the approaching shells. Cunningham frowned. Christ, they're long. Way too long. They're going to . . ." His thoughts were interrupted abruptly as one round exploded right above him on the dike. Within a microsecond three others exploded on either side of the dike. Cunningham knew he was hit by shrapnel but before he could even move more shells soared into the area, farther back. Then a third salvo crashed down. After the din had ceased, Cunningham could hear cries and shouts all along the line.

Cunningham groaned when he moved. His left shoulder felt like it was on fire and one of his legs was numb. He forced himself up, cursing, and tried to crawl toward Colonel Fowler. Gotta get on the radio. Tell Freeman those bastards are shooting at us. He halted abruptly when he saw the Colonel. He still held the radio but it was as shattered as his body. Fowler was dead.

Shaking his head to stop from fainting, Cunningham turned back. "Radio!" he yelled. "Radio! Anybody got a radio working?"

"Yeah, Captain, there's one back of me. But I can't get it to you. I'm hit bad," Tiny called. "Can't move."

Using one arm and one leg, Cunningham crawled through the mud toward Tiny. He found him soaked with blood. Then he got past him and found the radio.

"This is Green Charlie Leader. Roger, stop the firing. For Christ's sake, it landed right on us."

"Dave, are you all right? Colonel Nuan's sending the word out to stop shooting at you and get on the right target."

"They really plastered us, Rog. Fowler's dead and I don't know how many others. I know Tiny and I are all shot to hell. What the shit happened up there?"

"Nuan had the right coordinates for both positions but he must have got them switched when he told the Operations Officer who relayed them to artillery."

Cunningham ducked when he heard the artillery go into action again. "Goddam it, Rog!" he screamed. "We're getting it again!" He rolled into the mud and ducked his head. More rounds exploded along the dike. He finally lifted his head when there was silence and then talked into the radio weakly. "Roger, that really did it. I'd guess we'll be wiped out completely if we get any more of that."

The sound of artillery reached him again and he flinched. But this time one of the small wooden houses ahead exploded in flame, with a great secondary explosion. Must have been the mortar ammo, Cunningham thought. He saw a few black clad figures run from another house and disappear in the smoke when another shell hit close by. Within five minutes all the houses were demolished, but Cunningham was still fearful and stayed where he was.

"That's enough, Rog. But you'd better get some help up here fast. I'm closing down now to see who's left."

Cunningham was horrified when he crawled along the dike and saw the shattered bodies. Only a few of the South Vietnamese were alive. Harry Adams had been blown practically in half. Tiny, Jake Potter and Red Kennedy were seriously wounded and unconscious. Cunningham was in tears when he crawled back to the radio and reported the facts to Freeman. "We'll just have to lie here until help comes. Weather's starting to clear now, though, so evac choppers should be able to come in." The mike dropped from his fingers and he fell unconscious in the mud.

Captain Freeman's eyes were flashing dangerously when he reported the situation to a white-faced Colonel Nuan. Dick Sloan and the other newsmen were clustered around. Freeman went to the ARVN radio and contacted the helicopter base at Loc Than.

Sloan looked at Doc Elliott's strained face and tearful eyes. "Take it easy, Doc. Come on, let's move up. I want to see where this happened."

Elliott shook his head numbly and refused. "The evac helicopters will have them out before you get there."

"I know, but it'll give us something to do."

Elliott turned around and moved toward his black medical bag, picked it up and opened it. Sloan looked at him curiously and heard him cursing Colonel Nuan over and over. The newspaperman and several of his companions started to move out. Colonel Nuan sat on an empty ration box alone and stared into space as if he were in a trance. Sloan looked back and saw Elliott take something from his belt and put it in the medical case. Then the medic moved toward Nuan and sat down behind him, his hand on the black case.

Doc Elliott reached in and held the hand grenade tightly, staring at the ARVN officer. You dirty bastard, Doc thought, you did it before and now you've done it again. Killed Colonel Fowler and poor Harry Adams. And all the rest shot to pieces. My buddies. Well, you won't screw us up again, ever, he said wordlessly, and a small smile crept on his face. "Goodby Nuan, you bastard!" he called softly as he pulled the pin. The Colonel turned around suddenly and stared at him. Elliott's eyes were shut tight as he released the grenade.

It exploded, killing both Doc and Colonel Nuan immediately.

Freeman reached the bodies first, looking fearfully

273

around, wondering if the Viet Cong had done it. Dick Sloan beat the other newsmen back to the scene. He arrived just in time to see Roger Freeman carefully remove the grenade pin from Doc Elliott's hand and quickly stuff it in his pocket. Freeman sadly followed Sloan away from the vicinity, both sick to their stomachs.

"I saw the pin, Rog," Sloan said thoughtfully.

"Well, you aren't going to . . ."

"No, Rog. For my dough it was an accident. Doc Elliott was a fine guy. A damn good Green Beret and medic. And Nuan got exactly what was coming to him."

Freeman nodded and an angry look came on his face. "You know, giving those wrong coordinates must have been deliberate. He knew Colonel Fowler would try to crucify him for not getting going sooner and moving faster. I guess maybe he thought that if the guys were dead he'd get away with it."

Sloan agreed. "Rog, how about getting the chopper base on the radio again. I'd like to get the hell away from this ARVN outfit. Maybe we could stop and take a look at where Dave and the boys got it."

"Okay, I want to get moving too. We'll take Doc's body out with us."

Dave Cunningham was awakened by the light rain falling in his face. It took him a few seconds to realize where he was and what had happened. His first reaction was that he had to get moving and give first aid to his men. But his body wouldn't get going. He lay back gasping. Then he froze. Voices. Speaking Vietnamese. He started to thank God but then his reason returned. He'd heard no choppers and he couldn't have been out long enough for the leading ARVN units to approach this close.

It took him a couple of minutes but he finally managed to roll over and raise himself slowly on his right elbow. He peered through the grass up at the dike. Finally his eyes focused enough to make out several figures garbed in black and another in a khaki uniform. He listened carefully. The uniformed man was barking orders in Vietnamese, urging the others to hurry. Search the bodies and take all weapons and useful equipment. Kill any wounded. Cunningham's head dropped. Helmet in the mud. Oh no, some of those VCs must have been dug in deep and escaped the artillery barrage. He listened intently, trying to decide what he could do. The uniform passed above him. Instantly he made it out. A regular Army sergeant from North Viet Nam. He had one of the American-made automatic weapons in his hand and was looking toward the direction the evac helicopters would be coming from. Cunningham heard him say they would try to knock some of them down. And he knew they would be able to do it with the captured weapons.

Cunningham thought of his men lying there, half-dead. After they had worked so hard, fought so valiantly, and come so far. His teeth clenched. No, by God! They deserve the chance to live, he thought. One last chance. He watched the uniform go past again and suddenly his left foot went into action first. It dug into the mud and pushed. Cunningham felt himself moved upward a few inches. His right arm took over. Up the bank farther. Left, right, left, right. He almost laughed hysterically. Left right left right left right . . .

His automatic weapon was clutched in his right hand and he examined it quickly. The VCs had collected the weapons from the men on the other side of the dike and would be moving toward him shortly. He decided to try for the top of the dike. He'd have a clearer field of fire, although he would be exposed.

His left knee provided the leverage he needed to gain the top. He stretched out and rested for a second. Then he heard it. The drumming in the distance of the helicopter engines. The VC must have heard them, too, because the PARVN noncom yelled to them to hurry.

Rolling on his side, Cunningham sensed the deep-seated pain in his left shoulder and chest and had to fight to retain consciousness. The grass screened his movements but he cursed it for he could not see the enemy too well. He inched his rifle out ahead of him and gathered his strength.

275

One last check. On automatic fire. Full clip. It had to be good. He drew up his left knee and then with his good arm he got into a crawling position, but it was no good to shoot from. His balance was too shaky. He had to get upright on both knees.

In the distance he could see the choppers. The VC had their attention on them too. Cunningham saw his chance. He lurched up and, not bothering to raise the automatic weapon above his waist, let go. There were screams of surprise and pain. The PARVN was the first to drop, Cunningham saw with satisfaction, and he swung his rifle to the left and right. They were all down when his gun clicked empty. He wilted, wondering as he dropped if he had got them all. But he knew his gunfire would alert the chopper pilots. His men would get their chance. Suddenly it was as if a crimson veil had been dropped over his face. Everything was red as he closed his eyes.

Cunningham came to, screaming with pain, as something tore at his leg. The figure leaning over him was hazy but it made no difference. He struggled to sit up and grab his rifle. He was slowly forced back by another man.

"Easy, sir. Easy. It won't hurt much longer. Relax."

Only then did he realize they were Americans and he settled back. "The others," he whispered. "What about the others?"

"The Medical Officer is looking at each of them now. I think we can save most of them that are still alive. Thanks to you, Captain." The medic looked at him admiringly. "Our crew chief saw the whole thing through his binoculars, sir. Wounded like you are, I just don't know how the hell you were able to get up and knock those VCs off."

Cunningham barely remembered doing it.

"It's a damn good thing you did, sir," the corpsman continued. "We'd seen the VC. We wouldn't have been able to sit down, and couldn't get any air support. We'd have had to wait until the ground troops moved in and secured the area. Might've been hours. You guys would all have had it by that time."

His voice faded from Cunningham's hearing as the sedative took effect. The last thing he remembered was a slight bit of pain as he was hoisted onto a stretcher and moved to the helicopter where he was loaded into the big wide open rear bay below the twin tail booms.

Chapter 19

Later that day Dick Sloan talked to the doctors at the field hospital at Soc Trang.

"Yes, Mr. Sloan, they've all got a good chance to live," the senior medical officer said. "They'd lost a lot of blood. Luckily those three evacuation helicopters were all ready to take off from Loc Than. They were underway with a doctor and corpsmen in a matter of minutes. Captain Cunningham's heroic action was the clincher."

"Yes, I know. I talked with the evac copter crews and the medics over there. Can I see Captain Cunningham?" Sloan asked.

"Certainly. We'll be evacuating him shortly. I have recommended sending him back to the states for more surgery on that shoulder." the medical officer said.

Cunningham was flat on his back, eyes open, gaze fixed on the ceiling. His left shoulder was a mass of bandages and his right leg was encased in splints.

"How are you feeling, Dave?" Sloan asked, looking at his white face.

He turned his head slowly toward the newsman. His smile was weak. "Okay, I guess. You know these medics. They never tell you exactly what the situation is." He shook his head slightly. "God, we sure took a clobbering. I've been lying here wondering about that artillery foul-up. What have you heard?"

"It was Nuan's fault, all right. Whether it was deliberate or not, we'll never know," Sloan said, hesitating. "He's dead. And so is Doc Elliott." He told him about Doc and the grenade.

"Oh, my God!" There was an anguished look on Cunningham's face. "Now only four of us left. Red, Jake, Tiny and me. Out of a dozen." His eyes filled with tears. "God, that Doc. What a guy. What guts. He was worth a hundred Nuans. He shouldn't have done it, no matter what Nuan did." His voice faltered.

"Dick, there on the bedside table is an extra copy of Colonel Fowler's last report. I got them to send the original to Saigon. They took it off his body."

"Thanks, Dave. I'll need this for my story. Believe me, I'm going to write the whole damn thing, except about Doc's killing Nuan."

"Good. Maybe it'll stop any more messes like this one. Look, will you do me a favor. Stop by and see how the other guys look? Then come on back and I'll give you a rundown about what happened the last couple of days. Okay?"

"Damn right, Dave. I especially want to get your account of the VCs coming up before the medics arrived. That must be some story."

Sloan found that Jake Potter was unconscious but he left word with the nurse that he should be informed the newsman had inquired about him. Red Kennedy was also swathed in bandages, but his face was cheerful.

"The doc just told me I was headed stateside, Dick. Thank God! Man, I'm fed up to here with Viet Nam," Kennedy said. Sloan told him about Doc Elliott and Nuan and reported on Cunningham's condition. Then he sought Tiny Christopolous. The huge Greek looked worried.

"It's this leg of mine," he said. "Shattered the bone pretty bad. I just hope to hell I'll be able to play ball again. My hitch is up pretty soon and I was counting on playing in the fall."

"The nurse says they're evacuating you, too, Tiny. Hell, you'll be back home in a matter of days and be getting the best of care."

Tiny brightened. When Sloan started to leave, he said, "Dick, say hello to the Captain for me and the other boys. Tell him I'm awful sorry about Doc. And thank him for getting the last batch of gooks. We owe him our lives."

Sloan brought a chair and placed it beside Cunningham's bed. "You'll probably all be going home together. If Jake Potter can be moved, that is. Right now he's still in shock."

Taking notes, Sloan listened to his recital of the events from the time the VC attack began at Thuong Ninh until they were wounded. Finally the reporter rose. "I've got to catch a flight up to Saigon to file my story."

"Hey, wait a second. Did you ever hear any more about Monique?" Cunningham asked.

Sloan nodded. "I was afraid you'd bring that up. They fished her body out of the Saigon river. Her throat was cut."

"Oh, God, no!" Cunningham turned his face toward his pillow.

"Sorry to have to tell you that, Dave. I guess they did it to get even with her for putting me in contact with the black market people. One of my CID friends told me she was in pretty deep with a bad crowd, herself. That's where she got the dough for that beautiful home and all those clothes."

Cunningham nodded slowly. "Yes, I guess I realized that all along. But she was a terrific gal, Dick." He hesitated. "Do me another favor, will you? When you cable your story please ask your editor to call my wife and say I'm okay."

Sloan agreed and they shook hands. "Dave, you did a helluva great job out there. I'm sorry to see you go, although I'm glad for you. You've been through too much."

Cunningham pondered his last words after the newsman had left. Man, how true. The things I've seen and done. And I've grown a lot these past few months. It's as if I left Fort Sheridan a cocky kid and I'm going home an old man. A sick and tired old man. With a belly full of fighting, killing, and blood. Now I know what it's all about. What the score is. How precious life really is. I guess maybe Martha was actually a lot more mature than me. He went to sleep thinking of her.

The senior medical officer visited Cunningham in the morning. "I have some news, Captain. Your man, Jake Potter, is out of shock now. We've taken him off the critical list. His chances are good."

Cunningham was elated, but he felt physically lousy. In fact, worse than the day before.

"I hate to tell you this, Captain," the gray-haired doctor began. "But—over my protests—the word has been sent down from Saigon to fly you up there as soon as possible. Sergeants Kennedy and Christopolous, too. It shouldn't hold up your evacuation out of the country more than 24 hours, though."

Cunningham swore softly. They can't wait to get a statement from me. Those goddam politicians up there, he thought. I'll bet they'll try to whitewash the whole goddam business. He chuckled grimly. Well, I wonder what they'll think when Dick Sloan's story is printed.

Kennedy smiled feebly as the three Green Berets were carried from an ambulance to a small transport plane and carefully loaded inside. A doctor and two medics were the only other passengers. "By God, Captain, this is such a plush deal that it worries me," Kennedy said.

Tiny laughed, but then groaned as his ribs hurt. "Red, I've only been in the Army a little while, but I have learned to take advantage of every goddam thing they're willing to give me. Take it and question their motives later."

Cunningham waited until the doctor and the corpsmen were seated at the other end of the compartment. Then he turned to his men. "They're probably sending us up there to let the big brass question us. I know I don't have to tell you this, but I'm going to, anyway. You can do what you want to. They may put some pressure on you. I don't know. All I am sure of is this. I intend to tell it exactly as it all happened."

"Me, too, Captain." Tiny's smile was mean. "Don't forget one thing, sir. I may just be an SP/4, but I am something of a celebrity. I'm known from coast to coast as a damn good pro football player."

Kennedy spoke up, his voice suddenly firm. "I was a

newspaperman, Captain. We usually stick together. Tiny and I'll both back up anything you say."

Cunningham nodded, satisfied, and smiled softly at them. "Thanks, boys. But this is going to be a long session, unless I miss my guess. Let's get some sleep."

In Saigon they were met by ambulances and taken to the military hospital, escorted by armed men in jeeps. Tiny enjoyed the whole thing immensely.

Cunningham frowned when they were each wheeled into a private, single room and put into bed. He refused to be worried and luxuriated in the soft mattress and clean, crisp sheets. The presence of a solicitous Army nurse and a good American meal topped off the whole deal. After lunch he was thoroughly checked over again by a team of doctors.

He was allowed to rest for another hour before a U.S. Army-uniformed corporal entered and set up a tape recorder on a table by the bed. Oh, oh, Cunningham thought, now it comes. He whistled under his breath when the hospital Commanding Officer came in and stood rigidly by the open door. Cunningham had never seen in person the tall, four-star General who stalked in, but he had often noticed his photograph in the newspapers. The Commander-in-Chief of the Advisory Command, boss of all U.S. forces in South Viet Nam.

Cunningham's right hand automatically went up to his brow in a salute. The General smiled and returned it. Then he moved to bedside and held out his hand. His clasp was firm.

"Hello, Cunningham. I'm sorry about having to delay your evacuation. But the word came from Washington that they wanted a complete statement from you and your men just as soon as possible. To make up for the lost time, I've arranged for you to go by jet tomorrow. You're headed for Tripler General Hospital in Honolulu, as are Christopolous and Kennedy." The General swung a straight chair close to the bed, turned it around, and straddled it. "I want to also say right now that I'm sorry as hell about the whole damn thing. From leaving you down there at Thuong Ninh so long, right up to your getting hit by friendly artillery. It was a stinking mess."

"Thank you, sir," Cunningham replied softly, feeling he was expected to say something.

"I've read Colonel Fowler's report. As you may know, he was an old and valued friend as well as an outstanding combat officer. He had a lot of respect for you, Cunningham." The General sighed and sat silently for a moment. "Now, here's the drill for today. One of the colonels from G-3 will be in next. With a map of the area you covered. In your own words, I want you to dictate an hour-by-hour account of the whole period from the day you left Thuong Ninh until you were picked up by the medics. Try to pinpoint what your men, and Colonel Fowler, and any of the ARVN and SDF were doing. Try to use names where you can remember." He grinned. "Don't bother about phrasing it in Army terms. A doctor will be standing by in here. Any time you want to stop and rest, or take a nap or eat, just say so." He turned to the Colonel who had come in. "Understand that?"

The General rose and shook Cunningham's hand again. "You're a damn good officer, Cunningham. I wish I had gotten to know you personally out here. I'm going to see your two men now, and tell them the same thing I've said to you. Good luck."

Whew, Cunningham breathed after he had left. That sure was painless. He turned his head toward the colonel. "I'm ready to start any time you are, sir." Since he had recited the whole series of events for Dick Sloan the details were fresh in his mind.

He talked steadily for three hours, halting only when the radioman changed the reels on the tape recorder. The doctor finally stopped the session when Cunningham's voice began to slow and weaken. "Rest awhile, Captain. Then we'll send in something to eat."

Cunningham insisted on continuing during the evening. He stopped voluntarily at midnight. His account had reached the last day's action. He knew it was burned so vividly into his brain that he wouldn't lose his train of thought. They started in again the next morning, after the doctor had examined him.

The tape recorder was packed up at 11:00 and the Colonel shook Cunningham's hand. "That was one of the goddamnedest stories I've heard in 30 years in the Army, Captain. It's a shameful thing to have happened. Damn all this politics." He left the room shaking his head.

The three Green Berets were put aboard a jet assigned to carry an Assistant Secretary of Defense and an Assistant Secretary of State and their staffs back to Washington, via Honolulu. After the dignitaries had come back and fussed over them, Cunningham, Kennedy and Tiny were left alone. They compared notes and concluded the same thing. No attempt would be made to whitewash the incident. Tiny looked down at his bandages and chuckled. "Well, maybe things will get straightened out with the ARVN and the South Vietnamese government now. But I'd just as soon not had any part of it." His face brightened. "Hey, did I tell you? The head bone specialist at the hospital looked over my leg. He says he figures it will be as good as ever. With a lot of therapy, I should be able to play next fall."

They congratulated him and Cunningham punched the button by the built-in bunk. "Well, if we're going first class, let's enjoy it." An Air Force stewardess came in immediately. "Any chance of snagging three drinks from the bottles of those VIPs up there?" he asked her.

She smiled beautifully and nodded. "Fellows, anything they've got on board you can have."

"Now isn't that a helluva note! We get an offer like that from a doll as pretty as this, and look at the condition we're in," Tiny said, laughing loudly.

The girl flushed but didn't stop smiling. Two drinks apiece and an excellent hot dinner later, and all three of the Green Berets were sound asleep. They did not awaken until the plane touched down at Hickam Air Force base in Honolulu.

Cunningham was still half asleep when he was put to bed at Tripler. They examined him anxiously in the afternoon and kept him under sedation. The next day they operated on his left shoulder even though he was still weak. A chunk of shrapnel had been taken out originally, but they found others which had made a bigger mess of the joint than they had originally estimated. Cunningham was put under intensive care for another forty-eight hours. Slowly he regained his strength.

The third day the doctor finally let Tiny and Red see him. They were up in wheelchairs, each attended by a pretty nurse.

"We were pretty worried about your relapse, skipper. They say you've had a rough go," Kennedy said. He and Tiny exchanged amused glances. "You've got to get on your feet pretty fast, you know. To go to Washington for the ceremony."

Cunningham looked from face to face. "What the hell do you mean? I'm not getting Pentagon duty, am I?" His mind was still fuzzy from all the sedatives.

"A buddy of mine over in U.S. Army Pacific Headquarters here stopped by to see me. Seems the scuttlebutt over there is that the recommendation for a MOH for you is sure to be approved." Kennedy handed a sheaf of newspaper clippings to the nurse. "Here, when he's able let him read these. About what a bunch of heroes we are. Congratulations, Captain. I hear that in a couple of weeks I'll have to change that, too. They say you're a cinch for field grade."

His words finally registered on Cunningham as they were wheeled from the room. MOH—Medal of Honor. The nation's highest decoration. And field grade—he'd be promoted to Major. He lay back, almost exhausted. It was too much to comprehend. The nurse drew the blinds and he fell asleep.

He was still in a daze the next day and it was not until the rush of the morning hospital routine quieted down that he was able to sort out his thoughts. He still discounted the Medal of Honor bit. Getting his Majority, that was in the realm of probability. The nurse finally let him see the clippings. He was surprised at the publicity he and the

Green Berets had received. Sloan's articles had been picked up by the Associated Press and sent all over the country. Suddenly he wondered why he had had no word from his wife. Not even a telegram. Certainly Dick had passed a message through his newspaper, and she should have been officially notified by the Army that he had been wounded. He mentally shrugged. She'd probably written and there was some screw-up in the Army Post Office system, he decided. Then he wondered how long it would be before he could get into a wheel chair. He'd be able to get to a phone then and call Martha.

The next morning he felt much better and brought up the subject with the nurse. She smiled enigmatically and evaded the question. Later he was annoyed when a cleaning crew came in and gave the room a thorough going over. The hospital Commanding Officer entered and made a silent inspection. He directed that flowers and two over-stuffed chairs be brought in. Cunningham noticed the flurry of activity in the corridor as his nurse cranked up his bed, fluffed his pillows and smoothed his sheet, leaving him half-sitting up.

"I hope you're up to having visitors, Captain Cunningham," the hospital C.O. said. "VIPs."

"Yes sir, I guess so," Cunningham replied, still mystified.

The senior medical officer left and returned five minutes later, accompanied by General Moran, Commander-in-Chief, U.S. Army Pacific. Cunningham had met him once when he had visited Chicago to make a speech. After the preliminaries were over the General got serious.

"It is my pleasure to inform you that the recommendation that the Congressional Medal of Honor be awarded you has been approved in Washington. When you are fit again, you will be flown there and it will be presented to you by the President at the White House. Congratulations."

Cunningham could hardly believe his ears. His reply was hardly military. "Well, I'll be damned!" he said softly.

"The recommendations for the Army Distinguished Service Cross for your three men have also been approved.

They will be presented at the same ceremony." The General stood up and opened an envelope he was carrying. "Only one other item of business, Cunningham. Here is your appointment as a Major in the Army of the United States. Congratulations."

Cunningham dazedly shook his head and accepted the paper.

General Moran held out a small box and set it on the table. "It's also my pleasure to give you your first set of Major's gold oak leaves. Congratulations again."

There was a twinkle in General Moran's eyes as he moved toward the door. "Now I'm going to get the hell out of here, Major, without any further delay. I've held up your real important visitor." He opened the door.

Martha Cunningham rushed in, almost knocking the General aside. She ran to her husband, tearful but smiling.

Speechless, Cunningham reached out with his good right arm and pulled her to him.

Over and over she repeated, "Darling, darling, darling . . ."

Suddenly he felt almost faint. The nurse came closer, anxiously watching his pallid face. Cunningham took several deep breaths and felt his pulse settle back to normal.

"Mrs. Cunningham. Five minutes please, this first time. He is still quite weak." The nurse shut the door softly behind her and they were alone.

"I can hardly believe I'm not dreaming, Martha," he began when she was seated next to the bed.

"Oh, you poor dear. What you must have gone through. It seems like an eternity that they've made me wait to see you. I was so worried."

He smiled at her rush of words, studying the wonderful planes of her face. Suddenly his conscience nagged him. He had almost forgotten how beautiful she was. Then he frowned. "How long have you been here in Honolulu?"

"Days. When the word came to Fort Sheridan you were being evacuated from Viet Nam, the General called General Moran, and arranged for me to stay with him and his

286

wife. I flew out by jet straight from O'Hare, nonstop. They met me here and have been so wonderful."

Cunningham swore. "The least those bastards here could have done was to let me know you were around."

She put a finger on his lips. "Hush. They wanted to make sure you had complete rest. They said you were so run down at the time that you were wounded that the infection set in almost at once."

"Shit, they never said a thing about that to me."

Martha frowned. "David, you must watch your language." Then her face lighted with a flashing smile. "Oh, darling. It's so wonderful your being a Major and getting the Medal of Honor. You've been so terribly brave. And to think I argued against your volunteering for Viet Nam duty. You really knew your duty was to your country."

It was Cunningham's turn to frown. He decided to be honest. "Martha, we'll talk more about this later, but I want to get one thing straight. You were absolutely right. I was a goddam fool for volunteering. There was no patriotism or none of this damn 'duty' bit involved. I should have waited until they ordered me out there. Martha, I was just pissed off at the duty at Fort Sheridan. Bored by all the travel. Bored with the cocktail circuit. With life in general." He breathed deeply, now very tired. "Martha, I'm glad I got that off my chest. I've been trying to put it into a letter to you for weeks."

There was an incredulous expression on her face. Then it softened. "Darling, I know. It will take some getting-used-to being a hero. But don't be so humble, David. You've earned everything they'll be giving you. My dear, I just never realized what being a Green Beret meant to you."

Cunningham started to deny her words and plead for understanding, but then his lips closed. Why bother, he thought decisively. She'll never believe me. She'll never understand that I've finally grown up. That I've learned to face the facts of life. And now she has the chance to bask in the limelight. She'll love it. And she'll love the hero of a

287

husband she has even more than she did before. Why not give her that. She's earned it.

His hand closed on hers and he smiled up at her. "You've got a beautiful tan, dear."

Martha laughed lightly. "I should. I've been sitting by the pool waiting since the day I arrived. Oh, it's so beautiful in Hawaii." She glanced at her watch and looked at him calculatingly. "David, wouldn't it be wonderful if we could be assigned out here?" Her voice quickened with enthusiasm. "General Moran mentioned that you could be. He would like to have you for his Administrative Assistant. Anyway, they say it's going to be some time before you are able to go back to duty in the field. And there are some lovely quarters out here."

Cunningham listened to her prattle on and watched her fondly. He had changed a lot inside, he realized, but she had not. The same Martha. Exactly the same girl he had married. Well, Cunningham, he thought, you made your decision at that time and you've got to stick with it. She still has the same wonderful qualities and you should be thankful for that. Slowly his eyes closed and he drifted toward sleep. Yes, it'll be the same old rat race. I'll take the job here to make her happy. We'll get on the merry-go-round. But this time I will take everything as it comes. Do what she and the Army want me to do. She may never understand the difference in me now, but at least I'll know. Deep down, I'll know, and it will be my secret.

Sunlight streaming in the window of the huge hospital finally awakened him. He stretched with his good arm and decided he felt very, very good. At the same time he sensed pleasure that his analysis of his personal life and his relationship with Martha had been the right one. There was a firmer ring to his voice as he called for the nurse and asked for his breakfast.

And when Martha visited that afternoon she found him smiling broadly and wearing the gold leaves of a Major on his pajamas. His green beret was on his head at a jaunty angle. He wore it proudly.